FOLLOWED BACK

A NOVEL

FOLLOWED BACK

A NOVEL

Charlie Torino

CORREDORA
INDEPENDENT PUBLISHING

The Library of Congress Cataloging-in-Publication Data
Names: Torino, Charlie, author.
Title: Followed Back
Description: First edition.
Identifiers: ISBN: 978-0-9995768-5-4 (paperback)

Cover design: Ashley Siebels

CHAPTER ONE
Amanda Wagner

Amanda Wagner knew that she had a doppelganger in a neighboring town. On several occasions, random adults had greeted her on the street, then squinted and politely apologized for the mistake when Amanda responded with a blank stare or a wary smile. Amanda's peers were less tactful. A group of girls who looked a year or two older than her called her a "stuck-up bitch" when she walked by without acknowledging them at the Danbury Mall; and when she and a few friends decided to sneak into a random party at Fairfield University one weekend during her sophomore year of high school, she was promptly cornered by a nineteen-year-old boy who, while slurring his words, insisted that Amanda looked exactly like one of his younger sister's friends, except Amanda was "chubbier" but had "a smaller nose and better skin."

Her doppelganger's name was Jill. Or maybe Jen? The drunk guy at the college party had insisted that the other girl's name was Jen, but he also had vomited all over the ice luge fifteen minutes after their conversation, so it wasn't implausible that he would misremember certain details about his little sister's social circle.

Based on the offhand comments and misplaced accolades that Amanda received, this Jill (or Jen?) was an accomplished soccer player. One time, though, while Amanda was idly browsing

1

through a rack of blouses at J. Crew while she waited for her friend's shift behind the cash register to end, a forty-something woman with a posh bob haircut and a YSL handbag congratulated Amanda on her performance in a piano recital that took place somewhere in southwestern Connecticut. Amanda bashfully shook her head and made a self-deprecating joke about her utter lack of musical talent. The woman replied with a cordial half-smile and returned her focus to the embroidered camisoles. Amanda's curiosity, punctuated with a tinge of envy, deepened.

Attempting to learn to play the piano was a nonstarter, but Amanda did consider trying out for the school soccer team in the hopes that she might face her look-alike in a match someday. Two humiliating three-hour sessions of trying to dribble and shoot during a summer soccer camp, however, were enough to convince her that her mediocre career on the Trumbull High School girls' JV diving team constituted the outer limit of her athletic abilities.

The drunk guy at the Fairfield University party had mentioned that he grew up in Wilton, Connecticut, so it stood to reason that his younger sister, and therefore Amanda's doppelganger, probably went to Wilton High School. And thus, one autumn afternoon during her junior year, Amanda skipped diving practice to attend the Trumbull varsity girls' soccer match against Wilton High. It was an away game. Amanda kept her plans a secret and drove thirty minutes west along the Merritt Parkway in her used 2007 silver Nissan Versa, which she had finally saved enough money to buy (with the help of a small loan from her parents) earlier that September.

It was an embarrassingly futile endeavor. Aside from a teacher scolding her for loitering outside the school entrance, no one gave her a second look that day, and no one on Jill's presumptive team bore even a remote resemblance to Amanda. All that resulted from the excursion was Amanda's diving coach—who, through that mysterious network of teachers, coaches, and other adults, somehow learned where Amanda had been the prior afternoon—admonishing her that if she ever skipped practice again for such a frivolous reason, she'd be kicked off the team.

As her coach was lecturing her, it occurred to Amanda that the college kid and his sister could have gone to private or prep school, or they might have met Jill (Jen?) through a country club, or a premier sports league, or a charity gala, or any of the other ways that the residents of the wealthier half of Fairfield County interacted with each other. At this realization, her face flushed and she hung her head. Her coach, mistaking Amanda's humiliation for remorse, sent Amanda back to the pool with a pat on the shoulder.

In four years of high school, four years of strangers approaching her, four years of family acquaintances asking why she didn't return their greeting at the May Fair, four years of friends saying they thought they spotted her at the movie theater or shopping at Trader Joe's with a strange older couple, the closest Amanda ever got to seeing her doppelganger was when Westport, Connecticut's high school winter musical gained statewide notoriety after it was discovered that the school administration failed to properly remit the obligatory licensing fees to Music Theatre International for its student performance of *Rent.*

There, on the front page of the *Trumbull Times*, accompanied by three other student actors, was a girl who seemed to bear more than a superficial resemblance to Amanda. It was hard to know for sure. The black-and-white photo was blurry and taken at a distance, and Amanda had heard only that her look-alike was a gifted pianist, not a singer. But when she saw the newspaper sitting atop her parents' pile of mail, it was enough to make her heart skip a beat. This girl had the same long, slightly wavy blond hair and fair skin. Something about the shape of her jaw and the slope of her forehead felt distinctly and personally familiar. The camera angle and the costume might have been distorting Amanda's perception, but this girl seemed to be about the same height and have the same general body type as Amanda. Was this, at last, her mysterious "twin"?

The photo caption identified the students only as "local teens." Amanda was surprised to note her disappointment at how anticlimactic the chance discovery was. Although the girl really did look like she could be Amanda's sister, or at least a cousin, the fuzzy, black-and-white newspaper print rendered the picture too indistinct to know for sure. She tried to view the photo in the online edition of the paper, but web access required a paid subscription and, unlike most of those rich Westport kids, her parents didn't allow her to have a credit card.

Amanda sighed, defeated. Most likely, all those mistaken encounters were the result of strangers and casual acquaintances noting the two girls' eye-catching blond hair and taller-than-average height, and exaggerating their other similarities to be sociable or feel like they had something interesting to say. Amanda briefly considered trying to track down a copy of a Westport high school yearbook, then quickly dismissed the idea as foolish. Trying to find this Jill girl had occupied enough of her time and mental energy, and there was no reason for it beyond appeasing her curiosity—and, perhaps, her vanity. The girl in the newspaper photo didn't look that much thinner than Amanda, and Amanda couldn't help wondering who was actually the prettier of the two.

Throughout her senior year of high school, on the handful of occasions when someone confused her with this elusive "Jill," Amanda tried to maintain a casual indifference. She never had felt comfortable trying to press strangers for clues that might help her uncover Jill's identity or location anyway. Now, Amanda simply corrected them with a tired joke about her mysterious clone a few towns over. Privately, however, she continued to wonder how often the same thing was happening to Jill. Had Jill ever tried to find her? Perhaps she already had seen Amanda's pictures on social media or had glimpsed Amanda from afar, and had realized that their passing resemblance was so minor that she didn't bother introducing herself.

After graduating high school, Amanda prepared to attend the University of Evansville, a small liberal arts college in Indiana, that fall. She had done okay on the SATs but had struggled to maintain a B average in most of her classes, and U of E was by far the best of the few schools from which she had received an acceptance letter. She had no idea what she wanted to study, but she was excited to be a Purple Ace!

In addition to her regular job waiting tables at the upscale restaurant Parker Steaks & Scotch in Trumbull, Amanda spent the summer working as a lifeguard and assistant diving coach at Aspetuck Country Club. Most of the parents there were cordial. Some asked Amanda about her future plans, and when she told them about U of E, they tried to respond with polite enthusiasm, although Amanda suspected that they'd be horrified if their own children didn't attend Ivy League schools someday. Only one of the many ladies-who-lunched looked at Amanda with shock, even contempt, when Amanda responded to her inquiry about Amanda's post-graduation plans. The woman was certain that Amanda had received a partial scholarship to MIT, and she couldn't fathom why Amanda would try to hide that fact, much less choose a small, little-known school over one of her more prestigious options.

In the moment, Amanda didn't know how to respond. She dared not talk back or try to correct the woman for fear of incurring her further wrath and disgust. The lifeguarding gig was decent money and she didn't want to risk losing her job if the woman complained about her sass mouth to management. Employees there had been fired for far less.

It wasn't until she clocked into her shift at the steakhouse later that night that it hit her: in addition to being an athlete and a piano prodigy and possibly a high school musical-starring singer and actress, her doppelganger was also some sort of math or science genius. Amanda was an only child, but in that moment she felt the full weight of the sibling rivalry about which her friends sometimes complained. She was the "loser" twin.

CHAPTER TWO
Amanda Wagner

College was for Amanda, as for most of her classmates, a chance to start over without the weight of her hometown's expectations and assumptions boxing her in. She hadn't realized the burden of living in a stranger's shadow until she had left it behind. Amanda decided not to go home for Thanksgiving her freshman year and she stayed with her parents for less than a week over winter break, citing her desire to retain her part-time job as a waitress as an excuse. Although her manager at Mojo's BoneYard Sports Bar and Grille truly had been haranguing her about taking almost a week off work, one of her colleagues—a woman with two kids under age six whose expectations of Santa Claus far exceeded their mother's financial flexibility—had happily covered all of Amanda's shifts. Amanda could have extended her stay in Connecticut without risking her job, but she was anxious to return to the Midwest. She didn't want strangers approaching her in the grocery store or at church, asking how MIT was treating her. She couldn't bear their looks of embarrassed pity when she would be forced to confess that she was the dumb doppelganger. At U of E, she was just Amanda: a solid B student, waitress at one of the most popular local sports bars, and second baseman on a co-ed intramural kickball team. And that was enough.

Four years of college passed quickly. Amanda changed her major from Political Science to Psychology and back to Poli Sci again. She didn't know what she would do with her degree—law school, grad school, what else was there?—but everyone around her seemed equally confused as to their next steps, which alleviated some of the sense of urgency to make a decision. Deciding on her major had been difficult enough.

In the course of her four years in Evansville, Amanda had a few casual hookups, a few boyfriends (although none too serious), and even a steady girlfriend for two and a half glorious months, until Alicia declared that she only wanted to get serious with a "real" lesbian and unceremoniously dumped Amanda over Chick-fil-A in the Ridgway student center.

Amanda was heartbroken and remained casually obsessed with tracking down social media evidence of Alicia's subsequent love life, until she met Jeff at a bar after a kickball match. There were less than three months left until graduation, and most of Amanda's friends advised her that it'd be foolish to start up a new relationship right before everyone would go their separate ways, but she felt an undeniable connection with Jeff. Amanda was widely considered to be one of the prettiest girls in the kickball league, but Jeff was, by far, the best-looking guy ever to express romantic interest in her. He was charming and witty and commanded attention even though he wasn't boisterous like the other boys. He had transferred to their college from Dartmouth at the beginning of his senior year ("for unavoidable family reasons," he would say when asked why, in a tone that made it unequivocally clear that it was time to change topics), and he had *direction*. He had been accepted to Georgetown Law in Washington, D.C., the city where he wanted to work long-term. Over the upcoming summer, however, he planned to remain with his parents, who lived twenty minutes from the U of E campus, while he worked landscaping jobs to make some extra money.

From their traditional spot on Amanda's bed—out of sight and earshot of her nosy, bossy roommate, with a laptop playing reruns of *The Office* on Netflix poised on a pillow between their legs—he explained in a hushed voice that as long as everything was stable with his family by August, and he fully expected that it would be, he would pack the old station wagon his dad had handed down to him and drive across the country to get settled in his new apartment a week before law school orientation. After exchanging a few emails with two guys who had posted on their class message board looking for a third roommate, Jeff had decided to live alone.

"Won't you get lonely?" Amanda asked.

"No," Jeff said abruptly. A sardonic remark from Dwight filled the silence that otherwise would have lingered. Jeff and Amanda both chuckled at the line, despite knowing the entire episode by heart. Jeff's tone softened. "No, I need privacy to concentrate and study. Those guys I was messaging seem like good dudes, but everyone says that the first year of law school is the most important. I have money saved up, and my parents will help too. It's worth the extra expense to know that I'm giving myself the best opportunity to succeed."

Amanda smiled. On their second official date, Jeff had explained that he wanted to join a boutique firm specializing in white collar criminal defense. Amanda had nodded enthusiastically and spoke a few vague words of encouragement and support. Then, when she got home, she googled what the hell that meant.

In moments of insecurity, she wondered why he bothered with her at all. What was she bringing to their budding relationship that he couldn't find elsewhere? She saw how bartenders flirted with him, how drunk girls would rub up against him on the sticky dance floor at Lamasco Bar on Thursday and Saturday nights. He could get sex on demand from any number of girls with better bodies and brighter futures. One Friday night after too many tequila shots, she began to wail in the Buffalo Wild Wings parking lot about how she'd always be the fatter, dumber twin. "Fuck Jill!" she screamed, slamming her fist into the pavement.

The memories came back to her in a rush of shame as she looked at her bloodied knuckles the next morning. She and Jeff had been hanging out for three weeks at that point. She expected that she'd never see him again. Who would blame him for ghosting her after that horrifying display, she thought bitterly.

9

But two days later, he texted her to check in. He claimed that he had blacked out and spent the next forty-eight hours nursing the most brutal hangover of his life. Amanda was dubious. She was pretty sure he had spent most of the night sipping on a single beer. For some reason, he was forgiving her for the entire debacle and trying to spare her feelings.

Jeff never asked Amanda who Jill was, or if she had a twin sister. This wasn't entirely surprising. Jeff was very private when it came to his own family matters, and he was probably trying to show her the same courtesy and discretion he had made very clear she needed to extend to him in that regard.

Still, after that night, Amanda began jogging five days a week and embraced a low-calorie vegetarian diet plan. She might not be an athlete or an MIT scholar, but at least she could ensure that no one would refer to her as the chubby version of her smarter and surely more successful look-alike ever again. With two months of admittedly brutal effort, she was down ten pounds from the beginning of the semester. She couldn't tell whether or not Jeff was pleased with the change. As her waist slimmed and she began to see hints of definition in her arms, Jeff refrained from commenting. But he must have noticed.

"He probably doesn't want to offend you by saying the wrong thing," Amanda's friend Kiara mused during one of their thrice weekly coffee dates before their 10:00 a.m. Principles of Public Relations course. "He doesn't want you to think that he was unhappy with the way you looked before. Which he obviously wasn't. You were smoking hot before you started all this diet and fitness stuff, and you're still smoking hot now."

"I suppose so," Amanda replied dispassionately. She stared with envy at Kiara's double chocolaty chip Frappuccino with extra whipped cream. "So, what do you think, should we go to class today or what?"

Amanda hoped that Kiara was right, but Jeff was an enigma. He was so sweet and attentive whenever they were together. He seemed to truly listen to and remember every word she said. But sometimes he disappeared for days. "Family stuff," he would explain curtly. This meant that the conversation was over. It was hard for Amanda to criticize it. She never suspected he was cheating on her or deceiving her. She simply wondered what was going on with his family that weighed so heavily on him. Although he spoke often of duty and honor in general terms, Amanda sensed that his loyalty and responsibility to his parents and siblings in particular was what drove most of his actions, including his decision to move to D.C. and attend law school.

Amanda momentarily pondered how she might fit into his hierarchy of love and obligation in the long-term, and then scolded herself. They had been dating for less than three months, and they'd be graduating in just over two weeks. He was moving across the country, and Amanda was still searching for a job. So far, the four years she had spent waitressing and bartending at Mojo's qualified her for more opportunities than her college degree.

At Mojo's, she had outlasted several managers, each as capricious about scheduling shifts and firing employees as the last, and she was grateful (and a bit proud) that she had figured out how to placate each one, at least enough to retain her position. The restaurant had been a useful excuse to avoid spending time back in Trumbull during school breaks, and evidently it also had turned into the only way she'd ever make a living.

Jill flashed into Amanda's mind. She would be graduating MIT now. Would she go on to grad school? Take a position at a tech or engineering company? Spend a year volunteering with AmeriCorps or Teach for America before commencing a prestigious job with a six-figure starting salary? Amanda sighed. Whatever Jill was planning, surely it was more impressive than remaining in the same small college town, in the same dumpy apartment, waiting tables for the indefinite future.

Amanda and Kiara took the rest of their Starbucks to class that morning, but Jill was on Amanda's mind for the rest of the day. She hadn't actively tried to find out anything about her look-alike since high school ended, but that night Amanda spent an hour searching through Facebook, looking for any Jills who graduated from Westport's public high school three to five years prior or with whom she had mutual friends. She knew it was a long shot, but she was still frustrated when her efforts proved as fruitless as when they were teenagers. Plenty of people confused them, but no one had been willing to connect them. Although, in fairness, Amanda always had felt too timid to ask.

Amanda stared angrily at her laptop, lamenting her failure to act when she'd had the opportunity, until she was struck with sudden inspiration. She held out her cell phone and took a selfie, then uploaded it to Google image search. The results returned a collection of her public Instagram posts, as well as numerous selfies of other blond, fair-skinned women posed in front of similarly drab backgrounds. Amanda clicked on each, hoping that one might link to the profile of a girl named Jill. No luck. Aside from the blond hair, none of them looked much like her (or like that girl pictured in the old *Trumbull Times* newspaper article about the high school musical scandal) anyway. The bone structure was all off.

Amanda continued to scroll and click. It was becoming a silly game: snatching glimpses of these strangers' lives, judging their online presence, trying to divine based on one photo whether she should envy their lives or they hers. Amanda clicked a button at the bottom of the screen to load more results.

Second row. Third picture from the left.

Amanda felt her face growing hot. She leaned forward to scrutinize the thumbnail until the tip of her nose was four inches from the screen. She couldn't bring herself to click the page just yet. The image was her, but it wasn't her. She had never posed for a professional portrait like this one. She didn't own a blue pinstripe blouse like the girl in the photo was wearing. And her hair never had been quite that long. But otherwise, it was her face. Or it might as well have been.

Amanda looked at herself in her phone's camera and tried to mimic the girl's half-smile. Their features were nearly identical in every way. Even their eyebrows were threaded into the same shape. Dark brown eyeliner, mascara, matte brownish-pink lipstick, and a bit of bronze highlighter on the outer corners of her eyelids—it was exactly how Amanda did her own makeup before class each day. Was this girl wearing MAC lipstick in Velvet Teddy? That was Amanda's signature shade! It was her only cosmetics splurge, and she kept a stick in her purse and another on her bathroom counter at all times. The matching makeup may well have been the eeriest part of their overall resemblance.

Amanda recalled what that obnoxious drunk guy at the Fairfield U party had said to her all those years ago: Jill was fitter, but she had a bigger nose and blemished skin. Amanda was certain those were his words. Every time she felt crummy about being the dumb, chunky doppelganger, she would try to console herself with the knowledge that at least she supposedly had a prettier face. But this girl's skin was clear and bright, and her nose was shaped in the same delicate ski jump as Amanda's. Exactly the same.

Amanda's heart was racing. Had she sat for this photo years ago and simply forgotten about it? She clicked the image. Her eyes brimmed with tears as she read the caption. Jill Torres. She had won an award at MIT for some sort of code-breaking program that she had created and patented. For fuck's sake. Jill was even more brilliant than Amanda had imagined, and obviously at least as pretty. Amanda's heart sank. What did she have left to cling to now?

But she finally had a last name! And maybe the article would have more details about Jill Torres's future plans. Amanda hesitated. Did she really want to know, or would it just make her more depressed?

She needed to know. Hastily, she clicked the link to the article before she could change her mind.

Page Not Found.

Amanda slammed her hand onto the kitchen table. Then she opened two more browser windows, mystified by the sudden sense of panic she felt. She typed "Jill Torres" into Facebook in one, and searched for "Jill Torres MIT" in Google on the other.

Facebook returned two matches, both dark-haired women in their forties. A lot of Amanda's friends had long-since migrated away from Facebook in favor of Insta, Snap, and TikTok, but most of them at least maintained a "historical archive" account. Tech prodigies must not have enough time for poke wars and fielding friend requests in their busy schedules.

Amanda switched to the Google results and began clicking. The first three returned the same infuriating "Page Not Found" error. The fourth result linked to an MIT German language club. Amanda zoomed in and squinted at the group photo of smiling students. Jill Torres was listed as a member, but she must have skipped picture day. But it was another nugget of information—genius Jill spoke at least one foreign language—and Amanda was voracious for more.

The fifth result linked to an article in the MIT student newspaper. Junior Jill Torres was quoted in relation to a month-long, school-sponsored trip to China in which she had participated during the previous summer: "I'm grateful for the opportunity. Professor Yao organized a remarkable itinerary of excursions around the mainland for us. The trip was life-changing. And my ability to speak and understand conversational Mandarin has improved exponentially."

Amanda scowled. Somehow, Jill's one remark was infinitely more irritating than the incessant blathering of her classmates who came back from their semester abroad at Harlaxton College and fancied themselves sophisticated world travelers because they had taken a few daytrips around England. Amanda didn't even have a passport. She resolved to figure out how to apply for one soon, even though she knew she couldn't afford to travel anywhere that wasn't reachable by car.

But a photo gallery of the trip accompanied the article, and that was Amanda's immediate priority. She scoured every photo for the telltale glimpse of long blond hair, but Jill must have been camera shy. She didn't appear in any of the candid or posed group shots until the very last image of the entire group: students, professors, and their local guides, all huddled together grinning. Jill had ducked behind another female student. Amanda tried to zoom in on her face, but the resolution was poor; there seemed to be a strong resemblance, but with the pixilation, it was not nearly as shocking as the posed and polished press photo had been.

Amanda clicked back to the original image and shivered. They looked almost like identical twins. She returned to the group photo and readjusted the frame. There, they only looked like sisters.

Was that the explanation? Did she have a secret twin, just like in that old Lindsay Lohan movie she had watched almost a decade ago? She didn't think she had been adopted. She had seen plenty of pictures of her mother pregnant, and of herself as a newborn, being cradled by her father and lying on her mother's chest. Besides, everyone said she had her mom's eyes and her dad's chin and dimples. And it couldn't have been one of those crazy soap opera stories where the father has a whole other secret family and life. Right? Even if Amanda were willing to believe that her loving and loyal but sometimes scatterbrained father were capable of doing such a thing, and even if he had found another blond woman that looked similar to her mom, she and Jill ought to look like half-sisters at most. Not nearly identical.

Maybe she had a sister who was kidnapped from the hospital maternity ward! Or did her parents unexpectedly have twins and decide, perhaps for financial reasons, to give one of them up for adoption? Only to have the child end up living a few towns over? What did Jill Torres's parents look like? Now that Amanda finally had a confirmed full name, now that she had seen for herself why people had confused them for years, she was desperate to learn more. This was, after all, quite possibly the most interesting, unique, special thing about Amanda. Maybe some of her friends came from wealthier families or made better grades or had more Instagram followers, but how many of them had a secret twin?

Perhaps one of Jill's travel companions had posted additional photos on social media. Just because Jill didn't have any accounts and couldn't be tagged didn't mean she wouldn't appear, even if only in the background. Instagram wouldn't let her limit her results by university, so Amanda began to type the other students' names from the article into the Facebook search bar one by one. After several private profiles and dead ends, she was finally able to click through to Jean Paul Woo's profile. He had graduated from MIT the year before and was now working in Silicon Valley, but it had to be the same guy.

Amanda opened his photo page and found two dozen albums, most titled with the names of exotic foreign countries: "Russia Trip," "Costa Rica Adventure," "Winter in South Africa," "Glorious Return to France." Amanda wondered why she felt less jealous, less ashamed, as she skimmed through the photographic evidence of Jean Paul's journeys around the world, than she had felt moments before when she had learned of Jill's school trip to China and compared it to her own history of travel (which consisted, in totality, of two spring breaks staying at a sketchy motel in Daytona Beach).

She had always assumed that people like Jean Paul—who had traveled more by age twenty-two than she would in three lifetimes—simply came from a different world. They had rich parents. They didn't have to worry about finding someone to cover their shift at a crappy-but-indispensable job for one day, much less for two weeks. They never had to choose between filling their gas tank and paying their electric bill on time. It was fun to fantasize about what it'd be like to trade places with them; and between living in Fairfield County, waitressing at a high-end steakhouse, and lifeguarding at a country club, Amanda had seen more glimpses into their reality than most. But she had accepted her lot. She had been born into a solidly middle-class family, with parents who both worked in solidly middle-class jobs, growing up in a safe, stable neighborhood in Trumbull, Connecticut—a town that wasn't the wealthiest in the state, but it certainly wasn't poor.

But that was just it! Jill wasn't identical to her only in appearance. Amanda knew that unless Jill were an heiress or a trust-fund kid, her upbringing must have been nearly identical as well. Maybe Westport's houses were a bit larger and their cars a bit fancier, but their towns had more or less the same traditions, their residents had more or less the same values, and their public schools had essentially the same well-respected reputations. Each town had its own Panera Bread, its own Starbucks, its own Banana Republic, and its own Ulta Beauty; and in each, the older residents griped about how the chain stores were destroying their respective hometowns' old-fashioned charm. In both high schools, the popular girls played field hockey and the rebellious kids cut class to loiter in gas station parking lots smoking cigarettes. Amanda knew how Jill must have grown up, because she grew up basically the same way, albeit a few notches down on the income-bracket ladder. So how had Jill managed to transcend the path that had been set for both of them, to achieve so much so quickly? Was the gap between middle-class and upper-middle-class really so consequential? Why hadn't Amanda been able to do the same?

She scrolled farther down Jean Paul's page until she came to an album entitled "Summer in China." Seventeen photos in, the blur of a wavy blond ponytail in profile filled the right edge of the frame. Thirty-two likes. Four comments.

Darryl Jones: An elusive Jill appears in the wild. This is the closest our photographers have gotten to capturing her in her natural environment.

Jean Paul Woo: [laugh emoji] This humble documentarian claims to have heard her speak that day, albeit only in Mandarin. Other researchers are skeptical.

Darryl Jones: [indecipherable text, in what was presumably Chinese writing. Jean Paul Woo likes this comment.]

Tanner Fenwick: she looks hot bro how r her tits good to? blonds r hot

Amanda rolled her eyes and clicked through to Darryl Jones's profile. His basic info was available, but his photos and wall posts were set to private.

"Who is Darryl Jones? Should I be jealous?"

Amanda jumped out of her seat.

"Jesus, Jeff, you scared the shit out of me!" Amanda shut her laptop. Other than that one drunken, barely coherent outburst in the B-Dubs parking lot when they first started dating, Amanda had never told him about her doppelganger, and now she was more convinced than ever that this was the right decision. He didn't need to know that an upgraded version of herself existed out there. "He's no one. A friend of a friend of a friend. I hadn't been on Facebook on ages. I fell down the rabbit hole and was creeping on strangers."

"I didn't mean to startle you," Jeff replied. "I texted thirty minutes ago and I knocked when I got here. The front door was unlocked."

"My idiot roommate is doing laundry. I have told her a million times to lock the damn door, but she leaves the apartment wide open every single time she washes her clothes. I swear, a murderer could walk right in here and stab us both. But she doesn't seem to care."

"Two more weeks, right?"

"Yes, thank goodness. Her parents are going to drive her home right after graduation. Technically she has another two months on the lease with me, but at this point, I don't even care whether or not she pays her share. I just want her gone. Once she's gotten all her crap out of here, I'm going to clean this place up and start looking for a replacement roommate. Maybe a quiet, nerdy, responsible grad student."

"So you have your heart set on staying here after graduation, then?"

"I wouldn't exactly say that I have my heart set on it." Amanda smiled wearily. "More like, I've made my peace with it. I make decent money at Mojo's, and I figure I can get a second job bartending a few nights a week at the casino. My degree is apparently worthless in every major job market in the country, so my only real prospects are staying here or begging my parents to let me move back in. And frankly, there is a good chance they'd say no. Sorry. I don't mean to sound so defensive. It's just depressing. Why do you ask?"

"Well, that's what I wanted to come over to talk to you about. What would you think about moving to D.C. with me?"

"You want to move in together?" It was as much a joyful exclamation as it was a question. Jeff cringed and flushed a deep red. Realizing she had misinterpreted his proposition, Amanda controlled her expression as she continued. "Because I thought you were pretty firmly committed to living alone your first year of law school, and it's probably still a little soon for us to take that big of a step, right?"

Jeff looked so relieved by her follow-up remarks that Amanda had to suppress a giggle. Her feelings weren't hurt. Not really. They had been officially dating for less than three months, and she hadn't considered getting an apartment with him until she thought that he was suggesting it. Besides, it probably *was* too soon to move in together.

"Well, I've been thinking," Jeff began. "I think D.C. could be a really good place for you, and not just because I selfishly want us to be in the same city. It'll be a lot easier to get a job with a Poli Sci degree there than in the Midwest or back in your hometown. Or at least, you can probably find an internship. I'm sure there's a U of E alumni network there that you can tap into. And with all your experience at the sports bar here, you're not going to have any trouble finding a waitressing or bartending job in the meantime. Maybe you'll find a job lead with one of your customers. I know the cost of living is higher there, but the pay and tips will be better too. You'll need a new roommate either way, and I'm sure we can find some affordable housing options for you that aren't total dumps."

Jeff paused, trying to gauge Amanda's reaction. "I know this a lot to throw at you," he continued. "And this isn't an ultimatum. My family is here, so I'm going to have good reasons to visit pretty regularly. I'm sure we can figure things out either way. I know we haven't really talked about long-term stuff yet, and that's on me. I was going to wait until this summer, after graduation. I wanted to enjoy whatever time we have left together, in case you felt differently, like this relationship has an expiration date. But I don't want to be coy or play games. I like you a lot, and I think we could have a future together. I want to stay together and make it work, regardless of whether you stay in Indiana or you come to D.C. with me." Jeff paused again and looked into Amanda's eyes. "So, what do you think?"

Amanda was speechless. No one had communicated so maturely and openly with her in any of her prior relationships. Nor, to be totally fair, had she with them. Even with Alicia, her ex-girlfriend, Amanda hadn't said or done anything to try to salvage the relationship, despite her broken heart over how abruptly it had ended. Sometimes Jeff seemed a decade older than his peers. She was dating a man, not a boy or a guy or a dude.

He was staring at her expectantly.

"I'm not sure what to say," Amanda stammered. "I want to stay together too. Everything you said, I feel the same way. And you make a good argument for Washington. I had barely considered it before now, but you're very persuasive. You're going to be such a good lawyer."

Amanda looked down and fiddled with a leftover napkin. What would Jill Torres do? Well, she probably wouldn't follow her boyfriend across the country just because he asked. But she would seize an opportunity to change her circumstances for the better. She would take a calculated risk that could pay off personally and professionally. She would put herself in a location where her career could advance, where she wasn't resigned to indefinite stagnation in her job, salary, and life. Jill would be bold. Jill had gone all the way to China, and who knew where else. Surely Amanda could manage Washington, D.C.

"Can I think about it a little?" Amanda asked.

"Of course!" Jeff exclaimed. He collected himself and continued more calmly. "Yes, of course. I wouldn't expect you to decide on the spot. I can forward you the info of a few of the cheaper apartment complexes I looked into for myself, but obviously no pressure. I think it'll be helpful for you to get an idea of what's out there, but you might find something better on your own. One of buildings, though, is a two-minute walk from a popular strip of restaurants and bars. If you worked at one of them, you wouldn't need to bother with a car or public transportation until you found your dream job. And you could start sending out résumés now if you wanted. Maybe I'm getting ahead of myself again, though. I'll drop it for the night. I'm just excited that you're not ruling it out immediately."

Amanda grinned. He was just so handsome and charming. It was irresistible.

"The idea is already growing on me," Amanda said. "Let's watch something on Netflix while I process. Maybe I'll call my parents this weekend to run it by them and see what they think.

Oh, and I can update my LinkedIn profile to specify that I'm looking for D.C. jobs! Or thankless unpaid internships and bitch work, to be realistic. All these years as a waitress will have prepared me well for that."

Jeff chuckled and kissed Amanda gently. There was a lengthy, heavy pause. She wondered if he was going to say "I love you." She nearly blurted it out herself.

"They added a new *Trailer Park Boys* special this morning," Amanda said, stepping back. "I resisted the urge to watch it because I knew you'd be stoked to see it together."

"In that case," Jeff said, "let's grab a six-pack from the fridge and settle in for the night."

They retreated to Amanda's room. Jill Torres, MIT, China, that eerie press photo—all quickly seemed like a distant memory. Amanda was almost certain she was going to agree to Jeff's proposal. It was time for her to start creating an enviable, adventurous life of her own.

The next morning, Amanda's conviction that she should move to Washington, D.C. had only grown. She doubted that she'd ever meet a better guy than Jeff anywhere—and certainly not if she remained waiting tables in a Midwestern college town or if she moved back to Trumbull and lived in her childhood bedroom, which were her only other viable options at the moment. Besides, even if she and Jeff did break up for some reason, she would have her own place, her own sources of income, hopefully some of her own friends, and eventually maybe even an idea as to how she could build a meaningful career. Spending time with someone as ambitious and goal-oriented as Jeff was instructive and inspiring, and she'd always be grateful to him for that too.

So, Amanda reassured herself, she wasn't saying yes just for a guy. She was saying yes for herself too. She would be happy with her decision even if someday they did split up.

She really hoped they wouldn't, though.

Neither of them mentioned it the next morning until after they had made the two-block walk from Amanda's apartment complex to their regular coffee shop, where they ordered two large cups to go. On the walk back, Amanda announced her decision. The often stoic and inscrutable Jeff couldn't disguise his delight.

"I'll help as much or as little as you want as far as getting situated there," he began. He stopped walking, set his cup of coffee on the ground, and threw his arms around Amanda's shoulders.

"Be careful before I dump hot coffee on your back!" she squealed. This was the reaction she had hoped for, and it warmed her heart. She had made the right decision. "I don't want to burden you, but I will take you up on the apartment leads you mentioned last night. And I'll call my parents later today. I'm not going to wait until they're here for graduation to tell them."

Jeff picked up his coffee and they began walking again.

"Are they going to be mad?" he asked.

"I'm not sure how they'll react," Amanda admitted. "They'll probably be relieved that I'm not asking to move back into their house. They'll probably be glad that I have a plan beyond just waitressing here. Although, they won't like that I don't have a job, and they definitely won't like that I'm planning to dive back into the service industry once I'm there. I might have to ask them for money. I really don't want to, and they might say no anyway. But I don't have a choice. I had to load my schedule with six classes the past two semesters to graduate on time, which meant I spent more money on books at the same time that I was picking up fewer weekday shifts at the restaurant. I totally screwed myself. I should've taken all early morning classes and skipped them whenever I needed to close at Mojo's the night before. So stupid. But anyway, it means that I have almost nothing in my checking account. My idiot roommate made a couple cigarette burns in the carpet, but aside from that, we should get most of the security deposit back. That'll help."

Amanda unlocked her apartment door and glanced at Jeff.

"I'm just venting. I'll figure it out. I'll be here all summer, and I'll be able to work sixty hours a week now if I need to. That's going to make a huge difference. And I'll take a side gig at the Tropicana too. I'll be fine by August, even without my parents' help."

Jeff was hovering in the doorway.

22

"What?" Amanda laughed. "Just spit it out. You think I'm being a spoiled brat right now?"

"No!" Jeff said. "Not at all. Not even close. The opposite. I don't want to say it because I know you'll be mad." He sighed. "Look, I know how fortunate I am to have basically all my expenses covered. I've been able to save almost every dollar I've earned from landscaping in the summers since freshman year. So... just don't let money stuff dissuade you from doing something you want to do. If August arrives and you still don't have enough to put down for first and last months' rent on a place in D.C. and your folks can't help, I'll spot you the cash. Just don't change your mind because of a few hundred bucks."

"You know I'd never accept that," Amanda said. Part of her wanted to snap that she wasn't a charity case, but Jeff was so sincere. He looked terrified even suggesting it. Sometimes it was hard not to resent that he never needed to work; from rent and utilities to groceries and gas, his parents paid all his bills. As far as she knew, they'd be doing the same for him in law school too. She thought of Jean Paul Woo and his extravagant trips around the globe, and she marveled at how she could feel more envy and creeping bitterness at the substantially more modest parental support received by someone she actually knew and cared for.

"It wouldn't be a handout," Jeff was continuing. "It'd be a small loan, and I know you'd be good for it. But we don't need to talk about it now."

Amanda set her cup of coffee onto the kitchen table and smiled. "How about this: if August comes and I'm still short on cash, and my credit card is already maxed out, and a couple hundred dollars is literally the difference between me joining you there or staying in Evansville forever, I'll reconsider your offer, okay? But I know I can come up with enough money on my own. And maybe I'll wait until tomorrow to tell my parents. They might be more inclined to help me if I have a solid plan. Like, if I could tell them I want to apply to a grad school in Washington in a year or two and I'm trying to find a job there that'll make me a better candidate or something."

"Do you actually want to go to grad school for something specific?"

"I don't know. Maybe! Maybe I do! I never thought seriously about it before. I know a lot of Poli Sci majors do it, but it didn't seem like a realistic possibility for me until today. And now, anything seems possible! I feel like maybe I could actually achieve something special with my life in D.C., and now I'm excited to figure out what it's going to be!"

Jeff cupped his hands around Amanda's face and kissed her. "I think that's the sexiest thing I've ever heard you say."

CHAPTER THREE
Amanda Wagner

Early on a Wednesday morning in the second week of August, Amanda finished packing the last of her belongings into the back of her car. Jeff had left three weeks earlier to get settled in his new apartment. For Jeff, "settling in" meant getting a jumpstart on his required reading, attending networking events and mixers with 2Ls and 3Ls who had returned from their summer internships early, and tracing out the most efficient and reliable public transportation route from his apartment to the law school.

Amanda's new room in Washington, D.C., on the other hand, wouldn't be available until the middle of the month. She had found a space in a three-bedroom condo that was a fifteen-minute walk from Jeff's building. Amanda had only "toured" the property and spoken with the owner—a thirty-one-year-old resident in the oncology ward at MedStar Georgetown Hospital named Marta—via Skype. Marta seemed nice enough, albeit a little high-strung. She had told Amanda that her hours at the hospital were irregular, and that parties, loud music, pets, and any kind of smoking were strictly prohibited. It was even written into the lease agreement Amanda had signed; any violation was grounds for immediate eviction.

"I think those are great rules," Amanda had said, with forced enthusiasm. "I'm in the service industry, so my hours can be erratic too. And I've got a few leads on internships that seem promising. Whenever I'm actually in the condo, I'll probably just keep to myself and sleep."

"And your boyfriend?" Marta asked. "I don't mind if he's over here occasionally, but I don't want you to think this is some sort of two-for-one deal. He shouldn't plan on spending the night here with any sort of regularity, and if he does, he'll have to start paying rent too."

"He has his own place. And he's a law student. He's not a big partier either. Both of us just want to focus on the next steps of our respective careers."

At this, Marta smiled. "I don't mean to be a hard-ass. I just want to make sure you'll be a good fit. I've learned the hard way what happens if I don't do my diligence up front. I charge less than what you'd pay for a crappy apartment in this neighborhood, one without any of the amenities or security that my building has, so I have the luxury of being picky. But I do think you're the right person for the room if you want it."

"I do." This time, Amanda's enthusiasm was not at all forced. For however finicky Marta might be, Amanda could tell she was smart and stable, and the condo itself was noticeably cleaner and more spacious than the other options she had viewed online. More importantly, it was also over $200/month cheaper.

"And you're truly comfortable signing a lease without having seen the property in person? Even though I'm not an apartment complex, I'm still your landlord. It will be a binding commitment, and you can't, like, change your mind if you get here and decide you don't like it as much in person."

"Yes," Amanda nodded vigorously. "I appreciate you taking your laptop all around the common areas for me. I've done my research. Compared to the alternatives, the bedroom's square footage is bigger, the bathroom is nicer, and like you said, none of the other places in my price range have a doorman or their own gym."

"Okay, good. And remind me, since I've interviewed couple people for the space—oh, and by the way, even though you're the youngest of everyone I've spoken to, you seem the most mature.

You're exactly what I was looking for. Anyway, I can't remember, how did you find out about the opening? You know Irina already? Or do you want to talk to her first? Her work schedule is more consistent than mine, but she's rarely here during the daytime. She's a grad student. I think she's studying on-campus right now, or it might be her TA office hours, but I could text her and ask her to FaceTime you when she has a break if that'll help you make your decision."

"Thanks, but don't worry about bothering her. I haven't met Irina yet. I guess she's dating this guy Kristoff that my boyfriend met in the law school bookstore. Classes haven't started yet but they're already planning to form a study group together. I'm sure she and I will get along. It sounds like our paths would've crossed anyway."

"I think you'll like her. She's an interesting person. She's from Latvia, and she used to be a pretty well-respected professional ballerina. She toured all over the world with her old dance company and she speaks like five different languages. Now she's about two years away from her Ph.D. in math and I'm already dreading losing her as a roommate if she gets offered a professorship out of state. We've never fought once in the two and a half years that she's lived here. She always pays her rent on time, and she keeps her space and the common areas spotless. She's a pretty private person, but super kind and sweet once she opens up."

"That sounds exactly like my boyfriend! My last roommate was so nosy and irresponsible, so I can really appreciate the dynamic you're trying to create. Everyone respects each other, everyone gets along, but everyone also has their own life and commitments and gives the others the privacy and quiet they need."

Marta was beaming and Amanda was pleased that she clearly had said the right thing. In fairness, her personal preference would have been for roommates who were also her best friends and who shared all their secrets. It had been like that during her sophomore and junior years of college. Maybe part of growing up was accepting that most relationships were at arms' length. The forced intimacy and instant friendships of undergrad were a thing of the past now. It was sad, actually.

But this apartment was too much of a bargain to pass up. Amanda would find another way to make friends in the new city. If nothing else, she probably could count on her coworkers in whatever restaurant or bar she wound up working at to be her drinking buddies. And once she found her internship, surely that would lead to new connections too. Maybe she could befriend some of Jeff's law school classmates, or at least their significant others. She might not have much in common with a cancer doctor or a math genius, but at least there wouldn't be any melodrama in the apartment. At least she could count on getting a good night's sleep.

"... and I'll email you the paperwork as soon as we disconnect on Skype." Marta was still talking. Amanda worried that she must have been staring blankly into the laptop camera, but Marta didn't seem to notice or care. "And I'll let Irina know the good news when she gets home. She'll be happy. The girl in the room now, Laura, isn't awful. She's just a chatterbox and a bit of a ditz, and she's definitely messier than the two of us. She's certainly not the worst I've seen, though. Anyway, Irina is too polite to say anything out loud, but I know she's glad Laura is leaving. Even though Laura changed her mind about renewing her lease at the last minute, which really could have screwed me, it all seems to have worked out for the best."

"I agree! I'll read over everything and send it back to you by tomorrow morning, along with a Venmo of my deposit."

"Perfect. Laura's last day is August 14, although I'm sure you could see, she has already started boxing up her stuff. She might be gone a little sooner, but you should plan to be here any time on or after the fifteenth to be safe. Hopefully I'll be here to greet you, but if I have to work, I'll leave a key fob and instructions with the doorman so you can move in efficiently. Just update me by text to let me know your status. If Irina is around, she'll help out too. With getting into the building and getting situated up here, I mean. No promises about your furniture or boxes or anything. I don't think either of us will have time to help you with that."

Amanda chuckled. "I wouldn't expect it. I'm selling or trash-ing most of my stuff anyway. I'm just keeping whatever I can fit into my car. I'll need to buy a new mattress when I get there, and my boyfriend will help me with the rest."

"Okay. There's only one parking space for my unit, though, and it's mine. There are a couple of long-term public parking options two or three blocks away, but it adds up. Just something to consider."

"I appreciate it. I hadn't even thought about that. I'll use the public parking as a short-term solution until I figure out whether or not I should sell the car, I guess. Or maybe I could drive Uber or Lyft! Even thought my car is super old and not very fancy, I don't know if that matters." Marta looked impatient. "Anyway, that's my problem and I'll deal with it. Thanks for letting me know."

"Of course. Like I said, I've learned the hard way what happens if I don't set expectations up front. There's a penalty of two months' rent for canceling the lease early, and I won't waive it for any reason. I have the resources to take you to collections if I have to. But I really don't want that to happen. If you're committed to staying in D.C., you'll have a better experience here than anywhere else, especially if you're in the service industry. This neighborhood is already trendy, and it's only getting more popular."

Amanda thanked Marta for her time and they said their good nights and goodbyes. Within two minutes of disconnecting, Amanda received an email with the lease document attached. Her information had been pre-populated into the contract. All Amanda needed to do was provide her electronic signature.

She scrolled through the document, haphazardly skimming the provisions. These were the terms that would govern her living arrangements for the next year, or longer. Rent and her share of utilities would consume almost half of her expected income, maybe even more if business was slow or tips were stingy. And yet, reading through the lease was both embarrassingly confusing and cripplingly boring.

Was this the kind of thing Jeff wanted to do for the rest of his life? He had explained that he'd probably have to spend at least three or four years marking up documents and writing first drafts of legal briefs before his bosses would allow him to step foot in a courtroom under their supervision. And the goal was to resolve his client's problem long before a judge or jury got involved.

"It'll be like any other office job in a lot of ways," he had said. "Just longer, more volatile hours. And eventually, much better pay. But not too many grandiose speeches like on TV, unfortunately."

Amanda was tempted to forward the document to Jeff and ask him to review it for her, but she resisted. He wasn't actually a lawyer yet. There was no reason she couldn't figure out what the lease provisions meant just as well as he could. Besides, at that point he had been in Washington for a mere four days and he already had managed not only to find her this awesome lead on a spare bedroom, but also to make her a list of a few nearby bars and restaurants that were looking for help.

Amanda wondered if Jeff were nervous that she'd try to move in with him, or perhaps that she'd bail on the idea of moving to D.C. completely. Either way, he'd already accomplished more for her there than she'd been able to do for herself from Indiana over the preceding two months combined. She didn't want to text him about anything related to the move again until she could at least say that her living arrangements were officially settled.

Although Amanda's mother had cosigned her current lease in Evansville, Amanda didn't want to ask her parents for help either. So many of her friends' parents called their kids multiple times a week, freaked out if they took longer than an hour to reply to a text, and dictated exactly what classes they were going to take and what their major would be. One acquaintance's father had flown to the school to talk with a history professor when his son's midterm grade wasn't as high as he thought it should have been! Even back in high school, Amanda's parents were never like that. Her mom became a little overbearing at the start of college, with a strict schedule of nightly phone calls and forceful, frequently declared opinions as to what Amanda's major and extracurricular activities should be, but the input and interference had dissipated almost completely by the start of her sophomore year. So much for the idea that parents of an only child were the worst offenders of helicopter parenting.

Amanda knew of pushy parents who had applied for jobs on their child's behalf, had personally driven their kid to interviews, and had waited for them in the car or lobby until they were done. Kiara had heard a rumor about one mother who tried to finagle her way into the interview room with her son so they could answer the potential employer's questions together. Amanda and Kiara had mocked them for a good five minutes ("Where do you see yourself in five years?" "Well, perhaps by then my charming mother here will have weaned me off her titties." "Don't count on it, son."), but later Amanda wondered if her sense of superiority was misplaced. Most of those kids had real jobs lined up now. They weren't desperately applying to every random D.C.-based internship posted to LinkedIn. And two months earlier, Amanda hadn't had the motivation or direction to do that! Maybe those overbearing parents were on to something.

What were Jill Torres's parents like? Amanda was surprised by the sudden thought. Since the summer started, her idle musings about her doppelganger had nearly ceased. She didn't have enough mental energy to expend on anything other than preparing for her next steps, financially and otherwise. When she first called her parents to inform them of her decision, she was shocked by how supportive they were. They said they were proud of her! She had barely formulated a basic outline of her plans at that point, but her parents seemed thrilled that she was taking such a bold risk.

Then, when they visited Indiana for the U of E graduation ceremonies, they presented Amanda with a check for $3,000. She was flabbergasted. They weren't a wealthy family. Her parents didn't do handouts. It was far more than she could have asked for or expected.

"To fix up your car before the trip," her mom had said. "Or to cover your share of the security deposit once you find an apartment."

"Or just to help with general expenses until you can parlay your internship into a full-time job," her dad added. "We've been reading articles online. They say that the best opportunities in big cities like Washington go to the kids with well-connected parents, or who have trust funds and can afford to work for nothing. I wish your mother and I could afford to give you more to help you get started. It was different when we were your age. Going to college and working hard used to be enough."

"But we also read plenty of success stories about people who made it in D.C. without the benefit of political connections or family wealth," her mom jumped in. "Plenty of young ladies in your position have done it, and you can too. That doesn't make us any less proud of you for taking the leap all by yourself though."

Amanda felt her face flush and her eyes brim with tears. She appreciated her parents' kind words, but she couldn't stop staring at the check. Three thousand dollars. It was ten times more money than she'd ever been able to keep in her bank account for more than two days.

"Are you sure you didn't add an extra zero by accident?" Amanda asked, barely audibly.

Her father let out a hearty laugh and hugged her. He normally wasn't so affectionate, and certainly not in public. Amanda had to choke back her tears as her mom patted her on the arm. She never doubted that her parents loved her. They just expressed it in their own way. But they had never made her feel quite as cared for as in that moment.

Graduation weekend was a whirlwind. When it was over, Amanda picked up a second job at the Tropicana Casino downtown, bartending at the Brew Brothers Tap House. It was a good gig. The bar was adjacent to the casino floor and, unlike Mojo's, which always seemed to slow down a bit after the undergrads left for break, the casino stayed busy throughout the whole summer. Notwithstanding her parents' generous gift, Amanda was trying to plan ahead and save as much money as possible in advance of her move. Between at least sixty hours a week working, an hour or two almost every night applying to internships, and keeping up with her fitness program five days a week, Amanda was overwhelmed. And yet, somehow, it was also the happiest she could remember having been since she was a child.

She and Jeff never got around to taking a long-weekend trip to Nashville or St. Louis that summer like they had discussed. They never managed to schedule a good time for her to meet Jeff's parents. Most nights, they were content to collapse onto the couch in Amanda's blessedly roommate-free apartment. But their bond seemed to be growing stronger. It felt like a real adult relationship now.

Amanda looked up from her laptop. She had read the same convoluted provision in the lease half a dozen times and she couldn't recall a word of it. She wouldn't bother her parents with this either. She willed herself to focus.

Marta had emailed her ten minutes ago. Amanda didn't want to reply too quickly; she got the impression that Marta would look down on her if she knew that she was planning to sign the contract without really reading, much less understanding, it. Amanda figured she ought to wait at least another twenty minutes before sending it back, so she got up, grabbed a soda from the refrigerator, and typed "Jill Torres MIT" into Google when she sat back down. Just to see.

Amanda scrolled through the results absentmindedly. Somehow, parsing through Jill's accomplishments and trying to find clues about her identity didn't seem as important or interesting as it had several months before. There weren't any new links anyway. Maybe Jill had peaked early, whereas Amanda felt like her life was finally about to begin in earnest. She thought about browsing through the image results to see if there was anything new, or to take another look at that one unsettling photo that was basically an ever-so-slight distortion of her own face.

"Oh, who cares!" Amanda snapped. She blushed, even though the apartment was empty. Then she exited out of that browser window entirely and began to type out a reply to Marta.

CHAPTER FOUR
Amanda Wagner

Washington, D.C. was overwhelming. Overwhelming, but exhilarating. Jeff had asked Amanda if he should fly back to Indiana to help her pack, maybe even buy a one-way plane ticket so that he could accompany her on the eleven-hour drive from Evansville, but Amanda had declined. She was pleasantly surprised at how successful she had been at selling most of her furniture and apartment furnishings simply by posting them on a message board for incoming students. The remainder she had unloaded for cents on the dollar to a trio of locals who, Amanda suspected, would resell everything for a sizeable profit once more students had arrived for the start of the fall semester. Really, it was a win-win situation. Amanda was able to stuff the rest of her possessions into her car without throwing anything away, and she had an extra $1,500 in her pocket to boot.

The long solo drive was unexpectedly enjoyable. She stopped for bathroom breaks and snacks whenever she wanted, she had full control of the radio, and she was able to coast along in the middle lane without sensing Jeff's suppressed aggravation from the passenger seat when she opted not to zoom past drivers who were going "only" ten miles over the speed limit. Her old car held its own the entire trip, and as Amanda pulled into a long-term parking structure two blocks away from her new apartment, she thought of Marta's advice with a heavy heart. Even if keeping her car was financially impractical, irresponsible even, she didn't want to sell it quite yet. Ridding herself of her college belongings had felt like the first step to a fresh start and an adult life, but her faithful old Versa held a sentimental value that Amanda hadn't appreciated until she saw the price of parking per day and realized that she might be forced to let it go.

But, she thought, she should wait until she had found a steady job before deciding definitively to sell. If it took too long to find a bartending or waitressing position, or even if she simply wasn't picking up enough shifts, she might need to follow through with the offhand idea she'd had of driving for Uber or Lyft on the side. Although, wouldn't the type of person who could afford a private ride over public transportation expect to be chauffeured around town in a newer, fancier vehicle? If they were Very Important and in a rush, they were unlikely to be as restrained in their frustration as Jeff was with her cautious defensive driving. What would she do if her GPS signal dropped? What would she do if some big dude started being sketchy or aggressive?

Then again, Amanda remembered having similar fears before she started her very first retail job as a sophomore in high school ("What if someone tries to shoplift?" "What if no one takes me seriously because of my age?"), and again before she interviewed for her first waitressing job at the steakhouse ("What if I mess up someone's order?" "What if a customer tries to get handsy with me?"), and yet she had ended up being a natural at both. Any challenges she faced or mistakes she made never rose to a level that got her fired. She always tried to develop a solution before informing her supervisors that there was a problem, and that usually seemed to do wonders for mitigating their anger.

Never mind driving for Uber. Why was it so impossible to imagine that the skills she had acquired from seven years in the workforce would translate to an office job or internship? None of her applications, even for unpaid positions, had panned out yet. During the first few days of submitting her résumé to various opportunities, Amanda had been fueled by fantasies of strutting into the office and awing her new colleagues with her impeccable style, sharp wit, and brilliant ideas. Eight futile, demoralizing weeks later, and Amanda was struggling to envision herself ever doing any type of work outside of the service industry. Now, when she applied to open positions, her fantasies had turned dark, with her imaginary future coworkers scoffing at her inexpensive suit jackets and rolling their eyes at her lame ideas, whispering to each other that the new girl ought to shut up and fetch the coffee. She was, at least, eminently qualified to do that.

Amanda had arrived at the front of Marta's building. Most of her boxes and bags were still in her car. The parking lot seemed relatively well-lit and secure, and frankly she was more concerned about the cost of repairs if someone were to smash a window than she was about anything inside getting stolen. Unloading was going to take multiple trips. She didn't expect her new roommates to help her, and for some reason she felt shy about texting Jeff and asking him to come over. She was glad that she had motivated herself to get on the road several hours before dawn that morning and finish the full trip in one day. She was exhausted, but she had spared herself the expense of a hotel somewhere in West Virginia and she'd still have an hour or two of daylight to finish the task at hand.

As Amanda was reaching for the door buzzer, she could see Marta hurrying toward her while looking at her phone.

"I got paged thirty seconds after you texted me," Marta said as she opened the door. "You're Amanda, right? I recognize you from our Skype talk."

Amanda nodded and held out her hand. Marta was staring intently at her phone and didn't notice. Amanda quickly pulled it back, embarrassed.

"My Uber should be here by now. I swear, half the time, I'd be better off fetching my car and driving myself there. I could jog to the hospital faster. You didn't try to park in the building deck, right? It's all reserved spots. You'll get towed, guaranteed. There's nothing I can do about that."

"No, I'm in public parking about two blocks away. I'll carry my stuff over."

"What?" Marta looked up, irritated. "Where is this guy? Irina is here, so she'll let you in and get you a key fob and show you your room. Is that bag all you brought?"

"No, I'll have to make a few—"

"Damn it, what is this idiot doing? He's parked halfway down the street. Look, Laura left her mattress, but it's on the floor and it's grungy and old. And she had some disgusting habits. I wouldn't want to sleep on it under any circumstances, but definitely not without any bed sheets."

"It's okay. I brought some. They're still in—"

"Irina can tell you where the Target is. Or, you know, just GoogleMap it. I can't help you anymore right now. This clown is going to make me chase him down. I'll go over everything with you when I get back from the hospital. That might not be until late tonight or tomorrow morning. Assuming this jackass manages to get me there at all. Hey! Hey!"

With that, Marta ran down the street, waving her arms and hollering at the Uber driver. Amanda stifled a laugh. Marta was shorter than Amanda had expected and her face showed more lines in the sunlight than Amanda recalled seeing over Skype, but overall she was prettier in person. She was also abrasive and intimidating, for sure, but it didn't bother Amanda much. More than anything, she envied Marta's confidence, her seemingly unshakeable certainty that everything she had to say was important, that her time was important, that her work was important. The entire premise of Amanda's past few jobs was that her personal time was valueless. She was expected to drop everything to cover a shift on her scheduled day off, or to stay until closing even when she'd been told she'd be cut early and had planned to use that time to study for an exam the next morning. A false sense of urgency was foisted upon every task, from cutting garnishes to making sure table 14 got their food within fifteen minutes, notwithstanding all the "gluten-free, extra cheese, dressing on the side" substitutions they had made or how stoned the line cooks happened to be that day. As if it were a matter of life or death that someone in the kitchen forgot to sub in curly fries for potato chips and Amanda failed to catch the mistake before taking the order to the table. As if it merited reaming out Amanda for twenty minutes after her shift was over because she didn't pre-cut enough tomato slices before the lunch rush. As if the drunken whining of some washed up forty-something in town for the weekend trying to relive her college glory days, upset that a damn sports bar didn't have a sufficiently upscale selection of red wines and that her nineteen-year-old server didn't have a suitably developed palette to recommend the appropriate vintage to accompany the grease-bomb bacon grilled cheese sandwich dipped in a vat of ranch dressing that the cow had ordered, as if *this* should be treated with the same profound apologetic concern that you'd express if you accidentally ran over your lonely elderly neighbor's pet cat.

Would Marta ever know such indignities? Would Jill Torres? Was Amanda delusional to think she could make this D.C. experiment work? At least waiting tables was an evil she knew and understood. At least she had the camaraderie of her fellow servers, the late nights griping about the idiotic requests they'd confronted that day while spending half their tip money treating each other to rounds of shots at the dive bar down the street. Most of the paid office positions Amanda applied for sounded utterly soul-crushing. Amanda was almost relieved when she received her rejection letters, one after another. Although her efforts to obtain an unpaid internship were equally futile, at least the tasks set forth in the vague job descriptions for those roles hinted at the possibility of helping with meaningful research or projects. At least those organizational missions meant the opportunity to be a part of something bigger, something world-changing, instead of just resignation to life as a corporate drone. That was the point of this adventure, wasn't it? That she'd find her cause, her purpose, her passion, and it would inspire and energize her so much that she'd willingly spend her time outside the office waiting tables or serving drinks to make up for the lack of salary that pursuing noble ideals seemed to entail.

So Amanda stifled the urge to pick up her bag, run to her car, and drive back to the Midwest or to her parents' house without giving D.C. or Jeff or these lofty ambitions another thought again.

Irina was inside waiting for her. Amanda had to try to make this work.

Another resident was exiting the building. Amanda's focus snapped back to the present moment and she caught the door in time to let herself into the building, then slid into an elevator going up. She knocked timidly on the door of Unit 411. Almost immediately, it opened.

"I am Irina," a dark-eyed brunette said, extending her hand. "I did not mean to startle you. I saw you approaching on the security camera app." She held up her phone, which showed a blurry feed of the hallway just outside the door. Amanda stepped into the apartment and the back of her head fell out of the frame. Irina returned her phone to her pocket. "Marta left five minutes ago. Did you find her, or did the doorman let you in?"

"I'm Amanda, it's nice to meet you! I did see her, but she was rushing to work. I didn't notice any doorman in the lobby. I kind of let myself in."

"Oh, okay. Everyone knows that he often takes very long cigarette breaks. The neighborhood is safe, but you are supposed to have a key fob to get through the front doors or use the elevators. Here." Irina handed a small black disk to Amanda. "You put it on your keychain and wave it at the sensors. It will get you into the building's gym too, which is on the seventeenth floor. It is a decent gym, if fitness is something you value. It has all the basic equipment. You must not lose that fob thing, though. Building management charges seventy-five dollars to replace it, and they will act like you must have sold it on the street for drug money. Our apartment door is keypad access only. We each have our own code. I can help you set up yours right now." Irina paused and her expression softened. "Or, I can stop talking and give you a moment to catch your breath if you would like."

Amanda laughed more loudly than she intended, partly out of nerves and partly out of relief.

"We can do it now, that'd be great," Amanda said. "I didn't mean to interrupt your day. I'm sure you have better things to do."

"No, no, it is quite alright. I do apologize if I seem... agitated. I have a dozen more papers to grade by tomorrow morning's 10:30 a.m. class, that is why. It is probably good that I step away for a bit. It is frustrating, you know? The class is called Philosophy of Mathematics. My focus is applied mathematics, but I am TA'ing it because I need the money and the professor is a publishing star. Maybe two students in a class of twenty care at all. If any of the others bother to show up, they spend the whole lecture looking down at their phones and texting."

"It would suck to take the time to prepare a thoughtful lecture on a subject you care about, and then present it to the top of twenty students' skulls," Amanda mused sympathetically.

"Yes! Exactly!"

"At least you know which of the guys are prematurely bald-ing," Amanda added with a smirk. A heavy silence hung in the air, and Amanda felt her cheeks growing hot. Then Irina threw back her head and laughed in delight.

"Prematurely balding! Oh! I will tell your joke to my colleague! We will laugh for hours." Irina giggled. "Prematurely balding," she repeated with a smile. She looked up and stared intently at Amanda. "So, what has brought you to Washington? Your fiancé attends Georgetown Law with my boyfriend, yes? But what do you do?"

"Well, Jeff is just my boyfriend, we're not engaged yet." Yet? As if it were imminent? Amanda wondered whether she ought to clarify her words, but she hastily continued. "And as for me, I'm still applying to jobs and internships. A nonprofit, a think tank, even a startup—I'm trying to be flexible about the organization's structure, but I'm definitely trying to find a position related to environmental conservation."

Amanda paused again, shocked at herself. It was true that she had applied to several entities focused on environmental protection and similar concerns, but she had been spamming her résumé to all kinds of organizations as long as they were adver-tising a position for which she was remotely qualified. She had no idea why she had told Irina that environmental conservation was "definitely" what she wanted to do, as if it were some lifelong

41

calling that she was destined to fulfill. Nevertheless, this was the most clearly she had articulated her aspirations to anyone. For whatever random reason her mind had jumped to "environmental conservation," of all things, it was invigorating to declare a goal with such certainty and purpose!

Irina seemed to be giving her an encouraging look, so Amanda continued, "I haven't had much luck yet, but I'm hoping that now that I'm physically here, they'll know I'm serious and the interviews will pick up. I'm willing to be patient, although obviously not forever. I figure I can waitress or bartend in the meantime, and maybe drive Uber or deliver Postmates on the side if I need to."

"Huh. Do you have your own car here?"

"I do, yeah. It's where the rest of my stuff is right now. It's old, but it's still reliable. And I'd clean it up before I started driving anyone around."

There was a long pause. Irina's expression was inscrutable. Amanda wondered if she was bothering her, nervously oversharing her problems when all Irina wanted to do was get back to grading papers or focusing on her own research. Still, Amanda couldn't resist asking, "Do you think that's unsafe? You look skeptical."

"Not unsafe. Or perhaps it is, I do not know what security measures those companies provide to protect drivers. I do know other graduate students who have supplemented their income this way for many years. I think most of them only pick up passengers when they are driving to or from GW anyway, though."

"But you don't think it's worth it?"

"Well, if building your career is your priority, you might be better off focusing your attention elsewhere. Owning a car here is expensive, and driving in this city is very difficult and frustrating and time-consuming. And perhaps you have seen the self-driving cars? My recollection is that this city was one of the first jurisdictions to allow them. And my guess is that the government will begin phasing out human-driven cars within the district limits over the next few years."

"I've only ever seen one once on the road in real life, but it scared the shit out of me when I looked over at the stoplight and the driver's seat of the car next to me was empty," Amanda laughed. "I'm guessing the dude in the passenger seat could've done some sort of manual override, or whatever the technical term is, if he had to. At least, that's what I told myself. Although he looked like he was playing a game on his phone. Either way, I can't imagine people will be willing to give up driving within the next few years. I know things are different in the Midwest than on the coasts, but I don't think there was a single self-driving car in the entire state of Indiana. What is the government going to do, seize millions of cars against our will and force us to buy new ones?" Irina was looking at her with the same placid but enigmatic stare. "*Are* they going to do that here? Did you hear something in the news?"

"It is merely an inference. Certainly no announcements have been made, to my knowledge. But they are building parking structures just outside the city limits and renovating the public transportation system. Self-driving cars are being subsidized. There was a provision slipped into an unrelated federal bill about six months ago that would have banned the manufacture or sale of any human-driven cars within the next two years, but of course it was struck out long before the legislation was passed. As you suggest, that would have been too abrupt a change. But if you look at places that have publicly declared their intention to move toward self-driving vehicles, in this country and elsewhere around the world, you will note that Washington, D.C. is on a similar path. I suppose that commuters from the suburbs will have to leave their human-driven vehicles at one of the parking structures they are building and take public transport or a self-driving car the rest of the way. And eventually those structures will be transformed into holding stations for the self-driving vehicles themselves. Our grandkids will be amazed that anyone ever dared to drive a motor vehicle on their own."

Amanda hesitated. She had never engaged in a conversation quite like this, and she didn't know how to respond. Irina was absolutely nothing like what she had expected. Marta had described her as basically a quiet, reclusive math genius, and yet here she was, confidently expounding on technology and politics—with the slightest hint of a foreign accent and the occasional mispronounced word, reminding Amanda that English was not her first language nor was the United States her native land—with more insight than Amanda could remember having heard in four years as a political science major. Although, in fairness, she herself had been exactly the kind of student that exasperated Irina, spending most of her classes texting (maybe she hadn't been doing it as covertly as she had thought), and only briefly reverting her attention to the lecture when some cocky, overzealous classmate interrupted the lesson in an inane attempt to correct or argue with the professor.

Was this how everyone in Washington, D.C. spoke and thought and interacted with each other? It was humiliating. She couldn't think of one single intelligent thing to say in reply to Irina. No wonder she couldn't get an interview. She had been griping about how worthless her degree was, but now she wondered if she were at least partly to blame. Maybe the job market was oversaturated with applicants, but maybe hiring managers were sick of trying to coax coherent answers out of recent graduates on questions relating to the exact subject matter of their major.

"I do not mean to digress," Irina continued. "You are an environmental activist, not a city planner. Although, I suppose it is related. In this city, everything is politics and everything is interrelated. I suppose you will figure that out quickly. Anyway, let us finish up with this. You can type in your four-digit access code to the door now." Amanda had barely registered it, but Irina had been tinkering with the keypad to the entrance as they were talking. Or rather, as Irina was talking and Amanda was dumb-foundedly listening. Irina motioned for Amanda to proceed.

"Ugh, okay. Umm, eight, nine, nine, one," Amanda said aloud as she clunkily punched in the digits.

"Good. Now hit the pound key."

"Pound key?"

"Hashtag." Irina stifled a smile.

"Oh, okay. Shoot, should I have not said my code out loud?"

"It does not matter. Marta will ask you for it anyway. She will remove your access whenever you move out. And if you give it to someone untrustworthy and they break in, she will know who to blame." Irina shrugged. "Her place, her rules. Are you ready to see your room?"

Amanda nodded and followed Irina down the hall.

"You and I share that bathroom there, but I only use it to shower, so feel free to leave your stuff on the counter or wherever. I will not touch it. My room has its own half-bath with a toilet and sink, so I brush my teeth and do my cosmetics in there. It is a—what is the politer word?—a crappy deal for you, perhaps, but I think Marta charges you a slightly lower rent since technically you do not get a private bathroom. And this is your bedroom. Ugh, Laura was such a slob!" Irina bent over and picked up two empty beer cans. "This is the cleanest the room has been since the day she moved in, but you might want to give everything a scrub yourself. Marta told Laura that she would subtract a cleaning fee from her deposit if she did not tidy it up herself, but it does not look like Marta checked it or hired anyone after Laura left."

"It's really not that bad," Amanda said. "I'm excited about the big windows! And I'll sweep up the floor after I carry the rest of my stuff in."

"Is your boyfriend coming to help you? Jeff, right?"

"Yes, Jeff. I haven't even texted him to let him know I'm here yet. I wanted to get settled first."

"And you do not mind sleeping on that mattress on the floor? I have extra clean sheets you can use until you have a chance to buy your own."

Amanda felt like she was disproportionately touched by this offer. "That is so nice of you! Luckily, I have some in my car that are the right size, and I'll buy a bed frame and maybe a newer mattress as soon as I can afford it. Honestly, it doesn't look as bad as Marta made it out to be. It'll be fine in the meantime, and I'm sure I can find some cinderblocks or something from Craigslist to lift it off the floor a little. But thank you."

"Okay. I am sorry I cannot help you unload, but I really do need to get back to work."

"Oh, I never would have expected you to haul my junk in for me! I'm sorry I interrupted you at all. You've been so helpful getting me set up. I won't bother you anymore tonight."

"It really is no trouble. I needed an excuse to step away for a break anyway. Just remember to take the building key fob with you, and please shut our door on the way out. It locks automatically, and you can use your code to get back in now."

Amanda gasped and her face flushed a deep red. "I can't believe this. I've already forgotten—"

"Eight, nine, nine, one," Irina interjected, laughing. "You muttered it out loud as you typed it, remember? I am guessing it is your birth year backwards, no?"

"I'm an idiot. Yes, you're exactly right. I promise I'm not always like this. I'm just flustered and exhausted from the drive."

"You are fine. This is a big change. If you do need me tonight, just knock on my bedroom door."

"Thank you so much, Irina."

Irina smiled and turned toward her room. She halted in the doorway. "One more thing, and take this advice for whatever it may be worth. This is your first time being in this city, yes?" Amanda nodded and Irina continued. "Go see all the monuments, visit the museums, do all the touristy stuff this first week. Before you get into a routine and your job and the rest of your day-to-day responsibilities take over. Otherwise you will probably never get around to it. You will start to become, shall we say, immune to the city's charms. I have learned this from experience. Besides, if you end up bartending at a touristy place, you will want to talk to your customers about what is worth seeing from personal experience. But, to use the expression, this is merely my two cents."

"I think that's great advice! I mean it. Even if Jeff is too busy to come with me, I'll go by myself. Thanks!"

"I am happy to meet you, Amanda." Irina gave Amanda another smile and walked down the hall. Amanda glanced into her bedroom, overwhelmed but oddly proud. Then she set down her bag and left to fetch the remainder of her belongings from her car.

CHAPTER FIVE
Jill Torres

Jill Torres knew exactly who Amanda Wagner was. She had known for years. She knew why they looked nearly identical, and she often wondered what personality quirks and interests they might share. If they met, would their inevitable similarities cause them to clash or bond? But Jill knew she could never approach Amanda. She could never introduce herself and explain the bizarre connection they shared. They could never be friends.

Jill and her family were different. She couldn't remember a time when she wasn't aware of this fact. Although her parents never wished to conceal the truth from her, the tactlessness of total strangers forced them to initiate certain conversations before they otherwise would have preferred.

One of Jill's first memories was of a polished brunette woman accosting her mother, Jaya, at the playground as Jill and Jaya were walking back to their car. Jill had been misbehaving all day, and Jaya was pulling her along with a bit of force (albeit nothing egregious) while reprimanding her for her continued disobedience. The brunette woman, who had been observing Jaya and Jill through the tinted windows of her Mercedes GLS SUV, stormed up to them in the parking lot. In front of an audience of three other pearl-adorned, Waspy suburban moms, the woman yanked at Jaya's arm until she broke Jaya's grasp on Jill's shoulder, and barked out a disjoined series of questions and rebukes: "Who are you? Are you this girl's nanny? How dare you! How do you think her parents would react if they knew you were treating her this roughly? I could have you deported! Do you even understand English?"

Jill was only four years old. She desperately wanted to defend her mother but she didn't know how, so she began to sob. She couldn't remember how her mother had responded to the woman; Jaya had perfected the art of a stony face and an icy stare, but she almost never lost control of her temper. All Jill could remember after they had gotten away from the woman was her mother strapping her into her car seat, giving her a juice box to calm her down, and telling her, "The rest of the world doesn't like that our skin colors don't match. That nasty, nosy woman wasn't the first person to bother us, and she won't be the last. I don't care about any of them, and I need you to be tough and learn not to care either. Okay, my sweet baby girl? No more tears today. Drink your juice. I will always be your mother and Daddy will always be your daddy, and we are so proud and happy that you're our daughter. And that's the only thing that matters."

Jaya had been right, though. That woman in the park was far from the last to question Jaya's parental authority. They lived in Westport, Connecticut, where the residents were, almost without exception, as uniformly white as they were uniformly wealthy. Jaya often felt like her mere presence made many of them uncomfortable. And when she had her daughter with her, Jaya knew that they could not fathom that a petite Black woman with thick, tightly curled hair could be the mother of the fair-skinned, blond, robust young Jill.

It wasn't just strangers either. Jill remembered her tío Bruno admonishing her father, Mateo, in hushed tones during a family gathering, asking if Jaya had faked being pregnant. If Mateo and Jaya were going to feign a pregnancy to try to conceal an adoption, Bruno had continued, why the hell wouldn't they have sought out a Latina or Black baby? Her tía Rosa chimed in as well, angrily reminding her dad that pretty blond white girls would never have trouble finding adoptive parents. He owed it to his community,

Rosa had said, to choose an Ecuadorian girl, or at least a child with some Latin American roots.

Jill was barely five years old at the time and was eavesdropping on their conversation with only partial comprehension, but she was clever enough to deduce that her aunt and uncle were mad at her daddy and it was her fault because she was a bad kid. Her father caught her eye, and she remembered his expression darkening—Jill heard him holler about devious coworkers and unscrupulous merchants from time to time over the ensuing years, but she never again saw him as profoundly angry as he was in that moment—as he told them with steely ferocity, "Jill is my daughter. She is *our* daughter. She and Jaya are the most precious things in the entire world to me. You will respect my family and you will drop this conversation, permanently, or you can get the hell out of my home and don't bother contacting me again."

The three of them exchanged a few more words in Spanish—Jill could no longer recall what they had said—and then Bruno excused himself to get a beer from the refrigerator, while Rosa give Jill a half-hearted pat on the head and returned to the couch to sit with her grandmother.

The family moved past the encounter. Jill's cousins continued to visit the house from time to time throughout the years, and they always played happily together. But the younger ones sometimes liked to hold their arms next to Jill's, to see how closely their skin tones matched. It was one of the few instances in which Jill would be reminded that she was different from everyone around her, and she'd always think back to that day when she was five. She knew that her cousins liked her—they were guileless almost to a fault, and would have told her to her face if they didn't want to play with her—but she always wondered about their parents. They always seemed wary around her. Or was she just imagining it? Jill had decided at age six to speak to them only in Spanish, and by age eight she was independently preparing llapingachos, patacones, and other Ecuadorian snacks for family gatherings. As if, somehow, this would prove to them that she belonged.

Jill rarely saw her mother's side of the family. Zimbabwe was a twenty-three-hour plane trip away, and even the worst seats on the most frugal of budget airlines cost almost $2,000 per person. Nevertheless, Jill suspected that her mother's concerns about the financial expense and her purported reluctance to pull Jill out of school for several weeks at a time were a pretense to avoid returning to her native country more often than once every five or six years. Jaya clearly loved her family; she spoke on the phone with her sisters and mother almost every day, sent them money every month, and offered up the guest bedroom indefinitely to whichever distant cousin or step-uncle twice removed happened to be traveling within two hundred miles of Connecticut. But Jill had visited Harare with her mother three times, and despite being surrounded by family and despite Jaya's unabashed pride in her cultural heritage, Jaya's unease was palpable when she was on Zimbabwean soil.

Jill was too young to remember much of their first trip, but when they returned when she was nine, Jill was confused by the change in her mother's demeanor once the plane had landed. Although lacking the ubiquitous signifiers of wealth and status that Jill had become accustomed to seeing in Westport, her grandmother's neighborhood seemed safe and the family house was cozy and welcoming. Everyone spoke English and they even used American currency. Unlike the playgrounds and PTA meetings in their hometown, where svelte white women with silky shoulder-length hair wearing polo shirts and pearls reigned supreme, almost everyone in Harare shared her mother's complexion, hairstyles, and fashion sense. There, Jill, with her pale white skin, was the outsider! And yet, her mom was distracted and skittish.

When they returned together for the third time, a month after Jill had turned fifteen, her mom seemed even more uncomfortable than she had during their previous visit. The roads were in disrepair (Jill didn't remember nearly so many potholes on the last trip), there seemed ᵗ be more people in dirty clothes selling fruit on the side of the street, and the family car was pulled over on a pretense when they were driving to Jill's grandmother's house from the airport and her mom was forced to give the officer a small bribe before they could continue on. This wasn't the vibrant Harare that Jill remembered from six years before. This version of Harare was struggling to keep its spirit high. And yet, for reasons she couldn't articulate, Jill thought that her mother's agitation seemed to have more personal roots.

Then, on the second to last day of their eighteen-day stay, Jill overheard her Aunt Tawana talking with a friend. Jill didn't mean to eavesdrop at first. The two women were speaking in Shona, unaware that although Jill's command of the language was imperfect and she spoke with a westernized accent, she could understand almost everything they were saying. Her mother's occasional language lessons and her monthly Skype chats with her cousin Masimba—a handsome boy who lived in Avondale and was about the same age as Jill—apparently had taught her well. When Jill realized that Tawana and her friend were talking about her mother, expressing concern for Jaya's wellbeing, she couldn't resist listening in.

"It still affects her, doesn't it?"

"How could it not?"

"And the girl is the same age she was when it happened?"

"Almost. Jaya was sixteen. The girl is now fifteen. Jaya has barely let her out of her sight since they arrived."

"Can we blame her?"

"She is not so strict when they are in America. She lets the girl play sports for her high school. They travel to games by bus. It must be a small horror for her every time."

At this, both women dropped their heads and murmured to themselves.

"I still see the police officer who led the investigation at the market almost every Sunday," Tawana's friend continued. "He's remarried now. To an older woman. They don't have children. Can we blame him?"

"Imagine that first date. Do you introduce yourself as the man who caught the Kombi Killer?"

"Or as the man who didn't catch him until two more girls were murdered?"

Again, the two women dropped their heads and muttered expressions of sadness that seemed hollow to Jill.

"It's not why Jaya left," Aunt Tawana said suddenly. "But it's why she'll never come back. She's an American now. How can I resent her for leaving us behind after all that? How could she face her little friends' parents and siblings? Even after twenty years?"

Before Tawana's friend could respond, they were interrupted by an acquaintance offering them food and inviting them to join another conversation. Jill turned away and busied herself with her cell phone, trying to process what she had overheard. Despite how close she was with her mother, Jill felt embarrassed to ask Jaya for details. If her mom wanted to share this part of her past, wouldn't she have done so already? Her father had stayed in the States this trip, and she didn't feel entirely comfortable asking him about his wife's past either. Even if she had been willing to wait that long for an answer, she suspected he'd reprimand her for being nosy or a gossip. And maybe he would have been right, maybe it wasn't any of her business. But Jill's curiosity was consuming.

For all the strides she had made in speaking and understanding Shona, Jill's spelling abilities were still lagging. After three failed attempts at searching for the phrase her aunt's friend had used, Jill tried typing "Kombi Killer" in English into Google instead. It seemed like a good translation. Immediately, dozens of results popped onto the screen. She skimmed the links on the first page and, overwhelmed, tried a second search: "Kombi Killer Jaya Mnangagwa". Her mother's maiden name. Again, dozens of results popped up, and now her mother's connection to the tragedy was apparent.

When Jaya was sixteen, she and three of her classmates were going to take a kombi from their school back to their neighborhood, about ten kilometers away. The other girls had already boarded the van when Jaya realized that she had left her chemistry notebook behind in one of the classrooms. Jaya's friends had told her to leave it. One had quietly warned her that it would be too dangerous to take a van ride back by herself. But Jaya had insisted that she needed it to study that night, and if they couldn't wait for her, then she would just walk back alone. That was the last time anyone saw the other three girls alive. Their bodies were discovered four days later, tortured and mutilated. Jill felt dizzy as she read through the horrific details. Her mom had been interviewed repeatedly by the police. Despite being a minor at the time, her name had been widely published in the newspapers. Jaya had given as many details as she could recall about the kombi driver's appearance and demeanor, but her memories were fuzzy. The police sketch that was drawn up seemed like it could have been almost any short-haired man between the ages of twenty-five and forty.

Of course, Jill thought angrily, defensive of her mother. How could Jaya have known that justice for her friends would depend on her recollection of a single one of the hundred different people with whom she happened to cross paths that day? Besides, they weren't even sure whether the driver was the culprit!

Jill read on. After a week had passed, two more girls from a neighboring school went missing. The newspapers seemed almost gleeful to report it, to incite a panic in the local population. When their bodies were discovered two days later showing the same gruesome evidence of torture as Jaya's friends, a source inside the police department leaked the news that they had determined conclusively that the same individual was responsible for both killings. This was not a copycat. This was the work of a serial killer. A day later, reports leaked that the police had tied the murders to the death of an eleven-year-old girl two years before. Jill clicked on, trying to focus her attention on finding additional references to her mother's involvement in the aftermath, but diverted and ensnared by all the morbid details of the story.

A week later, a suspect was brought in for questioning, then released. Three days later, the same man was arrested. Jill checked the dates on the articles. Two years later, he was convicted on six counts of murder committed in aggravating circumstances. The court exercised its discretion to impose the death penalty. There was an automatic appeal. And then, the papers seemed to stop reporting on the case completely. The news cycle had moved on.

Jill tried one more search: "Kombi Killer Jaya Mnangagwa trial OR testimony OR witness".

She knew her mother had left Harare at age eighteen to attend Caltech on a full scholarship. She knew that her mother had remained in Pasadena year-round. Whenever Jill was being wasteful or greedy as a little girl, her mom never hesitated to tell her stories about how she had worked in the housekeeping department of one of the fancy hotels off-campus for twenty-five hours a week while still maintaining a 3.7 GPA in her biochemistry major. Her parents loved to tell the story of how they first met in a physics study group when they were freshmen, although they lost touch thereafter and didn't reconnect until they were both in graduate school.

But her mom never mentioned that she had left campus for two weeks during the fall term of her freshman year to return to Zimbabwe and testify against the man who had murdered her classmates and friends. The kombi van driver. The man who almost certainly would have killed her mother too, had she not forgotten her chemistry notebook and decided to walk the six miles home alone that day.

My God. Jill put down her phone. She had no idea if her father knew about any of this. She couldn't decide whether or not to tell her mother what she had learned. What purpose would it serve? Her parents always had been honest with her about profoundly difficult, complicated family secrets. For whatever reason, her mom wanted to hold this part of her life in her past. She wanted to act like it didn't exist. She didn't want to be judged for it. Jill understood this all too well. She never looked up the Kombi Killer case online again, and from then on she was careful not to ask her mom anything other than superficial questions about her teenage years.

As her Aunt Tawana had said, with more than a hint of bitterness, Jaya was an American now. After Jaya had graduated from Caltech, she attended Columbia University in New York to pursue her Ph.D. in Bioengineering. Unbeknownst to her, Mateo had made his way across the country after graduation as well, spending a year doing statistical analysis for an accounting firm in Chicago before getting accepted into the Courant Institute at NYU. The winter before he received his master's degree, he presented a paper at a conference on data analytics and personalized medicine.

"It's a trendy topic now," Jill's dad liked to say, "but back then it was a niche field. The same conference today would have a thousand attendees. But there couldn't have been more than 150 people, all highly specialized, who bothered to show up that year."

Jaya was one of them. Mateo recognized her instantly when she approached the foldout table where he was refilling his coffee and surveying the bagel options with dismay. He had never forgotten her quiet confidence or her beauty, and he found himself as intimidated by her then as he had been during their freshman year of college. Jaya gave him a penetrating stare, as if she were trying to recall whether she had met him at a past conference or seen him lingering around one of the graduate student lounges on Columbia's campus. Mateo blushed, then promptly collected himself, held out his hand, and reintroduced himself.

Jaya was as captivating as ever. Six years before, Mateo had been a handsome, cocky nineteen-year-old boy whose ego couldn't have stomached rejection from such a woman. He had convinced himself that he was better off playing the field and he never asked her out. Now, he no longer permitted himself such self-deception, and he had grown weary of first dates with ditzes and bores. After a few minutes of polite conversation, before their break was over and the next panel was scheduled to commence, Mateo practically begged Jaya to let him take her to dinner. Jaya had blushed and, after a moment's hesitation, agreed.

"Mi media naranja, mi alma gemela," he always concluded the story, irrespective of whether he had been telling it in Spanish, English, or the broken Russian he had learned later in life for his job. "God meant for the two of us to find each other." Whenever the family was alone, he would add, "Just as He intended for the two of us to find you, mijita preciosa."

They had dated for another two years before Mateo presented Jaya with a garnet solitaire ring set in antique gold that had been handed down to him from his bisabuela. He had finished graduate school and was making almost six figures working for a government contractor as an analyst, but when they had first started talking seriously about marriage, Jaya had made it clear that she would rather he save his money for a future down payment on a house than spend it on an extravagant diamond ring. Three months later, they rented out a bar in Fort Greene, Brooklyn, and got married in front of about thirty guests, almost all from their respective graduate programs. Only two of Mateo's siblings and no one from Jaya's family were able to attend.

CHAPTER SIX
Jill Torres

Jill's curious parentage could be traced back to a twenty-year-old pre-med student named Connor, who had just finished his sophomore year of college and was home for break during the summer of 1997. Connor's father, who was a long-time golfing buddy of Dr. Adrian P. Wu of the Meskhenet Center for Reproductive Medicine in Stamford, Connecticut, had arranged for the internship, which came with a $7,500 stipend. It was far more than Connor could've earned anywhere else, particularly with his dismal GPA, and he was terrified of losing the money—both the summer stipend and, potentially, the generous allowance his father sent him each month while he was at school. His parents were lenient, but his father had made it clear that if Connor didn't take this job seriously, if he tarnished the family's reputation in any way, there would be consequences.

Alas, on the fateful day in question, Connor already had arrived to work late and hungover. He already had been scolded by one of Dr. Wu's nurses for leaving confidential patient information in the waiting area, and Dr. Wu himself already had reminded him twice that day not to send text messages (on his bright red, very conspicuous Nokia cell phone) during office hours. The staff could barely disguise their contempt for him; instead of receiving a qualified, enthusiastic summer intern, they were stuck doing extra work to compensate for this spoiled, immature nepotism-hire's negligence and disinterest.

So when Connor accidentally shattered the vial containing Jaya and Mateo's embryo, he panicked. Dr. Wu may have been willing to look the other way for minor infractions, but this would get him fired on the spot. He wasn't even supposed to be in that room without proper supervision, but he wanted to impress his high school ex-girlfriend by describing all the "weird shit" in there to her while she was on her lunch break from her summer job at Abercrombie & Fitch.

Five weeks into his internship, Connor was, for the first time, completely focused. He swept up the mess on the floor and buried it in a trashcan under a mound of crumbled paper towels. The Wagner family had been in the office that morning for a procedure, and their three remaining embryos were being refrigerated in that room until they could be moved to long-term storage. Connor took one, relabeled it "Torres (1 of 2)," and placed it where the shattered vial should have been. Then he hurried out of the room and acted like a model employee for the rest of the day.

At 8:00 a.m. the next morning, Mrs. Mnangagwa-Torres came in for her implantation procedure. Connor was the one to greet her at the receptionist desk when she arrived. He recognized her name and he could feel his face flushing, but the possibility that the switched embryo's ethnicity might not match Mrs. Torres's didn't occur to him. Two weeks later, the internship ended. Connor switched his major to Marketing and never thought about the incident again.

Mateo's oldest sister was in the room when Jill was born. Tía Ana had been videotaping the birth, with the idea that Jaya would be able to send the joyous footage of their newborn baby to her family in Zimbabwe, since none of them had been able to make the journey to the United States at the time. The excitement when Jill's head began to emerge quickly turned into an uneasy silence among the nurses. Ana continued to record; amidst the commotion in the room, neither she nor Mateo perceived what was transpiring. It wasn't until Jill fully emerged and Dr. Wu held her in his arms that Ana gasped. If anyone had played the video tape, they would have seen Mateo standing in the right corner, wide-eyed and mystified, trying to understand what was unfolding before him. In the stunned silence of the room, the voice of one of the nurses could be heard from the doorway: "Lord have mercy, their baby is white." Tía Ana set down the camcorder. All copies of the video were later destroyed.

Dr. Wu continued to hold the baby in his arms. Normally he would have placed the newborn onto the mother's chest, but initially he was as flabbergasted as anyone. Then the reality of what must have happened hit him with a crushing, crippling force. But how? His practice was recognized as one of the best in the region. They had strict protocols and procedures in place to prevent exactly this kind of disaster from occurring. It was inexplicable. There would be malpractice suits. He would be kicked out of the partnership, assuming the Meskhenet Center wasn't shuttered entirely. He would lose his medical license. His career was over.

"She is my daughter." Jaya's voice interrupted Dr. Wu's broken, frantic thoughts. Wearily, she lifted her arms. "She is of my womb. Give me my daughter." Jaya looked at Mateo, who managed to nod his agreement, despite the fact that the room was spinning and the world seemed to be crumbling around him. His first thought had been raw, instinctive, and bitter: "I have been cuckolded. This baby is another man's." He immediately admonished himself for such a ludicrous suspicion. The right corner of his lip crept upward in what he hoped was a supportive smile.

"She is mine," Jaya demanded again.

Was she, though? Dr. Wu wondered as he placed the infant into Jaya's open arms. Legally, ethically, whose child was this? The Torreses might have paid over twenty thousand dollars out of pocket for the embryo implantation, and Mrs. Mnangagwa-Torres might have carried her for nine months, but it didn't take a genetic test for Dr. Wu to know that the blue-eyed baby with tufts of pale blond hair was biologically someone else's. Dr. Wu wanted to offer up some sort of apology or explanation, but the advice of the partnership's outside legal counsel rang through his head: "Do not admit culpability or say anything that could be construed as such. If an error occurs, regardless of when, where, or how, contact me first. Don't say anything to the patient without me present." Dr. Wu looked at Mateo sheepishly. How could he stay silent?

Jaya was lovingly caressing the whimpering newborn. "My sweet little Jill," she said with a laugh. "We always wanted to give you a traditional American name and a traditional American life. And look at you. You could be one of *The Brady Bunch* sisters. I used to love to watch them on TV when I was a little girl." She looked up at Mateo and instantly recognized the look of growing rage on his face. He was going to explode. She grabbed his arm. "Please, my love," she said. "Not now. Eventually. But not now. Let that not be the memory of our first moments with our daughter."

Mateo touched the baby's tiny hand with his pinky finger and in an instant, his fury melted away. Ana was sobbing; she knew not whether they were tears of grief or joy for the strange family that was huddled together beside her. Dr. Wu excused himself, saying the nurses would clean and swaddle the baby after the family had a chance to bond. Immediately, he regretted referring to them as a family. Legally, ethically, were they? He rushed out of the room to call his lawyer. His continued presence was providing them no comfort, and remaining with them would only exacerbate his own perilous situation.

Three days later, Mateo asked one of his former grad school classmates, who had gone on to become a patent lawyer, what they could do. She advised him that, although it wasn't her area of expertise, the legal precedent she uncovered after a brief Westlaw search strongly suggested that the genetic parents of the girl could theoretically make a claim for legal custody. Mateo felt woozy. She continued that he really ought to enlist both a medical malpractice specialist and a family law attorney, and, before hanging up the phone, cautioned him that if keeping the child was his priority, he should be prepared to temper his expectations for financial recompense and pursue a resolution out of court. The team of attorneys that the Torreses hired thereafter concurred with this approach, although they instructed him not to admit anything to Dr. Wu about their desire to settle quickly and quietly. Jaya was ready to abandon the prospective lawsuit in its entirety.

"Why risk it?" she asked Mateo. "Why stir up trouble? For however badly they have wronged us, there is no amount of money that is worth losing our daughter."

"They want this kept out of the public record even more than we do," Mateo replied. "This is a major scandal. If it gets out, it wouldn't just destroy Dr. Wu's career. It would ruin their entire medical practice. Even if Dr. Wu wanted to try his luck in front of a jury, his business partners won't let him. And we'll agree to a settlement long before this ever reaches a courtroom. The money will pay for her college education. Grad school. It will let her choose whatever career she wants without having to base her decision strictly on salary and paying off loans. Imagine if we'd had that freedom early in our careers? Why not set her up with every advantage we can?"

"Fine," Jaya said, after a long pause. "But I will take this child back to Zimbabwe before I let anyone take her away from us. Our names are on her birth certificate, no one else's. I will not lose her."

"Agreed," Mateo said. "Agreed."

Four months later, a resolution was reached among the interested parties—well, most of them, anyway. Dr. Wu had his suspicions about who the baby's biological mother and father were. A week prior to Jill's birth, he had delivered another baby girl to the Wagner family. He was grateful that an entirely different team of nurses had been in the delivery room that day. The resemblance between the two babies was so striking that at least one of them would have noticed and made the connection immediately if they had seen Jill as well. Mrs. Wagner had continued to visit Dr. Wu for her post-pregnancy checkups and she always brought little Amanda along. Mrs. Mnangagwa-Torres had, unsurprisingly, started to see a new OB-GYN, but when Dr. Wu finally caught a glimpse of beautiful baby Jill three months later outside his attorney's conference room, he felt nauseous.

The girls were nearly identical. He never told his lawyer. He convinced himself that the burden of the knowledge of the child's true parentage was his alone to bear. The Wagners were blissfully happy and the Torreses had been through enough already.

During their negotiations, Dr. Wu noticed that the Torreses seemed as anxious as he was to come to an agreement out of court. Privately, he suspected that they didn't want to get the judicial system involved. Doing so would risk a mandatory DNA test to discover the true identity of the baby's biological parents, and the possibility, however remote, that Jill would be taken from them. Needless to say, Dr. Wu and his business partners were also willing to do whatever was necessary to keep this debacle out of public circulation. Ultimately, they settled all claims that Jaya, Mateo, Jill, and any of their successors in interest might bring forth arising out of the incident for $370,000. Dr. Wu had been prepared to pay twice as much, or more. Both the Torres family and Dr. Wu signed ironclad nondisclosure agreements.

The looming threat that Jill's $370,000 (plus accrued interest) trust fund could be taken from her if she or her parents violated the NDA was not the only reason, or even the major reason, that Jill and her family kept her unique history a secret. After the brunette woman at the playground, after the incident with her aunt and uncle at the family party, after the momentarily puzzled expressions of Jill's teachers on the first day of school, after the perplexed stares at the grocery store and countless other little indignities, her parents did the best they could to explain, in age-appropriate terms, why their family was a little bit different but no less special than others.

Jaya and Mateo had expected to have serious conversations about race, ethnicity, and cultural heritage with their child from an early age anyway; as a Black immigrant woman and a Latino man living in a predominately white community, they had assumed that their future daughter or son would face many of the same prejudices and displays of ignorance that they each had confronted, in varying ways, throughout their entire lives. After Jaya became pregnant, they started to discuss in more specific detail how and when they would broach topics of racism and xenophobia with their child. They didn't want to make their daughter self-conscious, but they also didn't want her to be blindsided by a bigot (or, to be fair, Jaya added, what was more likely to be an impressionable child with bigoted parents).

Publicly, Jaya had insisted that she didn't care what the baby's sex was, just as long as it was healthy. She confessed to no one, not even Mateo, that she found herself relieved when Dr. Wu told her that she was having a girl. For whatever stereotypes and slights her daughter might face—and after a decade of living in the United States, Jaya was all too familiar with the many forms, subtle and obvious, that racism and sexism could take—she feared it would be all the more arduous if she were raising a son. As a girl, her child's life might not be any easier, but it would probably be less dangerous. Maybe the conversation about the police could wait a few extra years. Jaya would have to worry about clerks following her future daughter around the store while she playfully modeled clothes and accessories with her preteen friends, she'd have to worry about strange men sexualizing and harassing her little girl on the streets, she'd feel the same righteous indignation she felt for herself whenever her daughter confronted a dismissive boss or was passed up for a promotion on a pretense, but maybe she wouldn't have to be quite as fearful that her child would be shot dead for walking through their otherwise all-white neighborhood because some bigoted busybody thought the mere presence of a young Black boy was inherently "suspicious."

But instead, Jaya found herself trying to explain these same issues of social bias and institutionalized racism to a six-year-old girl who was getting a premature glimpse of that reality because of the way strangers looked at her mommy and daddy, even though the child would never face these injustices in the same way herself. Jaya had read five parenting books before Jill was born; none of them had covered the particular topic of what to do if you're a Black mother who finds herself with a white baby.

When Jill was eight, a new family moved into the large brick house down the street: two white men with five-year-old twins, a boy and a girl, whom they had adopted from Vietnam. This

63

seemed to make it easier for Jill to understand the concept of adoption and to accept that families can be structured in all different types of ways, including sometimes with two daddies. It seemed to normalize the idea that sometimes kids can look different than their parents, but it doesn't mean they love each other any less.

The Torreses and the Ahlgrens quickly became close friends. The twins dutifully followed Jill around their backyards and played whatever game she proposed, and she was as fiercely protective of them as any big sister by blood would have been. Meanwhile, their parents enjoyed the respite of the company of other adults, particularly other adults who also felt like outsiders in a town comprised almost entirely of straight, white, old-money couples. They sipped on beer and wine while they discussed everything from reality TV to neighborhood gossip to how to acknowledge and integrate their respective children's unique heritages into family activities and conversations.

Thanks to their dads' diligent efforts, the twins were fluent in English within six months, although not before they had taught Jill enough Vietnamese that the three of them could hold secret conversations within their parents' earshot. Almost a decade later, when Jill and Jaya were waiting in an airport lounge, they overheard a Vietnamese family bickering while they waited for their flight. Jill was surprised that she could understand their argument better than she could make sense of conversations in French, which she was taking to fulfill her high school foreign language requirement at the time.

Throughout elementary school, Jill was quiet, introspective, and studious while in the classroom, but she lit up during gym class, recess, and especially while playing soccer. Her parents fostered her athletic proclivities, signing her up for any sports team or activity in which she expressed interest. Depending on the season, Jill participated in tae kwon do, gymnastics, basketball, and the swim team, in addition to her year-round soccer practice schedule. Jaya and Mateo's natural inclination was to prioritize academic achievement above all else and to steer Jill toward what they considered more classically intellectual activities, but more than anything, they wanted their daughter to be confident and happy. To feel like she fit in.

Beside, Jill still had her weekly piano lessons, and she sat in with her dad when his private tutor came to the house to work on his Russian language skills for his job. Most importantly, despite the fact that they both worked long hours and frequently had to leave Jill with a teenaged babysitter after school, Jill always completed her homework, error-free, before bedtime, and had never received anything other than an A or A+ as a final grade in any of her classes.

By the time Jill was in high school, nearly every family in Westport knew her name. She easily made the varsity soccer team her freshman year, was all-state four years in a row, and was unanimously elected co-captain by her teammates both her junior and senior year. Having a co-captain was necessary, her coach explained, to complement Jill's natural disposition and to keep the team focused and motivated. Jill was the first to arrive for the team's early-morning long runs and she never uttered a single complaint; she put in total effort during every drill and every game all season; and three times a week, she'd jog straight to the weight room after practice was dismissed to work on the raw strength required to improve her throw-ins and corner kicks and make her a more well-rounded athlete.

Many of her teammates saw this and tried to emulate her. But Jill was far more comfortable leading by example, and Coach also needed a player who could confidently tell the other girls what to do. Not everyone was as self-motivated as Jill, and part of being a captain would mean adapting her leadership approach to the teammates that needed more personal encouragement and direction. Unless and until Jill mastered that skill, having a co-captain was vital for team cohesion. Jill took Coach's words seriously and tried to work on being more assertive during practice and games, but it ran contrary to her natural leadership style. She preferred to pursue her objectives with an intensity and focus that was unobtrusive but couldn't be ignored or denied. Although her ego was slightly bruised when Coach assigned a second captain again during Jill's senior year, she was grateful not to have to always be the one to scold her follow players when they were slacking at practice or gossiping on the sidelines when they should have been focusing on the game.

By her sophomore year of high school, Jill was taking all AP classes and, midway through the fall semester, the Torres family resumed their discussion with the school administration about whether Jill should be allowed to graduate early and begin college the next fall. Jill had sat for the SAT the prior year in anticipation of this decision, and had received a perfect 800 on the math section and a 760 on the verbal section. Privately, she felt humiliated that her verbal score wasn't better and she hoped that her parents weren't too disappointed in her.

At the same time, Jill wondered if perhaps the improvements she needed to make in critical reading would be a sufficient justification to postpone college for another year or two. Jill wasn't the most popular girl in her class and she'd never been on a date, much less had a boyfriend or girlfriend. Maybe she'd have better luck with friendships and romance in college, but leaving high school at age fifteen felt premature. Her life was weird enough already. She wasn't strong enough to compete against college women in soccer yet, and she didn't want to abandon her high school team. The school was running out of appropriate classes for her, but Jill had designed her own proposed curriculum of independent study to supplement her classwork, and her AP Physics teacher had agreed to act as a faculty advisor if the administration was on board. Her parents were prepared to support Jill in whatever she wanted to do, but in truth, they weren't ready to send their little girl away yet either.

Jill's proposal for independent study was accepted. In addition to three or four hours of regular classes with the other students each day, Jill was allowed to pursue her own academic interests, first using the school's resources and then, when she got her driver's license her junior year, off-campus as well. In addition to exhausting every single AP class the school offered, Jill completed independent course work in, among other areas, Russian History and Culture (with all materials in Russian), Applied Statistics, C Programming, Blockchain Technology, and Contemporary Art. Essentially, if a topic sparked Jill's interest, her school allowed her to pursue a deeper study of it and to receive academic credit. She was curious and diligent, and frankly, they didn't really know what else to do with her.

At her advisor's urging, Jill also took elective courses in Improvisation and Theater Production, which led her to one of the starring roles in the high school's winter musical. At last, her advisor had found a way to push Jill out of her comfort zone. Jill was widely congratulated on her acting and singing abilities, but while she enjoyed the camaraderie of working with the theater kids to pull together a successful production, she realized that she unequivocally preferred to remain out of the spotlight. She didn't like having her picture taken. She didn't like the extra attention. Most of all, she didn't like receiving accolades for what felt like nothing more than the competent completion of a responsibil-ity. When the drama teacher reached out to Jill her senior year to invite her to try out again for that winter's performance, Jill politely declined on the pretext that her academic and athletic obligations were too demanding for her to give the musical the time and energy it deserved.

CHAPTER SEVEN
Jill Torres

It was also during the fall of Jill's sophomore year, two weeks after they made the decision that Jill would remain at Westport's public high school and graduate on the same timeline as her peers, that her parents told her the full truth about everything: the mix-up with the embryo, the settlement, the trust fund, and above all else, the fact that from the moment she was born, she was their daughter, and no law or DNA test was going to change that. Jaya and Mateo had wanted to wait until Jill was eighteen for this conversation, but alas, on a Wednesday evening after Jaya was driving Jill home from soccer practice, the plan changed. They had already picked up dinner from a local Italian restaurant, but Jill remembered she was out of her favorite shampoo and needed tampons, so they made a quick stop at CVS.

Whenever Jaya encountered another person of color while running errands in Westport, she and the stranger typically exchanged nods, smiles, sometimes even a bit of friendly conversation; there was an unspoken sense of solidarity between them. So, when a slim Jamaican-American woman stepped in line behind Jaya, it wasn't unusual that the two women began to engage in idle chatter. Then Jill turned around.

"Hey, Mom, will you hold onto my stuff and hold our place in line? I just remembered I need to get more hair ties too. Coach has been hassling us about wearing our hair down during practice. I need more for myself and I want extras to give to the other girls."

"Yes, but hustle," Jaya replied. "It's almost our turn and our food is getting cold in the car."

Jill ran off and Jaya turned back to the woman in line, who was staring at her aghast.

"You are that white girl's mother?"

"I am." Jaya's tone sharpened and her smile disappeared.

"Are you her foster mother? Or her stepmom?" the woman pressed, mystified.

"She has been my daughter since the moment she was born."

"But you adopted her? Even if her father were a white man...." The woman's voice trailed off. Jaya tried to control her anger. It was bad enough when white people scrutinized and judged her and her family. This woman should have known better.

"But, why?" the woman continued when Jaya didn't respond. Jaya wasn't sure if the woman felt betrayed, angry, or just confused, but as she stared at Jaya her eyes seemed to be brimming with tears. "Why would you adopt a white girl when there are so many Black babies in desperate need of a family? There are more than enough white folks who would've fought for the opportunity to give a pretty blond girl a home. You could have given one of our own a chance. Why would you deny your own people?"

Jill held up a package of multicolored hair ties in her mother's line of vision. Neither woman had seen Jill approach, and Jaya wasn't sure how much of their conversation she had overheard.

"I found them," Jill said softly.

"We're up. Let's pay for this stuff and go home." With a glare, Jaya turned away from the woman, who was looking back at her with disappointment. Neither Jaya nor Jill spoke again until they had returned to their car.

"Why *did* you adopt me, Mom?" Jill finally asked. "I know the rest of our family wonders about it too."

"Did one of them say something to you?" Jaya cut in.

"No. Not since I was really little, and even then I don't think they were trying to be mean. But I can tell that sometimes they still think about it. Wouldn't it have been easier to choose a kid who was the same race as you or Dad?"

"None of those kids would have been you."

"I mean, that's not really an answer, Mom." Jill sighed. "I guess it doesn't matter. You know I don't care about meeting my bio parents. You and Dad are my real mom and dad, and my only mom and dad. But I just, I don't know, I feel like there is something you haven't told me. Did you have another kid? Is this, like, a weird social experiment where you traded babies with a white couple? I feel like I've seen an old picture of you where you were pregnant, but it is impossible that I could've gotten accidentally switched at birth at the hospital and no one noticed. The fact that we don't look like we're related is literally the first thing everyone notices, even if they think they're doing a good job hiding it!"

They were at a stoplight, less than ten minutes from home. Jaya glanced at her daughter. She would wait until they were off the road, but the time had come. Jill had repeatedly demonstrated her maturity and discretion to her parents. So that night, while the family was eating dinner and for two hours after, Jaya and Mateo told Jill the entire story and answered every question she posed to them as honestly and openly as they were able. Jill responded with stoic grace—so much so that it was disconcerting. There were no tears, outbursts, or condemnations for not telling her the full truth earlier. She spoke calmly, listened, and when there was nothing more to be said, she hugged her parents goodnight and went to her room to finish her homework.

But after twenty minutes of staring at the same page of her calculus assignment without any progress, Jill caved and intentionally allowed her mind to wander. She had meant what she said: she truly didn't care if she ever met the individuals who had donated the sperm and egg that created her. It was a small comfort, she supposed, to learn that they didn't intentionally abandon her or give her away. Based on what her parents said, in all likelihood they had no idea whatsoever that she existed. Trying to track them down now would throw their entire lives into disarray. It would be unfair to everyone, to say nothing of how it would put her trust fund at risk.

71

Jill smiled despite herself at this thought. She was secretly kind of rich! Her parents had made it clear that the trust fund money would be used primarily for educational purposes, and any monthly cash allowance she might get after graduating college would be conditioned upon her holding a full-time job. It wasn't like she was a billionaire. Many of her classmates had trust funds and inheritances worth ten, twenty, even a hundred times more than whatever her relatively measly $370,000 had grown to with interest by then. But it was still pretty cool!

Still, if the confidentiality agreements and the potential custody battles and the loss of the settlement money weren't a factor, would she be more tempted to try to meet her bio parents, just to see what they were like? Would she still be trying to convince herself that it would be cruel to introduce herself to them when, by now, they had either accepted that they would never have children or had settled into family life with a different son or daughter of their own?

This last thought gave her pause. If they did have any other children, that would technically make them her brothers or sisters. For as much as she loved her cousins and as much as she continued to think of herself as the Ahlgren twins' surrogate big sister, she had always wanted a younger sibling—and although she would never admit it out loud, she especially wanted a younger sibling who looked like her. The fact that such a person might actually exist but they could never know each other was bittersweet.

Jill suddenly recalled a particular soccer match during her freshman year. The game had ended in a draw, and after the teams had shaken hands, two girls in black and gold uniforms had pulled Jill to the side to ask her if she was related to... some girl that went to their school. Jill had long since forgotten the name. She had laughed and said no, but the girls were still staring at her.

"It's cool! You really do look so much like her." The shorter player took a step forward and tilted her head, as if to examine Jill's face from a better angle. Jill shifted uncomfortably. "I guess it's not as cool for you as it is for us though. Like, since you don't know her," the girl continued, laughing.

"And besides, up close it isn't quite as much," the other girl added. "Your nose and cheeks are different. And no offense to her, but she's gotten kind of pudgy."

"Oh my God, Hannah, you are such a bitch!" the first girl said, whacking her friend on the shoulder.

"No, I meant it as a compliment to this girl!" She turned back to Jill. "You are in much better shape, that's all I meant."

"Ugh, Hannah, you have to stop talking! Like, you're freaking her out."

With a few more giggles and another half-hearted exchange of "good game," the two girls trotted back to their teammates and Jill returned to hers.

Jill hadn't thought about that encounter since it happened. Now the smallest part of her wondered, could it be more than a coincidence? She was almost certain that match had been against Trumbull High School, which was only about a half hour from Westport and an hour or so from Stamford Hospital, where she was born. It was completely plausible that a family from Trumbull could've chosen the same fertility specialist as her own parents had. There was a chance, however small, that her look-alike from Trumbull High was her embryo-sister. Wasn't there?

Jill quickly admonished herself for indulging in such a convoluted fantasy and turned back to her problem set before it got any later.

The self-restraint didn't last long. The following Saturday night, when most of her classmates were sipping lukewarm beer in a junior girl's hot tub or making out with some eighth grade Lolita from New Canaan Country School at an impromptu party on the eleventh hole of a private golf course or loitering in the atrium of the Stamford Town Center mall, Jill decided that she would lock herself in her bedroom with her laptop and learn everything she could about her potential sister.

Although Jill's parents hadn't given her any information about the other family, she was able to find the right Facebook account within thirty minutes of clicking around random Trumbull High School profiles. The goofy oversized glasses the girl was wearing

73

in her profile picture weren't enough to obscure the sisterly resemblance, and scrolling through the rest of her publicly posted photos removed any lingering doubt: this girl, this Amanda Wagner, was Jill's biological sister.

Now armed with a full name, Jill was able to pull up previews of Amanda's Instagram, Twitter, and Snapchat accounts. After that, Trumbull High School's intranet was an easy hack. Jill was able to create a fake administrative profile and gain full access not only to information about Amanda's extracurricular activities and class schedule, but also her grades, family information, and other confidential records. She was horrified: any deviant or predator with comparable computer programming and network security skills could snoop around their system and find deeply personal and private information about any of the students.

More immediately pressing to Jill, however, was the fact that if she could find out all these details about Amanda with a few hours of casual research and some light hacking, then Amanda could do the same to her. As it was, the only social media account that Jill maintained was a shell of a Facebook profile. She used it sporadically, having posted a total of eight status updates and two pictures, all relating to her soccer teams, over the previous four years, and all of the features were set to "friends only," of which Jill had less than two hundred. Still, she took down her profile photo and adjusted her privacy settings so that even her friends would lack access to her old posts and photos. She also deleted her last name, so that she was identified only as "Jill T." Hopefully she hadn't waited too long to privatize her information.

Jill never hacked into the Trumbull High intranet again after that Saturday night. She had skimmed through Amanda's classes and grades (Amanda was an average student, earning mostly Bs, and she was taking one honors class and no AP courses) before she started to feel nauseous and ashamed for the violation of Amanda's privacy. She logged off the network and deleted the fake admin account before she had looked up Amanda's parents' names or their home address. She was better off not knowing.

Two weeks later, however, Jill was still clicking on Amanda's Facebook page every other night. She felt a jolt of adrenaline every time Amanda publicly posted a new picture, and she started to wonder if Amanda was posting more often, but with the privacy settings turned to "friends only."

It was a ludicrous thing to do. Jill would never admit it to anyone. But she pulled a stock photo of a moderately attractive young Pakistani man and created a basic profile of banal interests in broken English. Farhad Razavi, age seventeen, likes video games, cricket, American TV shows (especially *The Simpsons*), and fast cars. Then she spam friend-requested almost 250 auto-recommended contacts. Once fifty had accepted, the profile was ready: it seemed real enough that it wouldn't arouse any suspicions, but she doubted that it would entice Amanda to initiate a conversation in private messages either. Jill didn't want to catfish anyone, she just wanted to be able to observe.

Then she friend requested Amanda. Within five minutes, the request had been accepted. Farhad Razavi was Amanda's 1,156th Facebook friend. Perhaps Jill needn't have gone to such lengths to construct a realistic seeming profile. Regardless, it had served its purpose quite effectively. Jill now had access to Amanda's status updates, wall posts, and a dozen additional photo albums beyond those available publicly. For three weeks, Jill logged into "Farhad's" fake profile and compulsively scoured through Amanda's old albums and recent posts multiple times a day. Whenever a friend posted a silly comment or meme to Amanda's wall, Jill would stalk them as well. This girl was almost certainly related to her, Jill told herself, so her curiosity was natural. But then, suddenly, Jill had enough. She felt dirty. She logged out of the Farhad Razavi account and didn't sign into Facebook again, under his name or her own, for another four months.

This pattern continued through the remainder of high school and into college: every few months, Jill would check in on Amanda's Facebook and Instagram pages, scrolling through her photos, reading through all her old posts, and clicking through to the profiles of new friends and followers, until Jill felt creepy and disgusted with herself. Then she would force herself offline and wouldn't return to either site for several weeks, until something random would spark her curiosity about what Amanda had been doing lately and the cycle would repeat itself again.

That "something random" was usually nothing more than a sort of vague loneliness or a sense of wondering what could have been. Amanda appeared to have been reasonably "cool" in high school, and she seemed to be having an enviable college experience as well: costume parties and weekend road trips were Instagram fodder, skipped classes and dorm pranks generated a week's worth of inside jokes on Twitter, and every club or activity led to a new Facebook group joined and an influx of new connections. Occasionally, Jill felt bitter and jealous, and it took all her willpower not to ironically "like" a particularly vapid post or comment using her phony account. She always resisted. She knew her bitterness was fleeting and misplaced. For whatever genetic heritage they might have shared, Jill and Amanda each had made their own choices in life. It was futile to wonder about their differing college experiences, much less complain about them. Besides, Jill knew that ultimately, she never would have traded her own life for Amanda's, irrespective of how much more fun Amanda's may have seemed.

Despite over seventeen years of her parents subtly and not-so-subtly expounding the merits of their alma mater Caltech, Jill was attending her dream university, MIT. Although Jill had applied to a half-dozen schools to ensure that she would have options, she always expected that she would attend MIT and play for their varsity women's soccer team as a walk-on. She could have gotten an athletic scholarship at almost any Division I school, but she had the luxury of her trust fund to pay for her college tuition, and neither she nor her parents had been willing to prioritize sports over academics. Playing for a D3 school with an elite academic program seemed to be the perfect compromise and, Jill assured her parents, if balancing a varsity sport with her academic course load proved to be too much, then she could and would resign from the team. MIT didn't provide its undergraduates with their class rank or designate a valedictorian, but Jill assured Jaya and Mateo that her position hadn't changed: her primary objective was to graduate with a perfect 5.0 GPA, and she wouldn't let short-term distractions like sports or parties or romance interfere with that.

During her senior year of high school, after she had officially registered to attend MIT the next fall, Jill reached out to the MIT women's soccer coach with a choppily edited highlights video and a résumé of her athletic accomplishments. The coach, as well as the team's captains, immediately began recruiting her to play. Although Jill would have to go through tryouts prior to freshman orientation, they essentially offered her a spot on the team if she wanted it.

The spring and summer of Jill's senior year of high school, Mateo woke up at 4:30 a.m. every morning, including weekends, so that he could train with Jill before he went to work: six-mile conditioning runs, wind sprints, and the full gamut of ball handling, dribbling, and shooting drills. When Mateo returned home from work in the evenings, they often left for a second training session at the weight room of the Westport YMCA.

Decades later, Jill would recall these grueling daily workouts as some of her fondest memories with her father; and in the shorter term, they more than served their purpose. Jill arrived at MIT's soccer tryouts in peak physical condition. Unlike the other freshman, who looked scrawny and childish compared to the veteran players, Jill looked strong, powerful, like a leader, from the first day.

Most of the players were thrilled with the prospect of adding Jill to their starting lineup. But one of the incoming junior girls, Annaliese, who played midfielder like Jill, seemed to dislike Jill from the first team warm-up. She bullied her throughout the first day of tryouts on the pretense of "friendly hazing" and "testing her character," and she refused to let up during the group dinner later that evening. Aside from an occasional eye roll, Jill was visibly unfazed by Annaliese's provocations. If anything, it impelled her to work harder and be better.

Then, midway through the second day of tryouts, Coach Barrett put the girls through an intense set of three-on-three round-robin scrimmages. By the third round, it became apparent which players had slacked on their summer conditioning. Their passes were getting sloppy, they were missing easy shots, and whenever the ball was stolen from them, their attempts to recover it were half-hearted at best. Jill and her threesome were playing against Annaliese, who had continued to pester Jill throughout the entire morning. Jill could tell that Annaliese was struggling. Jill did not relent. After she scored three quick goals against Annaliese's team, she could sense Annaliese's ire growing. With two minutes left in their round, Jill had a flash of a premonition that the girl was going to do something to retaliate. She immediately disregarded it as absurd and willed herself to focus on scoring a fourth goal. Not more than twenty seconds later, Annaliese barreled into Jill, elbowing her in the nose and taking her out at the knee. Jill crumbled to the ground.

Coach Barrett was livid. The seniors would later whisper to the younger players that, in over three full years of playing for her, none of them had ever seen Coach Barrett so angry, including the time she discovered the small baggie of weed that someone had accidentally dropped on the team bus during an away game their sophomore year. It was unequivocally a cheap shot, despite Annaliese's protestations that she was just playing aggressive defense.

Jill hadn't gotten up. Two of the other players rushed to her with wet rags to try to stop her bleeding nose. Coach Barrett ordered Annaliese off the field. Despite the fact that she had started at left midfield the prior year, she was never invited to return.

After two weeks, Jill was walking without a limp, and after a month she had recovered enough that she was cleared to start playing again. Despite the injury and four weeks of unplanned rest, she still would have been one of the best players on the team. But Jill's heart was no longer in it. Nothing about her time on MIT's campus thus far had been what she expected.

Prior to freshman orientation, her presumptive teammates had encouraged her to move into Baker House, where several of them resided. Jill assumed that she would enjoy being around other student-athletes and didn't give any of the other dorms much consideration. In the interest of recovering from her knee injury as quickly as possible, however, she had kept mostly to herself after the school year started, hobbling to her classes but otherwise staying in her dorm room, studying and keeping off her feet. She could tell her constant presence was starting to irritate her roommate—a gawky brunette from Los Angeles who had recently dyed blue streaks into her hair and who was at last enjoying a semblance of popularity after four excruciating years spent at a high school where she was deemed not noteworthy enough to bother bullying—but Jill wasn't willing to exacerbate her injury by walking to the library or the student center. As a result, her roommate seemed to be turning everyone on the floor against her. And Jill's nose, which she had always thought was too big anyway, was now so crooked that she found it difficult to breathe at night. The balance she had found in high school by pushing her body and her brain to their respective limits had been stripped from her by Annaliese's petty spite, and there was no one to whom she could vent her grief and anger.

By the beginning of October, Jill had given up on trying to make friends, and instead spent her time doubling down on her assignments. Occasionally she wondered how things might have been different: if she hadn't gotten injured, if she had rejoined the soccer team once she had recuperated, if she had selected a different dorm, or even if she had been assigned a different roommate. Then she would admonish herself for losing focus. Was it any different than high school? Hell, was it any different than her own beloved family? Maybe she would always be an outsider. She might not ever be happy, but at least she could be productive.

Then, a single bedroom dorm opened up in MacGregor House. A sophomore girl had first landed there from Maseeh Hall, knowing no one, in the aftermath of a fight with her two best friends at the end of their freshman year. Unlike Jill, who maintained a stoic countenance and concentrated on her schoolwork, the sophomore girl was openly lonely and miserable. She was as desperate for a roommate as Jill was desperate for an escape from Baker House and some semblance of privacy and solitude. In both cases, the poor fit was affecting the morale of the entire floor. The graduate resident tutors intervened, the housemasters worked their magic behind the scenes, and by the start of the January independent activities period, Jill and the sophomore had switched living spaces and were settling into their new homes.

The change of environment wasn't a panacea. The first semester had transformed Jill, and she was ambivalent as to whether it was for the better. She was confident that she no longer needed companionship to be happy or successful; she was unsettled that, most of the time, she no longer wanted it.

Nevertheless, MacGregor House quickly proved to be a healthier environment. Jill was grateful to find other students like her, who avoided the nightly gatherings in the lounge, who preferred to stay in their rooms or spend their time at the library or in some quiet nook around campus studying or working on an independent project outside of their core curriculum. Jill wasn't unfriendly. She wasn't mean. She just couldn't relate to the students who seemed to crave the constant presence of others, the incessant chatter about nothing in particular. She had no desire to skip class to nurse a weekday hangover or pop 80mg of Adderall the night before an exam to try to make up for a half-semester's worth of negligence. The petty roommate fights, the perpetual cycle of procrastination and panic, the manufactured interpersonal drama over who was flirting with whose boyfriend: it was all unnecessary, avoidable chaos. The fact that so many of her classmates—especially those from Baker House, but more than a few at MacGregor too—seemed to invite it was mystifying to Jill. It served only to distract them from their greater purpose. When they complained about their workload or how challenging the subject matter was, Jill nodded with a sympathetic half-smile but found herself unable to relate. She enjoyed the challenge and fulfillment of mastering all the new material and, although she never vocalized it, she suspected that most of her peers would feel less burdened by their assignments if they spent less time messing around on their phones or drinking Natty Lights in front of the communal television.

Jill had heard so much about how people blossom once they get to college, so she was surprised to find herself surrounded by the same social hierarchies and posturing that plagued her high school in Westport. The dynamic at MacGregor House was a major improvement over that first semester at Baker Hall, but even there, pockets of cliquishness still existed, and she still thought many of her floormates seemed more interested in performing for some unseen audience than in making genuine connections or living in a purposeful way. She didn't resent them for it, strictly speaking, and she was happy to engage in pleasant conversation whenever she was approached, but she refused to participate in the intricate drama the bulk of them had constructed for themselves. It would have been unfathomable to most of her peers, but for Jill, somehow her simple acquaintances and casual, activity-specific friendships were plenty. Anything more would have been too much a distraction from her academic goals.

CHAPTER EIGHT
Jill Torres

Halfway through the spring term of her freshman year, Jill had finished her classes and her workout for the day and had decided that, rather than studying in her room with the door closed, she would head to her favorite study nook in MacGregor for a few hours that evening. When she arrived, there was only one other student in the room. Jill had seen him there before; he was a handsome, muscular Korean guy with a proclivity for black t-shirts bearing metal band logos. Based on his textbooks, Jill guessed he was a sophomore or junior. Unlike other students who came to the library area for an hour or two and spent half that time compulsively checking their phones and occasionally laughing loudly, as if to let everyone know someone had sent them a particularly witty text or meme, this guy was able to focus on his work for hours on end with the same ferocious intensity as Jill. They had never spoken, but Jill liked him. He was quiet, courteous, and diligent in the study area because that's what the setting called for, but Jill sensed he might have a more playful, mischievous side to him in his down time.

That day, he had taken off his headphones and was leaning back in his chair with his hands over his eyes. Jill could hear metal music blaring from the doorway. It didn't seem like he had noticed her enter. With his hands still over his eyes, he groaned loudly. Jill couldn't help but giggle. She knew all too well how a particularly tricky p-set could elicit such a response.

"Oh, my bad! I'm sorry for the disruption," the guy said, quickly sitting up straight and turning off his music. "I know this is a designated quiet space. I didn't realize anyone else had come in."

"You're totally fine! I just got here," Jill replied with a smile. He smiled back. Jill's heart skipped a beat. His smile was broad, his teeth were perfect, and he had a cute little dimple on his left cheek. She pointed to his shirt. "Iron Maiden, huh? My dad loves them. 'Up the Irons,' right? Is that who you were listening to?"

"Up the Irons! Yes!" He seemed delighted by the reference. "But that's not who I'm listening to right now. These guys are newer. Or, at least relative to Iron Maiden they are. They're this random band out of Australia called Parkway Drive. I've never seen them play live but they're already pretty big in Europe and I think they're going to blow up in the States soon too. Someone posted them to the metal subreddit a few weeks ago and I haven't stopped listening since." He paused and blushed. Jill's heart skipped another beat. Until then, she had only seen him expressionlessly bent over his laptop, but now his face had become animated. He fidgeted with one of the pages in his textbook and continued. "Sorry. I tend to get stoked whenever I find a new metal band and connect with their entire catalog. It makes wading through a hundred pages of genomics more tolerable, at least. But I don't want to bother you."

"They sound badass," Jill said sincerely. "Even coming through your headphone speakers at a distance. I would totally listen to that while I'm lifting, but it's getting me energized to study too."

"Oh, you lift! Ha, 'do you even lift, bro?'" He cringed at himself. "Right, ignore me when I meme-speak IRL, even in jest. Do you use the gym in the building? I don't think I've seen you in there."

"Nah, I usually just go to the Z Center. Our gym is decent, but Zesiger's equipment is much better."

"Yeah, I don't know why I just said that. I don't use our gym that often either. Most of the time I just go to the Z too. There and right here. That's basically been my entire life this term."

Jill laughed. "Yeah, me too. It's not such a bad life, though, all things considered."

"Agreed! I'm Jean Paul, by the way. A lot of folks call me J.P. I answer to either." He laughed nervously. "I see you in here all the time. I think you're the only other person who actually gets any work done."

"I'm Jill, and I was thinking the same thing about you! No hate to anyone else. I'd just rather concentrate on one thing at a time. Do my work efficiently, then shift my focus to something else more fun." This was a half-truth. Jill didn't really waste her time with things her classmates would consider traditional "fun," but she didn't want Jean Paul to think she was lame.

"Yes, exactly! Wow. It's refreshing to hear someone else say that, for real. Half my friends give me a hard time about always working, and the other half give me a hard time about occasionally neglecting work to go to a party or the gym or whatever. Are you in G-entry too?"

"No, I'm in Hex. I moved in at the beginning of the semester. It's a long story, but it ended up being for the best."

"I can totally see that. You've got a Hex edge to you. I mean that as a compliment. The Hex kids are all chill as fuck."

Jill laughed again. "I agree! No one cares that I just do my own thing. I lived in Baker first semester and people were a little judgy if you weren't part of the core floor crew and didn't take part in every little group activity. Hex was meant to be. The Gents are cool too though."

"Damn straight, we are!" J.P. hollered. Immediately, his eyes widened. His friends were used to his goofy sense of humor, but he didn't want to make a bad first impression on the cute blond freshman he'd been searching for an excuse to talk to for the past several weeks. "I'm totally kidding, obviously. I mean, we are cool, but..."

"You've got to have your entry pride," Jill interjected with a grin. "I can respect it. If I were more of a gamer, I'd hang out with you guys more. It looks fun, just not really my thing." This was another half-truth. Jill's dormmates did seem to be having a blast whenever she walked by one of the lounges while they were having a *Super Smash Bros* tournament. It would be blasphemous to confess, however, that it seemed like a staggering waste of time to her, particularly since it was usually the same people spending hours there every night.

"Oh no, believe me." Jean Paul rolled his eyes. "I swear, some of them are full-on obsessed. Unless you're actually making money off it—and to be fair, some of them are—you're better off spending that time here. Or at the gym. Or literally anywhere else. I fucking love them, but I know this from first-hand experience. You probably haven't even seen the true diehards playing. They will shut themselves in a room on Friday after classes and won't reemerge until Monday afternoon. The smell. My God, the smell."

Jill didn't think she had smiled this much over the previous six months combined. She needed to get to work on her math p-set but she didn't want the conversation to end. Although, she didn't want to bother J.P. either, especially if he was just being polite. Maybe he was anxiously waiting for her to sit down and be quiet so he could get back to his work. They were staring at each other. It was going to get awkward. Or maybe it already was awkward, maybe it had been for a while, but so much time had passed since Jill had socialized with anyone that she didn't realize it.

"You seem about as anxious to get to—what is that, Calc?—as I am to get back to Bio," Jean Paul said. "I hope you take that in the half-sarcastic, half-painfully true way I intend. So let's make a deal. We'll force ourselves to do two full hours of work: no talking, no texting, no Instagram-creeping, no distracting each other with our witty commentary. And then the two of us can take a real break. Like, together, if you want."

"Okay, yeah, I could be amenable to such a plan." Jill's first instinct had become to decline all social invitations immediately and unequivocally so she could focus on her work. She shoved that urge down. College was about growth, after all, and this would only be one night. Not even a full night, just a couple of hours at most, and she could always come up with an excuse to leave later. This Jean Paul guy seemed like a good dude, and Jill already knew he wasn't a slacker. They would probably relax as efficiently as they worked. "Any ideas as to what we can look forward to for this glorious break in two sweet, sweet hours?" Jill added.

"Yeah!" J.P. laughed. "I'm cooking oyster sauce chicken and rice for a couple friends later tonight. It's not as fancy as it sounds, but you should try it. It's a good crew. We take turns making dinner once a week."

"That sounds awesome. I live off grab-and-go salads and microwave meals."

"Are you vegetarian or anything? One of the other guys is, so we always make a plant-based option. Like, with tofu or something."

"I'm the last-minute intruder, so I will eat literally whatever you serve me. And you can play me the Parkway Drive album you're listening to while you're cooking. I want to hear more of it."

"Fuck yes. Deal."

"I'm setting my phone timer for two hours exactly," Jill said.

Jean Paul Woo was born in Sacramento, California, but he moved with his mother, father, and older sister to Seoul four months after he was born. Two years later, his mother's job took the family to Taipei, where they remained until he was eleven. After a nine month stay in Riyadh where he and his sister attended the American International School, the family returned to the United States so that both children could attend the Overlake School in Redmond, Washington, for all four years of high school. By the time J.P. arrived at MIT, he was fluent in English and Mandarin but, much to his grandmother's dismay, his Korean (like his Arabic) was barely passable.

Although his intense, studious nature was what had originally captured Jill's attention, J.P. turned out to be quite socially active. At least twice a month, he left MIT's campus to attend a random metal show in Boston or Worcester, and in addition to hanging with his friends from G-entry, he constantly had commitments to go to meet-ups sponsored by the Asian-American student association, or to lift with his gym buddies, or to volunteer with a group of other undergrads to tutor English as a Second Language. He wasn't afraid to decline an invitation to a random weeknight flip cup tournament or sorority mixer, but he was a sucker for costume parties.

J.P. and Jill dated for two months after their first meeting—or, something dating-adjacent, at least. Initially, Jill was happy that J.P. had so many friends and was involved in so many activities, because it meant she could continue to focus on pursuing her own ambitions. His social calendar was already overflowing. Everyone liked him, and when she occasionally ventured out with him, everyone seemed to make an extra effort to be nice to her for his benefit. Maybe they didn't see each other as often as the many inseparable couples that populated the campus—studying, eating, relaxing, and sleeping together every single day—and maybe they didn't flood their social media accounts with daily posts declaring their love for each other, but that didn't mean there wasn't a connection.

Jill was trying. More than once, she skipped her workout, or at least cut it short, to accommodate J.P.'s schedule. She registered for Chinese I on top of her regular course load for the next semester because she wanted to be able to chat with J.P. and a group of his friends who often seemed more comfortable conversing in Mandarin than in English. After three weeks, they slept together. J.P. had no idea it was Jill's first time. She couldn't confess that the sum total of her prior sexual experience had occurred during her sophomore year of high school, when she French kissed a boy at a house party. She was ashamed the kiss had been so gawkish and abrupt, and J.P. would have judged her if he knew the guy had started dating one of her soccer teammates less than a week later.

Besides, Jill had no illusions that losing her virginity was supposed to be something magical or special, and she didn't want him to make a big deal out of it. He always asked her afterward if she came, and she always stifled a sigh and replied with an honest "no," but reassured him she was close and it felt really nice.

Whenever she woke up the next morning with J.P. lying in bed next to her, she was conflicted. She did care for him, deeply, but she wondered what the point of it all was, and if perhaps her time with him wouldn't have been better spent studying or working on one of the software-based side projects that she hoped eventually to monetize.

With a week left in the semester before final exams, J.P. broke up with her. Jill had seen couples get in ferocious, melo-dramatic, public fights around campus, but she and J.P. ended their relationship with total cordiality. They had been together for two months, but he still felt like he barely knew anything about her. He was concerned that her work would always take priority over him. He appreciated that she was independent but wished she would have made more of an effort to go out with his friends, or introduce him to her own group, or even just initiate plans once in a while. He wasn't saying that she had an eating disorder or anything, because he liked to work out too, but she really did spend a lot of time at the gym.

Jill listened with perfect composure. He wasn't wrong. She really, truly had tried to love him as best as she was able, but he wasn't wrong. Why shouldn't he dump her for someone who could give him what he wanted? How could she argue with that?

She told him that she had valued their time together and that she was disappointed it was ending. She meant it. She told him that she hoped they could still be friendly and cool when they ran into each other in the future, and she meant that too. Then she gave him a hug and walked back to her dorm room in a daze.

Would he have wanted to stay with her if she hadn't busted her nose playing soccer? If her abs were more defined? If she had paid more attention to her makeup and hairstyle whenever he was around? She wondered if there was something inherently unlov-able about her. She wasn't the daughter her parents had wanted; her aunts and uncles and cousins had to make a concerted effort to accept her into the family; her longest (only!) romantic rela-tionship had lasted barely eight weeks before it failed on account of all the "good girlfriend" qualities she lacked; and nothing she achieved academically or athletically ever seemed to be enough.

But by the time Jill unlocked her dorm room door, she simply felt like she had gotten the wind knocked out of her: it was startling, dizzying, a wound to her pride, but it was something that had happened a dozen times on the soccer field and she knew that once she caught her breath, she was going to be fine. No permanent damage done. Nothing worth crying over. At least now she could prepare for finals without any distractions. She changed into her sports bra, ran to the Z, and PR'd her deadlift and power clean. Then she got back to work.

That summer, Jill got her nose done. It wasn't because of J.P. She had started researching the procedure long before the first night she spoke to him. If anything, the demise of their relationship made her more reluctant to go through with it since, more than ever, she didn't want to take the several weeks off from the gym that would be necessary to recover from the surgery. But now that her soccer career was over, and now that her parents had made a special arrangement allowing her to dip into her trust fund to pay for it, Jill could fix something that had bothered her since high school without having to worry about breaking her nose for a third time on the field and undoing the doctor's work. It would be worth it. She knew exactly, *exactly*, how good she could look.

A week after returning home to Westport for the summer, Jill had a consultation with a plastic surgeon. She didn't want to show the doctor a picture of Amanda Wagner's face. Even beyond the unwanted questions that doing so would generate, Jill found it especially humiliating that she essentially would be asking to be turned into a stranger's clone. So instead, over the course of the preceding spring term, she had developed a machine learning algorithm that was a refined version of the various types of facial recognition software she had been analyzing in her Computer Science class. In addition to modifying how the software normalized photos to match in head tilt and lighting, Jill's software was designed to identify matches based on the internal coordinates of specific, individual facial features rather than a holistic comparison of distinctive points across an entire face.

In truth, if there was any improvement over the then-existing facial recognition technology, it was modest at best, and only for certain demographics. Still, when Jill turned in the project as extra credit, her professor was impressed by both her initiative and her creative approach. It was clear that Jill hadn't merely been absorbing the lectures; she also had been thinking through their consequences and imagining alternatives and next steps.

Jill had presented the project to her professor on the premise that it could be useful in law enforcement whenever it was suspected that the subject was wearing a disguise—which could be anything from an amateurish fake beard to infrared light glasses and anti-surveillance makeup—or when available images of the subject were partially obstructed. In practice, however, Jill used the software to comb the internet to find pictures of the closest matches possible to Amanda Wagner's nose, both head on and in profile, which she then brought to her plastic surgeon.

The doctor examined the photos and reminded Jill that she should keep her expectations realistic. He told her that he would use the pictures to get an idea of what she wanted, but that there were a number of variables that would affect her results. Nevertheless, by the time Jill was preparing to return to classes the following autumn, her facial swelling had totally subsided and she had a nose that was virtually indistinguishable from Amanda's. Their resemblance beforehand had been unusually strong; no one would have doubted they were sisters. Now, they might as well have been twins.

Jill had used the time recuperating from the surgery to undertake an intensive independent study of Mandarin. In late July, she contacted the department head, tested out of Chinese I and II, and enrolled in Chinese III. She had adjusted her diet to compensate for the relatively sedentary first half of the summer and recommended lifting weights barely three weeks after the operation. All of her clothes still fit perfectly. She hadn't gained any fat, and any minor setbacks to her raw strength and conditioning were quickly recovered. After a random late-night discussion with her father about the use of encrypted messages by political dissidents in Latin America, she had outlined plans for a new side project to tackle during her sophomore year: a machine learning algorithm that would be capable of code-breaking and that, more importantly, would learn to create new codes that were increasingly difficult for unauthorized humans and other machines to decipher. She had been assigned a single dorm room on the same floor in H-entry, three doors down from where she had been the previous semester. It was a slightly quieter spot with a slightly better view. Jill was ready for the start of the new term.

On her second day back, she ran into J.P. in one of the ground-level hallways in MacGregor. They exchanged polite conversation about their summers and their class schedules that fall. He seemed impressed by Jill's rapid progress in learning Mandarin and mentioned a trip to mainland China the following summer that advanced students were eligible to attend. Jill had already heard about it and had made it a personal goal to be ready to apply by the deadline at the beginning of spring term. If J.P. noticed her cute new nose or more defined upper body, he didn't mention it.

Jill didn't see him again until 10:00 p.m. on a Friday night almost a month later. He was on the couch in one of the lounges, watching a movie with a few other people curled up around the room. He was cuddling a girl. Jill was pretty sure her name was Marisol. She was tiny and beautiful, with dark hair, dark eyes, and flawless cinnamon-colored skin set off by her signature deep red lips and large bronze hoop earrings. Even dressed comfortably and casually, her style was impeccable. She nuzzled into J.P.'s neck. She appeared to be the physical opposite of Jill in every way. And he seemed entranced by her. Neither of them was paying much attention to the movie, and neither of them noticed Jill, momentarily stopped short and staring. Jill wasn't sure if the bitter anger she felt rising from her gut was directed toward them or toward herself. She shook it off as quickly as it had come. It was late. It was his prerogative to move on. It was nothing worth crying over. She would save it as fuel for the gym the next day.

Jill returned to her dorm room, put in earplugs, and opened her Materials and Structures textbook.

Jill didn't date again her sophomore or junior years. Why bother? It still stung every time she saw J.P., whether or not he was with his precious Marisol (although they seemed to be more nauseatingly in love with each other every time Jill crossed their path). Why shift even a portion of her focus away from her work and her goals, why dim the flame of her ambition, if it was only going to end in heartache a few months later? Maybe she was obsessed with the gym and her schoolwork, but the gym and her schoolwork wouldn't get sick of her after a couple of weeks and leave her behind. She wasn't sure if she ever wanted to get married or have kids. It might be nice someday to have someone love her back and to feel like she belonged. But "nice" wasn't worth derailing her bigger plans. If she couldn't be loved, she damn sure could be respected.

In a moment of weakness on a Thursday night during her senior year, Jill took a ten-minute Uber ride to Grafton Street Pub in Harvard Square. She had a few casual female friends in the dorm she could have asked to accompany her, but she didn't want to get stuck there if she wanted to leave and they wanted to stay. Besides, the whole reason she sought out a Harvard bar was because she needed a break from MIT students. She was constantly surrounded by her peers and yet, for the past week, she had felt a suffocating loneliness. Jill was comfortable in solitude. It was her default position. But lately, something had been different. Jill dutifully went through the motions of her workouts, her assignments, and her side projects, but an overwhelming sense of ennui weighted her down the entire time. Was this really all there was?

Having a drink at Grafton Street would be an experiment. If it was boring or humiliating or horrible, then she could return to her work knowing that a solitary but successful existence was the best she could hope for. But maybe she would start to understand why her floormates got so excited about dressing up and hitting the bars a few nights a week. Maybe she would even have fun.

It was relatively early in the night when she arrived, just before 8:00 p.m., but the pub was aflutter with students drinking on the sidewalk patio, eating dinner at the tables inside, and socializing around the bar. There were two empty barstools left; Jill took the one toward the far end and ordered a pale ale on draft. For fifteen minutes, she sat alone, slowly sipping her beer while she listened to the animated conversations around her. Everyone else seemed to be having such a great time. They seemed so connected to each other. The experiment had failed. She didn't belong here either. She was ready to close out her tab and leave when the handsome bartender who had served her earlier appeared in front of her again.

"If you liked that beer, you should try the Dogfish Head we have on tap. They're a Delaware brewery, and we'll only have it for a limited time. It's a higher gravity than what you just drank, but it has a nutty undertone to it, so it goes down smooth. I can give you a sample if you like."

"Well... sure, I guess I can try a sample," Jill shrugged. She supposed she ought to spend at least as much time at the pub as the roundtrip Uber ride would take.

The bartender brought Jill a small glass filled with dark golden liquid and watched excitedly for her reaction. Jill smiled. She didn't want to disappoint him.

"It actually is quite good," she said enthusiastically. "I think I like it even better than the last one. Okay! Okay, I'll take one of these, please."

The bartender brought her a full glass. Jill wondered if he'd linger to chat, but he was waved down to the other end of the bar by another patron. She thought she saw a glimmer of disappointment on his face when he couldn't stay, but she probably was just imagining it. It was part of his job to be charming, after all.

"OkCupid or Match?" a voice behind Jill asked. It took her a moment to realize that the question was directed at her. She swiveled her stool.

"Huh?"

"OkCupid or Match? Or Tinder? I've seen you sitting here by yourself for a while. I'm guessing you're meeting an online date and he's running late?"

"I'm... no. No, I just decided to come here for a drink. It's my first time here. It seemed like a cool spot and I wanted to check it out." Jill laughed. "I'd probably be drinking vodka straight from the bottle if I were about to get stood up. It didn't occur to me that's what it must look like to everyone else, me sitting here by myself."

"Can I join you, then?" the man asked. The people to Jill's right were closing out their tab. "My friends are over there, and you're welcome to join us, but I wanted to get to know you one-on-one."

"Sure, of course," Jill said. He was so confident! It was a refreshing change from most of her classmates at MIT, even the graduate students. "Have a seat. I'm Jill."

His name was Jesse. He was twenty-six and in his second year at Harvard Medical School. He was from Winnetka, Illinois, which he made a point to clarify was an affluent suburb along the north shore and not one of those "bad" sections of south Chicago that politicians liked to invoke when pushing one agenda or another. His parents were both doctors: his mom, a gastro-enterologist, and his dad, an ear, nose, and throat specialist. He went to Brown for undergrad, where he majored in Economics and played rugby. He thought he'd make an excellent plastic surgeon, but he was considering becoming a general practitioner instead because he didn't want to deal with the extra years of residency and the cumbersome board certification prerequisites. He considered GPs no less prestigious, by the way. He would be the gateway to the specialists, he would be the one providing his clients with long-term care, and he would have to be well-versed in all areas of medicine, but he would start making a six-figure income long before any of his peers. He thought his classmates who professed lofty ambitions about practicing in third-world countries or underserved rural communities, accepting low salaries and grueling hours to be the engine of a greater social good, were deluding themselves. Statistically, almost all of them would succumb to the almighty dollar, especially if they didn't have extensive family roots in the geographic area they claimed they wanted to "save." Maybe some of his classmates thought he was arrogant or selfish for not pretending to admire their plans, but he thought they all fell somewhere between childishly naïve and willfully disingenuous. If forced to choose, he preferred to be a rationalist rather than a self-indulgent phony. This, at least, Jill could understand and respect.

Jill was more comfortable allowing others to talk than she was speaking about herself, and Jesse seemed more than happy to oblige. She remembered, however, J.P.'s complaints about her being impossibly closed off, so she tried to share a few tidbits about herself in response to the handful of times Jesse actually asked. She told him about her plans after graduation to work as a software engineer (at the time, she was still unsure whether she was better suited for a major corporation or a tech startup) and he seemed reasonably impressed. He thought it was cool that she was a "smart chick." Jill was starting her fourth beer by then, and she accepted the awkward pseudo-compliment with grace.

Jesse wanted to know about her family's background and what kind of town she came from, and he seemed genuinely excited to learn that she was from Fairfield County, Connecticut, and that her parents were both well-educated professionals. Jill wasn't sure why—he certainly hadn't said anything openly racist!—but she decided to omit the detail about her mom being an African immigrant and her father having Latin American roots. What did it matter anyway? It was irrelevant. Plenty of her dormmates and other acquaintances had no idea either, unless they happened to glance at one of the framed pictures of her family that she had placed on her nightstand or her desk in her dorm room, and then pressed her for the story of who the man and woman were.

She was over-thinking things. Jesse was trying to tell her about how he and his group of friends were prepping for the Boards, how this exam was basically the last hurdle they needed to overcome before they could start seeing patients as M3s, and here she was, absorbed by her own thoughts, wondering why she felt vaguely uncomfortable sharing her unconventional background or giving him any indication that she and her family had led anything other than the idealized southwestern Connecticut life. Maybe J.P. had a point. Maybe she wasn't cut out for relationships at all.

But Jesse hadn't seemed to notice Jill's brief regression into her own head. They had another beer. Five total for Jill. This officially constituted more alcohol than she had consumed over the previous year combined. She was drunk. She thought she was, miraculously, holding herself together pretty well—she wasn't slurring her words or slumping over the table or laughing boisterously about nothing or committing any of the other telltale signs she had seen so often from her dormmates on weekends when her return from the library happened to coincide with their return from the clubs—but she was definitely drunk. She didn't particularly enjoy feeling so out of control, but she couldn't deny that the inner monologue that normally would have reprimanded her for slacking off and allowing herself to get to this point had been delightfully subdued. She was having fun. This was what college was supposed to be about, wasn't it?

Their goodbye was a little clumsy, but not painfully so. Jesse seemed genuinely surprised when Jill politely declined his invitation for her to accompany him home that night. For a moment, she was nervous. Had she wasted his time? Was he going to become angry or aggressive with her? But the look of shock on his face quickly subsided until he almost looked pleased. He asked if he could take her on a proper date on Saturday, then asked for her number so they could coordinate their plans. Jill hesitated. She didn't know why. This was exactly the type of man she should be dating. Maybe he was a little cocky, but to be fair, he had the achievements and accolades to back it up. He was attractive and seemed to have a solid group of friends. He seemed to know exactly what he wanted for himself in this life, and now, apparently, one of those things was Jill. So what was the problem? Wasn't he the kind of guy that most heterosexual girls dreamt about dating and someday marrying?

Jill gave him her number, planted a soft kiss on his cheek, and tumbled into her Uber. Jesse had texted her twice before she arrived back on MIT's campus.

"You're making me crazy," he had said at the end of their second official date. This time, they had made out on a park bench for a few minutes before Jill once again declined his invitation for a sleepover and summoned her ride. "I mean that in a very good way," he continued. "You're not like other girls. Most of them hear 'Harvard Medical School' and jump right into bed with me. But I like that you're making me wait. You're making me earn it."

"I'm not doing it to play games with you," Jill shrugged. She had no idea how else to respond. She knew the cardinal rule was, allegedly, that a woman shouldn't sleep with a man right away if she wanted him to stick around. She found this notion repulsive, antifeminist, and hypocritical, of course; but more than that, it was also the sort of advice that often proved to be flat-out wrong. She knew plenty of people in her dorm, straight and gay alike, who were still dating partners that initially were casual hookups or meant to be one-night stands. And conversely, she herself had held off on sleeping with J.P. Woo at first, and how well had that worked out for her? She wasn't trying to lure or trick Jesse into a relationship, and especially not by using sex as a tool of manipulation.

But she wasn't sure why she was holding off. Sex held no inherent religious or moral value for her. She found Jesse attractive. She was a little concerned that she had no idea how to be good in bed, but sleeping with him would itself be an opportunity to rectify her almost total lack of experience. She wasn't even sure if she wanted to be in a relationship with him, but she wanted to want it, and she felt like she ought to want it. And she had an unshakeable sense that he felt the exact same complicated twist of emotions toward her.

Neither of them spoke a word of these internal monologues aloud, of course. It was easier for her to let him believe that she was the "good girl" he had been looking for: the intelligent, pretty, younger (but not inappropriately so) coed who would fit snugly into the perfect life he was constructing for himself, that he was destined for, that he was so certain he deserved.

Two dates later, they finally had sex. Jill had decided after their third date that she would, and over the days leading up to their fourth date, she had thought extensively about how it would play out. Thought about it, but not fantasized about it. Every time she imagined it, she assumed it would be somewhere between "mediocre" and "an utter debacle."

Perhaps this was a self-fulfilling prophecy. Jesse could barely get it up. He blamed the problem ("flaccidity, flaccidity, flaccidity," Jill screamed internally until she very nearly broke into a combination of deranged laughter and uncontrollable sobs) first on the whiskey they'd had at dinner, and then on the stress of finishing up his M2 requirements and studying for Step 1. Jill blamed herself. They fumbled through it and went to sleep. When they woke up and tried again a few hours later, it was marginally better. Jesse seemed reasonably satisfied, at least.

But first times were often awkward, weren't they?

They really did have fun together over the next six weeks. Notwithstanding his complaints about his workload, Jesse seemed to have a different social event to attend almost every night, from "Thirsty Thursday" beer tastings and "Taco Tuesday" dinners with his med school classmates, to rowdy weekend bar crawls with a group of graduate students from a miscellany of disciplines that he had befriended and almost seemed to lead. He invited Jill to most of it, and Jill tried to be flexible. He didn't seem interested in having any more one-on-one dates with her, as he had in the beginning, but that was okay. She couldn't imagine trying to add anything else to their packed social calendar. She already had needed to turn down several of his invitations to one random event or another so that she could study or prep for a job interview or finish up a p-set. Every time she did, she could tell he was frustrated, but she wasn't sure what more she could do. As it was, she felt like she was one step away from crossing the line between "making compromises for the relationship" and "compromising herself." She could justify a tiny bit of leniency with her workout regimen and study schedule, particularly since it was her final semester of college and she already had several excellent job offers from which to choose. But she was on track to graduate with a perfect 5.0 GPA, and she was not willing to sacrifice that. Not for Jesse, not for anyone.

And it was fun to spend time with him. Really. Two or three of the women in his social circle were occasionally smug and standoffish toward her, but they weren't openly hostile, and everyone else was incredibly welcoming. It was a cool experience to be a part of such a huge friend group; the faces at each event varied somewhat from night to night, but there was a pervasive camaraderie and familiarity among all of them. It reminded Jill of most of her peers at MacGregor, actually, especially the ones who wound up with an integral part of their identity being attached to their dorm entry. But for whatever strides Jill had made in getting to know the other students in Hex since her second semester freshman year, she was completely unable to relate. The only reason she had stayed in the dorm instead of moving off-campus was because she thought it was fairly priced for the locational convenience and because she had been granted a single.

The closest thing she had personally experienced to Jesse and his sprawling friend group was with her high school soccer team, but even that wasn't quite the same. Back then, they had bonded over grueling twice-a-day practices and a shared desire to win the state championship. There were weekly mandatory team dinners, and most of the girls got along well enough that they would have attended voluntarily even if Coach hadn't insisted on it. But their relationships with each other never seemed so... emotionally infused. Jill would have said that they identified primarily as fellow Wreckers soccer players, not as best buddies. She would have said that those girls were her friends, sure, but they were her teammates first and foremost. But they all had felt that way, hadn't they?

Regardless, Jill was adapting as well as she could to what she assumed was a more typical version of a twenty-something's social life. It was a little odd, Jill supposed, that Jesse had never asked to meet any of her friends. He'd never expressed an interest in it. But that itself was also kind of a relief. Who would Jill have introduced him to? The casual acquaintances at MacGregor who liked to cook dinner around the same time Jill did, or who gravitated to the same study spaces on Saturday afternoons? Or maybe the girl from her Thermodynamics lab, with whom she sometimes walked to lunch after class, laughing together about their professor's latest political tirade (which was always completely unrelated to the lecture until, about eight minutes into that day's digression, the professor would pause—a combination of aghast and self-satisfied for going off on a tangent for so long—and half-ironically claim that the federal government was the embodiment of the second law of thermodynamics in action, continually degenerating into a more chaotic state, and therefore his diatribe was directly relevant to the day's lesson)? That girl at the gym with the dark red hair and a proclivity for muscle tanks, who always exchanged a nod of recognition with Jill whenever they were the only two women in the weight room lifting heavy? Maybe Jesse could tell that Jill didn't have the same huge network of close friends that he did, and he was trying to spare her feelings by not asking to meet them.

Nevertheless, by the end of the sixth week they were together, Jill was physically and emotionally exhausted. She felt like she was growing complacent with her schoolwork and training; maybe she was doing the minimum necessary to maintain her current level of athletic and academic achievement, but that type of stagnancy felt as disheartening as regression. Her ambition and interests, which Jesse had praised in the beginning, now seemed to irk him, particularly when they interfered with her ability to accompany him to whatever was on his agenda for the week. Jill had decided to work for a year or two while she considered whether to pursue a graduate degree, and from the first week that she and Jesse began dating, she also was being courted by several major corporations that wanted to fly her to their headquarters around the country whenever her schedule might permit. Every time she mentioned that she had accepted another of their invitations, Jesse would congratulate her, but then immediately sigh and ask, "So I guess that means you won't be able to come with me to Random Event #183, then?"

Besides that, the sex was still... laborious. He was always either too drunk to get it up or unable to finish, irrespective of what Jill did to facilitate the process. She tried first being more aggressive, then being more passive, in bed. She asked him if he had any fetishes or kinks they might want to try together. She watched a couple of porn videos on her laptop in her dorm room one evening to make sure she was actually doing it right, then tried to incorporate the actresses' moves and style into her own performance when she slept over at Jesse's two nights later. It

101

barely occurred to her that she was getting absolutely nothing out of their budding relationship or their sex life other than a creeping insecurity that she was unsexy, unlovable, and terrible in bed.

Why didn't she just end it? That was the obvious solution. But Jesse seemed as frustrated as she was, and he wasn't ending it either. He probably felt like he ought to be attracted to Jill, that Jill was someone he ought to be dating, and after pursuing her so ardently in the beginning, he was simply too stubborn to acknowledge that he had picked the wrong girl.

The end of Jill's final semester at MIT was approaching. The entire thing was becoming a huge distraction, but Jill didn't want to admit that her first attempt at dating since Jean Paul Woo was destined to wilt away even more quickly than the last time. She didn't want to concede failure. But she also didn't know how much longer she could countenance shortchanging her workouts, neglecting her side projects, stressing over Jesse's satisfaction in bed, and coddling his fragile ego and his need to be constantly surrounded by a pack of friends. She was sick of always, always, being the one to trek over to Harvard, when he never once came to see her at MIT. She was sick of him always, always, making their plans without considering what she wanted to do, under the assumption that she'd dutifully tag along as his date. She was sick of patiently humoring his conceit about being a Harvard medical student, and she was sick of making herself smaller to placate his insecurity, bubbling under the surface of his bravado, that maybe, just maybe, she might be even smarter than he. She was just sick of all of it.

CHAPTER NINE
Amanda Wagner

"You've got to be fucking kidding me," Amanda muttered to herself. She set down the tray of entrees she was carrying and gestured to her coworker, Jasmine. "Hey, look who just walked in," she said more loudly.

"Holy shit, is that Jeff? With that bitch?" Jasmine was standing three steps from the kitchen door, but her voice was loud enough that two middle-aged patrons' heads turned with disapproval.

"Shush!" Amanda laughed, then scowled. "Angie sat them in my section too. Ugh. Angie never met him. She has no idea what she just did."

"What the hell is the matter with him?" Jasmine set her tray next to Amanda's. "Is he trying to provoke you?"

"Honestly, there's a chance he doesn't realize I work here. He visited me at Breaking News a few times, but that's because I was bartending and it was easier for me to chat. He's never come here before, at least not to see me. And I doubt he was paying enough attention to anything I said to remember that I work here too."

"So you think it was that bitch's idea?" Jasmine asked.

"Probably," Amanda replied. Her throat suddenly felt parched. "Jeff couldn't be bothered to remember where I work, but if anyone so much as mentioned it to her, she one hundred percent would not have forgotten."

"And then she suggested that they come here to... what? To rub it in your face?"

"Pretty much."

"That's him? Tu ex-novio? Came here?" Hector was Amanda's favorite busboy. He had walked up behind Amanda and Jasmine and had overheard enough of their conversation to piece together what was unfolding. Instinctively, all three of them looked around to ensure their manager, Nick, wouldn't catch them slacking. When they had silently confirmed his absence, Hector continued, "Y es ella? But she is ugly. Gorda y feísima. She has the face of a dog. What was the fuck he thinking?"

Amanda laughed again. The audacity of the two of them to show up at her place of work—irrespective of whether or not it was intentional on Jeff's part—made her flush with rage. She was trapped. It wasn't like she could just strut out the door with her head held high. Not unless she wanted to get fired. And she didn't. Ottimo had plenty of the same internal B.S. and melodrama as every other restaurant and bar at which she had worked, but these colleagues were by far her favorite. They were the only reason she was able to handle the unexpected appearance of Jeff and his... his whore! ... with any grace.

"I've worked in the service industry for almost eight years now," Jasmine was saying. "And, hand to God, I have never once fucked with a customer's food in any significant way. But say the word and I will stick every piece of bread that goes to their table so far up my—"

"Jesus, Jasmine!" Amanda squealed.

"If they order anything with the cream sauce," Hector added, gesturing toward his crotch and clearly amused with himself, "I give them mi crema especial, okay?"

"You are both fucking mental," Amanda said. "And I love it. I love both of you. Thank you. But don't screw with their food. I've already decided to rise above it."

Someone in the kitchen called for Hector. He took Amanda's hand, kissed it, and before turning away, looked her in the eyes and said, "Oye, you will not let the shit-man make you sad, okay, cariña? You are so pretty to be sad."

Amanda nodded. She was surprised to find herself blushing. She had long since become accustomed to Hector's sometimes-cheesy, sometimes-bold, Spanglish flirtations, but in that moment, his words were exactly what she needed to hear.

"I'll take their table for you," Jasmine proposed. "You can have one of mine. We seem pretty slow tonight anyway. Nick won't notice. Or if he does, he can go fuck himself." Jasmine and Amanda again instinctively looked around to make sure their manager hadn't snuck up behind them. "You don't need to make eye contact with them the entire night unless you want to."

"Actually, you know what? Take their order. Get them situated and comfortable. I still have to serve table 7, but I'm going to try to do it out of their line of sight." Amanda snickered. "I want them to be invested. I want their food order in, I want them to have to stay. Jeff is even more of a tightwad than I am, and once he has to pay for the food, he won't leave until he has it in his possession, even if they end up taking it to-go. And I'm still not sure if he realizes this is where I work. I'll bring their food out to them and hopefully that'll ruin their date. It might even cause a fight if she's the one who suggested this place."

Jasmine smiled wickedly. "This is why you're my girl. I'll do whatever it takes to make sure their attention stays on me. Let's dick around with them."

"It won't be nearly as bad as he dicked around with me," Amanda said. "But I dig this plan."

They way Amanda explained it to her coworkers at Ottimo, it all went down at Barrister's Ball, late in February of Jeff's 1L year. But when she was honest with herself, Amanda saw the signs well before then. There was always plenty of talk about how many couples break up during the first year of law school. Indeed, the 2Ls and 3Ls seemed to relish any opportunity to mention the incoming couples' terrible odds. Jeff and Amanda were characteristically humble about their chances. They understood the risks and temptations and, ostensibly, took preventative measures to avoid becoming an unwanted statistic. Amanda thought she had it under control.

When she met Beth at Jeff's first section mixer of the year, she felt... something. Not jealousy. Not suspicion. Just... unease. It was raw and instinctive. Something she had never experienced before, even with the girls in their intramural kickball league back at U of E who had shamelessly fawned over Jeff, and occasionally explicitly propositioned him. She asked Jeff offhandedly about her the next day.

"Don't be weird," Jeff said. "She's in my section. We're all trying to get along and not succumb to the malicious competition that the whole law school system is designed to impose on us. Don't make this harder for me."

Amanda was apologetic. She really wasn't trying to start shit. Her intentions were innocent. She didn't realize her question was so loaded. She wasn't trying to entrap Jeff in section drama. She dropped it.

She saw Beth twice more at Thursday "bar review" nights during the first semester. Both times she felt the same unexplainable sense of discomfort. Even the second time, when Beth was hanging onto the neck of a guy who looked at least seven years her junior, something just seemed off. But she remembered how upset Jeff had become the first time she brought up Beth, and she kept her mouth shut.

She didn't see Beth again until first-semester finals were over. Jeff's small section had gotten together to pregame before a class-wide party. By then, all of the long-distance couples in Jeff's small section had split up. One engagement had been broken off. Only two other unmarried couples who had been together at the start of the school year remained. And Amanda felt nauseous. Beth wasn't doing anything specific. In fact, she seemed to have her attention at least partially focused on another new guy, a sweet twenty-four-year-old from Sedona, Arizona, whose long-distance girlfriend had been flying in to see him every other weekend until their section's Legal Practice take-home exam in mid-November, at which point their relationship apparently had crumbled.

Amanda didn't know the details. In fact, she had heard more about it from her roommate Irina than she had from Jeff. She didn't want to care. But when she saw Beth and Jeff talking in the kitchen that night while the rest of the group played "Never Have I Ever" and got hammered off of Kraken rum and the cases of Four Loko and Boone's Farm boxed wine that someone had ironically-but-not-so-ironically purchased from a nearby convenience store, Amanda found herself trying to repress her fury. He had abandoned her.

She didn't understand it. She asked Jeff again the next afternoon, trying to control the pitch of her voice, trying to be as casual as possible: what was Beth's story?

"You're acting crazy. Stop it." It was the same tone he used whenever the topic of his family came up. End of discussion. Pursue further at your own peril. Amanda didn't want to be crazy. She wasn't one of those girls. She was a chill girlfriend. She trusted him.

Barrister's Ball was law school prom. It was important to Jeff. It also happened to coincide with the annual cocktail party hosted by the sponsor of Amanda's internship, the Green Resources Alliance Foundation, a mid-sized organization focused on developing and promoting environmentally sustainable economic and agricultural growth, particularly in rural and impoverished areas in the United States. Amanda had landed the position at GRAF the prior October, two days before Halloween. Irina happened to be friendly with several of the organization's executive-level employees and officers, and Amanda had no illusions: she never would have had a chance at the role without Irina's enthusiastic recommendation.

The internship was part-time only and came with a $6,000 per year stipend, renewable after the first year. By Amanda's calculations this amounted to approximately $2.78 per hour, a sum notably less than the wages she received before tips for bartending or waitressing. She didn't care. It was a minor miracle that the prior girl quit without notice to take a position at a fashion house in Milan less than two months after starting. It was the type of miracle that could turn a person religious that, less than a week later,

Irina happened to be at a happy hour for Baltic ex-pats with the organization's infuriated hiring manager, who just wanted to find someone reasonably smart, diligent, and willing to pay their dues without relying on "daddy's connections" to fill the remainder of the position's term.

Amanda understood that she was the beneficiary of a well-timed fluke and that another opportunity like the GRAF internship was unlikely to come along again for someone like her, and so she put her entire heart into the job. Every menial task—from scanning, digitizing, and electronically filing twenty thousand pages of old paperwork, to prepping the conference room with fresh fruit and coffee, to testing two giant cardboard boxes' worth of old pens and highlighters and sorting out the handful that were clean and functional—she completed with a smile on her face, even when her salaried coworkers were being particularly nasty or dismissive toward her. She wanted to impress Jeff. She wanted to be the type of girlfriend who was on his level. She wanted to be successful. And if that meant starting at the bottom and working her way up, step by excruciating step, she would do it. He had said that he found her drive and perseverance sexy. She believed him.

So their argument over GRAF's cocktail party was perplexing. This was an opportunity for Amanda to make connections. Maybe a chance to prove to her coworkers that she had value beyond completing tedious administrative tasks, an opportunity to show them that she was charming, clever, interesting. Maybe a chance to impress someone who could offer her a higher-paying job with a title other than "intern" someday. Maybe a chance to meet a mentor, or to get to know her bosses better, or even to subtly weasel her way into a more meaningful assignment. Not that she was complaining about her current responsibilities, but she was ready for so much more.

And maybe this cocktail party would be her way in! A lot of the people she had met in D.C. thus far seemed kind of socially awkward. Amanda often felt like they were mimicking basic human interactions based on something they had seen on a television sitcom, and when even that routine became too difficult to maintain, they defaulted to talking about politics and their past accomplishments, without ever really listening to what their conversation partner was saying back. If Amanda were going to distinguish herself, a cocktail party would be the ideal setting for her to shine.

Jeff was having none of it. Almost aggressively so. Uncharacteristically so. Amanda never suggested that they skip Barrister's Ball entirely. But GRAF was hosting the event and there was an expectation that she'd attend, so maybe they could do an hour or two at the cocktail party first, and then head over to Barrister's? They wouldn't need to change clothes and they wouldn't arrive more than twenty or thirty minutes late to the dance. Amanda would make sure of it.

Absolutely not. Jeff rejected the proposal outright and shut down any further discussion of the matter. Amanda was free to do whatever she wanted, he said, but he wasn't going to skip his section's pre-party for her cocktail party. It was her work function. She could attend it without him. He didn't care.

Amanda was baffled. She was also terrified. He had repeatedly claimed that he was most attracted to her when she showed ambition, when she acted in pursuit of a higher purpose. Yet here was an ideal opportunity to make headway with her aspirations, and he was trying to make her feel guilty for it. He was belittling her and trying to force her to reprioritize. It was unprecedented. She didn't know how to respond. She didn't want to be stubborn. She wanted to support her man. But she also felt like she would be compromising a part of herself if she skipped the GRAF event entirely.

She skipped it. Entirely. This was the part she replayed over and over in her head. The moment she decided to skip GRAF's cocktail party. The moment she chose Jeff over herself and her career. And then she got screwed over anyway.

She did the dutiful girlfriend act. She went to the section pregame. Beth was there, of course. Amanda's unease hadn't dissipated. She tried to talk to Beth, to befriend her. On some level, she must've known it was a futile gesture.

Everyone was drunk by the time they arrived at the venue for Barrister's. Amanda put on her best game face. She never would have said it aloud, but she knew: Beth may have been borderline "law school hot," but Amanda was actually hot. Real world hot. Jeff was a man. His actions were primordially dictated by one thing, right? Amanda would be fine.

Two and a half hours into the dance, Beth and Jeff disappeared. At first, Amanda only noticed that Jeff was missing. She continued to socialize with the other spouses and significant others and the handful of law students she was starting to count as her own friends too. But her smile was forced. Something was wrong.

Five minutes later, it clicked. Beth also had vanished. In an instant, their simultaneous absence became a flagrant, conspicuous, and deeply personal affront against her. The entire rest of their small section, to a person, was hanging around the two tables they had claimed with their handbags and coats earlier in the night. Jeff and Beth were gone. Amanda forced the smile. She danced in place to shitty early-2000s remixes played over the venue's sound system by a gaunt deejay in a pleather blazer. Fuck this. But smile.

After twenty minutes, Jeff and Beth both reemerged. Amanda didn't know if they had bothered to stagger their return for appearance's sake. Did one of them wait outside for two minutes after the other had walked back through the hotel's ballroom doors? Did it matter? She was livid. But she would try to play it cool. She was the chill girlfriend.

"What was that about? Where did you go?" Not five minutes had passed before Amanda yanked Jeff to the side. There was a fury behind her hushed tone that she couldn't control.

"Would you stop?" Jeff growled. "She is my friend. I'm allowed to hang out with my friend."

"You disappeared for almost half an hour and left me here alone with people I barely know. And you did it with the one person I have told you makes me nervous."

"You're being crazy."

Amanda dropped it. For the moment. They could pick it up the next morning when they were both less intoxicated. She was fuming. She had been disrespected. But they could get through it.

She briefly chatted with Beth before the night ended. It was superficial nonsense, but she thought maybe it would humanize her to this girl.

Then they left. She and Jeff. They were drunk. They were both angry. But they could figure it out the next morning.

"Hey! You're leaving with the wrong girl! What happened to your busty brunette, player?"

A tall, chubby white guy with dark hair, sweating through his dress shirt, was loitering in the doorway. One of Jeff's classmates. Not in his small section, but sociable enough that Amanda had crossed paths with him a few times. And he was calling Jeff out.

"He's full of shit," Jeff had muttered after they were both in the Uber. "He's hammered and coked out. He doesn't know what he's saying."

Amanda knew it was over.

They went back to Jeff's apartment that night. This was an aberration; usually they went to Amanda's place, waved to Irina or Marta if either happened to be hanging out in the common area, and went to bed. Jeff was drunker than Amanda had seen him since college. She was disgusted with him on every conceivable level. Out of some wretched combination of drunken habit and self-loathing, she initiated sex with him anyway. When he couldn't get it up after four minutes of half-hearted effort, they passed out in each other's arms.

Then, at around 6:00 a.m., they both woke up. What immediately followed wasn't the best sex they'd ever had together, but it was close. Perhaps the still-unspoken understanding that this would be their last morning with each other imbued the act with an emotional gravity of which they had been deprived for months. They fell back asleep and did it again at 7:00, and then again at 10:30. At noon, they left Jeff's bedroom and sat on the couch by his window. They both knew it was over. It was only a matter of who would say it first.

"Did you fuck her last night?" Amanda asked.

"No." Jeff said. He didn't look guilty. He just looked uncomfortable.

"Okay."

111

They stared at each other. Amanda didn't want to be the one to end it. She wasn't sure why. She supposed that she didn't want him playing the victim to his law school friends, acting like she had hurt him, betrayed him, dumped him suddenly and out of nowhere when he needed to be focusing on his schoolwork. The words still rang through her ears: "You're going home with the wrong girl." Or some shit like that. Some utterly humiliating shit like that.

But Jeff's dumbass acquaintance had only confirmed what Amanda already knew to be true. That sweaty, bloated asshole's stupid comment simply made Jeff's refusal to own up to his misdeeds that much more obnoxious.

It didn't matter. Amanda didn't need to be told the details anyway. She understood exactly what had transpired the night before. Jeff wasn't lying to her. Not technically. He hadn't fucked Beth. Not yet. But they had fooled around at Barrister's. Although Amanda couldn't objectively prove it, she was certain of it. Jeff probably was the one who reluctantly put a stop to it before it went any further. He probably felt noble when he did so. And then it had been decided: Amanda was something that needed to be handled first. Something that needed to be gotten rid of.

After a few minutes of Amanda's prodding and leading questions, Jeff broke up with her. If it had taken much longer, she would have sucked it up and done it herself. But she cried anyway. Her heart was still broken anyway. She was furious with him, but more furious with herself. She had skipped the GRAF cocktail party. She had been ignoring her intuition for months. She had convinced herself that she was making compromises for the benefit of their relationship, when the only thing being compromised was herself.

And he hadn't forced her to do any of it. That was the thing. Maybe she had been manipulated, maybe she had been strung along, but could she really place all the blame on him? He hadn't abused her, technically he hadn't lied to her, she just had wanted so desperately to make it work—even though she had felt in the pit of her stomach for weeks, months, that something was broken beyond repair—and now it finally had blown up in her face. My

God. It was almost a relief. She had no appetite, she wanted to curl into a ball and sob, she could barely resist the urge to punch a hole in her bedroom drywall every morning when she woke up, she was tempted to find a hot, rich, older man on Tinder and parade him around in front of Jeff and his classmates. But she couldn't deny that a weight had been lifted.

"Beth?" Irina had shouted. She angrily muttered something to herself in what Amanda assumed was Latvian, then threw her hands up and began pulling at her ponytail. This was, by far, the most animated that Amanda had seen her. "The chunky white girl with brown hair? That Beth? Pie velna! Es nesapratu. I do not understand how this woman has such a... a Helen-of-Troy magical pussy. Honestly, I am fascinated to know. What are these pheromones emanating from her vagina, that men cannot resist? This is at least the second relationship at the law school that she has destroyed. Arguably it is the third or fourth. She is not even pretty."

Amanda's jaw dropped and she cackled with laughter despite her anger and grief.

"I am sorry," Irina continued. "I forget how rude the word 'pussy' is for Americans."

"It's not just that," Amanda laughed. "I've never heard you talk like this."

"My English is correct though?" Amanda nodded and Irina continued, only slightly more subdued. "I just do not understand. My boyfriend told me about her. He says she is a 'law-school six,' which is a 'real-world four' at best. These are Kristoff's words. I know scoring women on their looks is dehumanizing, and I know I should scold him and never repeat such things. But right now, I do not care. I have seen her and he is right. If anything, his rating is generous. But you are gorgeous. You are a real-world ten."

"Jeff said I was gorgeous too. He kept repeating that exact word. 'Gorgeous.' Even as he was breaking up with me. A lot of good it did me."

"It is more than that, though. She also is not especially interesting or clever or fun. No more so than any other girl in their class. Kristoff does not understand it either. Everyone knows

113

she is the reason that Eric and Sarah broke up first semester. And you know Justin, the tall guy with the glasses? Kristoff says that Beth was a big part of the reason that his relationship ended too. I thought that was just gossip and was willing to benefit her the doubt that there was more to the story, but now I believe it completely. Oh, and two months ago she hooked up with Dante, who we all thought was dating a 2L at the time."

"Jeez. No one ever told me about any of that. I don't know if this makes me feel better or worse."

"It should make you feel better. She just likes the chase. I think she is bored. Or maybe it is more strategic. Maybe she is jerking around all the 1L men in the hopes that it will mess with their minds and mess with their grades, and then her class ranking will be better."

"Ha. I could almost begrudgingly respect that if it were true."

"Regardless," Irina continued. Her tone and temperament had returned to normal, but there was a fire in her eyes as she spoke. "She may have stolen him from you, but it will not last. She will move on quickly and leave him with no one."

"I don't even want to say that she 'stole' him from me, to be honest." Amanda shrugged. "Jeff made his choice. Whatever magic spell her vag may cast on 1L men, it didn't trump his free will. I got a bad vibe from her from the beginning, but she didn't owe me any sort of loyalty. I'm not going to debase myself by fighting with another woman over a man. Not over Jeff, anyway. Six months ago, I would've thought he was worth it, but he's proven me wrong. I don't know why I'm not angrier with Beth, but I don't really care about her one way or the other. I just expected more from Jeff."

Irina had wrapped her arms around Amanda and squeezed her tightly. It was a sweet, simple gesture, but it was enough to make Amanda's lip quiver. It was enough to make her realize how long it had been since Jeff had shown her any kind of affection, the kind of affection he had given so freely at the beginning of their relationship. When did it change? How long had he been forcing himself to go through the motions with her? For how long had he been miserable?

Sitting at a two-top in Ottimo, across the table from Beth, Jeff looked anything but miserable. Amanda could see them in her peripheral vision as Jasmine took their order. They weren't swooning over each other, groping at each other under the table, sticking their tongues down each other's throats, or referring to each other as "honey bear" or "baby girl" or "pumpkin," and loudly professing their undying devotion while taking pictures of each other from across the table, the way some of Ottimo's patrons did. In a sense, that would've been preferable. At least then, Amanda and the rest of the staff could have spent the duration of their shift hollering, "Five out on the risotto, BABE!" "Your fucking sirloin is dying on the pass, my poopsie schmoopsie!" "Atrás, my KING, fucking watch it!" while they were back of house. The public performance of some movie-cliché idea of romance would have been fodder for a night's worth of snickering and contempt.

But Beth and Jeff were far more reserved. They looked content. Comfortable with each other. Happy without being showy about it. They didn't have to convince anyone around them that they were good together. They just were. Irina was wrong about how this would end. Beth might have left those other guys—torpedoed their relationships, messed with their minds, and claimed her conquests, only to get restless and lose interest a few weeks later—but Amanda knew better than anyone that Jeff was special. Even if it had been a game for Beth at first, soon enough Jeff would have a hold on her the same way she had gotten a hold on him.

Watching them together as she jotted down the dietary restrictions and special requests of her four-top of thirty-something businessmen with a phony, flirtatious smile plastered on her face, she knew that Beth wouldn't want to give that up. She felt preternaturally calm one second and dizzy with rage and jealousy the next. She was going to screw up one of her current customers' orders, almost certainly, because she was so spitefully excited to bring Beth and Jeff their meal. She had no intentions of tampering with their food, but she wondered if they'd dare eat a bite of it.

Beyond that, Amanda had lost about eight pounds since she had last seen Jeff. As she explained to Jasmine, it wasn't intentional; she simply had been served so much bullshit that she lost her appetite. Regardless, this was the slimmest she had been in years. Her size 2 pants were fitting loosely around her hips again. Briefly, she remembered those nasty high-school era comments about Jill Torres having a much better body. Perhaps now that wasn't true anymore, although Amanda hadn't tried to find Jill on social media in ages to check. Had Jill ever confronted such disrespect? She probably was too smart to be tricked by someone like Jeff. Jill Torres would have trusted her intuition. And she never would have skipped a work event to placate a man.

"They didn't ask for you or anything," Jasmine said as she and Amanda were sticking their chits to the board. "They weren't looking around the room or acting shady either. I think you might be right that he doesn't realize you're working here. I'm not sure if she knows either. Although I don't see how it could possibly be a coincidence."

"Yeah, it doesn't make sense. It's not like this is a popular spot for Georgetown students. But maybe that's the point. Maybe they don't want their classmates to see them together. The gossip at that school is a plague even when it comes to mundane shit, and this is an especially juicy story."

"They should be ashamed to be seen together. Their classmates should judge them. It's disgusting what they did to you. Who does he think he is?"

"What did they order?" Amanda asked, ignoring Jasmine's question, which she had been repeatedly asking herself. Did he think he was better than her? *Was* he better than her? Was a fellow law student more on his level?

"Stop running your mouths and get back out there!" Their manager Nick was approaching. "A slower night doesn't mean you can slack off back here. Go refill your tables' water glasses and try to upsell some of that horseshit wine the owner forced on our sommelier. Clean something. Finish your sidework, and don't think I didn't notice that both of you completely half-assed it today. If there aren't enough customers for both of you, then I'll cut one of you now."

"Chinga tu madre, Nick," Jasmine said with a saccharine smile. They never understood why he seemed to think being cut early was some sort of punishment. And he never followed through with these empty threats anyway.

"¡Muy bien dicho, mi cielo!" their dishwasher Hugo shouted. He held the distinction of being the most creatively foul-mouthed of all the kitchen staff and seemed to take great joy in teaching Jasmine a variety of Spanish obscenities whenever their cigarette breaks aligned.

"After fifteen years in the service industry, do you think I don't understand you two? Go do your jobs, both of you. So help me God, Hugo, how many times have I told you not to stack the plates like that?"

"I sorry, señor. Lo siento, señor. No te entiendo."

Nick's attention was diverted. Jasmine and Amanda exchanged a look and stifled their giggles; Hugo's English was far better than he pretended whenever Nick was around.

"Do you still want to bring them their food?" Jasmine asked as they walked back to the floor. "Say the word and I'll 'accidentally' dump her entire plate on that frumpy-ass dress she's wearing."

Amanda laughed and shook her head no. She could see table 11 was trying to catch her eye. "Nah. I want to see them squirm up close. On the bold assumption that either of them has enough of a moral compass to understand that they ought to feel uncomfortable, that is." She gave Jasmine's shoulder a squeeze and took the roundabout way to table 11, being sure to stay out of Jeff and Beth's line of vision.

Fifteen minutes later, their orders were up: braised lamb shank and gnocchi for one, seared scallops with smoked bacon and mushrooms for the other. Amanda didn't know who had which dish. She still wasn't sure what she was going to say or do. Had she ever brought her shift meal home in a container with Ottimo's label on it, or told Jeff that if he came by with a few of his classmates, she would sneak them a free appetizer? Maybe they knew that she worked here after all. But what was the point? They seemed engrossed in their conversation: making direct eye contact, nodding their heads as the other spoke, oblivious to Amanda approaching. It wasn't too late to take their appetizers back to the kitchen and ask Hector to rub his balls all over the food. Amanda sighed.

"Who has the lamb and gnocchi?"

Jeff's head immediately whipped up. For a moment—just a moment—she caught a glimpse of horror and embarrassment on his face. He quickly controlled his expression.

"Oh, that's me!" Beth exclaimed. "That smells so good. Diet starts back up tomorrow. Today's my cheat day."

Amanda nearly choked. If this moment were scripted, she would have had a witty retort at the ready. Something about, wasn't every day with Beth a day for cheating? Or... or something like that, only more clever and cutting. But instead, Amanda's mind was a blank. All she could do was stammer, "I guess the scallops are yours then. Sir." She dropped the plate to the table from six inches up. The crash was louder than she had intended. She hoped Nick wasn't around to scold her for it.

"We didn't know," Jeff said. "Honestly. We never would've.... Our Torts professor mentioned this place offhand during lecture, that's why...."

Amanda said nothing. She glanced at Beth, whose eyes were moving slowly from the gnocchi to Jeff and finally to Amanda. She looked languidly puzzled. Then, finally, recognition.

"Oh," Beth said under her breath. That was it. She didn't appear particularly remorseful, nor did she seem particularly surprised. Her casual indifference was the most baffling and infuriating part of the entire encounter. Amanda wanted to grab her by her shoulders and shake her, make her realize that she was a damned sociopath. She wanted to slap Jeff across his face and tell him to do something other than stare at her with his emotionless eyes. He could scoff in her face, storm out, apologize, cry, demand another waitress, demand another chance, passionately kiss Beth right in front of her—literally anything would be better than this blank stare. How did she ever convince herself that he was simply

118

a stoic, and that this was something noble and old-fashioned? He was callous. He was a sociopath too. How had she shared a bed with this man for almost a year without realizing it? She was as disgusted with herself as she was with him.

"We really didn't—" Jeff started again.

"Enjoy your appetizers," Amanda said flatly before turning away.

It was so anticlimactic. Between the unexpectedness of their visit and the demands of her other customers, Amanda hadn't had enough time to envision how an elaborate confrontation could play out in her favor, but she had expected something more compelling than the blundering, banal interaction that had just unraveled.

"Are those two idiots actually going to stay here and eat?" Jasmine smacked another chit onto the board.

"I think so," Amanda shrugged. "They didn't tell me to cancel their entrees or wrap their food or anything."

"Holy shit, I thought lawyers were supposed to be smart. How could they possibly think it's a good idea to hang around here? Like, we have to screw with them now. We're morally obligated." Jasmine looked around, as if searching for inspiration for something to do.

"Table eleven in the window!" a voice shouted from behind them.

"I need to run that," Amanda said. "Look, will you pick up their table again? I know they're in my section, but since it's kind of a slow night and Nick won't—"

"Girl. Say no more. Of course." Jasmine smiled sympathetically. "They will get cold food and my shittiest service, and you won't have to speak to them again for the rest of the night."

"Drinks are on me after we close," Amanda replied.

Jasmine left their entrees dying under the heat lamp for an extra twenty minutes, and Amanda half-suspected that Hector and Hugo had rubbed their asses over the dinner plates first, but even with time to reflect on what sassy, spiteful things she could say, Amanda didn't interact with them again. She resisted the temptation to look over at them as she moved from table to table,

119

even when she could feel their eyes boring into her. Jeff and Beth finished their meals quickly, gave Jasmine a tip just short of twelve percent, and left without further incident.

"Fucking cheapskates," Jasmine griped.

"I mean, you did leave them awkwardly sitting there with no food or drink for a good thirty minutes," Amanda laughed.

"Damn right, I did. Her yellowfin was practically rancid by the time I dropped it. That shit was about to go bad to begin with, Nick has been up my ass this whole night to push it. I don't care, I stand by my original assertion: fucking cheapskates." Jasmine scowled. Then her face brightened. "Oh! Oh! I almost forgot to tell you! She was a ranch girl! For real. That dumb bitch asked for a side of ranch dressing to go with her tuna. Like we're a fucking Applebee's or something."

Amanda suddenly found herself laughing uncontrollably. Her anger, exhaustion, frustration, humiliation, shock—all of it came out in a torrent of laughter until her eyes were filled with tears. Jasmine began to laugh as well, which only exacerbated Amanda's hysterics.

"Would you two tone it down a notch? Holy hell. Literally nothing is that funny." Andrea was in her late-thirties and widely considered to be gorgeous *for her age*. She was also, according to the official rankings that Amanda and Jasmine had created at 3:00 a.m. one Saturday night after they were both borderline delirious from the double shifts they had just pulled, the biggest bitch out of all the servers on staff.

"Everyone knowing you sucked off Nick in the storage room is that funny," Jasmine retorted. "Especially since we all thought that was your special spot to suck off Marcus." She and Amanda fell into another fit of laughter as Andrea stormed away.

"Did I mention how much I love you?" Amanda said after Andrea was out of earshot and their chortling had subsided.

"Did I mention that I love you more?" Jasmine replied. "Seriously, without you and Angie, this place would make me lose my shit."

Amanda grinned. They both had worked at far worse establishments, with significantly more obnoxious coworkers and for substantially less money (the occasional 11.7 percent tip notwith-standing). They knew they had a pretty sweet deal at Ottimo. Even Nick wasn't that bad, despite their constant complaints. He was those rarest of managers who was occasionally willing to con-sider their other commitments when assigning shifts: for Jasmine, twice weekly bartending gigs at the nightclub Space Cadet, various private catering events, and occasionally a full week away touring the east coast with the pop punk band in which she played bass; and for Amanda, bartending twice a week at Breaking News (con-veniently located down the street from Space Cadet), and working three days a week from 7:30 a.m. until 3:30 or 4:00 p.m. at the Green Resources Alliance Foundation.

CHAPTER TEN
Amanda Wagner

Working at GRAF was simultaneously invigorating and exhausting, empowering and demoralizing, challenging and debasingly simple. One hour, Amanda might feel like she was going to change the world, and the next hour she would feel like they were all wasting their efforts—and she more so than anyone, since she was barely getting paid. There were times when she was certain that she was the smartest person in the room. Most of her coworkers (who Amanda knew were earning respectable five-figure salaries) were so well-intentioned, so earnest, but so excruciatingly short-sighted. They often seemed more interested in demonstrating their dedication to making a difference, convincing each other or some unknown audience of their sincerity and commitment to progressive ideals, than they were in actually strategizing and implementing any meaningful change.

Their Instagram and Snapchat accounts were filled with pictures of them holding signs at sparsely attended protests that received no media coverage, impassioned text posts demanding unspecified "legislative change," and tacky selfies with rambling captions about plastic straws or CBD oil that contained no apparent connection to their heavily filtered cleavage or their lush, well-groomed beards. They would lecture strangers at bars about the importance of going vegan or make angry but vague comments about the ineptitude of their current elected officials. When they held meetings with their volunteer activists, they could easily spend half of their scheduled hour together boasting about the various organizations with which they had been involved in the past and recounting their visions of a future global utopia—and then allow the volunteers twenty of the remaining thirty minutes to indulge in the same self-satisfied puffery—and they would happily justify what Amanda considered an egregious waste of time by framing it as "community building."

But when it came time to act? To develop a plan, establish milestones, engage in enough self-reflection (or institutional reflection, if self-reflection was too painful) to uncover and acknowledge what adaptations were required, where compromises could be made, what alliances (however uncomfortable) were necessitated in pursuit of their overarching goals? They all seemed to freeze. All of them. In those moments, their passion seemed to Amanda to be a childish indulgence. They were like three-year-olds playing house. A room of eight or ten spoiled adults playing activist. And then the workday would end and they would go back to their penthouse apartments, fully paid for by Daddy (although not all of them would admit it publicly), get ready for another night out at D.C.'s high-end lounges and nightclubs, and show up for work around 10:00 a.m. the next day, no less sincere in their purported commitment to saving the world notwithstanding their slight hangovers.

And Amanda would go to her second or third job. Or fourth, if one counted the sporadic TaskRabbit gigs she ran on weekends before a lunch shift at Ottimo or after serving the mimosa crowd at Breaking News. She had managed to hang onto her car. After listing it on Craigslist and receiving nothing but propositions for sex (how did these fools even know she was a girl, much less an attractive one?) and attempts to barter her vehicle for garbage ($4,000 worth of Legos? Really?), she had resigned herself to either paying for long-term parking indefinitely or getting ripped off by a second-hand dealership. She wasn't sure which outcome was worse.

124

Then she met one of Marta's neighbors, a guy who lived in the unit three floors directly above them, at a "Gnocchi November" mixer in the building's lobby. Amanda hadn't attended the event intentionally; one of her supervisors at GRAF had held her late to finish filing some documents from the early 2000s, and she wanted to change her shoes before she went to Ottimo. But the food was free and it smelled good. She had filled a disposable plate until it was overflowing and was preparing to sneak it upstairs, but a thirty-something University of Chicago MBA sparked a conversation with her before she managed to get to the elevator. She remembered he went to Chicago Booth because he had been sure to mention it twice within the first ninety seconds of conversation. Amanda knew she was supposed to impress him back, but she was daydreaming about the Diet Red Bull waiting for her upstairs.

He kept talking. At some point, for some reason (had she told him she worked for GRAF? She didn't know. Or care.) he mentioned that he had sold his BMW 4 Series and was planning to walk or take Uber Black (and maybe even try out public transportation!) to "do his part" to reduce auto emissions. Suddenly, the prospect of scarfing down some dumplings and recaffeinating herself became secondary.

"Wait a second. Do you still have a parking space?" Amanda had asked.

"Random. Yeah. Everyone who owns their place here has one. I'm an owner, by the way. It's not a big deal. I got in when the market crashed in 2008. It was a brilliant investment," he replied.

"Right. Great. So is your parking space sitting vacant now?"

"Yeah. What? Why? I guess it is. But I could afford to buy a new car at any time if I wanted to. An even nicer one."

"Okay. That's cool. Until you do, I have a proposition: would you rent me your space?"

"I don't understand. What?"

"Would you rent me your parking space? That's what I'm asking. I have a car sitting in long-term public parking right now, and it's fucking me over. Sorry to cuss. But it is absurdly expensive. If I keep using that lot, it's going to cost me over two hundred dollars a month, and I'd like to be able to leave my vehicle in the building."

"And you want my spot?"

"Yes, dude." Jesus. After running his mouth about his MBA, he was having a strangely difficult time recognizing an easy business opportunity when it was aggressively presenting itself. "I'd give you seventy-five bucks cash a month for it, if that seems fair? Until whenever you need it back. If it's just going to be sitting empty, that's probably a win/win, right?"

"I'll give it to you for free if you let me take you out on a date."

"Sorry, dude. I have a boyfriend. But, for sixty dollars a month, do we have a deal?"

"Because you're so pretty, I'll give it to you for fifty. Deal?"

"Fuck yes. Yes, we have a deal!"

It was, in a twisted way, Amanda's proudest accomplishment in Washington to-date. She had obtained a more secure and convenient parking space thanks to her creative thinking, and she would end up saving well over one hundred dollars a month courtesy of her smooth negotiation skills.

Maybe she did have some semblance of business smarts. She had barely focused on her classes in college, and she had no professional experience, and she was yet another twenty-three-year-old lost in D.C.—but maybe she did have some value to add. Maybe she at least had potential.

Amanda was barely two weeks into her internship at GRAF at that point. The next morning, a question about how to remedy the thus-far lukewarm response to a recently initiated letter-writing campaign came up in the 10:30 a.m. weekly department meeting. Riding on a rush of confidence from negotiating the deal of the century the night before, Amanda proposed they reach out directly to student leaders of environmental activism groups at local universities, who presumably would be easy allies with extensive contact lists. In fairness, it wasn't the world's most brilliant or unique idea. In fairness, it was also the smartest and most constructive thing that had been uttered in the preceding twenty minutes.

Her suggestion was greeted with silence and side-eyes. Amanda's face burned. She and Jasmine (who, back then, she was only starting to get to know) had both slammed several shots of well tequila at the end of their shift the night before. Amanda didn't feel hungover, but maybe she was still drunk? She didn't think her comment was so stupid as to merit a reception of baffled silence. After the meeting, Stephanie—a redheaded thirty-seven-year-old whose cloying pleasantries couldn't disguise her festering rancor toward herself and with the world, and who had admonished Amanda on her third day for wearing a pencil skirt (which Amanda had purchased for work because it was comparatively conservative) that was "distractingly sexy"—informed Amanda that unpaid interns don't normally speak up during staff meetings.

Three days later, Stephanie proposed the exact same idea. It was met with resounding approval.

But it was a job. A meaningful one, sort of. At least compared to waitressing. Ostensibly, her work at GRAF was in furtherance of a higher purpose. Right?

Even though Amanda's relationship with Jeff was now over, sometimes Jeff's observations still flashed through her mind. He had told her about several of his classmates who had worked as paralegals before attending law school. All of them, without exception, had vowed never to return to their old law firms. No matter how much value they had added back then, and despite everything they had accomplished since, their former colleagues would always view them as inferior in the firm hierarchy—even with the J.D., even with Law Review, even with Order of the Coif, even with a more prestigious law school and a better class ranking. If they were to return, they would forever remain a lowly paralegal in their coworkers' eyes.

And maybe it was the same for Amanda. Maybe, no matter how hard she tried, no matter what she accomplished at GRAF or elsewhere, Jeff would always see her as nothing more than a cute-but-dumb waitress. God. She didn't want to be resentful. She wanted to move on. She didn't want to creep on Beth's social media and try to figure out whether she was still with Jeff, or whether she had found yet another relationship to annihilate for the giggles.

But Amanda had moved to D.C. for Jeff, and now it was over. She thought she might marry him, or at the very least she thought they'd be together for longer than eleven months. But it was over. And what had she gained from it other than a generalized wariness toward men? Other than whispers of the type of cynicism and asperity she saw from Marta, whose entire social calendar, on the rare nights when she wasn't working late at the hospital, seemed to be dedicated to going on terrible dates with guys she had met off Hinge and OkCupid. Was that Amanda's future too?

Because the prospect of winding up like Marta was untenable. Since Amanda had moved in, the only thing that could throw the otherwise-unflappable Marta off-kilter was a guy. Always and only, a guy. By Amanda's unofficial calculations, Marta cycled through an average of three men per month. Sometimes there were stretches where Marta went on four dates per week, while other times a new guy—this new guy who was finally different from all the other assholes before him—would stick around for a month or two before disaster would strike.

As these various men were also the reason why Marta would sometimes stumble into their home belligerently drunk in the middle of the week, Amanda finally asked Irina, after four months of tirades, smashed wine glasses, and uncomfortable silences the next morning: were men in D.C. really so shitty, or did Marta actually deserve that dreaded, dismissive title of a "Crazy Bitch"?

"I have been her roommate for almost three years," Irina said, fidgeting. "I do not like to talk about her behind her back like this. But I suppose, since you have to live with it too, I will say that I honestly think it is an unfortunate combination of both."

Amanda was still blissfully in love with Jeff at the time and had only asked out of idle curiosity, so she dropped this subject with Irina immediately. Besides, she had seen more than her fair share of drunken tantrums during her undergrad days. Among innumerable other alcohol-fueled incidents of reckless stupidity, she had witnessed her friend Jordan, who was topless and barefoot at the time, lob a brick in the general direction of a cop, and she and Kiara once had to forcibly drag their friend Skylar three blocks back to Amanda's off-campus apartment after Skylar had keyed the car and slashed the tires of the guy who had a threesome with two sorority girls the night after he had told Skylar that he was falling in love with her. Marta's drunken rages weren't quite as outrageous or dramatic in comparison, and at least they were sporadic. And so, when Amanda thought about the issue at all—which was usually only while one of Marta's episodes persisted—she focused far more on the absurdity of Marta's actions than she did on the potential reasons behind them.

But now, her relationship with Jeff had imploded. And now, Amanda couldn't help but try to recollect every terrible date from which Marta had arrived home in a fury:

"Martha! He called me fucking 'Martha' the entire night. No matter how many times I told him, my fucking name is fucking Marta. With a hard T. Mar-tah. Mar-tah. Tah. Tah! Not -tha! How fucking hard is that? But he had no trouble saying the hot waitress's name perfectly, I'll give him that! The moron left an eight percent tip and his business card for her. Good luck with that, dipshit! I'm sure she's really impressed."

Or:

"He whipped out a dick pic at the table. Before they'd even brought us our appetizers. Just shoved his phone across the table into my face. And was like, 'So, you want to just get out of here or what? It's even thicker in person.' And I'm like, is this a prank? Am I being filmed? Has this strategy ever worked for him, even once? Because listen, I get plenty of guys sending me their nasty, pathetic, shriveled cocks, or asking me if I eat ass, or sending me selfies mid-wank. But this guy was different. He managed to message me for a full week on the app, plan a proper date, and actually show up on time without being visibly high or drunk. Granted, the restaurant was a tacky dump, but I had been so impressed with his ability to not be a pig up to that point that I was barely even judging. And then he says, 'You weren't going to eat anyway, right? You want to maintain your figure. Women just want to know that a man can pay for the meal, don't they?' As if I'm going to fuck some idiotic, double-chinned, washed-up ex-frat

129

boy because he can afford to waste seven bucks on mozzarella sticks! Fucking fuck!"

Or:

"We dated for six weeks. I stopped making plans with other people after our second date. I waited five dates to blow him and six dates to fuck him so he wouldn't think I'm too easy. I did everything by the book. He called me his girl. He said he'd never met anyone like me before. And then, out of nowhere, he just stopped texting. Look. Look at this shit, Amanda. Just read it. Look at what it says up here: 'I'm sold on you.' Right? So I invited him to hang out on Friday, when I actually didn't have to work for once. Look. Look at this! I told him I wasn't even on-call. And he didn't respond. So then I texted him again on Saturday, and look at this! 'I'll let you know.' But he didn't let me know. He didn't let me know shit. And he hasn't texted me anything since. Fuck this. I'm going to send him a message right now and let him know what I really think. He wasn't good enough to date someone like me anyway."

Or:

"We went out three times and slept together the last time, but now he won't return my texts or DMs. But he still likes every selfie I post on Instagram. Look, he even put three little flame emojis for the last one. What does it mean? Maybe he's just been busy? Should I hold off on the new guy I just matched with to try to work it out with him?"

Spare all three of you the trouble, Amanda had thought, and hold off on the new guy, and the old one, and anyone else on those godforsaken apps altogether. Take the flame emojis not as a sign that you look hot in your lightly FaceTuned, overly filtered, post-gym selfie, but rather as a sign that you should burn your cell phone, your laptop, and any other device you use to "meet men online," to ashes. Free yourself from the self-inflicted prison of unsolicited dick pics, copy/pasted pickup lines, strained text conversations, and shitty excuses for last-minute flaking. Marta was a doctor! A beautiful, wealthy, successful doctor! Up until Barrister's Ball, Amanda had been as baffled by Marta's plight as she was secretly smug about her own seemingly unshakeable relationship with Jeff.

Of course, Amanda never expressed any of this out loud in Marta's presence. Complaining about terrible dates and duplicitous men was one of the only times that Marta opened up to Amanda and Irina at all, unless snapping requests to rinse out plastic containers before tossing them into the recycling bin could be considered an attempt at interpersonal connection.

Marta did seem to soften a little when she heard about Amanda's disastrous breakup with Jeff. Granted, the extent of her sympathy and sisterly advice consisted of attempts to commiserate over the "undeniable reality" that "all men in D.C. are limp-dicked scumbags" while scrolling through and summarizing the various dating app options Amanda might want to consider. Marta prefaced each app she opened with the caveat, "but obviously all the shithead guys on here just want to fuck-and-chuck too."

These bizarre conversations were one of the closest things Amanda had to feeling like anyone cared at all about her losing Jeff and having to start over in what still felt like a new city. Marta was probably the one person in Amanda's life who could appreciate, on some level, how isolated Amanda felt. Even her own parents didn't seem to care much. She tried to call her mom two days after the breakup, but her mom sent her to voicemail after two rings. Amanda was so taken aback that she almost laughed as she punched out a text.

It Meeeeeee☺😳: Seriously, mom???! You sent me to vm?

The first semester of Amanda's freshman year at University of Evansville, her mom had insisted that Amanda call home every single night between 7:00 and 8:00 p.m. to let her know she was okay. She had been far more lenient while Amanda was in high school, and by the spring semester, Amanda's mom had relaxed the rule to at least one phone call per week. Even still, her mom had made it clear that under no circumstances would a text message suffice for her weekly check-in obligations. Nowadays,

Amanda couldn't get her mom to pick up the phone, much less initiate a conversation.

La Madre 🌸: me + ur daD r watching the BacHelor Can we tlk l8r?

Amanda sighed. She might as well give the news via text. Maybe her mom would pause the show and call once she realized it was serious.

It Meeeeeee😊😜: Don't worry about it. I just wanted to let you know that it's over with Jeff. It ended badly. But I'll be fine. He hurt me, but I moved to DC for more reasons than just him. I'm broken-hearted but I will move on.

For four full minutes, three little dots indicated her mother was typing. Amanda patiently awaited the words of wisdom and consolation that she could screenshot and reread when she needed a boost.

La Madre 🌸: Sry 2 hear that sweetie U deserve Bbetter

Amanda was, and would always be, absolutely alone in this world.

Cool reply, mom. Cool fucking reply. I can feel the sincerity and concern oozing through the phone. Maybe if I recommence my search for a husband on The Bachelorette, you'll actually give a shit about how I feel. Until then, hint fucking taken.

Amanda paused, her face flushed with anger and disappointment. None of this was her mom's fault either. She deleted the text before hitting send.

It Meeeeeee😊😜: Thanks. I'll let you get back to your show. Tell Dad I love him. xoxo

Another minute passed.

La Madre 🌸: Luv u 2 sweetiE

Amanda placed her phone on her bed and closed her eyes. She thought about FaceTiming Kiara, but they had drifted apart since graduation. They still liked and commented on all each other's posts and would occasionally send each other a particularly funny meme that related to some inside joke from two years prior, but it had been months since they'd texted about anything substantive, much less actually spoken to each other.

Besides, Amanda's first real conversation with Kiara after all this time couldn't be about a situation that made Amanda look utterly pathetic. Kiara's post-graduation life seemed to be going really, really well. Every day brought a new Instagram pic that received at least five hundred likes. Kiara, fitter than ever, taking selfies in another cute sports bra at her high-end gym. Kiara eating a forty-five dollar gourmet chorizo and roasted red pepper sandwich for lunch (the type of meal that Amanda could enjoy only if one of the guys in the kitchen screwed up an order and she managed to scarf down a few bites before anyone else front of house poached it). Kiara posed with three other equally gorgeous, perfectly made-up girls in tight dresses at a trendy nightclub, with a pack of hot guys lingering behind them holding their purses and drinks. Kiara lip-syncing to a pop song in the passenger seat of a BMW convertible, sunglasses on, the ends of her impeccably plaited hair delicately fluttering in the wind, while the slightly older man in the driver's seat quickly shifted his gaze from the road in order to give the camera a patiently amused grin. It was relentless.

She didn't want to be jealous of her friend. She was happy for Kiara, or at least she wanted to be. But how could their lives have fallen onto such divergent courses so quickly? Didn't Kiara have to work? Where was all this money coming from? How did she manage to gather a whole new crew of other carefree, young, beautiful people with whom she could enjoy leisure and luxuries, while all Amanda did was run from one under-paying job to the next, phlegmatically stomaching one blatant insult after another, before drinking her anger away with a few other people from the service industry at the end of their shifts, all of them knowing that this was their only chance for some semblance of happiness and camaraderie, because all of their dictatorial bosses, condescending customers, and overdue bills would be waiting for them the next morning.

Not that Amanda wasn't grateful for the friendships she had made at Ottimo and Breaking News, and with some of the staff at their respective neighboring establishments. Jasmine, in particular, had been a godsend since she and Jeff had broken up. If Amanda started moping, Jasmine was always there with a snarky comment or a shot of well whiskey or a hearty smack of Amanda's butt and a shout of "I'd take a bite out of that juicy peach, mama!" that would give Amanda the strength to greet another six-top of grouchy old white guy lawyers and lobbyists with a perky smile.

But Amanda yearned for something more than constantly getting hammered in the name of blowing off steam. She didn't want to be pitied. She also didn't want to bond over bitterness. She didn't want to listen to the trite advice of acquaintances whose life priority was convincing the world that they had the perfect relationship. She didn't have the energy to coo empty words of sympathy at any of the friends who would, within two minutes of Amanda initiating a conversation, shift the topic to their own romantic troubles or psychological struggles. Amanda couldn't think of a single person in D.C. with whom she would feel comfortable expressing the simple truth that losing Jeff had deeply hurt her.

So when, two weeks after the breakup, Amanda finally had her first full day off from all three of her jobs, she chose to lock herself in her bedroom. She slept until after 12:00 noon and then, without leaving her bed, began mindlessly scrolling through various social media apps while *Friends* reruns autoplayed on Netflix in the background.

Every vapid, pseudo-inspirational quote in gaudy font against a pastel background annoyed the shit out of her.

Every amateur butt model wearing transparent leggings and false eyelashes preaching that, by purchasing the thirty-dollar glute bands and a monthly supply of the bootleg dietary supplements they were currently shilling, their desperate followers could achieve the glorious booty that they themselves had obtained only thanks to Dr. McAssimplants, annoyed the shit out of her.

Every screenshot of someone's own mildly amusing tweet, which they had then posted across every other social media site, as if the banal observation that Amanda had already seen three other people post (all of which were slightly reworded plagiarisms of a joke originally written by a midlevel comedian workshopping material on Twitter two days prior) was so damn hilarious that they could not deprive any follower on any platform of their witticism, annoyed the shit out of her.

Every fawning, groping, "take a selfie while jamming your tongues down each others' throats" picture, accompanied by a caption declaring the other person "My Queen" or "My King," and prattling on for a paragraph about how special their love was—as if everyone didn't remember them making an almost identical post six months prior about a different person, as if anyone wanted to witness the digital equivalent of them having gross sex and calling each other stupid pet names—really, really, really annoyed the shit out of her.

And yet, she kept scrolling. Wallowing in her sadness and inflaming her anger with this unceasing stream of bullshit was the only thing she could bring herself to do. She was relieved that she was opening at Ottimo and closing at Breaking News the next day. The fourteen to eighteen hours of work would get her back on track to make her monthly rent payment, especially since her whole budget was blown after having spent $248 on a new dress and lipstick to don while getting cheated on and dumped at Barrister's Ball. Perhaps more importantly, the stacked shifts would get her on her feet and off her phone.

Ten more minutes of lying in bed scrolling, she negotiated with herself. When those ten minutes passed, she decided she would finish the episode of *Friends*. But there were less than six minutes remaining, so maybe, rather, she would just finish the next full episode.

She had been trying to resist the urge to refresh Beth's profiles every five minutes. She restrained herself to every twenty or so. Beth didn't post all that often, but she left her settings to public, so there was no harm in checking. Amanda could see if Beth had gained any new likes or comments.

On a whim—as something to do between refreshing Beth's social media pages and scrolling through the curated photos of various style influencers, whose most boring, basic days around their exquisitely decorated houses with their generically hand-some, doting husbands (whose bleached-white smiles seemed only a little bit forced) were far more glamorous and fulfilled and enviable than a single moment of Amanda's life would ever be—she searched for Jill Torres's account.

Amanda was baffled that there were still no relevant results for her mysterious doppelganger. Maybe Jill already had gotten married and changed her last name? That was the only logical explanation for why Amanda still couldn't find Jill's profile. She wished she could sneak a glimpse into Jill's life. Heck, she could probably steal some of Jill's photos and post them as her own! Jill, who surely still had a better body and a better job and a better home, who came from a better town, who probably took better vacations and had better boyfriends even before Jeff turned out to be such a cheating snake? That Jill probably had a perfect page filled with perfect posts, liked and commented on by thousands of adoring followers (followers that she didn't have to buy!).

If Amanda could locate Jill's account, she could screenshot all the best pictures and pass them off as her own. While Jeff and that horrid witch Beth were slogging around the GULC campus stressing about exams, Amanda could post a pic of herself (Jill) cuddled up next to some rich shirtless stud, who definitely would be taller and more jacked than Jeff, holding a glass of fancy champagne in a hot air balloon. While it rained incessantly for five straight days during a muggy D.C. spring, Amanda could post pictures of herself (Jill), now featuring perfectly defined abs, frolicking first on the beach, then on a yacht, then on some cliff overlooking the ocean, on vacation in the Greek Isles. While Jeff and Beth were stuck indoors all summer doing legal research for a professor for less than minimum wage, she would post a photo of herself (Jill) wearing a Lilly Pulitzer dress and eating lobster on a patio at sunset, captioned simply #nantucketstyle.

That would show them! Even if Amanda were actually covered in kitchen grease or in the midst of being berated by some entitled trust fund kid who didn't like the way Amanda had collated the meeting materials that day, they would see how much better her life had gotten after Jeff. Everyone would see.

It occurred to Amanda that perhaps Jill did know who Amanda was, and that maybe she had preemptively blocked Amanda from viewing her pages to prevent exactly this type of scenario from unfolding. Amanda chortled, then grew hot with rage. Was she really so pathetic?

There was a knock on her bedroom door. She glanced at her phone. It was now 9:16 p.m. She had been bouncing from app to app for nine hours straight and had run through a full season of *Friends* without even realizing it. Part of Amanda wanted to feign sleep so that she could be left alone for the remainder of this utter waste of a day off, but instead she sighed and muttered, "Yeah, come on in."

The door handle twisted without avail. Amanda groaned and pushed herself upright. If she had remembered that she had left the door locked, she definitely would have pretended to be asleep.

"One sec, I'm coming, I'm coming," she said groggily.

Amanda felt a twinge of guilt over how relieved she was to find Irina on the other side of the door. As much as she appreciated Marta's recent warming toward her, she didn't have the emotional energy to discuss whether Marta's outfit was something that a person in their mid-twenties would wear on a first date (Marta recently had cut eight years off her true age on her Tinder bio), or to decipher the hidden meaning behind a lack of punctuation in a curt text from a dude that Marta had been out with twice but with whom Marta felt the possibility of potential for eventually developing what could maybe be a genuine connection.

"I am sorry to bother you, Amandiṇa," Irina began. "I hope I did not wake you up."

"No, no, it's fine. I was just wasting time on my phone." With a gesture of the hand, Amanda invited Irina to sit on the edge of her bed, then plopped down beside her. "What's up?"

"I am ordering delivery from the nice Mexican restaurant we all like, but they have a twenty-five-dollar delivery minimum. Marta is working late tonight. I can order extra food for myself for tomorrow, but I thought I should check if you wanted anything first."

Amanda raised a skeptical eyebrow.

"I do not mean to pressure you," Irina added. "Marta cleaned out the refrigerator at, like, 4:00 a.m. this morning. It does not look like there is anything left in your section."

"Is there really a twenty-five-dollar minimum for delivery, or was that just a pretense to check and make sure I wasn't dead in here?" Irina's eyes widened, and Amanda internally scolded herself for the gallows humor.

"Honestly? It was both." Irina smiled. "I have been grading essays in the common area for many hours and I have not seen you all day. I hope you are not offended by the intrusion. I was concerned. And truly, you do not have any food left in the refrigerator! Marta went overboard with the cleaning again. So I figured I should check with you before all the good restaurants close."

"You're the best," Amanda said. "For real. You're talking about the Mexican place that has healthier options and uses those multicolored biodegradable containers, right?"

"Yes, that is the one! El Castillo Verde. I am ordering chips with black bean dip, a side salad, and the vegan enchiladas, but that is only seventeen dollars total so far."

"Okay, cool. Um, I guess I'll just get my usual. Will you hit the tofu taco salad with a side of guacamole for me? I have fifteen bucks on my dresser you can take. That should cover the food, and grab a couple of singles from my purse for my share of the tip and delivery fee."

Irina clicked through her phone.

"We are up to twenty-nine dollars now. Would you like anything else? Anything to drink?"

"No, I'm all set. I've been keeping my cases of Diet Coke and sparkling water in here, and not just because it spares them from Marta's manic cleaning binges. For some reason, I've been drinking almost everything at room temperature lately."

"How very European of you," Irina laughed. "Okay, it is saying thirty-seven minutes to arrive. I will not believe that until I have seen it, though. Do you want company while we wait?"

"I don't want to bug you if you have more work."

Irina's posture straightened and she frantically looked around the room. Amanda was bewildered, and all the more so when Irina abruptly stopped herself and started laughing.

"You must think that the undergrads have finally pushed me to the point of a complete mental breakdown," Irina spurted between laughs. "I am so sorry. This one word always confuses me and I do not know why I cannot ever remember it correctly. I heard you say 'bug' and I forgot it means, like, 'being annoying.' For a moment, I thought there was a roach in here!"

"God forbid!" Amanda cried. "Can you imagine how Marta would react if she thought we did something to bring a roach infestation into her picture-perfect home?"

"She would not even wait until we had left the flat before she had men spraying bug poison in here!" Irina placed her hands on her knees to catch her breath as her laughter subsided. "Oh, she likes you so much better than the last girl. I tried to stay out of it, but Laura really was a slob. It was gross. Sometimes Marta was being fussy, but looking back on it, most of the time she was right to be angry."

"Hey, can I ask you something? In confidence?" Amanda began, more seriously now. "Like I said, though, I don't want to interrupt you if you have more papers to grade."

"I am done!" Irina smiled. "I am finally done, and I need a break before I begin my own research tonight. I want to relax until our food gets here. So please, go ahead, you may ask."

"Okay. Well, I'm not asking to be a gossip or a bitch, first of all. I never would have thought about it much at all, except now I'm single too."

Irina gave a knowing half-smile, as if she had already guessed the potentially volatile subject that Amanda was about to broach. This was already a far more promising start than the last time Amanda had brought it up.

"Marta is so smart, so beautiful, and so successful, and I have so much admiration for her," Amanda continued carefully. "I feel like she would be the dream catch for almost any straight guy in D.C. Or anywhere in the world, you know? So, I guess I'm just wondering, since you've lived with her for so long and have seen up close some of the, let's call them 'challenges,' that she's had dating...." Amanda trailed off, hoping Irina wouldn't make her finish the question out loud.

"You are wondering—and I know I have already said to you how much I dislike when anyone, male or female, uses the term 'crazy' to undermine a woman—but you would like to discuss if she is a so-called 'crazy chick' and that is why she has so much trouble in her love life, or if you will have all the same difficulties even though you are most certainly not a 'crazy chick.' No?"

"Well, yes. Basically." Amanda bashfully fiddled with her phone. "No disrespect to Marta, obviously. I honestly like her. I mean, I'm slightly terrified of her too, but I do genuinely like her. More than that, I respect her. With all the people in this city who are so obsessed with their image and social status and all that, it doesn't make sense. Wouldn't a hot, smart, doctor wife like her be the ultimate status symbol, if nothing else? She's shown me some of these dudes' profiles. She's not being too picky. They'd be lucky to date her." Amanda sighed and looked down. "Not to throw a pity party for myself, but if someone like her, however temperamental she might be, can't get a man, then what chance does my broke, waitress-slash-intern-slash-human-punching-bag, flat-chested ass have?"

"You are not wrong. Well, I misspeak! You are very wrong about how you describe yourself. But the dating scene here does appear to be, as they say, a trainwreck shitshow." Irina was grinning mischievously. "If you will pardon the swear words, of course. I am trying to redeem my English-speaker credentials by showing off my knowledge of American cursing and slang."

"I really hope this doesn't sound condescending, but just so you know, you are way too hard on yourself about your English. Hell, my spelling and grammar are atrocious, and English is my first and basically only language, unless you want to count my shitty attempts at speaking Spanish with the back-of-house guys at Ottimo. Like, they had me proofread a staff memo at GRAF one time, and I'm pretty sure I did such a bad job that that's why they haven't asked me to do anything substantive since." Amanda scowled. "Whatever, I have no business editing anyone's writing

140

anyway. The rules are confusing as fuck, even for native speakers. Anyway. Let's agree that your English fucking rocks, and fucking curse words are fucking encouraged tonight."

"Fucking agreed!" Irina laughed. "And since you brought up your internship at GRAF, if I may change the subject for a moment to give you a compliment and perhaps some encouragement?"

"I could use a healthy dose of both right about now," Amanda nodded.

"I understand the reasons why you are frustrated, but perhaps what you cannot see is how the job has helped you. Respectfully, since you started there, you seem to have grown more mature. The way you talk has changed. You speak less like a college student and more like a businesswoman. The way you carry yourself is different too. You seem more self-assured."

"Really? Because most of the time I feel like a gutter rat."

"Yes, really. What happened with Jeff is distorting your perspective. But it cannot undo all you have gained over the past few months."

"They're so mean to me though!" Amanda cried suddenly. "They were never very welcoming to me from the start, but it started getting so much worse around, I don't know, maybe Christmas or New Year's. It doesn't matter how hard I work. And the passive-aggressive stuff is even more hurtful than when they're openly critical. They don't bother trying to hide the fact that they think they're better than me. They're elitists! And it's not like my family is poor! I mean, they would be totally out of line even if we were, but I'm from Trumbull, Connecticut! It's a nice area! Maybe I don't have a trust fund and my parents both have to work and I went to public schools, but that doesn't make me, like, uncultured swine. I dress as well as I can afford to do and I try to look polished. I do force myself to talk differently around them compared to how I talk at the restaurant. I make myself speak more formally. I don't cuss. I hardly use slang. I never realized that I sound like a hick to people like them. I mean, I worked at fancy restaurants and a country club when I lived in Connecticut. Did I come across so badly to all of those rich people too?"

Amanda paused and collected herself. She had been so focused on how upset she was over Jeff, she was surprised that her work frustrations were what she was choosing to vocalize in the moment.

"It's just not fair," she continued. She couldn't stop herself. "They aren't even smart. Not the way you and Marta are. And they have no new ideas. They waste so much time every day sitting around congratulating each other on how 'woke' they are, without accomplishing jack shit. Seriously, I might be as pissed off about that as I am about Jeff."

"I apologize, Amanda. If I had known, I would have warned you before suggesting that you pursue a position there. It seemed like such a good match for you."

"I don't blame you for their bullshit, Irina. Not at all. Honestly, I'm still incredibly grateful to you for connecting me with them. It's just that, I thought nonprofits were supposed to be almost like some idealized version of a hippie commune. Compassionate and cooperative and nonjudgmental, in practice too, not just in what they profess to believe in. But GRAF is just a bunch of spoiled little shits with incredibly well-connected parents, screaming about 'fuck capitalism' and 'fuck the government,' even though those are the exact things sustaining their ceaseless bullshit. At GRAF, everything is centered around your status in the social hierarchy. And I'm at the very bottom of the pyramid, at my job and in D.C. generally, without any realistic hope of rising."

"This makes me sad. The people that I know there—how should I put this? I thought more highly of them. I am surprised they would act this way or allow this behavior."

"Oh, no, I should clarify! The people you introduced me to at the very beginning are much more senior than me, and I think they truly do good work. They care. But they are *actually* important, unlike my immediate coworkers, who just like to think that they matter, without ever doing anything productive. I never interact with your friends anymore. Not since the first week I started. I doubt they're aware of any of this nonsense. They'd probably be pissed off if they found out how much time we waste, but there's not enough day-to-day oversight of the group I was assigned to for them to catch on. Oh! But my point was that I wouldn't have gotten an interview, much less have any job to complain about, if it hadn't been for you. It never occurred to me to be mad at you for any of this!"

"Think about everything you have said to me, Amandiṇa. All the intangible things you have learned already. Not only how an organization like GRAF works, regarding the power dynamics and the inefficiencies and all that. You are figuring out how to adapt to their corporate culture. You are tweaking the way you dress and speak, not because there is anything wrong with the real you, but because that is how you have to play the game."

"I fucking resent it," Amanda muttered.

"I fucking resent it too!" Irina exclaimed. "Please consider, my friend: you do not think that, for me, being in America does not involve adjusting to culture shocks on a daily basis? Being in the math department at GW with a bunch of fellow geeks and foreigners helps, but it is still overwhelming. You must decide for yourself which is more painful: conforming to the group's norms, or dealing with the consequences of rejecting them. This is only my opinion, but I think either is a perfectly respectable option, and it does not have to be 'all or nothing,' as they say, either way. And from what you have told me, the internship seems to be improving your ability to find the right balance between the two."

Amanda sighed and pressed the thumb and ring fingers of her left hand into the top of her eyes without responding.

"Did I say something wrong?" Irina asked. "I have been working very hard on expanding my English vocabulary and maybe I have confused a word? I did not mean to offend you."

"No, no, nothing like that." Amanda sighed again. "If anything, you said things too perfectly, and I'm just a fucked-up combination of upset and jealous. Your vocabulary is probably better than mine, and I even downloaded a 'Word of the Day' app to try to keep up with the private-school snobs at my job. They've mastered the art of sounding brilliant and sophisticated while saying nothing but stupid, senseless bullshit."

Irina thought about this statement for a moment, then grinned. "Yes! I understand exactly what you mean. They could have a career in academia! They would probably get tenure!" Irina laughed at her own remark and gave Amanda a look encouraging her to continue.

"You seem to have a better understanding of how to be successful at GRAF than I do, and you don't even work there. It's not remotely related to what you do. And more than that! You have something that you *do* care about, and you're good at it. And hell, even if one day you wake up and decide you never want to look at another math problem again, you could go be a translator, or a diplomat, or a spy! You could be a dance instructor and open your own studio. You could be a stay-at-home mom and live off of Kristoff's salary. I mean, I've seen your Instagram; if you started posting more often, you could be an influencer! For beauty or for travel!"

"God forbid," Irina snickered.

"You could, though! You have the abilities and the option to do any of that stuff. That's all I'm saying. That's what I don't have. I get your point about what I'm learning from GRAF and I appreciate your words. I really do. I'm not trying to be ungrateful. But it's humiliating to go there every day, make next to nothing, be treated like human garbage, and then go to my shift at the restaurant or the bar for more of the same."

Irina opened her mouth as if to offer some advice or insight, but Amanda was too agitated to stop.

"I know I could try to find a new job, but what's the point? Why would it be any different anywhere else? Assuming anywhere else would hire me at all, which is beyond unlikely. I have less than a year of experience, and all I've done is set up conference rooms, rearranging filing cabinets, and run errands for them. It's so ridiculous! Last week, they forced me to print off twenty paper copies of a twelve-page PowerPoint presentation on deforestation. Absolutely no one used a single copy. Because, like I tried to tell them before we blasted through an entire color ink jet and a thousand pages of paper, everyone in the conference room wanted to pull up the deck on their laptops, and they were all dicking around on social media for the whole meeting anyway. Idiots! They don't even realize what hypocrites they are! It would have been better for the environment if we had all stayed home that day."

"Have you thought about going back to school?" Irina offered.

"Sort of. But, like, what's the point of that either? Would I go for environmental science? Business school? What else is there? Find whatever shitty tuition-scam law school would admit me and get a J.D. to spite Jeff? Come on. In undergrad, I was a mediocre student at best. I'm not qualified for anything. All getting another degree would do is sink me further into a debt that I'll never be able to pay off."

Amanda paused to collect herself. They sat in silence for almost twenty seconds, until Amanda decided she needed to say something to keep Irina from making an excuse to leave. This was pitiful. But all of Amanda's supposed friends from Jeff's law school class had, intentionally or not, abandoned her. Aside from Jasmine, Irina was the closest thing Amanda had to an actual "even when we're sober" friend in Washington, D.C.

"Thank you for letting me vent," Amanda said. "I'm sorry. I thought I was just upset about Jeff. And believe me, I am. But at least with him, I have a good reason for it. I'm right to be angry. I wasn't a perfect girlfriend, and maybe he always knew he could do better than me, but I know that him cheating was not my fault. But my job? My nonexistent career prospects? Like, I thought I did everything I was supposed to do. I got the college degree. I've been working since I was in high school. I go to the internship every day and do whatever they tell me. I try to contribute. I try to share my ideas and I try to stay enthusiastic. I try to help. And what has any of it gotten me?"

Again, Irina opened her mouth as if to reply but stopped herself. Instead, she placed her hand on top of Amanda's. Amanda's eyes filled with tears, but her voice became more controlled.

"Okay, I'll shut up now. I don't mean to be such a whiny little shit. I know there are plenty of people in this world with real problems. Intellectually, I know that. But it's not fair. I'm always exhausted. I'm trying so hard to matter, but I feel like I'll never catch up to everyone else. I don't know how I could. You're a math wizard. Marta is a doctor. Angie isn't just a hostess; she has seventy thousand Instagram followers and is dating some million-aire tech entrepreneur. Jasmine is going to be a famous rockstar someday. Jill graduated from MIT and she's the fittest person I've ever seen in real life." Amanda nearly gasped. She had never once seen Jill in real life. Indeed, Amanda's entire conception of Jill's physique was based on nothing more than a glimpse of Jill's shoulder in an old Facebook photo, the rough outline of her figure in slim-fitting a business shirt, and a few rude comments from a drunk fratboy almost a decade earlier, with Amanda's imagination filling in the details. She had no idea why she would mention Jill out of nowhere, as if they were old friends. Even though Irina probably assumed Jill was another one of Amanda's coworkers from the restaurant, Amanda was anxious to change the subject.

"I'll shut up for real this time," Amanda said with a forced laugh. "What were we talking about before I started rambling about my job?"

"You were lamenting the thought of entering the D.C. dating scene."

"Lamenting! That's such a good word for it. That's exactly what I was doing."

"Oh good! I hoped I was using it correctly." Irina glanced at her phone. "Our food is on the way. It says twenty-three minutes. There must be traffic."

"Of course there's traffic."

"Ha! Yes, of course." Irina set her phone back on the bed. "So, my sweet American doll, do you want to spend the next twenty-three minutes lamenting the difficulty of meeting a good man in this city? Or might we use this time to think up ways for you to gain new marketable skills or make more professional connections from your internship? And we could think together of possible alternative career paths in case you decide that the nonprofit sector is not what you want! Perhaps there are grad programs you have not yet considered where there are scholarships available to you."

"Ugh, I know I'm supposed to choose the second option. The productive one. And I really would like to take you up on

146

the career counseling mini-session at some point. That would be amazing. But—"

"But you just went through a terrible breakup and you are not in the mood?"

"Just not tonight. I want to eat my food in bed like a fat piece of trash, wearing the same stinky-ass sweatpants I've put on after work every night for the past five days, and wallow in my misery and uselessness."

Irina looked appalled.

"I'm kidding!" Amanda added. "Well, mostly kidding. I was exaggerating and trying to be funny. I guess I failed at that too."

"May I give you one small bit of advice?" Irina asked.

"You're what? Five years older than me, max? And you already have your whole life together more than I ever will. I'd be stupid to say no."

"I am not sure about any of that, but my advice is this: be sad and angry tonight. Stalk Jeff's social media pages for another few days."

Amanda whipped her head toward her laptop and phone, both of which had fallen into sleep mode.

"Everyone does it. I was guessing," Irina said, waving her hand as if to brush aside this detail as unimportant. "Feel jealous or bitter or lonely if you must, but give yourself a deadline for when this stops. Let us say, next Monday. Then, no more pitying yourself."

"But I'll still be upset next Monday," Amanda pouted. "Unless Jeff and Beth both get expelled from law school and break up and someone punches them in their stupid faces, it'll still hurt."

"Well, you must start behaving like it does not. I am not saying you should download Tinder and start accepting dates with every creep who contacts you. All I am saying is, you wash these sweatpants. You wash your hair. Perhaps you put on some lipstick and smile at an attractive man at Starbucks. At the very least, you stop locking yourself alone in this room every moment that you are not working. And you stop scrolling on your phone looking at pictures of people you do not know and being jealous of the lives you imagine them to have. And you definitely stop looking for pictures of Jeff and Beth."

"And just fake being happy?"

"In a way, yes. It is how you survive until you actually are again."

Amanda knew Irina was only trying to help and that this was her version of tough love. But Amanda didn't want to hear it. It was obnoxious. As if plastering the same bullshit smile on her face that she used for the rancorous customers who bitched about everything from the smell of the unscented candles on their (unacceptably located) table to the size of the ice cubes in their (unacceptably flat) cola, would somehow cure her malaise. All she did was work, and all she wanted to do in her rare moments of downtime was wallow. Fuck anyone who tried to stop her.

"I can see I have offended you," Irina said gently. "That was not my intent. I did not mean to—how should I say it?—make little your problems or your feelings. Sometimes one must talk to a doctor or take medication to be relieved from their sadness."

"That's not what this is," Amanda snapped. "I'm not clinically depressed, I'm just fucking pissed. I'm fucking pissed that I moved here to be with a man who cheated on me at a cheesy-ass school dance while I was literally in the same building! It is the single most humiliating thing that has ever happened to me, and my life is a fucking failure, and no one seems to give a shit, including my parents. Damn it! I'm sorry! I'm not angry with you, Irina, I swear. Now I feel awful. You are, like, the best part of this entire godforsaken city. I don't mean to yell at you. I'm just so fucking angry. None of this is fair."

"And you are right to be angry, and it is not fair. What he did was so disrespectful. It is shocking." Irina paused, frustrated. "Perhaps I am not expressing myself properly. What I wish to say is, you should be angry at him, but do not take it out on yourself. He should be the one sitting in his room all alone and feeling shame. He should be the one who is too sad to shower or put on clean clothes or shave his beard."

"That dumbass can't even grow a proper beard," Amanda scoffed. "It comes in all patchy and looks like shit. Stupid fucker."

"Yes, stupid fucker!" Irina cried, delighted. "Stupid fucker with a terrible beard! He is not a real man!"

Irina, who was typically so reserved and formal in her speech, was so giddy over the revelation of Jeff's substandard facial hair that Amanda started to laugh. The tension over their near-argument quickly dissipated as they egged each other on, sputtering out remarks about how Jeff "looks like he has soul patches superglued all over his ugly-ass chin" (Amanda) and how "patchy beards can be caused by fungal infections, so we may infer that the gross jerk probably has athlete's foot on his face" (Irina), between giggles.

"I needed that," Amanda said after they finally began to calm down. "I'm sorry. I've been so in my own head that it was starting to feel like I'd never laugh again." She realized that this was probably Irina's point all along and she felt ashamed for how harshly she had reacted toward the one person who had consistently treated her not only with kindness but also with respect. Still, Amanda decided it would be preferable to drop the subject rather than apologize again.

Amanda really wanted to ask if Kristoff had said anything to Irina about how his law school classmates were reacting to the breakup: if any of them were taking Amanda's side, or wondering how she was doing, or were planning to reach out to her after the GULC gossip cycle had moved on to another topic. She wondered if any of them liked her or respected her at all, or if she was never anything more to them than Jeff's bimbo girlfriend. For all she knew, they had placed bets as to how long it would take Jeff to dump her for someone better. Although Irina and Kristoff weren't as social as many of the other couples at Georgetown, Irina was still in with their crowd and she probably would know.

Amanda restrained herself. She didn't want to come across any more pathetic than she already did.

"So, like, I guess I should resign myself to the same fate as Marta?" Amanda said at last, as casually as she could muster.

"Oh. That is a heavy question." Irina looked at her phone again. Amanda could practically hear her mentally begging the delivery driver to hurry up so that she could avoid answering.

"Like I said before," Amanda added, "I'm only asking because I'm trying to understand: if it truly is hopeless for someone as beautiful and accomplished as Marta, what chance do I have? Why should I bother trying for anything more than the occasional random pointless hookup?"

"No, do not say these things!" Irina tossed her phone down and looked intently at Amanda. "Okay. I will tell you this much, although it might not be entirely comforting or what you wish to hear. When I first moved in, I thought that Marta brought all the trouble onto herself. I did not understand why she wasted so much time on dating apps when she should have just met a nice man at the hospital or had one of her married friends set her up. She always said she was too busy to meet men or date the normal way, but then she spent so much of her time with losers from the internet who treated her badly or stood her up. So I figured, she is seeking out bad boys because she enjoys the chaos.

"She used to come home very drunk and trash the kitchen and the common area and sob so loudly that it would wake me up. This was before Laura. We had a girl named Danielle living with us then. And sometimes Danielle would come home wasted too. Usually she came straight into this room here and passed out, but sometimes Drunk Danielle and Drunk Marta would be in the common area at the same time, and all hell would break free. Break free?"

"Break loose," Amanda corrected. "But it doesn't matter. I understood you. Go on."

"I thought I was living with crazy people. Not the insult. Literally, with mental illnesses that needed a professional helper. I do not like to see people take so much alcohol. The rules for dancers in a professional ballet company are very strict, so for many years I was forbidden from alcohol entirely. And in Latvia, ladies do not become intoxicated in this way. Well, there are exceptions, of course. But I had never seen such an extreme up close, and now there were two of them in one household. My household!"

"So, what changed? Or, has anything changed?"

"I started to grow sympathy for her," Irina shrugged, "even though I do not agree with her reactions. She forgets that before I met Kristoff, I also was single. I was very frustrated in Latvia, and I remember being frustrated here in America too. All her friends and colleagues are married, and she probably wonders when it will be her turn. I understand this too. I have three sisters, and all three of them were married by the time they turned twenty-four or twenty-five. And to very wealthy, influential men. Two of their husbands are British, and the other is German. My mother does not let me forget this."

"But when you were single, you didn't go out with four different dudes every week and end up crying over each one of them?"

"No. No, I did not. I met Kristoff at a grad student house party. Really, it was a group of nerds like me drinking beer and playing board games, not a 'party' in the sense you think. Kristoff was friends with the host. He was working for a lobbyist at the time. He—oh, what is the word? He brought me flowers, he planned thoughtful dates for us, he wrote me a love note on real paper..."

"He pursued you? Oh! He courted you?" Amanda offered.

"Yes! He courted me! Really, he was simply treating me like a human. Like I was someone worthy of time and attention and care, even though he was very busy with his job back then. I always knew I mattered to him."

"And Marta never gets that."

"Never! In fact, it is the opposite. These boys, the ones who do not text her pictures of their penis right away—and at least those guys have the decency to reveal that they are creeps from the beginning—some of these boys write her charming texts and make plans for drinks and tell her they want something real. Every time she gets so excited about them, and every time she is so disappointed. Her heart breaks. They do not show up. Or they look nothing like their photos. Or they try to make her leave right away for sex, and they tell her that if she will not give it to them, they have many other, younger options."

"And that's what I have to look forward to now too."

"Well, not exactly. The problem is, whenever she finally does meet a reasonably nice man—not necessarily someone spectacular, just a man that shows up on time for their date, does not talk over her too much, can make civil conversation without demanding a blow job, those basic courtesies—she convinces herself that he is The One. She will ignore all his flaws and all their incompatibilities, and she will start to smother him. She will become possessive and jealous after two mediocre dates because she is so desperate for something to work."

"And then the guy runs away terrified."

"Exactly. Even the best ones who are patient and willing to benefit her the doubt at first, they become scared off soon enough. It is too much for them." Irina rolled her eyes. "I should be getting my Ph.D. in psychology or sociology instead of applied mathematics. After three years in this house, I could write a dissertation."

"But you haven't found another place to live yet."

"No. I could not afford it even if I wanted to, not in a nice neighborhood like this. And ultimately, this is not so bad for an arrangement at all. It is not forever. And whatever quirks or shortcomings Marta may have in matters of love, she is a good roommate and a good landlord. She is a good, honest person with a big heart, and she makes sure her home remains a safe, clean, quiet place for us to live. It is much better than most of the graduate student housing, I am certain."

"Thank you," Amanda said. "Honestly, hearing all this gives me, I don't know, some compassion for her, I guess. And in a weird way, it gives me some hope for my own situation."

"That is good to hear. This is the only reason I feel comfortable talking of her and her love life at all. Her issues do not have to be yours."

"Thank you," Amanda said again. She wanted to tell Irina how much she valued becoming friends with her, how profound of an impact these conversations had on her perspective and her mood. She wanted to invite her out for coffee or drinks or some sort of—official hang out session? Friend date? How did adult women solidify their bonds with each other? It had been so much easier during undergrad.

"It looks like the delivery guy is close." Irina had retrieved her phone. "I am going to go meet him in the lobby. Or chase him down the street, depending on how much trouble he has finding the building."

"Do you want me to come with you?"

"That is not necessary. I missed Kristoff's call while we were talking, so I will see what he wants while I wait."

"Do you two always voice-call each other?" Amanda asked, surprised. Irina looked confused for a moment. Then she started laughing.

"Yes! I guess I am old-fashioned. I insisted on this from the beginning, and now he does it from habit."

Irina was still laughing to herself as she waved to Amanda and walked into the hallway.

CHAPTER ELEVEN
Jill Torres

Jill's relationship with Jesse—if it was fair to call their time together a "relationship" at all—had ended months ago. She didn't think about him often anymore, and when she did, it was mostly prosaic musings about how his Step 1 exam might have turned out or whether he ended up dating anyone from his incestuous friend group. She was vaguely irritated with her lack of control over her own thoughts nonetheless.

Their "breakup"—again, if it could be fairly labeled as such—was really more of a slow, awkward fizzling out, until they finally agreed over text that they each were so consumed with studying for their respective exams that they didn't have enough time to give their relationship the attention it deserved. It was a polite and mutually convenient excuse. Jill wasn't broken-hearted, although she typed out the proper expressions of melancholy in her text replies. Truthfully, she felt more relieved than forlorn.

And Jesse would be fine too. He would find his woman. Her Tinder profile would include interests of "laughing, fun, friends, and travel lol," even though this girl would have been out of the country once, seven years ago, to London or maybe Montreal. And they'd probably be reasonably happy together. This chick would be a basic bitch. But why bother hating on a basic bitch? She'd only have to post a Marilyn Monroe meme, no caption needed, and all Jill's criticism against her would be vindicated. Jesse would love how she loved him. He would marry her. And, at least from the perspective of the rest of the world, the basic bitch and her cheap leggings and her dull repartee would win.

In flashes of bitterness, Jill wondered what would have happened if Jesse hadn't approached her that night at Grafton Street Pub. Would she have sparked something with that hot bartender who she thought might have taken an extra interest in her? Would she have met someone her last semester at MIT who liked her, and not just the idea of her? How far back had their pointless time together set her?

And who were these "other girls" that she was "not like"? Because as far as Jill could tell, at MIT she had been surrounded by women who embodied all of the things that Jesse claimed made her different: intelligence, ambition, beauty, intensity, all of it. Harvard couldn't have been much different. When Jesse half-heartedly complimented her on her self-confidence, all Jill could think was that she was doing a good job faking it. And also that, apparently, she was not permitted show any vulnerability in his presence. But there actually *were* girls who seemed effortlessly self-assured. They were the ones who were actually not like other girls. She *was* one of the "other girls." Or was everyone else just faking it too?

But now Jesse was in the past, as was her undergraduate career. She had lost interest in finding a boyfriend, or at least that's what she told herself. Neither the pursuit nor the relationship itself was worth the effort. Aside from a two-week trip to Ecuador, she had remained in Boston since graduation, mostly keeping to herself. She refused to download any dating apps, but every so often she would head to a nearby bar solo, vaguely hoping that she might find someone to... make out with? Chat with? Have a one-night stand with? Connect with? She didn't know what she wanted from these excursions, but she knew she wasn't getting it. When she found herself fooling around with a stranger in the darkened corner of a patio, and even when she decided to accompany someone home, the entire experience felt hollow and perfunctory. She didn't understand why a spark had been missing with

Jesse—or with J.P. for that matter—and these listless experiments didn't seem to bring her closer to an answer.

Jill tried not to take it personally. She tried to convince herself that sex was only one component of the human experience. She tried to reassure herself that chemistry is fickle and she couldn't be expected to have it with everyone. She tried to believe that she had just been unlucky so far.

But the question nagged at her: was everyone else in the world except for her having great sex? The kind of sex one sees in the movies, where every couple finishes together, totally blissful and satisfied, every fucking time? Jill couldn't remember ever having seen a film where the man couldn't get it up or couldn't complete the act. At most, one of the male characters might come too quickly, but only in a scene meant as comic relief. In Hollywood, sexual dysfunction was treated like a joke, if it was referenced at all, instead of like a problem that generated insecurities, if not out-right self-loathing, for both partners involved. They never showed couples talking about these issues, or avoiding talking about these issues, or the damage it caused to their relationship.

Was that because this was a problem essentially limited to Jill alone? Was there something wrong with her specifically? Was she impossible to love? To want? To desire? Her body wasn't perfect, perhaps, but damned if it wasn't close, and damned if she didn't work every day to make it better and better. And she had fixed her facial flaws, spending thousands of dollars to straighten her nose and clear up her skin. What more could she possible do?

On a random weekday night a few months after starting her new job, Jill went to a bar in Beacon Hill, met a gorgeous nineteen-year-old with green eyes, a broad chest, and a respectable fake ID (his phony driver's license introduced him as Jake from Vermont, but his real name was Kyle and he had lived in Massachusetts his whole life). Within three hours, they went back to his place. She didn't know why. She supposed she wanted to prove something to herself. It was, obviously, only a one-night thing.

The experience was bizarre and unsettling, although ultimately no worse than her previous exploits had been. The entire evening after she and Kyle had left the bar felt like a performance, and Kyle had obediently adopted his role and recited his lines. Every utterance, every touch, every moment after they had taken off their clothes had all the external appearance of a passionate love scene, but it was completely devoid of any genuine emotion. Jill could practically hear him trying to calculate how many "likes" they would generate if their encounter were posted on PornHub.

Before they fell asleep, he called her a "sex demon." He meant it as a high compliment. It seemed borderline ridiculous under the circumstances. Had he sincerely enjoyed himself for even a fraction of the time they had been alone together? Had he come? He had been wearing a condom, and the entire experience felt so staged and surreal, that Jill wasn't entirely convinced that he had. Her moans and coos notwithstanding, she certainly hadn't.

The next morning, while Jill was standing over his kitchen counter finishing a second cup of coffee, Kyle's roommate Chaz meandered into the kitchen: shirtless, hair tousled, seeking orange juice. Jill had met Chaz the night before. He was as young and attractive as Kyle, a little bit taller and not quite as jacked. The three of them had spent almost an hour chatting at the bar until it became evident that Jill and Kyle had certain intentions for each other, at which point Chaz had excused himself politely but with a knowing smirk.

The entire situation was so absurd that Jill felt no embarrassment whatsoever when Chaz immediately perked up upon catching Jill's eye, hoisted the carton of orange juice over his head, and practically shouted, "Aw yeah! Get it! I know you showed my boy what's up. How was it?"

Jill smiled coyly and said, in good spirits, "It was nice, and that's all you need to know, you perv."

This reply, however, did not suffice for either Kyle or Chaz.

"Incredible," Kyle began. "We both came five times each." Make that less than zero for Jill and at most—at most!—once for him. "I ate her pussy." Jill had been drunk, but she was pretty sure she would have remembered that. "And then she ate my ass." What the fuck? Jill *definitely* would have remembered that. "I'm basically ready to make her my girlfriend after last night." God forbid.

It was a baffling response. In reality, they hadn't been that far off from having perfectly mediocre sex. Kyle's enthusiasm had seemed exaggerated, but it was certainly better than, say, Jesse's drunken borderline-indifference had been. Overall, it had been about as lousy as any other night with anyone else on Jill's (admittedly still limited) list of past partners. And Jill was willing to hold herself accountable for her role in the interpersonal disconnect. She also chose to perform a part for an imaginary audience, rather than try to experience some sort of genuine human connection— even if said connection amounted to nothing more than a fuzzy memory of a few hours of lust and superficial conversation.

She wasn't mad about Kyle's dishonesty, she was confounded by it. Why the fabrication? And why did he seem to believe, sincerely, the fiction that he had just created for the benefit of his roommate? The whole point of an otherwise pointless hook-up was....

God, what was the point? To savor a fleeting moment of reciprocated attraction? To enjoy the analog-world equivalent of having someone super-like your Tinder profile or follow your Instagram account? Kyle didn't need to slide into her DMs—she had willingly slid into his bed. And all that resulted from it was another fiction, another fiction as boring and exhausting as a filtered photo or a copypasta profile bio. There were no selfies in bed the night before, no TikTok snippets of their asinine conversation that morning, but nobody knew how to act outside the strictures of those laws, the self-imposed panopticon ensuring almost everything they did or said would be documented, posted, scrutinized, and ultimately mocked or envied accordingly.

Was that not how their value was assigned now? Jill had no illusions that Kyle had approached her the night before because he was impressed by her cumulative GPA at MIT or because he was intrigued by the headway her team was making on a code debugging project at TravelBlot. He had sidled up to her at the bar because he had noticed her long blond hair and her long muscular legs. Or perhaps he had just noticed other men noticing her hair and legs. Half the time, that was enough.

And Jill had dressed to flaunt those features that night. That was the point. It worked. Kyle sat next to her and initiated a loud, boastful conversation with Chaz—specifically, about the new car he was thinking about buying and the music festival he had recently attended with VIP passes—that was intended primarily for Jill's benefit and attention.

She noticed him back. He was six foot one and the outline of his pecs pressed through his shirt. She could tell he was younger, but he was hot and cocky in a way that made her roll her eyes and decide, "Why the hell not?"

Wasn't that the point? He was hot, she was hot, and in that moment, Jill's accomplishments and ambitions were more irrelevant than ever. She had changed out of her blazer and jeans and into a push-up bra and a tight skirt that hit at mid-thigh before leaving the house to lean into this very irrelevance. And Kyle had followed the script perfectly. He and Chaz had paused their inane conversation just when they needed to, and for just long enough, for Jill to interject with a banal comment of her own. The night's conclusion was an inevitability from that point on.

But in the kitchen, as Kyle boasted about the supposedly incendiary chemistry between them and the fantastical, idealized night of love-making that allegedly had unfolded, Jill wanted to scream. She wanted to howl with laughter. She wanted to shake both of these two dumbass, smoking-hot nineteen-year-olds by their shoulders, and ask them, "What the fuck are we doing here? Why are we pretending like any of this is real? Did any of us get what we wanted out of last night? Would any of us even know if we had? What is the fucking point?" She wanted to confiscate their fake IDs. She wanted to school marm them into making better choices. She wanted to convince these two barely legal, gorgeous fools that there must be something better out there worth waiting for, mostly because she already knew she'd never be able to convince herself.

But Jill didn't do any of that. Wouldn't it just be another skit? Wouldn't it be futile? Or was she simply too hungover to care?

160

"Yeah, we thought about texting you to join us for a devil's threesome." Jill smirked and swirled the rest of her coffee around her mug before looking Chaz directly in the eye. "But I figured you'd probably be too vanilla for that."

"I'm not too vanilla for that! Not for anything!" Chaz's voice had gone up a full octave. Kyle looked nothing short of delighted by Jill's comment. Jill was already daydreaming about the bottle of red Gatorade waiting for her at home.

They said their goodbyes. It was less awkward than Jill would have expected. Maybe because she no longer dared expect anything. What was the point, what was the point?

Midway through her Uber ride home, Jill barely suppressed an audible snort: if she hadn't deleted her Instagram account less than two weeks after creating it, she probably would've gotten herself two new followers. And she probably would've felt like that was enough of an accomplishment that she could justify spending the rest of the day napping and watching Netflix in bed.

But instead, Jill would drink that glorious bottle of red Gatorade, pound two zero-calories purple Monster energy drinks, do forty minutes of hill sprints on the treadmill in her townhouse complex's gym until the previous night had been sweated out of her system, and take a fifteen-minute scalding hot shower to rinse off the remnants. (Manny, the complex's current superintendent, had adjusted Jill's water heater, very much against state housing regulations, three months earlier after they had bonded over their shared addiction to those godforsaken Monster energy drinks and spent twenty minutes listening to Slipknot's newest album and cracking jokes in Spanish while he fixed an unrelated leak in Jill's bathroom ceiling. Jill was the only tenant who never lacked for hot water.)

And then she would spend the next ten to twelve hours working from home (a glorious perk of TravelBlot's startup culture), debugging a new feature in her employer's latest app update: a data-mining enhancement buried in the app's code—completely extraneous to its ostensible function of finding the best discounted hotel options based on the user's budget, interests, and multi-day sight-seeing (or bar-crawling) itinerary, but unequivocally consented to somewhere within the ten thousand brilliantly written words of legalese comprising the app's mandatory terms and conditions—which would allow TravelBlot to create and eventually sell targeted advertising strategies not only to anyone who downloaded the app, but also to that person's followers, connections, online associates, or whatever bullshit consultant-speak term would come into vogue next to describe these digital pseudo-relationships, which in some hypothetical alternate universe, Kyle and Chaz would have just become for Jill, notwithstanding that they'd probably never interact in real life again.

The fact that such an alternate universe essentially did exist—that Amanda Wagner was out there, earnestly trying to make a name for herself (currently in Washington, D.C., at least as of the last time Jill had checked), probably with one of the apps that Jill had a hand in creating already downloaded onto her phone, and therefore with what was essentially legalized corporate malware to be pushed onto Amanda's device when the app's next major update was released, unwittingly exchanging Amanda's and her friends' (virtual or otherwise) data and text messages and shared locations with TravelBlot—none of this was lost on Jill. She didn't feel good about it, necessarily; but she didn't necessarily feel bad about it either. Very much an equivalent reaction to her encounter with Kyle.

It wasn't that the passion and conviction of her undergrad years had been supplanted by an apathetic amorality. It was just that, in that particular moment, in the back of a tan 2011 Volvo driven by a Middle Eastern man named Zahid, whose sporadic, broken attempts at conversation suggested to Jill that he had taken this particular job in part to improve his English skills (and her lukewarm response to Zahid's overtures was giving her far stronger pangs of guilt compared to any qualms she might have about the social ramifications of her work or the ethical implications of her random hookup with Kyle), she was simply too hungover, too exhausted, too overwhelmed by everything she needed to accomplish, to give it more than a cursory thought, much less allow herself to care.

CHAPTER TWELVE
Jill Torres

Jill knew she had changed. And she knew it was not for the better.

The worst part was, the first nine months after graduating from MIT were incredible. Notwithstanding her inauspicious forays into the Boston young professionals' nightlife scene, it was the most transformative and rewarding period of Jill's life. She was finally starting to feel like she had found her place in the world.

Much to the surprise of many of her MIT peers, she had accepted a job at TravelBlot, an app-based startup headquartered in Boston. Jill hadn't wanted to remain in Boston specifically, but she hadn't been categorically opposed to it either. And she certainly had weighed her options, fielding more than her fair share of phone calls, dinner invitations, and miscellaneous (and sometimes quite pricey) swag from every major player in the technology, pharmaceutical, and telecommunication industries.

Amazon and Google each had flown her out first-class to their headquarters after her on-campus interviews, had put her up in the Fairmont Olympic hotel in Seattle and The Grand Hotel in Sunnyvale, respectively, and had stacked her interview schedules with their company's most affable, attractive, and important personnel. AT&T had taken her and three other top-priority recruits to tour the Dallas Cowboys' stadium and practice space in Texas;

Jill herself wasn't a big fan of American football, but Mateo's excitement upon receiving the blurry cell phone pics she texted him throughout the day made the entire trip worthwhile. Even Antecessus Pharmaceuticals had taken her to dinner at Atera in New York City, although Jill began to suspect that she might not be a good fit with their corporate culture as she picked at each course of their $285/plate tasting menu and tried not to pound each selection off the $365/person reserve wine pairing menu as soon as it was poured into her glass, while Antecessus's Chief Technology Officer, a VP of Product Development, and an HR lackey explained to her that the career path at Antecessus would *basically* be as prestigious as a Wall Street investment banker's and could *essentially* be as lucrative after a couple of promotions. She declined their invitation to attend a nearby nightclub after they had eaten—yes, even though they'd be VIP, even though they'd get bottle service—and went back to her hotel alone.

It was too late for Jill to call her mom so they could laugh together about what a debacle the evening had been. (The gauntlet of interviews that Jill had gone through earlier in the day had been comically uncomfortable in much the same way; everyone with whom she had spoken seemed either desperate to prove to Jill how successful, cool, and happy in their role they were, or desperate to prove that Jill's admiration or approbation of their life choices meant less than nothing to them.) Jill already had finished all the homework she had brought with her, and she wasn't in the mood to rewatch a movie on her laptop, nor was she tired enough to go to sleep yet. Instead, she exchanged her pencil skirt and blouse for running shoes and a sports bra, and cranked out five tipsy, exasperation-fueled miles on the treadmill in the hotel gym.

So no, Jill hadn't expected to join a Boston-based startup, but after her glimpse into Corporate America, it was a fairly easy sell. The concerns that steered many of her classmates to more stable jobs at major companies simply didn't apply to her. She had no student loans or credit card debt. Settling down and eventually supporting a spouse or kids was the furthest thing from her mind. When it came to health insurance, Jill figured that all she really needed was catastrophic care coverage and she'd be fine. She had to nod her head and feign enthusiasm when the corporate recruiters extolled the benefits of their platinum-level medical, dental, and prescription drug plans. Was this really supposed to entice someone her age?

Even basic job security was less of a concern for her relative to her peers. If the startup folded overnight, if it got sold to a mega-conglomerate, if the founders were forced to lay off half the staff to meet investor demands, if... if, if, if. Jill knew she could handle any of it. It wouldn't break her. MIT didn't give class rankings, but she had maintained a perfect 5.0 GPA over the preceding seven semesters. If disaster struck and her grades the final semester somehow slipped, even then, no one would doubt that she was at the very top of her class at one of the most respected universities in the world. She had her trust fund. Since her sophomore year of college, she had a stream of passive income, in perpetuity, from a patent she had registered and licensed with the help of a friendly paralegal in MIT's technology licensing office; she received only $285/month of the total licensing fee, but every time she saw the direct deposit into her checking account, it gave her a jolt of confidence and pride to know that there were businesses out there willing to pay for access to her inventions. If she did it once, she could do it again. Heck, she wasn't even limited to opportunities in the United States; she could move to China or Spain or South America or really anywhere in the world if the startup didn't work out!

She could even move back home with Mateo and Jaya—although, for as much as she cherished her parents, that would be an absolute worst-case scenario. But she was fortunate to have the option. A shocking number of Jill's classmates were struggling to find gainful employment after graduation, and they openly bemoaned the fact that their parents would not be so accommodating.

Given the dismal job market—even for students at MIT, and even including those with reasonably decent grades—Jill's dormmates and acquaintances were baffled that Jill would choose to work at TravelBlot when she had standing offers from some of the most eminent, desirable employers in the country. And, if the rumor mill were to be believed, at least two of those corporations had substantially juiced up Jill's proffered compensation and job title compared to any other MIT prospect. Jill did her best to ignore or dismiss this chatter, however flattering to her ego some of the speculation might have been, and she reiterated to herself that a year later she wouldn't remember or care what her peers thought about her decision or how her offers compared to theirs.

And ultimately, it wasn't about starting salaries or signing bonuses or job titles, much less some nebulous concept of prestige or a laundry list of perks, most of which Jill knew she'd never utilize. After six or seven rounds of in-office interviews, the big corporations all seemed interchangeable. She could practically recite what each interviewer was going to say to her verbatim, because she had already heard it at least three other times that day, and a barely modified version of it from every person at every other company she'd spoken to before that point.

Throughout the entire process, Jill willed herself to keep her energy high, asked all the right questions, and managed to charm almost every person with whom she spoke, because that was the dance. That was the game. That was what was required to get the offer, and Jill liked to win. But it was excruciating. And it hit Jill during her sixth corporate interview—when yet another VP of Digital Management (or midlevel network architect or HR benefits partner or whoever the hell this guy was) was explaining how, at their company, "we work hard but we play hard, our company holiday party is epic!"—that if she joined any of these places, she would have to adopt the same bullshit persona that she had taken on for these interviews, with the same seemingly effortless grace of a ballerina and the same existential soul-equivalent of a dancer's mangled blackened toenails, every day that company remained her primary source of income.

At half these places, it hadn't been clear what she'd be doing on a daily basis. Several of her interviewers couldn't articulate at the highest, vaguest level what her potential department's mission and objectives were, much less what her day-to-day responsibilities would be. That in itself was disconcerting, but ultimately beside the point. It didn't matter what she'd be doing.

She'd be an interchangeable cog doing it. And she'd have to pretend, constantly, that she was fine with that fact in order to continue to collect her (admittedly sizeable) paycheck.

The change from her life at MIT would be too drastic. She didn't want to be a professor or get her Ph.D. Not necessarily. She simply wanted to be able to go to her job with at least a semblance of the excitement, curiosity, and eagerness to learn and challenge herself that she felt when she attended her classes. And at any of those corporate jobs, this would be unthinkable. These places were staffed by, if not run by, the very same people who in college complained about every assignment, skipped two thirds of the lectures, and called the professor an asshole when they made a middling grade on the final exam (a grade which, in actuality, was inflated far beyond what they deserved).

Jill knew she was weird. Or if not weird, an aberration. She could understand why someone would prefer to talk about the latest drama on *Real Housewives* or *The Bachelor.* For real, Jill understood it! She wasn't an elitist or an intellectual snob or... or some sort of lady neckbeard! She found dumb shit entertaining too! But she also was deeply curious about biomedical ethics and neuroimaging techniques and civil engineering... and, really, she could become interested in virtually anything! Heck, she didn't know she was interested in neuroscience until she had to fulfill her communication-intensive HASS requirement and the 10:30 a.m. Monday/Wednesday/Friday course on Philosophical Issues in Brain Science was the only thing that would fit in her schedule. She bought all the books on each class's syllabus from the campus bookstore (yes, yes, she was woke enough to realize that, thanks to her trust fund, she was one of only a handful of students who could afford to), and she read them all. Sometimes beyond what the professor required, if she was curious about the additional context behind the assigned passage or chapter.

But this made her a gunner. An ass-kisser. A teacher's pet. She learned quickly that, even at MIT, some of her classmates were more interested in demonstrating that they were too cool for the education for which they (or, more likely, their parents) were paying hundreds of thousands of dollars, than they were in... for heaven's sake, not even in listening to the professor or participating in the class discussions themselves! How about just allowing the students who actually did give some semblance of a fuck to focus on the materials, to answer the professor's questions, or to engage in spirited debate with each other, unencumbered by their eye rolls and scoffs? How was mindlessly scrolling through their phones and posturing like some sort of wannabe badass more interesting or enjoyable than being mentally present for long enough to learn the materials that they'd have to figure out soon enough for the next p-set or exam anyway?

And if Jill accepted any of the corporate job offers, with their enticing, glorious paychecks? Those people would be her bosses. Those people would be her colleagues. Those people would set the social and intellectual standards to which she would be expected to conform.

MIT had been a blessing. More students than not genuinely did care. More students than not were at least two standard deviations away from the stereotypical college norm of generalized apathy toward anything beyond finding the next kegger. But Jill knew—somehow, without understanding how or why, she knew—that if she took a job in Corporate America, the same students that made her hesitate to raise her hand in class, the same students whose sporadic presence in seminars caused her to refrain from contributing more than twice in a session to the group discussion, would be the people with the authority to deem her worthy or not for a raise, a promotion, even a desirable assignment. They were consistently the worst part of MIT, and accepting any of her pending job offers would have meant accepting a position where her fundamental responsibility would not be to create or improve or problem-solve, but rather would be to placate them, to make them feel smart, in exchange for money and stability. Neither of which, bluntly, Jill actually needed.

So she decided to entertain TravelBlot's interest. Maybe there were other startups that were headquartered in more desirable locations, or whose missions more closely aligned with Jill's core values, or where Jill would have met her soulmate or her future lifelong best friend. But TravelBlot reached out to Jill at just the right time, and they were different from her other suitors in all the right ways. Even their initial interview process was unorthodox. TravelBlot was based in Boston, but they didn't bother with on-campus interviews. In fact, Jill's first significant contact with them outside of email—what she quickly realized was a screening interview, although they never expressly stated so—was conducted via Skype, even though it would have taken her less than twenty minutes to get to their offices in an Uber.

She was almost insulted. After the puffery and pandering of the preceding eight weeks, it was almost a deal-breaker. But before they had disconnected from the video chat, she had made a commitment to speak in person with Akari, TravelBlot's hiring manager (who was also acting as the director of HR, and as the company's public relations manager), at 11:00a.m. on a Tuesday. Jill had emailed her Matrix Methods professor to let her know that she'd be missing the lecture and would send that day's home-work via email by Monday night. There was no backing out. Not for Jill.

Jill knew within thirty minutes of arriving at TravelBlot's office that if they made her an offer, she would accept. There was something intangible, something that she couldn't quite articulate, that was different. Special. Was this what people meant when they spoke of their spouses and said that, from the moment they met, they knew that they had found the one?

TravelBlot's offices were bright and functional. They were vaguely reminiscent, on a much smaller and more modest scale, of the layout and décor she had observed when she had toured her other prospective employers' buildings across the country. Jill found TravelBlot's version refreshing. The Silicon Valley offices that Jill had toured were verging on becoming caricatures of themselves in pursuit of some movie-set ideal of how they were supposed to appear and operate, and the offices she had visited in Dallas, New York, and Los Angeles had been Silicon Valley's cloying store-brand knockoffs. TravelBlot wasn't wholly immune to the phenomenon—maybe there weren't any ping pong tables or hammocks, but they did have an inordinate number of modular work pods personalized with the company's logo, as well as a collection of bizarre abstract sculptures placed in inconvenient spots throughout the floor—but somehow it seemed less forced. Less phony.

Jill wasn't sure why she noticed, much less cared. It shouldn't have made a difference. She could have made her decision based on salary, title, where she could buy a home within a year, heck, even which city was closest to her parents or which role would allow her to maintain her workout regimen and pursue her side projects with minimal interference. Almost anything would have been a more reasonable metric than fixating on each company's interior design approach and its respective recruiters' unreasonable pride therein.

But that was just it. No one from TravelBlot mentioned a thing about their workspaces until Jill asked about their policy on telecommuting. No one mentioned "work-life balance" or uttered the godforsaken phrase "work hard, play hard." Everyone seemed genuinely excited about TravelBlot's mission, but they weren't reciting pre-scripted, generic talking points. Instead, they spoke about their specific duties, their specific challenges and frustrations, their specific visions for the future (regarding both TravelBlot's long-term potential for growth and their personal career trajectories). They asked Jill twice as many challenging questions within the first two hours of the day than she had been asked over the course of the preceding seven corporate interviews combined. And she loved it! These people had direction. They had meaningful, well-defined goals and they pursued them relentlessly. They were candid about the stresses of the job and acknowledged that TravelBlot's dynamic wasn't for everyone. The day was almost completely devoid of business-school jargon and self-important consultant-speak.

Jill talked to eight different TravelBlot employees, from the founder and the CFO to the company's two most recent hires, an entry-level coder and a mid-career product designer. Halfway through the interview rounds, TravelBlot's head of engineering and Akari, in her capacity as hiring manager, treated Jill to lunch at Archie's, a popular deli that was a five-minute walk from the office. The outing took less than forty minutes, and even that was mostly due to the unusually long line at the deli counter that afternoon. There was no four-course dinner that night. No fancy excursion to a professional sporting event. No VIP list at a trendy, noisy nightclub. TravelBlot made no extravagant gesture to woo Jill other than a personal phone call from Nathan, TravelBlot's founder, two days later, stating that the team unanimously agreed that Jill would be a great fit and that Akari would be in touch within the next twenty-four hours to present her with a salary and benefits package that they hoped she would accept.

Jill would have made fifty percent more money starting anywhere else, and she would be losing out on the prestige of having a Fortune 100 company name as the first item under the Job Experience heading on her résumé. To her surprise, as she was preparing to make her final decision, a part of her ego recoiled at the thought of giving that up. She had never considered herself particularly status conscious.

Jill wanted to believe that this unexpected visceral reaction stemmed from concern for her parents. In a town where nearly every family could afford a multimillion-dollar home, a luxury car for each child's sixteenth birthday, and summers split between the country club and Nantucket or the Cape, filial accomplishments became a status symbol, the way to distinguish yourself, the way to make your neighbors jealous. Didn't Jaya and Mateo deserve that? They hadn't gotten the kid they had planned for, but they had decided to keep her anyway. Didn't she owe it to them to show them that they had made the right choice?

But that wasn't it. Or, rather, that wasn't *just* it. The right analogy wouldn't come to Jill until that summer, a scorching June day in Quito, Ecuador, where Jill was attending her baby cousin's baptism along with Mateo and thirty other members of her extended family. In a modest ballet-slipper pink dress, kneeling, standing, and sitting in the crowded pews of La Iglesia de Santa Faz, her mind began to wander. She thought first of the ten days of solitary travel she had ahead of her—hiking in the Yanacocha Reserve, then heading south to Cotopaxi National Park and onward by auto to Guayaquil—before she would return to Quito to spend another two nights with her abuelo and then fly back to

Boston. She thought of the unpacked boxes sitting in her new two-bedroom townhouse in Belmont, where she had signed an eighteen-month lease that commenced the day before her flight to Ecuador left Boston Logan airport. She hadn't even purchased a bed yet, but she'd have almost a full month when she got back to the States to take care of the boxes, buy furniture, stock her pantry, and adapt to life in Boston outside of the college bubble. She thought of the handful of classmates she casually knew who also had decided to remain in the city after graduation, and she wondered if she'd ever see them socially. But if she hadn't really hung out with them before, why would that change now?

Jesse. He definitely would still be there. Jill felt herself cringe. She bowed her head, hoping that none of her family members had noticed her expression, or if they had, they'd mistaken it for some twisted, overly intense display of reverence as they recited the Act of Contrition. "Con todo mi corazón, me arrepiento...."

Thinking of Jesse, she was penitent indeed. Glory, glory, hallelujah, that the whole debacle had transpired at the end of her senior year, and had wrapped itself up before finals and before it could do any lasting damage to her GPA. Or her mental health. How many red flags had she ignored? How had she deluded herself into thinking that he was the right person for her? She had been so convinced that he was the kind of man she was supposed to be with, that she hadn't bothered to ask herself if she actually wanted to be with him.

She had made excuses for so much—his dismissiveness of her ambitions, his constant need for approbation from everyone with whom he came into contact, her own forced displays of passion during sex and his forced displays of affection during pillow talk after—on the supposition that "relationships take work." On the supposition that, if she wanted to achieve something, she had the intelligence and work ethic to make it happen. Even if that "achievement" was a happy, functional relationship.

Never mind that Jesse was unwilling to make any compromises himself. Never mind that Jill could see from observing Jean Paul and Marisol, who were still dating and who (based on her ongoing, not-so-casual stalking of their social media pages) seemed to be more deliriously giddy for each other than ever, that maybe not all relationships required arduous effort to survive past three months. Even if—especially if!—the other person was seemingly remarkable on paper.

And the offers from Google, from AT&T, from Antecessus Pharma, all of them? They were her Jesses of the corporate world. Sparkling presentation. Stable. Credentialed. Impressive. It was flattering to be wanted by them. They were the ideal for people who craved predictability and who were comfortable generating their satisfaction and self-worth by tying themselves to someone else's status and creating a believable illusion of a blissful life.

Jill had gone out with Jesse for seven weeks, and although she refused to admit it to herself at the time, she felt like the world was closing in on her after their third or fourth date. The sum total of her identity would not be The Doctor's Wife. The initial allure of being brought into a huge clique quickly wore off when Jill realized that she did not give one single semi-solid shit about the meddling, machinations, and melodrama of a group of twenty- and thirty-something graduate students who were constantly interfering in Jesse's romantic life (as, Jill quickly realized, he was in theirs). By dating Jesse, she basically had been dating his entire, often toxic, friend-group as well, and Jill found it appalling that they hadn't outgrown their particular brand of middle-school style nonsense years ago.

But she had put up with it. She had convinced herself it was worth it, because Jesse was The Type of Man She Should Be Dating.

And those corporate gigs? They were The Type of Job She Should Be Taking.

Somehow, for as inept as Jill was at recognizing how misguided her instincts were with respect to the former, she intuitively knew she was ill-suited for the latter.

And so, trusting her intuition in a way that she was incapable of doing when it came to matters of her love life, Jill turned down every Fortune 100 company and accepted TravelBlot's offer. She was grateful. ¡Gloria a Dios en las alturas! Yes! Smushed between Mateo on one side and her second cousin Isabel on the other, in a time-worn Catholic church in Ecuador featuring a newly installed air conditioning unit that simply could not compete with the midday sun, Jill was grateful (amen, amen, hallelujah, amen!) that although she apparently was utterly devoid of basic sensibility or a sense of self-preservation when it came to men, at least her judgment was spot on when it actually mattered.

CHAPTER THIRTEEN
Jill Torres

TravelBlot's primary consumer-oriented product was a travel-booking, itinerary-building, and deal-hunting mobile app, which also happened to monitor its users' behavior to determine how much vendors could statistically get away with charging before the potential customer would opt for another carrier, hotel, or tour package. Is F/25-29 more likely to plan a trip abroad after seeing a fitness influencer's travel posts on Instagram? If M/30-39 liked a friend's geo-tagged vacation photo album on Facebook, is he any more inclined to stay at the same hotel within the next twelve months? How many times does F/18-24 check flight prices before booking? How much of an impact do points and rewards programs have on how frequently M/25-29 travels? And how long does F/40-49 look at ads from airlines, cruises, car rental companies, and resorts before continuing to scroll through her social media feeds? TravelBlot's proprietary algorithms aggregated and monitored all this data, as well as its users' demographic information, social networking connections, and a myriad of other online activity.

As a Junior Software Engineer, Jill's primary focus day-to-day was to improve these algorithms by uncovering new ways to refine target populations and market to them more effectively. By the end of her first day on the job, Jill had downloaded the app onto her corporate phone to facilitate impromptu user experience testing. She registered her account under the name "Farhad Razavi" after resurrecting her fake Facebook page, which she had let sit idle for almost a year. She noted immediately and with strange satisfaction that Amanda Wagner still hadn't defriended her.

In the two years since TravelBlot had been founded, the app had exploded in popularity, reaching 1.2 million active accounts by the time Jill was hired, maintaining an outstanding seventy-four percent quarterly retention rate, and exceeding its projected seven percent quarterly growth rate thanks to a surge in popularity among European twenty-somethings. Jill mostly understood its appeal: the app was ideal for coordinating flights and hotel reservations for large groups, and it made the process of paying for the trip, including particularly splitting group expenses, seamless. Plus, the app was free, and it really did offer some great discounts and cool features.

Jill was particularly proud of her idea to aggregate all of a user's hotel, airline, and car rental loyalty programs onto one page for easy viewing; it incentivized the user to link all of their travel-related accounts to the TravelBlot platform by offering a convenient, one-click way to track their points and view available promotions. It wasn't her fault that no one bothered to scroll through the app's terms and conditions before disclosing (however unintentionally) all their personal information. It wasn't her fault that the people downloading the app didn't realize that *they* were TravelBlot's product, and that TravelBlot's actual clients were the companies who purchased the right to understand their online behavior and market to them accordingly. Thanks to Jill's contributions, data collection was cleaner and engagement and session length metrics rose so significantly that Nathan, TravelBlot's founder, took personal notice of Jill as a high-potential employee.

Nathan's approbation and endorsement of Jill became a self-fulfilling prophecy. Eight months after she had started, her official title remained Junior Software Engineer, but her responsibilities had been extended far beyond writing new code and debugging systems. She worked closely with the Design team to ensure the security and smooth integration of planned upgrades, and she refined TravelBlot's data mining algorithms in a way that immediately and permanently endeared her to the entire Research & Analytics team. She also offered to monitor the company's ongoing compliance with international data privacy regulations as they expanded into European markets. Lorraine, TravelBlot's in-house counsel, initially balked at the seeming intrusion into her domain of authority, but she quickly relented when she realized that, without Jill's help, she would have to engage outside counsel to handle GDPR oversight, and she wanted to reserve that line item in her limited budget to hire a law firm in the event of litigation.

Jill then expanded the (mostly automated) system she had developed for monitoring privacy regulations into FTC guidance, COPPA compliance, and the patchwork of other federal and state regulations applicable to the company. Lorraine still had to review and sign off on everything that Jill prepared, but it saved Lorraine countless hours of work and provided Nathan all the comfort he needed that the organization was operating within the strictures of the law (or at least that he could make a cognizable argument that they had made a good faith effort to do so). Jill and Lorraine affectionately referred to the program as "Toni," named after Lorraine's favorite paralegal at her former employer. It took Jill less than five hours to create Toni's core features on a relatively slow Friday afternoon, but the value it added to the company placed her even further in Nathan's favor.

Jill and Lorraine spoke daily. She met Lorraine's wife, Maggie, and their three-year-old son, Max. Lorraine's family even came over to Jill's townhouse for dinner one evening. They were the first visitors she'd had since moving in. Before they arrived, Jill was unsettled by how unsettled she felt carrying through with such a simple display of basic emotional intimacy, but the conversation was pleasant and her guests seemed to enjoy the meal (which Jill decided to have catered, as she dared not attempt to cook three courses herself). By the time Lorraine, Maggie, and little Max said goodnight, Jill was glad that she had opened up her home for a few hours.

Jill and Lorraine disagreed surprisingly often, about everything from work issues to local politics to the best place to buy bagels in Belmont, but they always talked (or bickered) through the matter with unwavering mutual respect. It was almost like having a sister; Jill never worried that any one disagreement would cause their entire relationship to collapse.

Their friendship was something special even around the TravelBlot headquarters, where the long, intense hours tended to form equally intense bonds, and it was especially special for Jill. Jill recalled her high school soccer teammates, a few of the girls that lived down the hall from her in MacGregor House, even two of Jesse's more mature and level-headed friends with whom she'd had several extended one-on-one conversations. Had it really been so long since she'd had a close female friend? Did Lorraine even count as one? Lorraine had a gorgeous, brilliant artist/graphic designer of a wife, an adorable, chatterbox, budding-musician of a son, law school friends, LBGTQ+ friends, rec street hockey league friends.... Most likely, Jill was barely a blip on her social radar.

But life at TravelBlot naturally facilitated the development of deep friendships. The hours were too long and the work was too demanding to avoid it. The details of whatever semblance of each employee's personal life that existed outside of TravelBlot's walls became communal knowledge as quickly as any rumor that Nathan had met with a venture capital firm or that another series of funding was imminent. There was virtually no privacy. Not out of malice, not out of some pernicious joy of spreading gossip, but simply because they were constantly and unavoidably in each other's presence. With few exceptions, secrets were impossible to keep.

Which was why it was so shocking, so inconceivable, when eight months after Jill began working at TravelBlot, the company was acquired by Ingentis Holdings, Inc., a multinational conglomerate headquartered in New York, but with offices all over the United States (as well as abroad), including Boston. Ingentis's motivation for acquiring TravelBlot was nebulous. Although its subsidiaries encompassed interests in the telecomm, financial services, media, real estate, and consumer electronics industries, the corporation had no apparent stake in anything relating to hospitality, aviation, or tourism.

Nevertheless, over the preceding twenty-four months Ingentis Holdings had purchased several other startups reasonably similar to TravelBlot. Indeed, six months into Jill's tenure at the company, the *Wall Street Journal* had printed an article speculating that TravelBlot was in Ingentis's sights. Within three days of its publication, however, the piece was rarely mentioned around the office anymore. It was conjecture. The same article had identified a dozen other startups as potential Ingentis acquisitions as well. The TravelBlot theory was unreliably sourced. And if there had been any validity to the rumor, word would have gotten out. Secrets were impossible to keep.

But Nathan, who pursuant to the directions of their biggest investor had moved into the role of COO two months earlier, and James, the acting CEO, *had* kept this secret. It turned out that the prospect of an acquisition had been broached over a year earlier, right around the time of Jill's initial in-person interview. The details of the deal had been essentially finalized six weeks before the documents were signed and the agreement was announced. Nathan and James managed to keep it entirely between themselves the whole time, hiring a team of outside attorneys and consultants so that not even Lorraine or her colleagues in the legal department were aware of what was transpiring.

"They don't give a shit about the app itself," Nathan said plainly at the all-hands meeting in which he announced the acquisition internally. What did he care anymore? "They want our intellectual property, and they'll adapt it for their own purposes. I doubt they'll collapse TravelBlot immediately, but they'll phase it out as soon as it's no longer profitable or interesting to them. It doesn't dilute their brand, but it doesn't add much to it either."

"We're not selling them a travel platform," Lorraine reiterated later, when she and Jill huddled by one of the espresso machines to discuss the news. "Honestly, what they really want is what you and your team created, Jill. They want to use your advertising algorithms, but in areas where the profit margins are better. And

179

they want to understand how you guys managed to achieve such ridiculous retention rates, so they can apply those techniques where their churn is higher."

Jill gave a half-smile of relief. This probably meant her job was secure.

As if reading her mind, Lorraine continued, "Don't get too cocky, girl. No one at Ingentis is going to give a single fuck about what you've done here. And unless Nathan or James tells them that you were the brains behind our recent growth, and reminds them of that fact on a daily basis, you'll be starting fresh there. Only now you'll be situated squarely in the middle of a cluster-fuck of burnt-out engineers, all of whom are carefully monitored to ensure they do their job exactly as management dictates, with no leeway for independent thinking or creative approaches. Which means there's no way to prove your worth without being arbitrarily plucked by Leadership On High as one of the chosen few to be mentored and promoted."

"Do you think Nathan will st—" Jill started to ask.

"I give him four months, maximum," Lorraine interrupted with a laugh. "More likely, four weeks. He's young. He's like you. You can both easily start over somewhere else. But you heard him at today's meeting: James managed to spew out the canned corporate line with a fake smile on his face, but Nathan couldn't control himself long enough to get through a five-minute speech. Being a vice president of whatever division TravelBlot gets absorbed into is a major demotion for him. At least, he'll think it is. And he's too arrogant to tolerate taking orders from Ingentis's hierarchy for long, irrespective of whatever retention package they agreed to. I almost mean that as a compliment. I've worked with the kid basically since he created TravelBlot, and I respect the shit out of him, but his ego will not suffer kissing the asses of people who are not nearly as smart as he is. And regardless of whatever 'happy corporate family' jingoism they force-feed us when we transition over, kissing Big Papa Ingentis's ass is going to be our new primary job responsibility. Frankly, I doubt James lasts through the year there either."

Two weeks after the acquisition was announced, the final form of the corporate integration plan was circulated. Two weeks after that, all sixty-two TravelBlot employees were to move to Ingentis's payroll and, more importantly, to commence their new roles with their new titles under Ingentis's managerial structure. No one would be made redundant, per se. Ingentis was offering a small payout for immediate voluntary severance, but otherwise was going to rely on "natural attrition" to "align workforce with need." Although Jill didn't have much of a basis for comparison, Ingentis's payout offer for TravelBlot's employees was far less lucrative than she had expected.

"You think it's stingy? I'm surprised they offered us anything at all," Lorraine said with a snort. Their usual spot by the espresso machine was occupied by three other whispering employees, so Jill and Lorraine had absconded to an empty corridor ten minutes after the severance package structure was laid out in a company-wide email. Productivity and morale had plummeted since the announcement of the acquisition, and with this latest development, every break area in the building was occupied by colleagues undertaking similar gripe sessions. "A severance payout this size is either proof of how oblivious Ingentis is to our company culture or proof of how badly they want all of us to resign. Most people here would have quit on their own volition even without the voluntary termination package. My only guess is that their pittance fuck-off money is to try to prevent anyone from sticking around out of spite alone. Ingentis Holdings is a stable employer, but it sure as shit is not interesting or 'cool.'"

"I mean, it is kind of weird that they're willing to bring me on as an engineer without doing any sort of technical interview or test," Jill replied. "I'm sure Nathan gave them my bio, but—"

"It's because this isn't an acqui-hire. Ingentis was never interested in acquiring TravelBlot's intellectual capital beyond what we've already produced. We're not the merchandise. We're an after-thought at best, and probably more of a nuisance. Nathan and James know damn well that most of us have no interest in assimilating into Ingentis's bloated mass of mid-level employees. They probably accepted whatever payout structure that Ingentis's corporate development people proposed—no negotiation, no debate—so they could expend their bargaining leverage somewhere that actually mattered."

"I'm not convinced—"

"Also," Lorraine interrupted, "don't be so sure that they're taking you on as an engineer. Ask James. Nathan doesn't give a fuck anymore. James assured me that I'd end up 'somewhere in Legal,' but who fucking knows what area they'll have me manage. Intellectual property or corporate governance would be the most logical, but they could dump me in real estate or employee benefits or somewhere else where I have a sliver of experience. You could just as easily end up in Ingentis's compliance department or behind their on-call IT help desk or in fucking HR, as you could in software engineering or analytics."

At the time, Jill had shrugged. The decision-makers at Ingentis and TravelBlot had guaranteed the most important thing: no one would be fired. If some of her colleagues freely chose to quit anyway, and they received a little bit of cash in return, all the more power to them. But Jill had less than a year of real-world experience. Resigning now would be risky, and it might even make her appear irresponsible or flaky to future employers. When she got back to her workspace, Jill reread the severance package email once more before deleting it and returning to her code.

Almost a third of TravelBlot's employees, most of whom had been through similar transitions with different startups in the past, had tendered their resignation within three days of the severance package announcement. Two months after the corporate integration, nearly three quarters of them were gone.

In retrospect, Jill almost wished Lorraine had left TravelBlot (now a division of Ingentis Holdings) with the initial mass exodus. Maybe then, Jill would've felt the full weight of the change sooner. Maybe then, Jill would've updated her LinkedIn profile and started reaching out to MIT alumni connections at the same time Lorraine was working with a legal recruiter to obtain a new position. Maybe then, Jill wouldn't have found herself five months later, after Lorraine finally had quit, spiraling through a corporate dystopian nightmare jarringly alone.

Not that Jill begrudged Lorraine for leaving. Quite the contrary. Lorraine had been brutally transparent with Jill about the entire exasperating process. Half of Lorraine's workday was occupied by calls from headhunters trying to add her to a roster of potential candidates to present to corporate clients (even when Lorraine fulfilled less than half of the client's prerequisite qualifications) and law firm hiring managers explaining that they'd be willing to consider bringing Lorraine into the practice if she were willing to join as a mid-level associate (despite eleven years of professional experience and a network of business contacts that should have made her a viable candidate for non-equity partner). She entertained options all over the country, including in states where she wasn't licensed and would have to apply for reciprocity, and in cities where she knew she'd have a difficult time convincing her wife and son—who were quite content with their life, home, and school in Belmont—to relocate.

But as Lorraine repeatedly and emphatically told Jill, all the aggravation was worth it to escape the flaming dumpster fire that was Ingentis's legal department. One of her colleagues should have been disbarred for gross incompetence. Another seemed to outsource literally all of his responsibilities to the most junior attorney in the company, a recent middle-of-the-class graduate of a middling law school whose mother was the Senior Corporate Counsel's husband's mixed doubles tennis partner—although, to be fair, the pitiable kid was more diligent about attending to his assignments in a timely, coherent manner than most of the functionally illiterate buffoons who had seniority over him. As far as Lorraine could tell, at least two, possibly three, other in-house attorneys, a boutique law firm on retainer, and a staggeringly overpriced outside consulting firm, all were responsible for the exact same set of duties she was. Responsible, but not accountable: according to Lorraine, the only reason Ingentis Holdings hadn't been audited and fined for several glaring regulatory violations was either sheer luck or a series of well-timed kickbacks to various midlevel government officials. Most likely a combination of both.

Since no one seemed to notice or care what she did all day, Lorraine had no problem conducting her job search, stepping up her share of Max's daycare drop-off and pickup, and handling the family's grocery shopping and other errands during work hours. As long as she showed up to a handful of "essential" meetings (using a very loose definition of the word "essential") and announced herself at the beginning of every pointless conference call, her colleagues mostly ignored her. She didn't need to say anything. No one was interested in her input anyway. The management clowns running these godforsaken circle jerks just wanted to be able to say that Legal was present for the discussion, and her coworkers were more than willing to spew out long-winded, ambiguous non-opinions that management could interpret however they deemed useful. Everyone was happy. Everyone, that is, except Lorraine.

Jill understood all too well. Even before Lorraine left the company, even when Jill was using the inordinate amount of free time her new position provided to pick up occasional work consulting for MemeographyNet (a startup offering a foolproof way to plagiarize memes and reaction GIFs and, in theory, also to create one's own) and to focus on her independent projects, even when she still held out a modicum of hope that if she did enough good work and kept a positive attitude, she could have a future at Ingentis, Jill was restless. Discontented. She didn't think she was succumbing to the same unbridled misery and rage that plagued Lorraine. Not yet, anyway. But she felt untethered in a way that was theretofore foreign to her—even with the side gigs, her workout regimen, and a newfound weekend hobby of pottery-making at a local artisans' collective to give her life structure and a sense of purpose.

"As our two corporate cultures merge, we look forward to incorporating the best elements of both to create an organization that is newer, stronger, and always more innovative," an email from HR read.

"You know that message was only sent to legacy TravelBlot employees, right?" Lorraine scoffed. "The reality is, adapt to the old guard or die."

"I think I *can* adapt, though," said Jill. "It probably would've made more sense to place me with the network architecture team from a skill-based standpoint, but I am genuinely excited about doing data analytics full-time."

"But do you really want to adapt? To this shit?" While they were at TravelBlot, Lorraine was always unflappable no matter the crisis at hand. She could find a solution to almost any problem, legal or otherwise, while maintaining perfect poise and professionalism. Now, she constantly seemed on the verge of exploding. Sometimes Jill wondered if Maggie, Lorraine's wife, had noticed the change too. "Do you really want to spend the next thirty-five fucking years until retirement dragging yourself to this hellhole, feigning productive work for eight hours a day with a team of ten other dipshits who don't even understand the game, then schlepping back home to watch some laugh-track sitcom on CBS every night so you have something to say to them the next morning other than 'I hate you and everything you represent'? And what, look forward to your one vacation a year to a hotel off the side of a highway in Orlando fucking Florida, where you'll have to crop out the methheads huffing paint in the background of your family photos before you can post them on Facebook in a futile attempt to prove to your former classmates and distant cousins that your life hasn't tumbled directly down the shitter and that all those sacrifices you made for your career early on were totally fucking worth it? That you aren't just another zombie who has to drink her 'Mommy Juice'— L-O-L, Jill, L-O-L, by that I mean, anesthetize yourself with wine, or bourbon, or Drano, or whatever you can get your hands on—to suffocate the lingering, nagging voice in your head reminding you that you chose to waste your potential. You chose to remain at Ingentis. You chose it! Fuck!"

Three days after that particular outburst, Lorraine quit. She quickly accepted a job in Boise, Idaho, working for a major health insurer. Her title would be Deputy General Counsel—not quite as prestigious as the Chief Legal Officer title she held at TravelBlot, but Ygeia Group Health Co. was a much larger institution than TravelBlot had been, and it was certainly a step up from the meaningless "Staff Attorney" moniker she held at Ingentis. It meant that Lorraine would be a decision-making authority again, her voice would be respected again, her law degree and eleven years of professional experience would have their value restored to something above the level of used toilet paper again. Placating fools and appeasing overblown egos would comprise a much smaller portion of her daily task list. Lorraine was thrilled. Maggie, although initially reluctant to abandon their home in Boston when Lorraine first mentioned her dissatisfaction with the post-merger changes and commenced job hunting several months prior, was perhaps even more enthusiastic.

"I got my wife back," Maggie said when Jill stopped by their Belmont townhouse four days before the moving truck was scheduled to arrive. They had barely started to pack, but they'd already found a preschool in Boise for Max, and Maggie's employer had agreed to let her work remotely on a trial basis. "I can learn to hike or ski or mud-wrestle cattle or whatever the heck they do out there for fun. I'm just happy that Lorraine is happy again. The moment she accepted the offer from Ygeia, a cloud was lifted from this house. And we already found a renter who will more than cover our mortgage here until whenever we decide to sell. Or maybe someday, hopefully, we can come back."

"Selfishly, I don't want you guys to go," Jill admitted with a smile, "but I'm genuinely happy for you both. I don't know what I'm going to do without her there. She was my daily sanity check before the merger, and a thousand times more so after. I wish she had found the right position in Boston, but this was too good of an opportunity for her to pass up."

"Maybe if something opens up in Ygeia's business analytics department? If they even have one..." Maggie started.

"No, no, I'm not looking for a job hookup! Even though the pictures Lorraine showed me from her interview trip make Boise look stunning. No, I'm going to tough it out at Ingentis for a while longer. They've been telling me they've got some projects in the pipeline that will require higher-level coding expertise in addition to data analytics experience, and they know I'd happily get back to my software engineering roots."

"Have they given you a timeline? Or guaranteed that if and when that type of work does materialize, it will be assigned to you?" Lorraine had walked up behind them in the kitchen carrying Max, who was squirming and reaching for his sippy cup. "You want your juice? I just offered it to you and you rejected it, you little maniac. Fine. Go trash the puzzles in the living room again." Lorraine set Max to the floor and shrugged as he scampered off, then turned her attention back to Jill and her wife. "Look, I only caught the tail end of your conversation, but I'm guessing Maggie was bemoaning my godawful attitude since TravelBlot got sold off, and she was encouraging you to get the fuck out before those fuckwits do irreparable damage to your spirit too. Right?"

Jill looked sheepishly at Maggie, who chuckled. "Yeah, babe. Pretty much spot on." Maggie glanced back into the living room and muttered, "I can't believe Max still hasn't picked up on the incessant F-bombs that have been hollered throughout this household over the past few weeks."

"Sorry. I know I promised to be more careful about my language around him." Lorraine gave Maggie a kiss on the cheek and returned her focus to Jill. "I'm telling you this as your friend and as someone who has been in the business world for over a decade longer than you: Get out. Now. The only reason I stayed for five months was because I wanted to make sure that our family wouldn't lose my paycheck. In retrospect, that was arrogant and stupid. We have emergency savings for a reason. I'm lucky Maggie didn't divorce my ass for being such an utter nightmare."

"I mean, all the extra Trader Joe's trips and daycare runs you took on, in exchange for my happy, vibrant, gorgeous boss of a wife? Close, but not quite worth it." Maggie and Lorraine shared a glance that made Jill's heart twinge. What must it be like to have that kind of bond with another human being?

"If I had known that picking up some frozen ravioli and pasta sauce was such a turn on, I would've stopped ordering Uber Eats every single night years ago."

"And if you had done that, we could both afford to retire by now," Maggie winked.

All three of them laughed; Lorraine's affinity for ordering delivery, even when the restaurant of choice was a four-minute walk away, had been an ongoing joke around the TravelBlot offices as well.

"We're digressing from the matter at hand, though," Lorraine continued. "I'll say my piece one last time, since I won't be around Ingentis to say it to you in person anymore. Thank God. There's a reason why all of our best people fled as soon as the merger was announced. Or if they have families or other ties to Boston, and the job market for their specialty is rough in this city, then that's why we've had the stragglers who are leaving as soon as it's feasible. But you, Jill? You were one of the best employees, full stop, at TravelBlot. I've seen your résumé. And there doesn't seem to be any reason that you need to remain in Boston, much less at Ingentis. No kids, no mortgage, no older relatives to care for, no one you're dating, unless something has changed in the past two weeks, right? So the only reason I can think of that you wouldn't have left behind this shithole joke of a company and all of the morons there who regularly undermine and denigrate you to prop themselves up, is either because you don't know any better or because you think you don't deserve any better.

"That's not a dig on you. When I was in my mid-twenties, I didn't know my own worth and I didn't have any mentors to steer me in the right direction. If anything, it was the opposite. At my first job, the older female partners had been so ingrained with the mentality that there was only room for one woman at a time in the boys' club, that they viewed me as a threat and went out of their way to make me miserable. This one woman I was assigned to work for could have been an amazing role model, but instead she sabotaged my projects, berated me in front of other attorneys for things I had no control over, and told co-counsel that my incompetence was the reason she missed her deadlines. She said that she'd never recommend me for a promotion because, among my many other flaws, my 'frizzy hair' was 'unprofessional' and she couldn't trust me not to embarrass the firm if I interacted with clients. It's hard not to internalize that stuff when you're subjected to it day after day by an authority figure. I don't think

I fully appreciated how toxic it all was until I had been out of that environment for two or three years. And I see all the same manipulative, gaslighting bullshit, just in a slightly different form, at Ingentis.

"But Jill, you're fucking brilliant. You could've been a killer attorney, although damned if I'd advise anyone else to go into my sinking forty-year depressive episode of a profession. You could get a job anywhere. Anyone who worked at TravelBlot would recommend you. Anyone with any connection to, or even awareness of, MIT would hire you on the spot. Ingentis enjoys having someone like you on its employee roster, and upper management will leave you there indefinitely without you having to do a damned thing, but they'll never appreciate you for all you have to offer. They'll never let you challenge yourself, much less push their own corporate boundaries, because that's simply not what an organization like Ingentis Holdings is designed to do.

"And you could see the change in me, right? I know we bicker about work stuff and politics and the Bruins, but I also know that you're too polite to call me out on anything truly personal. Which is why I know that, despite the fact that you haven't said anything, you've seen me develop the world's shortest fuse over the past three months. You've seen me suffer and become insufferable. Fuck, I can barely suppress my rage thinking about it even now! But I'm going to be less delicate with you than you've been with me. Bluntly, Jill, I've seen you change too. When I first told Maggie about you, I said you were a blond Sydney Bristow. Like, from the TV show *Alias*? With Jennifer Garner and her perfectly sculpted arms playing a super-spy who kicks ass and speaks a dozen languages? Oh for fuck's sake, you have no idea what I'm talking about. I'm really showing my age now, aren't I?"

Jill shrugged and glanced at Maggie, who was cutting up carrot sticks with a slight smirk and purposely avoiding eye contact with either Jill or Lorraine. Lorraine threw her hands up and continued.

"Anyway, the point is that, you are ferociously smart. You have this uncanny ability to develop a solution to any problem with whatever limited resources are available, even when the issue is outside of your area of responsibility or expertise. Plus, physically you're so ridiculously strong and fit and so beautiful, and kind of mysterious, that we joked that you basically must be a television superhero character come to life.

"And Ingentis will stomp that out of you. Maybe subtly, maybe shamelessly, but I promise you, I'd wager my life savings on it, that sooner or later they will curb-stomp that super-spy, superstar, something special out of you. And their preference is for sooner. They have to. There's no room for variance in a machine, even if it would otherwise be a drastic improvement. The machine relies on regression to the mean. The machine needs you to be mediocre and complacent and compliant so that you don't disturb any of the other peons from their own mediocrity and complacency and compliance.

"Don't look so hurt! You're still beautiful. You're still in such stupidly good shape that it defies the comprehension of my gloriously thick ass. A few months of their brainwashing analgesic bullshit isn't enough to dismantle your natural intelligence or undo the past quarter century of knowledge and experience you've gained. Those parts of you haven't changed. But I can see them dimming your spark. You can fight against it all you want, but you can't beat the machine when you're beholden to it for your livelihood."

"I'm trying to play their own game against them," Jill said dispassionately. She wasn't defensive. Not really. She didn't like what Lorraine was saying, but that was primarily because she feared that everything Lorraine was saying was true. Otherwise, she felt emotionally numbed. "They'll keep giving me my paycheck and I'll keep showing up and working on my consulting gigs or my latest software project whenever I can, between whatever menial task or false crisis I'm supposed to handle that day. It's easy for me to tune out the nastiness and melodrama on the floor. And Maggie will tell you, I can glaze the shit out of a vase now. I never had the time or energy for a weekend hobby while we were at TravelBlot, or even when I was at MIT, for that matter."

"And that's worth it to you? You're willing to trade your career and your potential, so you can paint some abstract designs onto a fucking pot every Sunday?"

"Jesus, Lorraine," Maggie interjected. "Ease up."

"No," Lorraine replied. "No, I won't ease up. Look, Maggie has texted me pics of your pottery. It's actually fucking awesome. Half the shit you make looks like it could be in a modern art museum, and it would be a part of the five percent of exhibits that I don't gripe about my wife making us go see. It is yet another thing you are good at. Which is the point. It is literally my entire fucking point and the reason I won't ease up. If you told me you were going to quit Ingentis tomorrow, just flip them the double bird and kick over a few cubicles on the way out, to pursue a career as a full-time fucking POTTER, I would hand-to-God have more confidence in your financial and emotional future than if you were to tell me you were planning on staying with Ingentis indefinitely.

"Because they will kill you. Bit by bit, slight by slight, unconscionable idiotic decision by unconscionable idiotic mother-fucking decision, they will kill you. They will promise you the world and they will never deliver. They will say they'll reconsider when the next quarter's numbers come in. They will say that your promotion fell through because the sales team didn't hit their account goals last year, or because share values fell unexpectedly, or because your performance review numbers weren't up to par, even though they won't give you any insight as to what specifically you need to improve, and it wouldn't matter even if they did. It will be an endless litany of false promises and cheap excuses for the rest of your career, and it will never change."

"Why don't we open the Macallan 18?" Maggie suggested. "I don't trust that it will survive the move, and I'd rather enjoy a little of it now in case the bottle breaks."

"Yes, let's open the fucking Macallan. And yes, babe, I hear your completely unsubtle hint. Let me say one more thing to Jill, and then we can enjoy our scotch in celebration of the good things to come. Rather than in unmitigated fury over the current reality imposed upon us when TravelBlot was sold." Lorraine paused to

191

peek her head into the adjoining room and check on Max, who was happily playing with his train set. Maggie had taken three tumblers out of the cupboard and was pouring them four fingers of whiskey each. Lorraine grabbed the first glass, took a swig, smiled, and then sighed. "I am ashamed of myself for staying for over four months. Literally, ashamed. The last time this happened, I said 'never again.' I swore I'd learn from my mistakes. This was back when I was a baby attorney, before I'd even met Maggie. And I stuck with the fucking Big Law equivalent of Ingentis because I didn't want to be a quitter. Or because the status quo was easier. Or because I was afraid, probably justifiably, that one of the firm's evil psychopath partners would have me blacklisted throughout the Boston legal community and it would've cost me five grand to break my lease and move to another city. I was too junior to apply for reciprocity and I didn't want to retake the bar in another state.

"Fuck whatever my reasons were. Fuck them. They were excuses. And they were a mistake. I allowed them to beat me down to a shell of my former self for over two years. And when I finally got out, after that fog of misery finally lifted, I swore on everything I held sacred that I'd never allow myself to be in that position again. Fast forward to now, when for twenty weeks straight, I betrayed that promise.

"And all the fucking fury that both of you have seen, that both of you have dealt with in a way that is far more than I deserve? I hope you understand that it is fury with myself. Fury and shame. And Jill, if I'm being hard on you now, it is only because I don't want you to come to this same realization a year from now, or five years from now. Or, God forbid, I don't want you to get so sucked into their horseshit that you stop realizing how fucked up it is and how much more you deserve, and you never escape."

Lorraine paused to take another sip of her Macallan.

"Rocks, honey?" Maggie asked stoically.

Jill snickered. A bright smile immediately crept onto Maggie's face as well. Lorraine tossed her head back and laughed.

"No, I do not want any ice." Lorraine feigned an irritated look, which quickly transformed into more laughter. "Fine. Point taken. If you weren't so damn beautiful, Maggie, I might be

192

mad." Lorraine and Maggie shared another glance that, again, Jill couldn't help envying.

A crash came from the living room, followed by mischievous giggles. Neither Lorraine nor Maggie seemed particularly concerned.

"I suppose we should go check on him," Lorraine said after a pause and another sip of scotch. "I'm guessing he got into the packing materials again. We could have saved on a few thousand dollars' worth of toys and puzzles and games for the kid if we had known he'd be happiest with some empty boxes and a few sheets of bubblewrap."

"You've got to get in a picture with him, Jill," Maggie added. "What's your SnapChat handle?"

"Oh, you can just text it to me," Jill said as they picked up their glasses and started walking toward the living room. "I don't have a SnapChat account."

"Your Instagram?" Maggie asked. "Actually, now that I think about it, I don't think we're friends on Facebook either."

"No. I know I'm a weirdo, but I don't have any social media. I mean, I guess technically you could count the dummy accounts I set up for UX testing at work, but that's just to check platform compatibility. I forget their login information all the time." Jill shrugged. It wasn't a lie, and she certainly wasn't about to suggest that Maggie send Farhad Razavi a friend request.

"Ugh, no wonder you two get along so well! Lorraine is against all that stuff too. I don't know how you survive without it."

"We thrive because we *are* without it," Lorraine muttered. Maggie raised an eyebrow. "Not that I'm judging!" Lorraine added more loudly. "Just because we've decided not to give away our private data in exchange for the dubious privilege of posting selfies with cartoon dog ears doctored onto them, doesn't make us better people."

"Doesn't it, though?" Maggie replied dryly. Jill snickered again.

"Whose side are you on, superwoman?" Lorraine exclaimed, grinning at Jill. "Come on, Max adores you. Let us take a couple pictures of you with him in his fort. We need something to remember you by. We'll print off the best one and send you a hard copy. Aw, Maggie, I bet she's too young to remember when that was the only way to view photos."

"I think I remember my great-grandmother mentioning something about it," Jill deadpanned.

"She's got jokes!" Maggie laughed.

Jill plopped to the ground by Max's side, in between two empty cardboard boxes, the scattered pieces of an overturned puzzle, and a toppled stack of blocks. "This is a cool fort, buddy," she said. "Can you give me a tour of the property?"

Max nodded his head and grabbed Jill's hand. Jill glanced up at Maggie, who had her phone at the ready. Jill smiled.

"Nailed it!" Maggie said. She tilted her phone to show Lorraine. "Look, babe. The second one is perfect. This is going on our mantel in the new place. Jill, we'll be sending this to you in a nice picture frame. Special delivery from Idaho. Assuming the postal service operates all the way out there."

"Oh for fu— for fudge's sake, we will be in Boise! It is a decent-sized city!"

Jill forced a laugh. Lorraine and Maggie were the only friends she had in Boston, and they were moving on. They would be gone so soon that there wasn't enough time left to print off a picture. What was she going to do without them?

CHAPTER FOURTEEN
Amanda Wagner

The fourth time that Eddie Medina called the Green Resources Alliance Foundation, it was a fluke that Amanda picked up the phone. At that time of day, Amanda usually was sitting cross-legged on the floor, rummaging through manila folders of paperwork from the early 2000s, or bent over a scanner, digitizing whichever documents she guessed her supervisors might deem important enough to save. But that Wednesday, almost everyone on her floor had left the office to participate in a demonstration near the Capitol building, leaving Amanda behind to answer the phone—although she had been sternly instructed not to say or do anything other than emphasize that the senior members of her work group were "on the streets, engaging in political activism in support of the environment," gather the caller's contact information, and state that the appropriate person would be in touch promptly upon their return from the protest.

"Y'all do realize that Congress is out of session right now, correct?" Eddie replied politely, but with more than a hint of amusement, to Amanda's mechanical recitation of her scripted lines. "As I mentioned, I'm calling on behalf of Representative Elizabeth Gable of West Virginia's Second District, but she isn't in town at the moment. Almost everyone in Congress will be back in their respective home district for the next week or so."

"So my coworkers are protesting to no one?" Amanda was barely able to stifle her mirth. "I mean, at least not to any legislators? Because that's why they were so adamant about doing this in front of the Capitol building."

"Well, I suppose word of the demonstration could still get to them if it hits the national news," Eddie said. "What media outlets have you contacted?"

"To be honest, I'm not sure if they notified any old-school media. When I suggested it in the past, they told me that Boomers are the only ones who read newspapers or watch the news on network TV."

"But that's precisely the demographic they should be trying to reach."

"That's what I said! Almost word-for-word, that's what I told them!" Amanda knew her glee was unprofessional, but she felt vindicated. Maybe her ideas weren't so dumb after all. "But I think they focused exclusively on promoting it on social media. Someone might have churned out half a draft of a press release, but I'm pretty sure they never made it to the 'releasing' step."

Eddie was laughing, and Amanda began to worry that she had overstepped. She had been on the phone with this guy—a person who had introduced himself as a congresswoman's deputy chief of staff at the start of the call—for less than two minutes, and she was being as casual and candid with him as she would have been with Irina or Jasmine. She leaned forward in her chair, her cheeks growing warm and lightly flushed, trying to think of a way to backpedal.

"You said your name is Amanda, right?" Eddie asked, as his laughter subsided. "You are delightful. I'd almost given up on reaching anyone who might be responsive to our overtures, but I'm glad I tried again. This is the most refreshing conversation I've had all week." Eddie started laughing again. Amanda had no idea how to reply. "Look, there isn't much I can do about the other four hundred thirty-four representatives in the House, but I'd be happy to pass along the news of the demonstration to Congresswoman Gable on your behalf. What would you say is your group's key message or goal today?"

Amanda hesitated. The others had spent a substantial portion of the previous workweek brainstorming hashtags and making signs, but the slogans lacked a consistent theme: "Friend, Not Food"; "Our Planet Is Getting Hotter Than Chris Hemsworth"; "Overthrow Big Oil"; "Destroy the Patriarchy, Not the Planet". Some of signs were, admittedly, kind of clever. Most of them showed a surprising amount of artistic skill, and the group seemed to have a great time making them. If Amanda hadn't been sorting through a mound of paperwork from 2008 at the time (pulling out the duplicates and, for reasons unbeknownst to her, rearranging the files by the date of the communication, rather than by subject matter, as some prior beleaguered intern seemed to have done), she might have held an idle hope that she'd be allowed to join in the fun. How could she distill all that into a single sentence or two that Eddie could pass along to his boss?

"Hey, Amanda? Are you still there?"

"Yes, of course! I'm sorry. I was thinking. The hashtags they wrote on the whiteboard before they left were #sustainability, #savetheplanet, and a random, less generic one. Oh yeah, #loveyourmotherearth. And they do #GRAFactivism for everything. I guess they are just trying to raise awareness again?"

"Awareness about anything specific, though?" Eddie pressed.

"Well... shit. Sorry! Pardon my language, jeez. Environmental justice, I think, is the best answer. They are raising awareness about the need for environmental justice," Amanda stammered. "I'm so sorry. You're not a plant, are you? Please tell me you're not secretly spying for them! They'd kill me if they knew how badly I am bungling this call."

"I really do work for Representative Gable, and I'm not a double agent," Eddie chuckled. "But may I offer you a nougat of advice? It might not be relevant to you personally yet, but perhaps it will be someday soon."

"Yes, please do!" Amanda said eagerly. The closest thing to any sort of mentorship or professional guidance she would receive since starting this internship (aside from the consistently helpful career insights she got from Irina) was going to be whatever this affable stranger on the phone might proffer. "I'm still a D.C. newbie and I'd appreciate hearing whatever you have to say."

"Your sincerity is great. Maybe sincerity isn't the word I'm looking for. Lack of smarminess? Lack of duplicity or lawyer-speak? I'm thirty-one, which isn't all that much older than I'm guessing you are, although it probably seems like it to you. Anyway, regardless of what I should be calling this quality, this town beat it out of me and nearly everyone else I know here ages ago. Depressing as that sounds. And is. Hang onto it as long as you can."

"Okay," Amanda squeaked.

"That wasn't my advice, though!" Eddie chortled. "Just an observation I couldn't resist making. My advice is that, if and when you are the person tasked with organizing one of these demonstrations, you need to have a clear objective that you can succinctly express to government officials and other thought-leaders and decision-makers, and you need to have a strategy to achieve your goal that extends far beyond a few hours of public protest. When you execute your strategy, you should be able to identify how the tactics you utilize—whether that's letter-writing campaigns, fundraisers, in-person meetings, or public demonstrations like your coworkers are trying to do today—will help you achieve meaningful progress toward that objective.

"Frankly, this is a personal pet peeve. Representative Gable is one of a handful of Republican congresspersons who truly wants to engage with the enviro community. But it's hard to be an ally when you focus all your energy on things that I'm sure are fun, and I'm sure they make for great social media posts, but they don't actually help your mission. You can't seem to articulate a single focused goal or message. Not you personally, Amanda. Not even your organization. Or at least, not exclusively. 'You' being an appalling percentage of the environmental activists and NGO workers I've had reason to interact with. This problem is ubiq-uitous, and it makes it politically impossible for Representative Gable to support you. Again, 'you' being the enviro community broadly, not you personally. Where would she even begin?"

"Yes, I understood your meaning. I didn't take any offense. The opposite. This is extremely helpful for me to hear. Thank you." Amanda meant it.

"As we've been talking, I've been scrolling through the results on Twitter and Instagram for the hashtags you gave me," Eddie continued. "Their results are lumped in with a bunch of random other stuff, but based on the timestamps, I think I'm looking at the right group. It looks like about forty or fifty people are out there today. That's not earth-shattering, but it's not bad, especially for a random Wednesday. I still can't figure out why they're demonstrating, though. It doesn't appear to have anything to do with environmentally sustainable agricultural and economic rural development, which is what we thought y'all focused on and was the impetus behind our reaching out to you. Even that's not a dealbreaker, strictly speaking; but this doesn't seem to be about *anything*.

"Look, if I could figure out how to say something specific, or even better, make it personal to Representative Gable's district or one of her initiatives, I would bring this to her attention immediately. I might even go out there myself to meet with one of the leaders. But this?" Eddie sighed. Amanda suspected he was still scrolling through his phone. "In most of these pictures, they're posing. With shit-eating grins. And the photos are filtered to unholy hell. For Pete's sake. That's not a problem in itself, necessarily, but with the lack of any clear point to you guys being out there today, it might as well be a photo shoot of them drinking wine in the park. It's a bunch of big kids skipping work to goof off. At least, that's what it looks like to me. And it will to every other staffer on the Hill too. What are they trying to achieve? What would they want from Representative Gable? What's the ask here? Specifically?"

Amanda wanted to cry. Tears of gratitude. Eddie—a total stranger up until a few minutes ago, and someone she had never met in person—had articulated a frustration that she had felt since her first week at GRAF, but which she hadn't known how to define, much less remedy. Her coworkers wanted to play "activist," the same way she had enjoyed playing "house" when she was in preschool. Even though she had fallen into this internship almost entirely by chance, she had started to care deeply about its high-level ideals, which was why it was so disturbing that she left work almost every day feeling more disgusted than energized or inspired. Rolling silverware at Ottimo usually felt more meaningful and productive than whatever she and her colleagues at GRAF had done to fritter away the day.

Eddie was waiting for a response. Amanda didn't want to be too effusive in her reply, but he *had* said that he appreciated her sincerity.

"That was probably the single most helpful thing anyone has said to me since I started here." Too much? Amanda exhaled and continued in a more subdued tone. "That probably sounds melodramatic, but what you just said explains so much about why I feel like, I don't know, like we're just going in circles sometimes. Most of the people here are genuinely passionate about the environment and want to make a difference, but even when it seems like we're doing important work in the moment, we always wind up in the same place we started. And part of me feels like maybe we shouldn't always blame it entirely on 'the government' or 'the capitalists' or on other people's ignorance or indifference. I'm just an intern, so what do I know, right? But hopefully someday I'll be in a position where I can help channel all that energy into, like, a straight line instead of circle. You know, so we can actually move forward."

"Yes, I follow the analogy."

"Right! So basically, I want you to know that I really heard what you just said to me. And thank you. After all, to make any real changes, we'd need to get congressional support, right? And who would know better what a congressperson wants to hear than their chief of staff?"

"Well, *deputy* chief of staff."

"Oh, right, deputy chief of staff. Either way, regardless of your exact title, your experience and your relationship with the congresswoman make me value your thoughts that much more, I guess. So, thank you!"

"Huh. Wow."

Amanda's heart sank. "I'm so sorry. Did I say something disrespectful? I promise it wasn't intentional. I was just babbling."

"No! No, no, not at all. This is your first job in Washington, right?"

"Yes. Technically, it's just an internship, part-time a few days a week."

"Okay. Well, I can't remember the last time anyone thanked me for my input. I can't remember the last time anyone from the other side of the political spectrum treated me like anything other than an enemy. Even people whose politics align with my own have a nasty habit of acting like I'm the main barrier to reaching Congresswoman Gable, rather than, you know, her trusted advisor who can facilitate a smooth and productive interaction on their behalf."

"That's bizarre. How short-sighted and obnoxious of them."

"Yes, indeed. It's both. Although I supposed that's the game I signed up for." Eddie paused and sighed. "I hate to wrap this up, but I have half a dozen more calls I need to make before my next meeting. Amanda, it truly has been a pleasure talking to you. Pass along the message that I called to your boss, but I'm going to give you my personal phone number as well. Call me directly if you need anything from me or Congresswoman Gable. That's an offer that will stand irrespective of whether or not your team wants to work with us and whether or not you remain with GRAF long-term."

Amanda jotted down Eddie's office number for her supervisor and plugged his personal cell number into her contacts list. After a split second of hesitation, she gave him her mobile number as well; nothing about their conversation up to that point made her think that he was fishing for a date or that he had some other sketchy ulterior motive that should induce her to keep her info private.

"I'll find you on LinkedIn as well," Eddie added. "Even if the meet-and-greet with your team doesn't work out, it doesn't change Representative Gable's desire for bipartisan collaboration on environmental matters or her interest in appealing to a younger demographic. I'm looking forward to telling her about our call."

Amanda hung up with Eddie, ecstatic. The next morning, however, when she told Stephanie and Braxton, the lead supervisor of GRAF's community outreach group, that Congresswoman Gable's office had called while they were out, they grilled her about whether she had disclosed any confidential information about their strategies to Eddie ("What strategies?" Amanda wondered), and were openly disdainful once she had assured them that she had not.

"All I told him was that you were leading a demonstration in front of the Capitol building. I gave him the event's hashtags. I figured that it was public information and, if anything, you'd want them to see it."

"Yeah, that's fine. Anything else?" Stephanie asked. Braxton let out a histrionic sigh, typed something on his phone, and wandered back to his desk without another word. Stephanie remained, hands on hips.

"Not really." A little white lie wouldn't hurt here. "I answered the phone the way you told me, and I was polite to him the entire time. I used the script you left me as much as possible."

"Okay. You don't need to be polite to him if he calls again. That guy is just a staffer, and besides, Gable is a Republican. I'm not sure why they'd reach out to us at all. How stupid."

"Really?" Thanks to almost a decade of experience dealing with obnoxious customers, Amanda had perfected the art of keeping her face expressionless and her tone even, but Stephanie, who had happily taken the lead in this particular debriefing even before Braxton had meandered away, was so haughty that it strained the limits of Amanda's composure. Amanda had assumed that Eddie might have been exaggerating about the way he was treated on previous calls, but apparently his assessment was spot on. "Couldn't a relationship with them be mutually beneficial? Doesn't West Virginia have rural communities that could benefit from environmentally friendly development practices?"

"Seriously, Amanda? You're an intern. Know your place." Stephanie started to walk away, then whipped around dramatically and stuck her finger in Amanda's face. "You sound like our executive director. Thank the Goddess that she is too far removed

202

from our day-to-day interactions to spread this kind of garbage any farther than her own office. Let me explain something to you. The facts are on our side. We are in the right. And real change is not something that can be negotiated away. Do you really think that a West Virginian, Republican congresswoman's office called because she wants to help us? Are you such a naïve little hillbilly? Compromise is not an option. They will see the truth and join us, or they will be left behind."

"How?"

"What?"

"How? How will they see the truth when we aren't even allowed to have a conversation with them?"

"What kind of a stupid question is that? You literally just said that you told what's-his-face that the reason why we weren't here is because we were staging a demonstration. You just told me that you gave him our hashtags. I don't even know what to say to you, Amanda. I don't have time for this. Rather than politicking for the Republican party, why don't you start reorganizing and digitizing the 2007 records. Or you can make a Starbucks run for the real activists here. Either way, go do your job."

Amanda watched in stunned silence as Stephanie stormed out. A year ago, she would have burst into tears. Now, the lump that briefly appeared in her throat was quickly overwhelmed by the desire to scream. Or to break into hysterical laughter, or to run through the office throwing the trash bins full of single-use coffee cups, plastic straws, half-eaten lunches, and crumbled printed-off (single-sided, of course) emails at every hypocrite in the building. The comments about being a "hillbilly" or a Republican apologist were too risible to be hurtful; she was a moderate Democrat from Connecticut, for heaven's sake!

She wanted to quit. She had wanted to quit a hundred separate times since she had started, but this moment was the closest she had ever come to following through with one of the elaborate "screw you!" scenarios she played out in her head every morning in the shower. But quitting would hurt her more than it would hurt any of them. Without this job, and without anything else lined up to replace it, she would be a full-time server. That hopeful hyphenate (student-bartender, intern-waitress) had always offered her the glimpse of a future beyond the restaurant industry. If she lost that, if waitressing became her entire identity, she wasn't sure she could ever get it back.

Besides, her share of rent was due in a week and they probably would make her pay back a portion of the stipend money if she quit.

Amanda resolved she would stay. She would stay to spite them; she would stay because there was still more she could learn about nonprofit operations; she would stay because she truly did want to save the planet; she would stay because she needed every extra cent she could get and, for as stingy as the stipend was (particularly given how hard she worked compared to the rest of them), she wasn't likely to make that much more money if she spent her time working the morning shift as a barista instead; and she would stay because this was the best chance she had at making some sort of connection with someone who could give her some sort of opportunity to do something that mattered. She didn't know who, or what, or how. She had no plan for that, and Stephanie and the others seemed, perhaps intentionally, to keep her from interacting with anyone important.

But she hadn't anticipated meeting Eddie either! She needed to be more strategic about building and maintaining those kinds of relationships. That seemed like a good first step. And maybe she could use some of GRAF's resources to start working on a project of her own. A small project, but one with a specific obtainable goal in mind, like Eddie had suggested. Amanda had no idea what this mini-undertaking should entail but, driven by a twisted combination of indignation and good intentions, she felt as inspired as she did overwhelmed.

CHAPTER FIFTEEN
Amanda Wagner

Amanda didn't speak with Eddie again until three weeks later. Braxton had reaffirmed (albeit in a much nicer tone) everything Stephanie had said to Amanda after he had left the room: Congresswoman Gable's office was a low priority and Amanda didn't need to bother calling them back to decline the invitation. They'd get the hint. Amanda left Eddie a voicemail anyway. She was disappointed when she didn't hear back from him right away, but she also was relieved to have more time to figure out what her mission should be and how she could impress him.

In the meantime, Amanda's responsibilities expanded to answering the community outreach group's main phone line every day over lunch, from approximately 11:00 a.m. to 1:30 p.m., plus whenever Claire, the office manager, was busy with another task. Amanda was thrilled with the opportunity to do something of practical value that didn't involve shuffling decades-old files from one drawer to another, and Claire had complimented her—twice!—on how well-organized and professional she was. Notwithstanding Stephanie's recommendation that Amanda be given "one of those wobbly old stools from the closet, or maybe she should just stand so she doesn't get your stuff all sticky," Claire even let Amanda sit behind her desk in her luxurious ergonomic chair while she was on phone duty!

And so, it was Amanda's cheerful voice that picked up the phone when Eddie called the community outreach group's extension again.

"I apologize it took me so long to return your voicemail," Eddie began. "I had some family stuff I needed to take care of. Actually, I've been back at my parents' house in West Virginia for the past two weeks."

"I didn't realize you were actually from West Virginia personally!" Amanda replied brightly.

"Oh! Yes! Born and raised. Do you have a connection to the state as well?"

"No, not really." She was excited to chat with Eddie again, but her initial reply was a bit overzealous for his offhand remark. She tried to recover. "I've been meaning to plan some hikes there along the Appalachian Trail or maybe in one of the state parks or something if you have any recommendations."

"Absolutely! I've always been more into hunting and fishing than nature walks, but I still have plenty of suggestions all over the state for daytrips. I had never traveled outside of West Virginia until I left for Yale."

"Really?"

"Actually, no, that's not true. We took a family vacation to Pennsylvania when I was a boy: Sesame Place, a tour of historic Philadelphia, and Hershey Park. Believe me, it was an eight-year-old's dream."

Amanda laughed. "My parents took me to Sesame Place and Hershey Park when I was about that age too! I still have the photos. Like, actual, real-life printed-off photos in frames."

"Me too! My pop is the quintessential gun-toting, pickup-truck-driving, tobacco-chewing, God- and America-loving redneck, and damn proud of it. He has a tattoo of a bald eagle carrying a flag-draped cross covering his entire right arm, for Pete's sake. But I've never seen him looking as happy as he is in the photo we have of him on an autumn day in the North, arm-in-arm with two giant smiling Hershey's Kisses."

"That sounds amazing! Please, you have to show me a copy of that photo someday."

"When I get to my apartment tonight, I'm going to take a picture of it and text it to you."

"I will forever be in your debt if you do."

"It must be the standard family vacation in this part of the country."

"Oh yeah, I meant to tell you when I saw you went to Yale on your LinkedIn profile. I grew up in Trumbull, in Connecticut! It's like thirty minutes away from New Haven."

"Ugh. I know exactly where it is. My college girlfriend used to make me drive her to the mall there on weekends sometimes. Most of the times. Suffice to say, that relationship didn't last."

"I mostly worked in restaurants while I was in high school, but a few of my close friends worked in that mall! I used to go distract them until their managers booted me out of the store. That's so weird. I wonder if our paths ever crossed."

"If you ever saw a tall blond guy in a tattered Mountaineers t-shirt lugging around a dozen shopping bags and looking like he was about to pull a fire alarm to get away from a hot redhead who wouldn't stop whining that her feet hurt? That was me. Jeez. The things a nineteen-year-old guy will do to get... never mind. Wow. Ignore me."

"Ha! You don't need to worry. Like I said, I've worked in restaurants and bars my whole life. Still do, actually. Pretty much nothing shocks or offends me anymore."

"Well, that's a relief."

"What, you thought that just because I work for an environmental organization, I must be another crybaby liberal snowflake?" Amanda asked playfully.

"No! Oh no, that's not—"

"Eddie. Dude. I'm teasing you."

Eddie chuckled, then quickly cleared his throat to try to cover his laughter. "You are always a pleasure, my dear Ms. Wagner. I really do apologize that no one got back to you to let you know where I was. One of the college interns was supposed to handle messages while I was away, but he's even younger than you are and I think he might have an actual phobia of talking on the phone.

As far as I can tell, not a single person received a call back from him, and only a handful of people received emails."

"Maybe he did try to contact me and the email got stuck in our spam filter?"

"I doubt it. You don't need to cover for him. He's not a bad kid. He's another Yalie from West Virginia, and his mom is a prominent doctor and a major donor in the Second District. He seems pretty sharp, but he's a lot more liberal than his mother, and apparently a lot less into networking and constituent outreach. He'd be a good policy wonk at a lib think tank, but our office isn't the right fit for him."

"Yeah, that can happen. I'd be lying if I pretended like I couldn't relate a little." Amanda doubted that Stephanie and Braxton were as generous as Eddie was being when they discussed Amanda's job performance.

"If we had any open positions whatsoever, I'd schedule you for an interview on the spot. Although maybe it's for the best. If our phone calls are any indication, we'd never get anything done."

"We'd both have a lot more fun at work, though!" Amanda glanced over her shoulders and lowered her voice. "I still have several more months left in this stage of my internship, but unless something incredible comes along and they'd be willing to cover whatever portion of my stipend I'd have to pay back, I'm going to tough it out. There are a few more things I want to accomplish here before either the internship ends or I resign and move on anyway."

Amanda didn't want to admit—either to Eddie or to herself— that this "something incredible" would have to materialize by magic or divine intervention. Other than occasionally scrolling through job listings on LinkedIn, Amanda hadn't put forth much effort into finding a new position over the past few weeks. First of all, for whatever complaints her coworkers may have had about her purported failings as an intern (and as a human being), Amanda knew they were far more resistant to the prospect of training a replacement, and they never would debase themselves by undertaking any of the clerical tasks that she handled. They may have devalued her contributions, but they couldn't deny that the work needed to be done. And Amanda was willing to do it for dirt cheap. Besides that, and perhaps more important in their decision-making process, Amanda suspected that they liked having her around as the designated outsider and a ready scapegoat.

Regardless of their reasoning, GRAF had already extended her internship for an additional twelve-month term, and Amanda was confident that, as long as she were willing to continue to accept an annual 0.8 percent increase in her stipend and another year of mooching off of her dad's health insurance plan, they'd keep her on staff indefinitely.

"So you're leading a big project at GRAF now?" Amanda snapped back to attention at the sound of Eddie's voice.

"Not exactly. It'll be more of an independent thing, although I think I'll be able to utilize some of GRAF's supplies and contacts or whatever if I need to." Amanda paused. She had been percolating on the idea of initiating some sort of small—very small!—environmental conservation or restoration project since she and Eddie had last spoken, but her progress had been exasperatingly slow. Every idea she generated seemed impractical for someone with her limited resources and experience, or redundant to projects being undertaken by other activists, or simply meaningless in the scheme of things. In a way, it gave her compassion for her coworkers' lack of cohesion and their misdirected zeal. Finding a way to effect change was, in turns, overwhelming, confusing, tedious, exhausting, and disheartening. It was hard! No wonder her colleagues preferred to make pretty posters in the conference room.

"So, are you going to elaborate on what this project is? Or is it a Top Secret Mission for now?" Eddie asked with a laugh.

"I think it ought to stay top secret for now, until I work out the details." Or even the basics, Amanda thought to herself. "I took what you said to heart. More than I think you could imagine. I don't want to waste your time blabbering until I have a clearly defined end goal in mind, and a step-by-step approach to how I'm going to get there. There's still a whole lot I need to pull together before my ideas are worth sharing."

"Well, I'm excited for you. Even though it's top secret, I'm looking forward to getting my security clearance and being read in." Eddie paused and groaned. "Ugh. I'll call myself out so you don't have to: that was an especially lame joke."

Amanda giggled. "Lame jokes, dad jokes, bad puns—I would accept all of them in exchange for your willingness to provide me five minutes of your input on how my approach could be improved once I have more of the details sorted."

"I'll tell you what: if you're willing to appease my ego and force a laugh whenever my jokes fall flat, I'll give you a whole hour's worth of advice. Write out your strategic plan and send it to me in advance, and we'll meet for a working lunch to discuss it. If you'd be up for that, of course."

"I would definitely be up for that, yes!" Amanda opened a new browser window and typed "how to write a strategic plan" into Google.

"Assuming that what you want to do isn't contrary to Representative Gable's interests," Eddie continued. "I should have said that first. She does want to broaden her appeal to younger, environmentally conscious constituents, but she isn't going to be amenable to me offering you advice if your plans run directly contrary to her platform or the interests of a major donor. She's a politician, that's just how it is."

"I understand," Amanda said. "I'm in a little bit of a similar situation. If we meet, it would be in a personal capacity. I won't be acting as a representative of GRAF. I mean, I guess who cares either way. It's not like I'm campaigning for the congresswoman or taking publicity photos with you or anything. But my supervisors would be furious if they knew I was discussing any kind of strategy with—"

"With an evil Republican?"

"Yes! With an evil Republican!" Amanda laughed and quickly lowered her voice. "Not all of them are like that here, though. I swear. It's just bad luck that I happen to work directly with the handful who instinctively hate anyone who isn't on the far left. Knowing that we get along would probably irritate them enough that they'd make me reorganize all the pre-2015 paper files for a third time."

"So, you're getting at the reason I called in the first place. I wanted to catch up with you, but I also wanted to confirm that lunch with Congresswoman Gable and your higher-ups is definitely a no-go?"

"Yeah, I'm sorry. Wait! Actually, you should try calling Heather Jenson! It's definitely a no-go for the group I work with, but she is basically the 'me' of a much higher level. She even works with the organization's board sometimes. I could give you her email or her direct line?"

"I appreciate it, but Heather is the one who originally connected me to your subgroup. I like her! She was pretty candid with me. She said that Community Outreach was my best shot and suggested I be 'persistent but not optimistic.' I got a kick out of that! Anyway, all things considered, I'm not disappointed. Even if a meet and greet with the congresswoman won't work out, at least you and I are getting a lunch date out of it." Eddie paused and cleared his throat. Amanda had pulled up his LinkedIn profile again while they were talking: he had the clean-cut, poised appearance of someone who had served in the military, with blue eyes and a professional but inviting half-smile, and even with his suit jacket on, Amanda could tell he was broad-chested and fit. He seemed like the type to rarely lose his composure, but in that moment she could sense him squirming on the other side of the line. She wondered if he had pulled up any of her pictures too. "Not a *date* date, I mean," Eddie continued. "Not that it would be inappropriate if I were asking you out. Or maybe it would be. But—"

"A lunch appointment?" Amanda offered, hiding her amusement at his sudden verbal clumsiness. "Maybe in two or three weeks, depending on your availability? I would suggest sooner, but I want to make sure I have enough time to prep a decent outline or presentation for you to consider."

"That sounds great. Since I was gone those two weeks, I'm playing catch-up now, so it might end up being closer to a month. But I'll send over a couple of days and times that I have free. I'd like to block off an hour or so on my calendar as soon as possible, otherwise something else will come up. I'm sure you understand how that goes."

"Yes, definitely." Amanda rolled her eyes at herself. She had no work-related engagements beyond showing up whenever and wherever she was told, and her social plans primarily consisted of spontaneous late nights drinking at one of the bars that were walking distance from Ottimo when she and Jasmine or Angie got cut early. Occasionally she got to enjoy low-key get-togethers with friends outside of the service industry who happened to be passing through Washington, D.C., but she had to coordinate those evenings weeks in advance and hope that Nick remembered she had requested time off when he was building the staff schedule. So yes, she vaguely understood Eddie's predicament, but for a totally different set of reasons. "Let me know whenever is convenient for you, and we'll go from there. I'm genuinely looking forward to it."

"As am I," Eddie replied. "Feel free to text me or email or whatever between now and then. You still have all my personal contact info, right?"

"Of course. And I'm counting on you to send me that picture of your dad with his sick tattoo and the dancing chocolate bars later tonight anyway."

"Ha! That's right. I won't forget. As always, it's been a pleasure, Amanda."

"Talk to you soon, Eddie."

After they disconnected, Amanda realized her cheeks were sore from grinning so hard. She couldn't decide if she was developing a crush on Eddie. Other than their phone calls, all she had to go on was a LinkedIn picture, and who knew how outdated that was. He was handsome, but not hot. Handsome like Jeff, but not hot like the random local musicians and bartenders she had been casually interested in since everything with Jeff had crumbled. Handsome in a way that was so polished that it made Amanda wary. That kind of seeming perfection was a deceit. The guys she was meeting at the bars after work were gritty, they were selfish, they were noncommittal, and they were all talking to a dozen different women in addition to Amanda—but at least they were honest about it. Jasmine had accused her of switching her taste in men from "rich preps" to "bad boys," but she was only half-correct; as far as Amanda could tell, all of the men in D.C. were bad boys, and she was simply focusing her attention on the ones who weren't perpetuating any illusions about it.

Amanda sighed. She had started absent-mindedly scrolling through one of the interchangeable "dating sucks" meme pages on Instagram. Post after post of lamentations, self-pity, misdirected anger, hopelessness. Amanda didn't even remember opening the app, much less consciously choosing to click on that account. She suddenly felt... icky. She was alone at her desk (which was actually Claire's desk) and alone in this world, trying to find comfort or commiseration in the pervasiveness of this empty, frustrated, loveless feeling, but these inane posts were only fomenting her bitterness and anger. It made her miserable, and it was entirely addictive.

She slammed her phone face down on the desk, harder than she intended. Immediately, she picked it back up to make sure she hadn't smashed the screen and then, out of sheer force of habit, unlocked it and opened Snapchat.

"What the actual fuck is wrong with me?" she muttered as she tossed the phone onto the desk again, with more exasperation than fury this time, turned back to her computer, and started scrolling through the results of her Google search on strategic business planning. Each link she clicked bombarded her with plenty of popup ads, irrelevant stock photos, and filler content, but offered none of the substantive details she needed to help her prepare for her meeting with Eddie. If she had been a finance or management major in college, would she know what to do already? Would any of these websites make sense to her? Or was business—as a concept and in practice—just more buzzwords and posturing?

After twenty minutes of clicking and skimming, Amanda had scribbled down a handful of notes into the moleskine journal she kept in her handbag. This was her first time opening it. Jeff always carried one around with him after starting law school, and Amanda had mimicked him because she thought it made her seem smarter and more prepared. It was exciting to finally have a reason to use it!

At the same time, rereading her notes was demoralizing. She had no marketing plan. She had no cash flow. She had no key performance indicators, whatever the hell those were supposed to be. She would be able to articulate a mission statement and organizational goals at some point, but not until she decided what idea or issue she was going to pursue, and even the finality of this most basic step was incapacitating. What if she chose wrong and ended up wasting her time (and Eddie's, and who knew how many other people's) pursuing something stupid or useless or counterproductive?

Amanda blushed. Since her first conversation with Eddie, there had been moments in which she envisioned herself appearing on the cover of *Newsweek* magazine, with televised interviews on *The Tonight Show* and *Jimmy Kimmel* to follow, and the entire country hailing her as an environmentalist hero. What an absurd, childish fantasy. Amanda had been criticizing her coworkers for their lack of a coherent vision and their disjointed action, but now she understood: the problems were so numerous and so grand that anything they tried to accomplish beyond "raising awareness" was quite possibly futile. And Amanda didn't even know what she wanted to raise awareness about! If she hadn't thought of anything decent by the time Eddie emailed her with his availability for their lunch meeting, Amanda resolved, she would come up with an excuse to cancel completely.

That night, while Amanda was working at Ottimo, Eddie texted her the picture of his dad laughing with two giant Hershey's Kisses, as well as a second photo of his dad, two decades later, in a sleeveless tank standing next to Eddie and his brother. It looked like they had just returned from a hunting trip; all three were carrying rifles and wearing camouflage pants and boots. Eddie's brother, who was shirtless in the picture and heavily tattooed, had darker hair and a full beard. Eddie, with mussed hair and a scruffy face, was wearing a muddy t-shirt that showed off his muscular physique. Amanda smiled to herself. Eddie was handsome in his

LinkedIn picture, but in this photo, she had to admit it: he was pretty hot. She flashed her phone to Jasmine when they both were in the kitchen.

"Not bad for a bunch of white boys." Jasmine raised an eyebrow. "Not bad at all. Which one is yours?"

"None of them are mine!" Amanda laughed. "But I'm talking to the one on the right."

"The preppier redneck, of course." Jasmine grabbed the phone out of Amanda's hand and scrutinized the photo. "Yeah, he's not my type at all, but I can see why you like him. He's got a great body, at least. And he looks tall!"

"I don't like him that way!" Amanda protested. "He's just the only person who is nice to me at my other job."

"Well, that's a bunch of bullshit. I can tell by the dumbass grin on your face," Jasmine laughed. "You're lucky there's a table of management consultant pricks that I need to get back to, otherwise I'd really call you out right now." Jasmine handed the phone back to Amanda. "At least your boy has a nice shoulder tattoo," Jasmine called on her way out. "Maybe there's hope for the both of you yet."

Amanda zoomed in on Eddie's shoulders and squinted. Jasmine was right. Amanda could see the outline of some sort of tattoo under his t-shirt. She smiled and thought about how to reply.

It Meeeeeee😀😳: Thank you! At the restaurant right now and this made my whole shift better. Your dad is a boss.

It Meeeeeee😀😳:Btw, what is your tattoo?

Whenever she had a moment away from her customers, she checked her phone. Ten minutes later, Eddie had texted her back.

Eddie M (WORK!): Hey, you were only supposed to zoom in on my dad. Not me. Haha.

Eddie M (WORK!): It's an Army star with some personal in memoriam stuff. I got it after my first four years of active duty were up.

Eddie M (WORK!): No regrets.

Amanda couldn't tell whether he was annoyed by the question or just being matter-of-fact.

It Meeeeeee😊😳: That's cool!! I was just curious. No tattoos for me yet. I'd want to get one that's personally meaningful like yours.😊

Amanda did a lap around the restaurant, refilling her tables' water and checking if they needed anything. About five minutes had passed but Eddie still hadn't replied. Amanda went to the kitchen with an idea. Most of the guys were goofing around and enjoying the relatively slow night.

"Hey, Arturo!" Amanda tapped one of the line cooks on the shoulder. "Yo poder... um, ver a tus, um, tattoo, por favor? And hacer pictura?"

"Oh, mi flaquita, porfa pídale a Jasmine to help with Spanish next time!" Arturo laughed. "What are you asking? You want to make painting of my tattoos?"

"Ugh, I'm trying to do better!" Amanda laughed too. "At least I know the Spanish names for most of our food now! And the best cusswords."

"Okay, princesa." Arturo glanced dubiously at the head of lettuce he was holding and tossed it onto the counter, giving Amanda his full attention. "What do you need?"

"The tattoo you got after you got your green card. Can I take a picture of it?"

"Sí, pero por qué? Why?"

"Just to show to my friend. We're talking about cool patriotic tattoos and yours is perfect."

Arturo, looking vaguely flattered, shrugged, took off his white coat, and rolled up the sleeve of his black t-shirt to reveal a colorful and intricately detailed tattoo of the U.S. and Honduran flags intertwined, with a bald eagle and a white-tailed deer nobly posed on each side. Amanda quickly snapped a photo, which she showed to Arturo, who nodded his approval.

"It's really badass, Arturo. Oh! 'Es muy chingón,' right? And it's because the deer is the national animal for Honduras? I just want to explain it correctly."

"Yes, you understand it! My two countries, like two sons, I love equally." Arturo shrugged again and put his coat back on with a little smile.

"You are the best! I have to get back to work before Nick catches me slacking, but thank you!"

Arturo said something to her in Spanish as she walked back to the floor, but Amanda's attention already had been diverted back to her phone. Eddie still hadn't texted her back, but now she had a good reason to send him another message.

It Meeeeeee😇🤓: P.S. Speaking of patriotic tats, check out my coworker's. Not quite as epic as your dad's but a nice combo of US/ Honduras pride.

She attached the photo of Arturo's tattoo and hit the send button. Then she reread her text and immediately followed up with one more line.

It Meeeeeee😇🤓: He got it in celebration of his green card!

Amanda cringed. She had added that last bit because Eddie was a Republican and she didn't want him... what? Calling in an ICE raid because she had mentioned one of the cooks at her restaurant was originally from a Latin American country? Eddie hadn't said or done anything that should've led Amanda to suspect he was racist or anti-immigrant. She didn't remember judging others so harshly based on their political affiliations before she moved to Washington, and particularly not anyone who was as kind and supportive as Eddie had been to her so far. She tried to think of a goofy follow-up message she could send so he wouldn't misinterpret her remarks, but she could see that her six-top was flagging her over. By the time she brought them their bill and had the chance to check her phone again, she had two new messages.

Eddie M (WORK!): I like that a lot! Artist did great work. Cool way to commemorate a huge life event for the guy too.

Eddie M (WORK!): Didn't mean to bother you at work though. I don't know how you do it with the multiple jobs.

Amanda read their exchange up to that point twice before deciding how to reply.

It Meeeeeee😇😳: You're definitely not bothering me.😊 Esp b/c it's a pretty slow night.

It Meeeeeee😇😳: And btw, GRAF isn't even full-time for me. I don't know if you knew that. If you call there and no one answers, it's not b/c I'm dodging your calls haha.

Eddie M (WORK!): I'm still impressed. With your top secret project on the side too, I don't know how you find the time.

Was getting hammered after work that night and confessing to Eddie via text (or even better, via a slurred voicemail) that she had absolutely no idea what she was doing—not only with respect to her still-completely-hypothetical activism project but with her entire life—a viable option here? If letting him down, and letting herself down, was inevitable, wasn't it better to just get it over with? Because she had no idea how else to reply to his text, other than with a meaningless scramble of random emojis.

Eddie M (WORK!): One more thing, then I'll stop distracting you at your job…

Eddie M (WORK!): Actually, it'd probably be easier to call you if that's okay?

It Meeeeeee😇😳: Sure. Looks like I'll probably get cut around 10 tonight, but maybe later, so maybe tomorrow is better?

It Meeeeeee😇😳: I could take a break now though if it's an emergency!

Eddie M (WORK!): It's not urgent at all. It's about a land conservation question in Rep Gable's district. I'd be interested in your thoughts.

It Meeeeeee😇😳: Don't get your hopes up about how helpful I'll be.😉 But let's talk about it for sure.

Eddie M (WORK!): Don't sell yourself short. If your schedule wasn't already so packed, I'd ask for your direct involvement with this thing. But will settle for your input.

Why was he being so nice? Jasmine and Angie would say that he wanted to sleep with her. And Jasmine surely would add that Amanda wanted to sleep with him too. To be fair, they did have a lot of chemistry on the phone. And it was entirely possible (even probable?) that he had looked up Amanda's various social media profiles, just as she had tried to look up all of his.

Amanda opened her Instagram account and skimmed through the first eight or ten rows of her pictures. Did she really think that Eddie would fall in love with her based off a smattering of random gym selfies and pics of her and Jasmine goofing around in the break room? Then again, it wasn't like she had any sort of social status or political influence, and she had even less money and experience, so what else possibly could motivate him to want to help her? Or even more bizarrely, to ask her for help?

Amanda made a conscious decision to give Eddie the benefit of the doubt. His motivations were probably innocuous, possibly even selfless. He was a military man, after all; that probably meant that his actions were driven by a sense of duty and honor, right? And if all this attention did turn out to be because he wanted to sleep with her? Well, he wasn't being a creep about it, he wasn't in a position of power over her, and she wasn't under any obligation to him either way. Plus, he was, admittedly, kind of hot. She had nothing to lose.

It Meeeeeee☺☺: That's sounds good. And if I can help, I want to! I'll be at the GRAF office tomorrow. Call me whenever. Use this number tho. Our chat will probably be the most productive thing I do all day.☺

Amanda stuck her phone into her pants pocket and tried to focus on work. The broad smile with which she greeted her tables for the rest of the night was, for a change, genuine.

CHAPTER SIXTEEN
Amanda Wagner

Eight months had passed since the first time Eddie had texted Amanda. Amanda had long since deleted the picture of Arturo's tattoo, but she still kept the photo of Eddie with his brother and dad saved to her phone. It was her only photo of him. Contrary to popular belief, she and Eddie were not dating or hooking up or involved in any sort of romantic or sexual way.

Jasmine was half-convinced that this was bullshit and that Amanda just didn't want to confess to fucking a Republican. Angie was more generous, conceding that perhaps nothing had happened yet, but adding that the two of them were wasting time they could be spending naked together, and that Amanda ought to jump on the opportunity ("literally, if you have to") before their chemistry started to fade. Irina thought Eddie sounded like a great catch, and even Marta—who finally had found herself a radiologist sixteen years her senior, who apparently was as anxious as she was to check "marriage" off his to-do list—preached to Amanda about the importance of getting into a stable relationship with a good man like Eddie before she got any older.

But they really were just friends! Friends, collaborators, business allies, and confidants, but not romantic partners. To be fair, Amanda had imagined what it would be like if they both had too many drinks one night and wound up in bed together. She would never admit that aloud to anyone, of course, but would it really be that outlandish of a confession? She had thought about what it would be like to hook up with at least half of the mildly attractive men and more than a handful of the women at GRAF, and she hated most of them! It was a function of proximity, nothing more.

Besides—and again, contrary to what nearly everyone around her assumed—most of her conversations with Eddie were professional. Or, at least, their primary focus was professional, even if they did tend to meander off into sharing their frustrations with their respective jobs, or grousing about the D.C. dating scene, or talking about their weekend plans. But that only further proved Amanda's point that their relationship was platonic! Why else would Eddie tell her about the often awkward and occasionally horrifying first dates he went on, unless he viewed Amanda simply as a gal pal who could offer a woman's perspective on why his OkCupid matches, who were charming and put-together online, acted so bizarrely in person?

Amanda wouldn't have wanted to sully their bond even if he *were* interested in her. This was the first time in her life that she felt like she had any sort of direction, and it was the most content she could remember having felt in years. This, despite the fact that she had quit bartending at Breaking News and she was constantly worrying about whether she and Irina would be left homeless when Marta and her new boyfriend inevitably got engaged. Her financial stress had never been more pressing, her GRAF coworkers still hadn't accepted her into their inner circle (although they now seemed to have contented themselves with ignoring her, rather than actively insulting her), and she basically had given up on finding a boyfriend.

But somehow, it all seemed manageable now. She had stopped stalking Jeff's and Beth's social media accounts multiple times a day. In fact, she couldn't say with certainty whether or not they were still together, and for the most part, she didn't care. She hadn't googled Jill Torres's name in months, and now it seemed silly and pathetic that, less than a year prior, she genuinely had wanted to steal pictures of Jill's life and try to pass them off as her own. She had deleted her Twitter and TikTok accounts completely, and she was becoming evermore disciplined about limiting her Facebook, Instagram, and Snapchat use to promoting GRAF community outreach events or sharing other environmental news and updates.

Eddie had been the driving force behind initiating the land conservation project that was bringing the newfound structure and satisfaction to Amanda's life, and he had been indispensable in helping Amanda navigate the political landscape since. The morning after they had first exchanged texts while Amanda was mid-shift at Ottimo, Eddie called her as promised. As he explained it, an ongoing land dispute had arisen in the unincorporated territory outside of Martinsburg, the largest city in Berkeley County and a key constituency of West Virginia's Second District.

Eddie had grown up near Charleston, on the opposite side of West Virginia, but he had visited the contested parcel once, during the early months of his employment for Representative Gable, to attend a community cookout. The eighty-seven acres of land always had been dedicated for public use, and it was a reasonably popular local spot for mountain biking, trail running, and picnics. A quaint pond in the western corner had become a locally trendy location for wedding photos, while a mostly untouched segment of land near the southeastern end was a beloved meeting place for a large group of elderly birdwatchers. A local volunteer group did basic trail maintenance and litter pickup for the park, and they even had managed to raise a few thousand dollars to install security lights and waste bins in the parking area a few years prior.

The parcel generated no revenue for the county, but it operated at no cost to the taxpayers either. It was an unobtrusive and mostly unremarkable piece of land, existing outside of the conscious awareness of most residents of the surrounding areas, yet priceless to a non-negligible but unorganized few. Locals had referred to it as Octavia Park for years, although the name was never registered in the county's office of records, and the myriad explanations for its origin were riddled with speculation, myth, contradiction, and shameless factual inaccuracies.

Then, seemingly out of nowhere, Ansley Development Corp. proposed buying the land from the county in order to turn the plot into a strip mall. The story broke when a popular West Virginian blog, *Montani Semper Liberi*, posted an eleven-hundred-word article disclosing that plans were in the works for a Berkeley County shopping complex that would contain a Walmart (the county's fourth), a Payless Shoe Store, a credit union, a Cricket wireless outlet, an H&M, and a Jared diamond jeweler, together with ample parking spaces and at least two higher-end fast food outlets to be determined. Several potential locations for the construction site were suggested, but Octavia Park was said to be the front-runner.

Quickly, rumors abounded. Whether they were feigning ignorance or they had been excluded from some under-the-table dealings, several local government officials admitted (off the record or on condition of anonymity) that they had no idea how the parcel got onto Ansley's radar as a potential development site. Nevertheless, in order to sate the voracious press and stave off any further rumormongering, the county began to release more information about the proposal. As it happened, the blogger had reported nearly all the relevant details correctly, including that Octavia Park would be the locus of the complex.

Almost the entire parcel would have to be razed, although the developers conceded that the pond could remain on the outskirts, perhaps as a nice location for employees to have their smoke breaks. The development would bring jobs: construction jobs in the short term, and retail jobs in the longer term. The development would bring exciting stores to the community. Ansley Development Corp. made grandiose claims about how their investment would inject cash into the local economy and line the county's tax coffers, eventually leading to improvements in everything from roads to public schools. The county board was so impressed that they fast-tracked ADC's plans for approval, with ground-breaking planned for spring of the following year. If nothing else, the much-emphasized promise of an estimated 350 new construction jobs, plus another 300 retail positions to be created after the shopping center opened, would invigorate each council member's reelection bid.

Which was why the county board found the near-immediate opposition to the proposal so baffling. They initially dismissed the objections as the whining of environmentalist radicals or the manufactured complaints of their political opponents. But the concerns were coming from unexpected voices as well. The hunting and fishing communities were upset about the precedent that the county commission's aggressive action was setting. Local businesses from Martinsburg and other surrounding towns were divided; some anticipated that any increase in traffic in the area could improve their bottom line, while others worried that they wouldn't be able to compete with the big box outlets on prices, that the increased congestion would destroy the old-fashioned small town feel of their neighborhoods, and that Ansley Development Corp. lacked the strong roots in the Martinsburg area that would help ensure decisions would be made with the community's best interest at heart.

Since then, there had been several thoughtfully written letters to the editor in *The Journal* and *The Shepherdstown Chronicle*, as well as an influx of curse-laden vitriol in the respective comment sections of each newspaper's online edition. Several of Congresswoman Gable's constituents had called her office to express their concern about the matter, and her staff had promised them she would look into it. This task was promptly delegated to Eddie.

"The issue ultimately will be decided by the local county," Eddie said when he first called Amanda to explain the project. "And bluntly, Representative Gable's default position is pro-business, above almost all else, so we might need to pull back. But for now, she considers her limited involvement to be a politically safe way to endear herself to the environmental community and to a surprising number of elderly constituents. Obviously, it will align her with many of the small business owners in the Martinsburg area too, which could pay dividends when her reelection campaign gears up. She would frame her motives much differently, of course, but I feel like I can be candid with you."

"That makes sense," Amanda said. "But how would I be able to help?"

"That's really up to you," Eddie replied. "Since this is technically a Republican-led effort, you probably wouldn't bother suggesting to your directors that GRAF participate at an organizational level, correct?"

"Yeah, I'm sorry," Amanda said. "I know it seems like this is pretty closely aligned with the type of community outreach that would advance our mission, but there's no way that Braxton would sign off on it. Honestly, I don't think I'll mention my involvement to my supervisors here at all, unless they ask me a direct question about it. I wouldn't lie, but I don't need to broadcast it either. You know how some of them are. Does this mean I would be working for Congresswoman Gable?"

"Well, no, you wouldn't be on our payroll or formally report to her, if that's what you mean. This would be more like a collaborative effort. I'm still confirming that Gable is going to want to be involved in a meaningful way at all. I'm telling you about it now because it seems like the kind of thing that speaks to your interests and strengths, and I already know that I enjoy working with you. It would be a good platform for a first-time lead organizer."

"Wait, lead organizer? I don't know if I'm—"

"You are perfectly suited for this work and more than capable of carrying it to a successful completion. I don't want to pressure you. If this project doesn't appeal to you, or if you have too much on your plate already, or if you get to Martinsburg and decide that you don't click with the people or the place, or for literally any reason whatsoever, you are under no obligation to me or to anyone else. The only thing I cannot countenance is you writing yourself off for the role because you don't think you're experienced enough. Or whatever other reason you were about to give me before I so rudely cut you off a moment ago."

"But I'm really *not* experienced enough," Amanda replied with a nervous laugh. "Maybe I've learned a little about what not to do by watching my coworkers here. But I've never led anything before in my life."

"It's probably not my place to push you too hard out of your comfort zone. I mean, you seem like an old friend at this point, but I haven't forgotten that we've never met in person. Actually, why don't we change that? Let's sit down, have lunch, and I'll show you some pictures of the land and tell you what I know about the opposition to the development so far. From what I can tell, it's a lot of strong but disjointed individual voices, each with very valid reasons for wanting the land to remain as-is. If you want to focus your attention elsewhere after that, believe me, I won't take it personally! In fact, I'll do what I can to help you with whatever your alternative project is. But I thought I should mention this opportunity because it seemed like you were looking..."

"Looking for something meaningful to direct my attention toward?" Amanda jumped in as Eddie's voice trailed off. "Yes. Looking, but having a tough time finding it. So I hope I don't seem ungrateful. This already sounds like I'll have a better chance of making a tangible difference compared to anything I've come up with on my own so far. I just don't want to let you down. Or let down the people of Martinsburg!"

"I can do a better job of explaining all this in person. Are you free for lunch today?"

"They usually have me sit at Claire's desk to answer phones over lunch while everyone else is on break, but I don't think I'll get scolded if I leave for an hour or two today."

"Really?" Eddie sounded excited. "This was meant to be. My lunch appointment had to take a last-minute flight to Florida this morning, so my calendar unexpectedly opened up. We can use my existing reservation at The Monocle if you want: 12:30, table for two."

Amanda hesitated. She didn't want to admit that she could order nothing but a small salad and tap water from a place like that, and her budget would still tremble from the strain. Or that, while her cute-but-cheap pantsuit from Express might technically comply with the restaurant's dress code, it was unlikely to meet the other patrons' standards (to say nothing of the fact that she probably would have chosen a more flattering outfit if she had known that she'd be meeting Eddie in person for the first time that day).

As if reading her mind, Eddie continued, "I can expense it, so it'll be my treat, of course. But there are plenty of delis and diners convenient to both of us if you want to do something more casual or the time doesn't work for you or whatever. I have a hard stop at 2:00 p.m., but otherwise I'm flexible after 12:00 noon."

"Okay," Amanda said. She wasn't from West Virginia, she didn't know anyone other than Eddie from West Virginia, she couldn't remember whether or not she had so much as passed through West Virginia on her drive to D.C. from Indiana, and she had never organized anything more important than a surprise birthday party for Kiara during their sophomore year at U of E... but what did she have to lose by sitting down for a lunch? "Okay, I'm in. I'm honored that you'd choose me for your rare free lunch hour! I hope you don't end up feeling like this is a bad use of your cool reservation. But 12:30 at The Monocle would be great. I'll text you when I get there. See you soon!"

It was 11:05 a.m. when Amanda hung up the phone with Eddie. Including the three and a half hours she had spent watering plants and filling out personal paperwork for Braxton that morning, Amanda had worked twenty-three hours that week. Although contractually, she wasn't supposed to be in the office for (and wouldn't get paid for) more than twenty-five hours each week, Braxton had asked her to come in and set up conference rooms the next day as well. So, Amanda reasoned, she would be completely justified in sneaking out for lunch. If she left immediately, she'd have time to run back to the apartment, change into a more suitable outfit (befitting a nice lunch at a popular spot on the Hill, not because it was a date!), and freshen up her hair and makeup (because she wanted to make a good first impression on a new business contact, really, not because it was a date!). Unless Stephanie or one of the others was in a particularly foul mood and looking to take it out on Amanda, chances were that no one would notice or care that Amanda had left at all.

Amanda grabbed her purse, stood up, and glanced around the room, filled with a giddy sense of mischief that sent her mind back to a random spring day her senior year at U of E, when she and Kiara had caught each other's eye outside their Public Relations classroom door two minutes before the lecture was scheduled to begin.

"Ditch?" Kiara had asked.

"Ditch," Amanda agreed.

Shrieking and laughing, they bolted down the hallway together and spent the next four hours drinking Kiara's homemade sangria on a park bench, scanning the quad for subjects of a forty-round game of "fuck, marry, kill," and debating whether their impending graduation should be mourned or celebrated, until Amanda had to stagger off to her shift at Mojo's.

Mourned. Unequivocally. Graduation should have been mourned. Amanda used to loathe when her parents told her that college would be the best time of her life. If her life peaked at age twenty-two, then what the hell was the point of the next sixty years? But that afternoon with Kiara was the last time she had felt this sense of joyful spontaneity, and all she was doing was modestly shifting her work schedule so she could meet up with a congressional staffer for a business lunch. Maybe her parents had a valid point.

Amanda nearly plopped back into her office chair in defeat. She was the one who had insisted to Kiara that they were both destined for greater things, that the world outside Evansville would welcome them as queens. Kiara had been the skeptic. And yet, Kiara was now the one who had been dating the same handsome rich guy for over a year, and who was herself making bank as the manager of a high-end eyelash and brow boutique in Chicago. They hadn't texted in months, but Instagram and Snapchat told Amanda everything she needed to know. The contrast between her pre-graduation hopes and her post-graduation reality slaughtered the burst of enthusiasm she had felt mere moments before. Perhaps everyone would be better off if she texted Eddie right then to apologize and say "never mind."

Amanda had been hovering over the desk for several seconds now, and it would soon become conspicuous that she was up to something. Her own indecisiveness grated at her. The obvious solution was to act—preferably to walk out the door immediately, but resolutely sitting back down and canceling lunch would be fine too, as long as she did so without further internal debate—but she was stymied by an inertia borne out of her constant sense of futility and inadequacy.

Her left knee buckled. Snippets of a coworker's insipid cell phone conversation vaguely entered her consciousness: "I think he's a Peloton instructor... way too much collagen in her upper lip... no, but her dad's really well-connected at the DoD...."

There had to be something more for her than this.

Amanda draped her jacket over the chair as if to say, "I'll only be gone for a moment, not even leaving the building," and walked quickly toward the exit, holding her head down to avoid eye contact with anyone who might halt her path.

When Amanda arrived in the lobby of The Monocle, she congratulated herself on having had the good sense to stop back at the condo to change her clothes and freshen up her makeup before meeting Eddie. Her new outfit—a form-fitting navy blue pencil skirt with dark yellow pinstripes and a crisp white blouse from Banana Republic—was almost certainly the least expensive ensemble in the room, but it was a timeless style that highlighted her figure without being overt that this was her intention. She undid her top button to show off a simple silver necklace and just a hint of skin, which she hoped would suffice to divert attention away from her basic nude pumps, which she had purchased on clearance from DSW almost two years prior. As anticipated, almost every woman who crossed her path, including several members of the wait staff, was wearing designer heels.

She was inexplicably nervous. She had worked in high-end restaurants since she was a teenager, so notwithstanding her inferior footwear, it wasn't because she was uncomfortable in the fancy setting, per se. Nor could she attribute it to meeting Eddie in person for the first time; she had agreed to (ill-fated) drinks with strangers she had met off Tinder with less trepidation, and she and Eddie had already established a rapport on the phone. She wouldn't have to impress a congresswoman (at least, not directly and not yet), and Eddie couldn't possibly expect her to be prepared to contribute much to a discussion about a random parcel of land in West Virginia, the existence of which she had learned about two hours prior. There was no need to be anxious about the prospect of politely listening and formulating a few reasonably intelligent questions.

"Pardon me, is your name Amanda?"

Amanda turned to her left. Unlike the majority of her Tinder matches, Eddie looked exactly like Amanda expected based on his pictures. Indeed, if anything, he was taller and fitter than Amanda had realized, and more attractive in person. His charcoal grey, lightweight Italian wool suit was tailored perfectly to his silhouette, his shoes were shined to perfection, his pocket square was folded with military precision, and his gold watch projected importance and wealth without being ostentatious. Thank goodness she had rushed home to change her outfit and redo her makeup! And even still, the other patrons probably were wondering what someone like her was doing there with someone like him.

"I am! Yes, you must be Eddie." Amanda hoped the extra layer of powder she had dusted onto her skin would conceal how hard she was blushing. "It's so great to finally meet in person."

"We do feel like old friends after so many phone calls, don't we?" Eddie said affably. "The pleasure is truly mine. I'm flattered you'd throw your whole schedule into disarray to meet me for a last-minute lunch. You haven't been waiting long, I hope?"

"Oh no, not at all. I just arrived. Your timing is perfect. I hadn't even had the chance to text you yet."

"Fantastic. It's 12:30 on the dot. Shall we sit?"

Amanda nodded her head and dutifully followed behind Eddie while he approached the hostess's desk and an elegant brunette woman led them to their table. Eddie remained on his feet until Amanda had taken her seat. The last man to show her any such old-fashioned gesture of gentility was Jeff. She didn't miss that scumbag, but maybe she did miss his impeccable manners, maybe just a little.

Their server, Amanda noted with unspoken approval, allowed them the perfect amount of time to get situated and review the lunch menu before returning to take their order. Eddie chose the 107 Club Sandwich. The vegetarian pasta was tempting, but premonitions of herself slurping noodles off her plate like a savage or staining her blouse with tomato sauce preempted Amanda's appetite. She decided on a Greek salad.

Ottimo's food may have been of the same high caliber as The Monocle's, but it was a far different experience to dine in the midst of politicians and D.C. power players than it was to scarf down a staff meal in a corner of the kitchen. The conversation with Eddie flowed as easily as it always had over the phone, although Amanda couldn't shake the nagging sensation that she was obliviously committing some sort of social faux pas that marked her as an outsider to Eddie and everyone around them. After all, the rich kids at GRAF had immediately identified her as poor and uncultured (at least, relative to them), despite all her efforts to adapt her style to theirs and to comport with their behavioral norms.

After fifteen minutes of pleasantries, punctuated by four brief interruptions during which other classically handsome, well-dressed, poised men in their thirties approached their table to greet Eddie and exchange bits of Beltway gossip (and during which Eddie always made it a point to promptly introduce Amanda by her full name and to describe her as an up-and-comer in the nonprofit sector), Eddie finally shifted the conversation to the West Virginia project. He reiterated the basic facts he had set forth earlier that morning and handed her a small stack of photographs.

"I suppose I could have texted you these pictures," Eddie shrugged. "But there's something to be said for holding a photo in your hand. It makes it more real. At least, that strategy seems to work with our older constituents."

"It seems like a cool little spot," Amanda said as she shuffled through the pile. "It's pretty! I especially like the pond. I wish we had a park this size here, especially one that's relatively untouched. I'd go trail running a few times a week if we did."

"You should check out Rock Creek Park one of these weekends, if you haven't yet. It's worth battling the northbound traffic, which is saying a lot," Eddie said. "Anyway, what do you think? Octavia Park obviously isn't as spectacular as the Grand Canyon or Glacier National Park or whatever, but it's not trying to be. It's important to the local community, and that's enough for Congresswoman Gable to take notice."

"I think it would be a shame if this place were bulldozed for a strip mall. Are there seriously no other viable location options available for the developers?"

"You're thinking the right way. Part of this project almost certainly is going to involve proposals for alternative construction sites, but I personally haven't researched that component at all yet."

"So that would be one of my tasks, I suppose," Amanda mused noncommittally. She sighed and furrowed her brow. "Okay, I hope this isn't a stupid question, but are you sure they really want my help? Or need it? I would have thought that it'd piss off the locals to have a bunch of Washington, D.C. busybodies coming into their town, telling them what to do."

"You are *definitely* thinking the right way," Eddie smiled. "As a rule—and I say this as a proud son of West Virginia—you are absolutely right. Frankly, if you started randomly meddling in the Octavia Park issue while acting on behalf of GRAF or some other D.C.-based organization, or because you were a rich city-slicker with too much time on your hands, it would not play well. But Congresswoman Gable's constituents are actively reaching out to her, asking for her to intervene. One of them, in particular, is a woman named Julie Locklear-Rhodes, who I think you'll get along with if you want to move forward with this. Julie has been the de facto leader of the local movement to prevent the construction, and she's eager to have an experienced ally in Washington to help guide her through the process and alleviate some of the workload."

Amanda winced. She doubted that her coffee runs and menial office tasks at GRAF rendered her "experienced," but she held her tongue as Eddie continued.

"I haven't met Julie in person yet, but we've spoken on the phone twice and we've exchanged a few emails. Based on what you've told me, working with her will be a very different experience than what you're used to at GRAF."

"Well, that doesn't sound like a bad thing, but how so?"

"Julie is very efficient in everything she says and does. Some might call it abrupt or gruff, if they aren't used to her particular kind of temperament," Eddie chuckled. "She's a Navy veteran. She had an exceptional career serving as an aviation rescue swimmer."

Amanda had no idea what that meant, but she could tell that she was supposed to be impressed. She nodded enthusiastically and hoped her facial expression didn't give her away.

"She and her team flew helicopters out to sea and rescued troops from downed aircraft and capsized vessels. And they saved U.S. civilians who were trapped or in imminent danger because of natural disasters. Things like that. So she's highly proficient in project planning and logistics, and her ability to perform under pressure is off-the-charts. What she needs from us—from you, really—is help translating those fundamental skills directly to the context of an environmental conservation operation." Eddie paused and smiled absentmindedly, as if he were reflecting on an amusing anecdote this Julie woman had told him. His face grew more serious as he snapped back to attention. "Are you old enough to remember Hurricane Katrina?"

"Not really," Amanda admitted. "I was in elementary school when it happened and I didn't really understand what was going on. We learned about it again in high school though. I remember thinking that the pictures were horrifying."

"Well, she was part of that search-and-rescue effort. She got her Naval Aircrew wings a few months before it happened, and it set the course for the rest of her career."

"I mean, wow," Amanda stammered. "Just, wow. I can't imagine doing something that heroic. What an absolute badass!"

"Yes!" Eddie seemed pleased by Amanda's awed response. "She is a badass. I think she could be a great role model for you, if you're still looking for that. I know you've mentioned that you aren't getting the mentorship that you'd hoped for at GRAF. Julie probably would know better than anyone what it's like to feel like an outsider and to be dismissed by her peers, and to use that as fuel to succeed."

Amanda faced flashed blank.

"You know, because there still aren't nearly as many female aviation rescue swimmers in the Navy as there are male ones. Not even close. She had to meet all the same physical and performance standards as the men, and I'm sure most of her team respected her for it. But, and I hate to say it, there's always that one dipshit in every unit who thinks women don't belong in the military at all, and who will vocalize his idiotic opinion at any opportunity."

"Oh, of course," Amanda blushed. "Jeez, compared to the adversity she must have confronted, my whining about not fitting in or being respected at GRAF must seem stupid and childish. I'm sorry. Are you sure I'm the right person to work with someone like her? I won't annoy her by being too young and inexperienced? Or just too..."

"The only thing that will annoy her is if you keep selling yourself short and apologizing over nothing. I hope that doesn't sound harsh, but I think that's the reality here."

"Is she going to, like, bark orders at me?" Amanda mumbled meekly.

Eddie let out a deep, guttural laugh, which Amanda could tell was louder than he intended. He immediately controlled himself but was still chuckling when he responded. "No, no, no. She'll probably end up being more the 'face' of the project since she's the local leader, but there's a shared understanding that you'll be more like partners. She's not your boss or your supervisor. And she's not a drill sergeant! In fact, she's retired from the Navy now. Active duty until a few months ago, when she hit her twenty-year service mark. She joined when she was eighteen, so I guess that'd put her in her late-thirties now. She has two kids and she works as an EMT part-time. And she's taking a couple classes at Blue Ridge Community College."

"She sounds so impressive, it's intimidating."

"She is impressive, but you shouldn't be intimidated! She has zero experience with community organization or environmental matters, and no time to waste with ineffectual busywork. She's smart enough to know that she needed to start delegating responsibilities, so she asked us for help. Her criticisms about the local movement reminded me of some of the things you've said about

GRAF. She told me that their efforts so far have made a little bit of noise, and perhaps they've put up some interesting social media posts that make some of them feel important, but ultimately their activities aren't part of a broader strategic approach and none of it results in a lasting impact. That was what made me think you would get along."

Eddie paused. He looked like he had something more to say but was weighing whether he ought to proceed. Amanda pushed her salad around her plate and looked at him expectantly.

"Candidly," Eddie said after several seconds of silence, "I think she'll also appreciate that you care about health and fitness as much as she does. You like to run outside, you like to lift weights, you see the value in outdoor recreation. To be honest, she's not really motivated by environmental conservation concerns per se. I'm hoping and assuming that's not a dealbreaker for you, but I still want to be upfront about it. She's ticked off that they are going to eliminate a convenient, safe, well-loved place for the community to get some exercise and fresh air, and they're replacing it with, as she put it, 'yet another spot for us to waste our money and sit on our ever-expanding asses and eat crap.'"

Amanda laughed. "I'm not sure we'd want to frame it precisely that way to the broader public, but I have no objection to making this about something more than just saving the trees or whatever. Maybe it'd be useful to raise funds and build a playground or one of those cool outdoor fitness stations for adults on part of the property to make the park's value to the community more obvious. Maybe I can work behind the scenes to help unite the runners and mountain bikers with the local businesses who aren't thrilled that they'll have to start competing with a Walmart. Maybe there are older residents who don't want the area to change anymore from the small-town vibe they grew up with. Hell, I feel that way about Trumbull whenever I go back to visit my parents and see that another small business from my childhood is gone or another green space has been replaced with an apartment complex!"

Amanda looked at Eddie and returned his bright smile. She was embarrassed that she had allowed her trepidations about whether she was qualified for this role to turn her into a sniveling, insecure baby for the majority of their lunch so far. Eddie probably didn't appreciate having to constantly reassure her any more than Julie would. His entire face had lit up when she started sharing her own ideas, and the more she spoke them aloud to an encouraging audience (as compared to the dismissive eye rolls she received at GRAF), the more convinced she became that she was capable of helping to lead this endeavor. Amanda took a sip of water to calm her nervous excitement.

"Okay," she said. "I'd like to meet Julie, and I'd like to help. I think I can do this. I know I can do this!"

"I know you can, too. I wouldn't have asked otherwise. And you are okay with the fact that Gable's office can't pay you for your support? We can assist with expenses, but that's about it. I know it's obnoxious to ask you to work for free—"

"That's essentially what GRAF expects from me, so believe me, I'm used to it," Amanda interrupted.

"Don't get too used to it," Eddie advised. "I'm aware of my hypocrisy for saying this at the same time I'm telling you that we can't pay you, but your time and skills are valuable, Amanda. You should be compensated accordingly for them. What I can offer you, at least, is a promise that I'll set up a personal introduction with the congresswoman, and her office will be happy to provide you with a letter of reference whenever you need one."

"By 'her office,' do you mean handwritten by you, Eddie Medina?"

"Most likely, yes!" Eddie laughed. "I probably will be the one to write it, although you'd need to be a cryptologist to decipher my penmanship. But the letterhead of someone from Congress will hold some sway almost everywhere in this town." Eddie paused and smirked mischievously. "Even the letterhead of a Republican from my humble home state."

"That honestly would be fantastic. I've always known that I wouldn't work at GRAF forever, but I had hoped it'd at least give me some exposure to professional contacts or job leads. Somehow I've stuck it out for two years, but they still think of me as their lame, disposable chore monkey, to be kept hidden away in a broom closet whenever anyone important is around."

"That reminds me. You should put this venture on your résumé and LinkedIn as of today. You can call yourself "Lead Special Projects Liaison" as your job title. Google how to format it properly, or just send me a message when it's up if you want me to double-check. Even though technically you aren't on Gable's payroll, the employer line should still read something like 'U.S. House of Representatives, Representative Elizabeth Gable, WV-02.'"

"Seriously?" Amanda put down her water glass mid-sip. "I can write that I'm working for a congresswoman on my résumé and post it online?"

"Yes! I'm glad you're excited about that! I cleared it with her in advance, obviously. We have a system for documenting stuff like this, so if anyone calls in the future to do a reference or employment status check, we'll be able to confirm your relationship with us. Gable knows that offering a nice job title is a necessary precondition to getting anyone who is reasonably competent to do unpaid work for her office."

"Regardless, thank you for pressing for it. They only recently bumped me up from 'Titleless Intern' to 'Junior Staffer' at GRAF. I've tried to list out my responsibilities in the best way possible, so it will seem like I've gained some sort of transferable skill set from my time there, but being able to write that I've been—what did you call it, Lead Special Projects Liaison?—for a congresswoman will take my résumé to a whole new level."

"Let me ping you Julie's contact info before I forget." Eddie took his cell phone out of his pocket. His eyes narrowed.

"Is everything okay?" Amanda asked.

"Yes, yes, it's fine. I should probably handle this, though. I didn't realize how late it had gotten. Hang on. Sending you Julie's number and email address right now. Let me know if it doesn't pop up in a moment."

"I hope I haven't held you up from anything more important," Amanda said as she reached into her purse to take out her phone. "For whatever it's worth, I did notice that you kept your phone in your pocket this entire time. You didn't check it once. No one does that anymore. It was, like, retro and genteel."

"You did the same thing!" Eddie laughed. "And I agree, it's a gesture of basic courtesy that has almost vanished. But in the interest of full disclosure, I've programmed special ring tones for Representative Gable and our Chief of Staff that would have sounded if either of them had called. They're the only ones though! Oh yeah, and I have a special ring for my mom too."

"Got it!" Amanda said, holding up her phone to show Eddie that she had received his text. "Thanks! I'll call her later today, and I might be able to make the drive to West Virginia this Sunday. Normally I work from brunch to close, but our manager threw everyone off their normal schedule this week because we have two new trainees. Never mind, that doesn't matter. I'm babbling and you need to take your call."

"I really don't. It's just an email, and while it's not nothing, it's also not as urgent as he's pretending it is. I'd rather use the walk back to the office to think about what I'm going to say and then discuss it in person. We probably ought to get the check, though. Like I said, my treat."

If this had been a first date, it would have been Amanda's best ever. If this had been a first date, she probably wouldn't have been able to set her phone down for more than three minutes at a time, waiting and hoping for Eddie to text and ask her out again. If this had been a first date, she would have boasted to Irina and Jasmine that she was deleting her Tinder and Bumble accounts permanently this time, because she had finally found a keeper.

But it wasn't a first date. It was a business appointment—albeit with a guy who happened to be reasonably handsome, reasonably successful, and definitely a gentleman—and after this meal, they would go their separate ways. Eddie would walk back to his office and probably match with his future wife on one of those god-forsaken dating apps that very afternoon. Amanda, meanwhile, would sneak back into to GRAF to snag the suit jacket that was still sitting on Claire's chair and that she couldn't afford to lose, before heading to Ottimo, where she would wait on attractive couples who were basically the same age as her, but who somehow had already figured out the secret to acquiring money and love.

It made Eddie's interest in helping her all the more perplexing. She desperately wanted to ask him, why? Why her? Just because she had been sweet to him on the phone? Did he think of her as a little sister he needed to protect and guide? Was it simply part of his character, or his military training, an almost compulsive need to help others wherever he could, the same way Amanda found herself unconsciously tidying up strangers' dropped napkins or steadying precariously stacked plates when she was socializing at a random bar or restaurant?

Eddie caught their waitress's eye with a friendly smile and motioned for the check. Amanda decided to keep quiet. Appeasing her curiosity wasn't worth the risk that her question would make Eddie feel uncomfortable, or worse, that he'd interpret it as a veiled hint that she thought he was being shady and wanted him to back off. Whatever his motivations were, Amanda was grateful that he wanted to be her friend and ally.

Amanda and Eddie said their goodbyes with a friendly handshake, and Amanda promised him that after she had contacted Julie, she would let him know how it went.

"Do you want me to send you daily or weekly status reports or anything?" Amanda asked when they had reached the street and were about to part ways.

"That's up to you. We can keep it more informal if you'd like. Daily reporting would get cumbersome for both of us. You might find weekly reports to be a useful way to document your progress and keep track of what strategies worked or didn't, though. If this process drags out, you'll be happy you have a written record to refresh your memory. And if nothing else, a week-by-week playbook could come in handy for you, personally, if you take on another project like this in the future."

"I suppose that for an assignment like this, Representative Gable is more interested in the results than the details. You probably are too, for that matter."

Eddie chuckled. "I think you must've worked on the Hill in a past life. You've got good instincts, Amanda. I know too many folks with terrible judgment and terrible people skills, and for however book-smart or well-connected they are, they can't seem to get out of their own way. Or it's the reverse: their judgment is meticulous but it's self-interested and manipulative, and their so-called charisma is calibrated and weaponized to exploit everyone around them. It's refreshing to be around someone who is simply smart and kind and easy to talk to."

"Thank you," Amanda said. She smoothed her skirt and bashfully shrugged. "I'm just trying to do my best, even when I feel a little lost, that's all."

"I appreciate it, and so will Julie. Please don't let the weekly reports become a burden. And you also shouldn't feel like you need to limit yourself to them! You can call or email me whenever. And we should set up another lunch meeting in a few weeks. This one has been the highlight of my week."

"Mine too!" Amanda said. "I'll look forward to it. Thanks again for lunch, Eddie."

"Enjoy the rest of your day, Amanda."

Amanda walked down D Street and back toward the GRAF offices in a contented daze, pondering what she could say to Julie to make the best first impression possible.

CHAPTER SEVENTEEN
Amanda Wagner

Amanda woke up to the sound of her phone's default alarm buzzing at 9:00 a.m. on Sunday morning. She had closed at Ottimo the night before, and even though she had declined the invitation to join Jasmine and a handful of industry friends for drinks at Space Cadet, she didn't get back to the condo until after 1:00 a.m.—at which point she was so wired that she ended up watching reruns of *N.C.I.S.* on Netflix for another three hours. She knew she would regret it the next morning, but she hadn't been able to stop herself from binge-watching since Eddie had told her about Julie.

Would Julie look or act like any of the female characters on the show? All Amanda had to go on was a four-minute phone call. Julie had been polite, articulate, and gracious, but Amanda was glad that Eddie had warned her that Julie also tended to be terse. In their brief conversation, they had agreed that, since Amanda was planning a daytrip to the Martinsburg area anyway, she and Julie would meet Sunday at 1:00 p.m. sharp (was that 0100 or 1300 hours in military time?) so they could discuss strategy and delegation of responsibilities over a cup of coffee. Although Julie wouldn't be able to act as a tour guide, she had recommended that in addition to Amanda's planned walk through Octavia Park, Amanda also should take some time to familiarize herself with the businesses, churches, and landmarks in the surrounding area before commencing her drive back to Washington, D.C. that evening.

By the time Amanda had showered and blow-dried her hair, applied a bit of concealer and eye makeup, settled on a comfortable-but-not-sloppy outfit, and gathered up her things, it was approaching 10:00 a.m. How was she already behind schedule? She had never been more pleased that she had hung onto her beloved silver Versa and her rented parking space in the building. At least she wouldn't have to worry about retrieving her vehicle from long-term parking.

Irina was in the kitchen, reading from a stack of papers she was holding in one hand while fixing herself her habitual cup of coffee with the other, when Amanda finally left her bedroom and headed toward the front door.

"You are sure this is a safe trip to make by yourself?" Irina asked, setting the papers onto the countertop.

"I'll be fine. The drive will take two hours at most, even with Sunday traffic, and I'll head back before sunset. And I have a stun gun in my car, so I can shock the shit out of anyone who messes with me." Amanda laughed. "To be honest, I'm far more nervous about making a fool of myself in front of this badass Navy lady and making Eddie look bad for recommending me than I am about traveling alone."

"You will do great and she will like you! And if anything happens, you may always call me. I will make Kristoff drive us up there and we will help you."

"You're the best, Irina. Hopefully I won't need to be rescued, but I feel better knowing you have my back if I do." Amanda caught a glimpse of the digital clock on the microwave in front of which Irina was standing. "And on that note, I ought to get moving. I don't know much about this woman, but I'm certain she's not someone I should keep waiting. See you tonight!"

The drive to Martinsburg was uneventful, although Amanda became preoccupied with the changing scenery outside her car window after she had passed through Leesburg. She couldn't recall if she had driven this route in the other direction during her move from Indiana to Washington, D.C., nor could she recall if she had been struck by the same inexplicable, vaguely unsettled sensation at the time. Evansville was a decent-sized city, but U of E students didn't have to drive far off-campus before they were surrounded by cornfields, farms, and dilapidated gas stations, so it wasn't simply that rural settings made her uncomfortable. Regardless of its source, a nebulous innervating energy had crept up on her somewhere in northwestern Virginia, and once it arrived, it was unshakable.

Amanda turned up her radio and willed herself to stop stealing glances at the faded billboards advertising auto accident attorneys, hunting supply stores, fundamentalist congregations, and truck stop diners, and to focus on the road in front of her. Although she never deduced what was so peculiarly eerie about that empty stretch of paved road, the feeling had dissipated by the time she reached the city limits of Martinsburg. It was just before 12:00 noon. Her visit to Octavia Park would have to wait until after her meeting with Julie.

Amanda found an empty parking space on a side street near a church (actually, by Amanda's count, near at least five churches within a three-block radius), and she decided to count her blessings and park. With one service letting out and another that appeared to be getting started, there was an influx of activity in the area and, according to GoogleMaps, she was a five-minute walk away from Latte Da Cupcakery, where she and Julie were scheduled to meet in just over an hour. The space was metered, but while Amanda was fishing through her purse for spare change, she noticed a small sign indicating that parking downtown on weekends was free. This was a good omen.

As Amanda meandered down Queen Street, peeking into storefront windows and occasionally pausing to snap a picture of an old-fashioned VFW sign or an interesting banner hanging on a lamppost, she started to feel self-conscious. Most of the residents she passed greeted her with a nod, a half-smile, or a mumbled, "G'morning, miss," and went about their business, but she couldn't shake the feeling that she was drawing undue attention to herself without intending to. She didn't think she was imagining it. People were stealing glances at her. She sensed that it was more out of curiosity, or perhaps wary suspicion, than it was animosity, although she couldn't pinpoint why.

What was marking her as an outsider? Amanda slipped her phone back into her purse. She took just as many random photos when she was walking around D.C. or her hometown in Connecticut, but maybe she looked like an overzealous tourist doing the same thing here. Or was it her outfit? She was wearing basic black leggings, a form-fitting silky maroon tank top, her favorite oversized light grey cardigan, and an older pair of Nike running shoes that were still in great condition. She looked sporty but not slovenly, a casual style befitting afternoon plans of coffee and a nature walk. At least, that's the look she had been going for. Should she have been dressed in her Sunday best?

Amanda tried to surreptitiously examine the apparel of the women on the street around her. Several were wearing simple flower-patterned knee-length dresses, but they each had one or more children in ruffled skirts with white patent leather shoes, or in pint-sized dress shirts with tiny clip-on bowties, in tow. All the young women who appeared to be in their twenties, and who weren't dragging along fashionable but rambunctious children, were dressed almost identically to Amanda. If she had worn those ubiquitous chestnut-colored, faux-shearling-lined boots or traded her grey cardigan for a loose-fitting flannel shirt, would that have been enough to prevent the covert glances and curious stares?

Or was it because she was alone? Upon reflection, Amanda realized that she had walked past only two other solo pedestrians, both of them men who looked like they were rushing to meet up with their families at one of the nearby churches. Everyone else was in pairs or groups. Amanda took her phone back out of her purse to check the time. 12:06 p.m. What was she going to do for the next fifty-four minutes?

After circling a six-block stretch of sidewalk twice, Amanda decided that it would be preferable to sit in the coffee shop alone, rather than to continue aimlessly wandering the streets. At least she could mess around on her phone and make it look like she had electronic companionship and a purpose. And surely Julie would appreciate her punctuality. She found an empty table for two at their designated meeting spot and sat down with a Black Dog coffee (a local favorite, according to the barista) with a splash of almond milk and cinnamon sugar, and a piece of snickerdoodle coffee cake. The latter, Amanda intended to either finish or throw away before Julie arrived; she didn't want to portray herself as anything less than the embodiment of self-discipline and high standards.

Amanda polished off the coffee cake within fifteen minutes and, although only two thirds of the café tables were occupied, she immediately began to wonder if she was irritating the staff by sitting there alone without ordering anything else. It was now 12:48 p.m. Amanda furrowed her brow and looked intently at her phone, hoping it would appear as if she were preoccupied with something more important than the explore feed on her Instagram account. This feed, incidentally, was focused almost entirely on butt models and CrossFit chicks, hot artsy shirtless men with facial hair and tattoos, modern home-decor inspiration, and, presumably as a remnant of her online interactions post-breakup with Jeff, "online dating sucks" meme pages and *The Bachelor* fan accounts. Oof. Was this what Instagram's artificial intelligence bots (or whatever the hell was tracking her activity) thought of her? Was this what people in real life thought of her? She could scarcely imagine a more vapid collection of images.

Despite her attempts to appear preoccupied by a Very Important Business Matter on her phone, Amanda's head whipped up whenever anyone walked into or out of the store. It was perturbing that she couldn't even focus on pretending to be focused. It proved to be useful, however, when Julie walked in at 12:55 p.m., exactly five minutes before their designated meeting time.

Although Amanda had never seen Julie's picture and all Eddie had told her was that Julie was a brunette, she knew instantly it must be her. She was taller than average (about the same height as Amanda), and wearing blue jeans, hiking boots, and a crisp grey t-shirt with "United States Navy" written across the chest in dark blue font. Her arms were chiseled and heavily tattooed above the elbows, and she wore her long, dark hair in a thick ponytail braid. She stepped into the café with poise and purpose, and promptly caught Amanda's eye. Amanda could feel herself blushing as she nodded her head eagerly and gave a slight wave. Julie strode toward her confidently, hand outstretched, and Amanda sprung up from her seat to shake it and introduce herself.

"You must be Amanda, correct?" Julie asked with a slight smile. "Julie Locklear-Rhodes. It's a pleasure to meet you, ma'am."

"Yes, hi! I'm Amanda. Wagner. Amanda Wagner." Amanda exhaled. There was no reason she should be this jumpy. "The pleasure is mine. Thanks for taking time out of your Sunday to sit and chat with me for a bit."

"Are you all set on your coffee?" Julie gestured toward the counter with her chin.

"I've still got half a cup left, thanks," Amanda replied, lifting up her drink and giving it a slight shake. "But I can hold our table if you'd like to get something."

Julie nodded her head and, with another half-smile, turned toward the counter to purchase her beverage. She returned less than a minute later.

"No line, black coffee," she said with a shrug as she sat down across the table from Amanda. "I've always liked this place. Even when it's busy, they're efficient, and they serve the best cup of coffee in town."

"It's fantastic," Amanda agreed. "The barista said Black Dog is a West Virginia company. That's cool."

Julie looked pleased. "Yes ma'am, their roastery is in Shenandoah Junction, I think. We have a lot of business like that here, that are as good as anything you'll find in Washington, D.C."

Amanda was afraid anything she said in response would sound either patronizing or disingenuous, so she simply nodded her head enthusiastically.

"Anyway, I suppose we should get right into it," Julie continued. "Have you had a chance to visit Octavia Park yet?"

"No, I'll head over after this. I figured that way, I won't be rushed."

"Okay. There are a few different trails, but the outer loop will take you past the pond that everyone likes. From what I understand, even if they go forward with the construction, that small section of the land will remain relatively untouched. All the native wildlife will be screwed either way, obviously, but apparently not even Ansley Development Corp. has the political capital to drain that pond and replace it with more parking spaces."

"Or it's just more cost-effective to leave it there and build around it," Amanda muttered.

"You're probably right," Julie snorted. "But they're doing a really good job of portraying the decision as a 'gift' to the community." She paused, sighed, and took a sip of her coffee before continuing. "So is it fair to say, then, that you have at least a high-level understanding of the major players here and the dynamics between them? I don't need to re-summarize what our mission is or what I expect from you?"

"Well, between our phone conversation earlier this week and talking with Eddie, I'm clear on our objectives. And I've done my research on the issue and the area, mostly based on the information Eddie and the congresswoman provided me. So I don't think there's any doubt we'll be aligned on all that. But maybe we should talk about what you're hoping to get out of my involvement." Amanda paused, thinking Julie would jump in. Julie arched an eyebrow but remained silent. Amanda fiddled with her coffee cup and continued. "By 'my' involvement, I mean Representative Gable's office, of course. There's a pretty wide range of what that could entail—basically anything from attaching her name to the project as a formality and leaving you alone, to having us take over the entire operation on your behalf. And I just want to make sure our expectations are aligned from Day One, so you get what you need out of our participation."

"Right. Well, the short answer is, somewhere between the two extremes you just described." Julie tilted her head to the right and stared into Amanda's eyes without changing her expression. "I'm sure I could have found a student at Shepherd University who would have been willing to help out for college credit or because it would look good on their résumé after graduation. And we should reach out to those kids as a resource: they're smart and energetic and can help us rally support from the younger members of our community. The only way we're going to convince local citizens is through other local citizens. But for better or worse, our town councils and county councils and even the state government have a fickle, fucked up, love/hate relationship with Washington. They resent y'all, but they also want y'all's respect and they'll listen to you, so having Representative Gable on our side means something. And that's where you come in. You are... what to her? Eddie wasn't clear about that."

"I'm her Lead Special Projects Liaison," Amanda said. God bless Eddie for giving her such an official-sounding title. At this moment, her credibility was entirely dependent on it.

"Okay." Julie looked dubious. Amanda held her breath as Julie continued. "Frankly, I'm surprised she was interested in sending us an emissary at all. The development is being positioned as an engine of economic growth. Trying to stop it is radically off-brand for her. Is she pissed off that she was cut out of the deal or something?"

"I think defending the community's best interests is her biggest priority," Amanda stammered. "I think she knows that the development probably will create some jobs, but it also will probably put a lot of small business owners out of commission. She's still pro-business, but she's pro-local-businesses run by her constituents above all else."

"Is that the official party line?" Julie scoffed. "Eddie said almost the exact same thing."

"It's not! I promise. At least, no one has said so to me. Eddie didn't tell me what to say, and neither did Congresswoman Gable." Amanda could feel her face burning red. "Honestly, if I had known that you'd be asking these questions, I probably would have made Eddie give me instructions about how to respond. But everything I just said was from the heart. If anything, I'm relieved Eddie said something similar, because part of me was worried that Congresswoman Gable would be really, really angry if she knew I was here speaking on her behalf with my own opinions."

Julie's expression softened. "Eddie told me you were—what's the word he used?—'guileless,' and that if I were ever going to get along with a big-city girl, it'd probably be you." Julie's laughter was kinder now. "He was right. I'm just giving you a hard time."

"For what it's worth, I never would have considered myself a 'big-city girl.' Living in D.C. is still a head-trip for me most of the time. I grew up in a pretty small town, and I went to a small college in southern Indiana. This is the first 'big-city' job I've had, and I still work as a waitress full-time to make ends meet. Always have. Obviously that's still pretty different than growing up in the rural south, but I haven't led anything close to the life of a Kardashian or a New York City socialite either."

"He told me that too. That was part of why I warmed up to the idea of this meeting." Julie took a sip of her coffee, set it down, and held Amanda's gaze. "Understand, we're all too used to outsiders coming here with grandiose promises that cloak their shitty self-serving motives. That, or they have the attitude that we're just a bunch of dumb rednecks and we should bow down before their ivory tower brilliance. I know I'm the one who solicited Gable's help, but it's an issue of time management and political connections, not incompetence."

"I completely respect that and I know Representative Gable and the rest of her staff do too," Amanda said. Part of Amanda felt like she was being personally attacked, or like she was being punished for the sins of people whom she had never met (and probably wouldn't have gotten along with if she had), but another part was relieved that Julie was being forthright about her mistrust and concerns. If Amanda were honest with herself, she'd have to acknowledge that she drove across the state line carrying a number of stereotypes about West Virginians, not all of which were positive. "I could tell you that I'm not some D.C. elitist," Amanda continued, "or that I love the natural beauty of this state and I have a tremendous amount of respect for your residents and your work ethic here, or that I'm different from everyone else who has come here in the past promising to help. But all of that will just make me sound like another politician or developer pandering to you. I know it's not going to matter until I can prove myself and earn your trust. So I guess I just want you to know that I'm willing

251

to do that. I'm here to help you with this cause for however long you want or need my help.

"I know I'm an outsider, so maybe I should be honest with you about my own motivations for caring about this project first. I want to impress Representative Gable, obviously. And I really like the idea of preserving natural green spaces and not bulldozing them down for more Walmarts. Even though Walmart has been a godsend on my budget! In the course of the ten minutes we've been talking, I've already realized how my involvement could be misperceived. Like, people might think I believe that saving a few trees is more important than their ability to work a decent job and put food on the table for their kids. This development must have a base of local support, otherwise they would have scrapped it already, right? But I know the resistance to it must be significant and well-founded too, otherwise Representative Gable and her team never would have bothered having me get involved. I know I'm rambling. I'm thinking out loud when I ought to shut up and listen. Maybe if more people in my position in the past had shut up and listened, we wouldn't need to have this conversation or strategize around these issues now."

Julie took a long, slow sip of her coffee before she responded.

"You said you're a waitress, right? So you know how to placate difficult customers? And I must seem like another one of those pains-in-the-ass that you have to calm down by any means necessary, correct?"

"Not at all! It's more like, if one of my regulars told me that the last time he came to the restaurant, he ordered, I don't know, the scallops without mushrooms, but someone messed up and served it to him with mushrooms. I would reassure him that I'd mention it to the chef and personally double-check his order before I or anyone else took it out to him—and then I'd actually follow through and do so! And I'd be happy he told me, otherwise I wouldn't have known that we had done something wrong and I wouldn't know that I might need to adjust my behavior to help make it better and regain his trust. I know the analogy is a little strained, but...."

Amanda's voice trailed off and she smiled weakly. Julie's expression was inscrutable. Amanda sensed that Julie still had her guard up, but it also seemed like she was warming up to her, at least a little. Between a decade's worth of finicky restaurant customers and two years with her temperamental colleagues at GRAF, Amanda thought she had mastered the art of adapting to every type of bad mood and unreasonable demand. But with Julie, neither her impromptu wordsmithing nor her perfectly timed disarming smile seemed to be a viable strategy. Not only would Julie see through that crap, she would resent it. Amanda didn't blame her. She also didn't know how to fix it.

Amanda reflected on the analogy she had just proffered. Did she make things worse for herself by saying something so stupid and convoluted? Was Julie going to call Eddie immediately after this meeting and demand that he assign someone else to work with her? Amanda was going to have to delete "Lead Special Projects Liaison" from her LinkedIn bio less than a week after she had posted it and broadcasted it to her network. Yet another disgrace in the infinite parade of her career-related humiliations.

"... and if you were raised here, if you live here, if your family goes back generations here, you'll understand this implicitly. If you don't, it's impossible to explain and equally impossible to comprehend in a way that's anything other than academic." Julie had been speaking while Amanda was lost in her own thoughts. Amanda finished the last drop of her coffee and furiously willed herself to pay attention while Julie continued. "And now we have these slick, smarmy men, wearing suits that probably cost more than some of us make in a year, bragging to us about how humble they are, oblivious to their own absurdity. Half of our local government is comprised of corrupt imbeciles, but we could comfort ourselves with the fact that at least they're *our* corrupt imbeciles. But now they're letting these outsiders from Ansley Development Corp. take over."

"How did they do it?" Amanda asked, trying to deflect the conversation back to Julie to cover for the fact that she had let her mind wander. "I think I remember reading that ADC is, what, a Delaware company? Or whatever state it is, like you said, they're not from West Virginia. So I guess I'm thinking, maybe if we understand how they weaseled their way in, we can figure out how to push them back out."

"Their employment projections," Julie said matter-of-factly. "Full stop, that's all it took. Although I personally suspect their numbers have been propped up with a healthy dose of bullshit. We're desperate for jobs and desperate to believe their data, but it's based on hopes and not facts. Normally a team of greasy, condescending businessmen like that would be chased out of town within the hour, but they were smart. Once rumors of the project got out, the very first thing they did was guarantee jobs, including some full-time jobs that'll pay several dollars an hour above minimum wage. They said that the manager-level positions could even have subsidized health insurance." Julie shook her head in frustration. "At the first public hearing on this shit, everyone in the room was immediately enraptured, because everyone in that room was unemployed or underemployed, or close to some who is.

"But the Ansley reps conveniently forgot to mention all the existing, not-totally-hypothetical jobs that will be lost because of this development. And for what? Most of us already have access to a Walmart. There are multiple options that are reasonably simple bus commutes from downtown Martinsburg, and it's an even easier drive for people who have access to a car. Maybe they're counting on customers coming from Hedgesville or Jones Springs. And yet, they also forgot to mention that we'll be competing with the residents of those towns for the new job openings too."

"And no one wants to hear it anyway?"

"Exactly! Everyone is so relieved to have some semblance of hope, that they aren't interested in listening to any facts or logic that could shatter the dream. But what I really don't understand is that the county has plenty of vacant lots from bankrupt department stores and other failed strip mall developments sitting empty. They aren't used for anything other than drug deals, vandalism, and teenagers committing petty crimes. Why not revitalize one of those places? How is destroying our beautiful little park more financially feasible?"

Amanda started to shake her head helplessly. Then, abruptly, she stopped herself and straightened her posture. She wasn't helpless. Julie certainly wasn't helpless. They weren't there to wallow or complain. They were there to organize and construct a plan of action. She thought back to the list of discussion questions she had jotted down in her moleskine notebook in preparation for this meeting. In her hurry to get on the road that morning, she accidentally had left the journal on her unmade bed, but she was glad she had gone through the process of writing down her thoughts in advance, even if she didn't have them at hand at the moment.

"So I guess," Amanda started, "that the first big question is, who around town already agrees with everything you just said and might be willing to join us in the fight?"

As she crossed the state line back into Virginia later that evening, Amanda had swelled with pride. Julie was someone who commanded respect by virtue of who she was, what she had achieved, and how she carried herself. She had a clear vision, and she was looking for a partner—not a doormat, and certainly not someone to boss her around—to execute it. And now, Amanda was going to get to work with Julie as a peer. Maybe some of that strength and composure would rub off on her. Maybe enough that her colleagues at GRAF would start to see her as something more than their annoying-but-too-useful-to-fire, lower-class, former intern.

Either way, the Octavia Park project felt like the first major step forward in her career since she had landed the GRAF internship over two years earlier. And she was driving back home with a set of specific tasks that she needed to accomplish before she and Julie planned to meet again the following Thursday, Amanda's next scheduled day off: set up a professional-looking social media presence to coordinate and publicize the project, compose a list of local business owners and other stakeholders who might support their efforts, and arrange initial meetings with as many potential allies as she could.

Two years prior, being confronted with the same demanding list of tasks on such a tight deadline would have paralyzed her. Amanda always thought this was one of her immutable flaws. Every semester of college during the week before midterms and finals, she had grown so anxious trying to prioritize what subject to study first, that she simply gave up. She sent out mass texts trying to goad her friends into getting drunk with her. She spent six hours watching mediocre rom-coms on Netflix for every twenty minutes she had dedicated to typing out an eight-page paper that was already overdue. She had deemed all of this "self-care." Why wasn't she crippled by the same anxiety now? Why wasn't she tempted to pull her car into a rest stop and text Jasmine to meet her at Space Cadet in an hour and a half?

Amanda turned up her radio and focused on the road. Whatever the reason, she didn't want to jinx it.

The next day at Ottimo, as she and Jasmine were lingering by Angie's hostess stand waiting for the Monday dinner crowd to arrive, Amanda explained why she would need to bail on after-work drinks for the rest of the week. Immediately, Angie and Jasmine perked up with offers to help.

"Once you get your Instagram page set up, I'll blast it to my followers and encourage them to follow you too," Angie offered. This was not a small favor: the last time Amanda had checked, Angie had built her reach to almost 115K. "If even a small percentage of them do, it'll look like a popular cause and the momentum will build on itself."

"I'm not nearly as insta-famous as our beloved style influencer queen Angie," Jasmine added playfully, "but I'll do the same thing. I'll do it on my band's page too. Our fans tend to be really pro-environment, anti-establishment, anti-megacorp-fuckery, so it would be on brand."

"You guys are amazing," Amanda said.

"If you want," Jasmine continued, "I can design a logo or something for you. I'm pretty decent at it. I've done all the merch for the band, and we make way more money off that crap than we do from ticket sales or the fucking seventy bucks a year we get from Spotify plays."

"Yes! Please! That would be incredible." Amanda did her habitual over-the-shoulder glance to check if Nick was nearby (an act which Jasmine and Angie instinctively parroted), before continuing in a lower voice. "I don't want to go overboard with swag, but it would be awesome if we could have, like, a sticker or sign to put in storefront windows that says something like, 'I Support Octavia Park Preservation.' Nothing flashy. And then have the same logo on our social media and maybe a really small number of shirts that Julie and I could wear or give to key local leaders."

"I can totally do that," Jasmine replied. "In fact, I'll do it tonight. The past few Mondays have turned into complete shit-shows. Did I tell you that Hector came out with us last week? Good Lord, that man can drink. Anyway, I could use the excuse to stay in. I need to stop blowing all my tips in one weekday night."

"I don't even know what to say. If I could have something to show to Julie tomorrow, and we could move forward with printing before the end of this week? I can't think of a better way to get on her good side." Amanda wrapped her arms around Jasmine and Angie's shoulders for a quick group hug. "Thank you both so much. I don't know how I can ever repay you for this." Amanda pulled back, looking mostly at Jasmine. "Um, I kind of mean that literally too. I'll double-check with Eddie, but I'm not sure if I'm going to be able to actually pay you money for your services."

"Get Angie's millionaire boyfriend to make a donation to the cause, and then give the money to me," Jasmine joked. "That should cover it."

"Oh, fuck yourself," Angie grinned. She nodded toward the entrance, where a dully handsome guy in his early twenties was awkwardly holding the door for a slightly older woman with delicate features, flawless makeup, and an Hervé Léger dress that was a smidge too small for her frame. "First date incoming. My money's on a Hinge match. I love you both, but get out of here. To be continued."

"Dibs!" Jasmine cried before she and Amanda headed back to the kitchen. "Put them in my section, please."

"Fine by me," Amanda laughed. "You know that's going to be painful to witness, right?"

"That's exactly why I want them. The comedy gold will be worth the inevitably shitty tip." Jasmine shrugged as Amanda shook her head with mock disapproval and they both returned their focus to work.

Despite having no more to go on than the half dozen cell phone photos that Amanda had taken during her brief walk through Octavia Park after meeting Julie, Jasmine managed to create a stylish graphic overnight, which she emailed to Amanda before Amanda's lunch break at GRAF the next day. The logo was eye-catching but not ostentatious, with the slogan "Preserve Octavia Park" prominently featured in an inspired choice of font, set below a simple but serene background image of a pond surrounded by trees, birds, and a running trail, all rendered in shades of blue, green, and golden yellow. Jasmine somehow captured the very essence of the park and the project in vector graphics, and she had done it in less than twelve hours. When Amanda opened up the attachment, she was so impressed that she immediately abandoned her desk and rushed to the ladies' room so she could FaceTime her friend. In these circumstances, a text message or email reply simply would not suffice.

Jasmine was lying in bed, makeup-free and with her hair still wrapped in a silk scarf, when she answered Amanda's call.

"Oh shit, I'm so sorry! Did I wake you up?" Amanda asked. "I figured it'd be okay to FaceTime since you just emailed me."

"No, no, it's fine. I woke up a half hour ago. I'm just hanging out in bed. I finished most of the logo around 4:00 last night, but I wanted to take a second look at it and make a few little tweaks before I sent it to you." Jasmine adjusted her pillow against her headboard and sat up straight. "Wait, gross! Are you calling me from the toilet, you maniac?"

"No! I'm just hiding in here! I had to call you right away. Jasmine. Seriously."

"What? Is it okay? I can make some modifications if you have, like, feedback. I want to put the design in my portfolio, so treat this like you would if you were a paying client and you had hired me."

"Jasmine, it is fucking perfect. It is insane. I cannot believe how talented you are. I literally could've paid someone five hundred dollars to do the work, and they wouldn't have done half as good of a job as you did."

Jasmine didn't say anything, but she was beaming.

"Can I send it to Julie right away? She's going to love it as much as I do, I know it. I can't believe you're not charging us for this."

"You can send it to Julie. If she has any comments, she can give them to you or she and I can talk separately. I'm stoked that you dig it, but if she wants me to make adjustments, I totally can."

"Okay. But I seriously can't think of anything she would want to change. I don't know how you managed to nail it so perfectly on your first try. I wish there were some way we could repay you."

"I'm trying to get more freelance gigs with this graphic design stuff. They've raised the rent on my apartment and on the band's rehearsal space, and the money I make at Ottimo and Space Cadet isn't cutting it. Anyway, if you want to repay me, the best thing you can do is make this project a success and let me use you as a reference in the future. And tell people about me if they need graphic design work, obviously."

"Absolutely," Amanda said. "If there's, like, a Yelp for designers, send me a link and I will write you a glowing recommendation. You can give your future clients my personal phone number or email or whatever too. And I can give you a testimonial to put up on your website!"

"Cool, okay. For now, that's a good trade for me. I had fun doing it. So you're at your bougie job right now?"

"Yeah, that's why I had to hide in here. I'm going to spend the rest of the workday getting this logo printed on t-shirts and stickers and stuff. Are you working at Ottimo tonight?"

"Every night until Friday, then I'm at Space Cadet the whole weekend. You?"

"I'm closing tonight and tomorrow, but I've got Thursday off. Nick is hiring another new person this week. If he throws them into the fire this weekend, at least you won't have to deal with that mess."

"Praise the Lord," Jasmine smirked. "Although either way, we can just dump the newbie on Andrea. If it's a girl, Andrea will want to play some bullshit big sister role and poison the chick against us, and if it's a guy—"

"Then she'll want to be the first to bang him!" Amanda finished, delighted. "We won't be allowed within five feet of the dude. Oh, Andrea."

The opening of the door to the restroom interrupted their laughter.

"Someone's here, I've got to go," Amanda whispered. "See you tonight."

"BYE, BITCH! I LOVE YOU! I LOVE YOUR SEXY—"

Amanda quickly disconnected the call, barely able to suppress her laughter. She remained in the stall until she heard the adjacent door click shut. She couldn't tell who was next to her based off shoes alone, and she was cautiously optimistic that her basic black heels were too nondescript to give away her own identity. Tucking her hair into her blouse and covering the side of her face with her hand in an admittedly puerile attempt to conceal her identifying traits, Amanda raced past the stalls back to her desk.

As soon as she sat down, Amanda forwarded the logo to Julie. Amanda was eager to hear Julie's thoughts, but between Julie's classes and homework, her EMT shifts, and her kids, Amanda knew she might have to wait awhile for Julie to check her messages and respond. She decided to pass the time by getting everything else in order: reserving the handle "PreserveOctaviaPark" on Instagram and Twitter; finding a reliable but inexpensive vendor who sold customized stickers, signs, and t-shirts in bulk; and compiling an initial list of the businesses, churches, and what appeared to be a handful of small houses on moderately sized wooded lots, within a two-mile radius of the park, all of which would be impacted by the proposed development.

When Amanda finally checked her phone again, it was almost 1:30 p.m. She had worked straight through lunch without so much as an urge to check her social media or send anyone a random text. Lunchtime usually was quiet on Amanda's floor, with most of the staff spending at least ninety minutes at the gym or running home to take their dogs for a walk or sitting down for a see-and-be-seen meal at a trendy nearby restaurant, but Amanda still was surprised that none of her colleagues had interrupted her focus. Amanda scrambled to come up with an explanation: did they assume that someone important had assigned her a time-sensitive project that required her total concentration, or was her involuntary termination of employment so imminent that they didn't care how she occupied herself for these last remaining hours?

Or were they just going about their business the same way Amanda was going about hers? Jeez. She had to stop with these runaway fatalistic thoughts. She had been having a great day, and the only thing dampening her mood was her anxiety over the hypothetical motivations of people who, ultimately, were indifferent to her existence unless and until they needed her to handle an office chore. Her dad used to have some pithy bit of relevant advice when she was a teenager. How did it go? If you always care about what other people think, you will always be their prisoner? That wasn't quite right, but it captured the general idea.

But it was impossible not to care! She had needed to care what her professors and peers at U of E thought about her in order to pass her classes and not be a total loner, just as she needed to care what her colleagues and bosses at GRAF (and at Ottimo, for that matter) thought about her so she wouldn't get canned. She needed to care about impressing Eddie and Julie by nailing the Octavia Park project, otherwise she would spend the rest of her life rotting as a lowly office drone for whomever would tolerate her presence. She needed to get along with Irina and Marta, otherwise her living conditions would be miserable, and she didn't want to give the soon-to-be-engaged Marta any excuse to kick her onto the street! They all had power over her anyway, whether she liked it or not. She was already their so-called prisoner. She might as well get, like, a slightly larger cell or extra time in the courtyard.

Hadn't her dad faced all of the same nonsense at his job? He was a middle manager at a company that manufactured automotive parts, not some high-powered executive who could do whatever he wanted. They weren't rich. He must've cared, at least a little, about what his own bosses and coworkers thought about him. Had he just been talking about her personal life? Her online life?

Amanda cringed. He had first offered her that nugget of wisdom when she was a freshman in high school, fourteen years old. She had been crying at the dinner table because one of the junior boys had started a campaign to get everyone to unfollow her on Instagram and unlike all her selfies, after she had refused to give him road head while he was driving her home from another junior's house party. Dan Ratowski was his name. Ugh. About a year ago, that douchebag had friend-requested her on Facebook. Before smashing the "Decline" button, she had noticed, with unabashed glee, that although he had a reasonably hot wife (with long blond hair that looked a lot like Amanda's) and a bratty-looking kid, his hairline had receded past his ability to disguise it and his smug, stupid face had gotten fat and bloated. Dan Ratowksi. What a prick.

She had dared not explain the full story (hanging out alone with a junior boy in his car!) to her parents at the time, and crying over lost internet points seemed so absurd now, but maybe her dad's advice held more weight than she had been willing to acknowledge back then. She needed to care a little, right? But maybe not quite so much, and maybe not about everything and everyone.

Suddenly, she wished desperately that she could call her dad to ask him what he thought: about his old advice, about her current job at GRAF, about the Octavia Park project, about Eddie, about all that had changed for her since she had graduated college. Why couldn't she? Plenty of girls her age spoke with their parents all the time. Heck, Marta—who was a doctor, a homeowner, and almost a full decade older than Amanda—was on the phone with her dad multiple times a week! Amanda didn't really mean to eavesdrop on them, although she never walked away when the opportunity to listen in arose. Marta took her calls on speakerphone and Amanda could hear them through Marta's bedroom door. Sometimes she and her father bickered, usually in Spanish spoken too fast for Amanda to understand what about, but they always, always, ended every call saying by "I love you." Marta probably heard "I love you" from her dad more times in a month than Amanda had heard it from her own father in her entire life. It hurt. She knew her father loved her, but not hearing it from him ached in a vague, indefinable way.

Amanda looked down. Her thoughts were, graciously, interrupted by the arrival of an email reply from Julie:

```
Excellent. I like it. Let's move forward
with that. My class is starting but I will call
you tonight to discuss. Good job.
```

Good job! Amanda already knew that Julie didn't hand out compliments casually, and she had given Amanda the green light to take the next steps. Dealing with Julie was refreshing. Amanda didn't have to guess what she wanted or search for subtext that might or might not exist. She was so pleased that she decided not to send Julie a reply reminding her that she would be working at Ottimo that night and likely would be difficult to reach. She would find a way to connect with Julie on a five-minute break or a fake trip to "haul trash" to the dumpster out back.

Instead, Amanda put a rush order on a sample shirt, sticker, and sign, which she paid for out of her own pocket. The swag wouldn't be ready by Thursday, but maybe she and Julie could postpone their meeting for a few days until the products were delivered. Amanda could switch shifts with someone or offer to train the newbie in exchange for an unplanned day off the following week. And she could reach out Eddie to ask about expenditures; they had exchanged a few texts since she had gotten back to D.C. the night before, but he explicitly had said he was looking forward to hearing the full story about how their first meeting went. Surely that meant it was okay to call.

CHAPTER EIGHTEEN
Jill Torres

Delia was, irrefutably, the single dumbest person that Jill had ever met. It was baffling enough that she hadn't been Darwin'd out of existence entirely; and yet somehow she had managed to keep a job at Ingentis Holdings, Inc., for almost twenty years. Delia was incapable of focusing on anything for more than twelve seconds (Jill had started timing it in meetings), and she was incapable of comprehending any email that was more than two sentences long. Delia froze like a frightened dog when confronted with an Excel spreadsheet, then barked out an email insisting that the data be summarized and delivered to her in a three-by-ten chart pasted into a Word document. Whenever Jill managed to decipher Delia's bizarre, incoherent messages, her most common reply was, "please see the yellow highlighted text in my original email below for the answer to your question." When Lorraine was still with the company, Jill would occasionally forward her Delia's most egregious offenses against the written word:

the so call spredsheet is allready. "when" will you have returned them4? i am monday.

Was she having a seizure on her keyboard? What the hell was she trying to say?

Mockery would have felt cruel if English wasn't Delia's first and only language; if she had any sort of learning disability; if she wasn't a woman in her late forties who spent the entire workday shuffling between the Twitter, Facebook, Snapchat, and Instagram accounts of online "celebrities" twenty or thirty years her junior; if she hadn't aimlessly drifted from group to group within the company over the past two decades; or if she ever accomplished anything besides initiating frantic email chains about issues that had been discussed, decided, and resolved weeks prior. But any time Jill started to feel some semblance of compassion toward her, Delia would do something else to waste Jill's time or provoke her ire, and Jill's guilt about privately ridiculing her would dissipate as quickly as it had arisen. Delia was an imbecile, and it was an outrage that Jill was subjected to her bungling, inattentive foolishness at all.

Jill had been relieved when Delia was moved from Corporate Strategy (where Jill and her colleagues in Business Analytics sat) to Talent Acquisitions, although the thought of Delia as the face of recruiting for the company was risible. And somehow, also, apropos: a middle-aged white woman who was mystified by the type of technological advancements that actually mattered and whose brain had been fried by social media, but who considered herself "tech savvy" because she eventually figured out that anyone could read the private exchanges she had been posting onto her friends' public Facebook walls. For all their posturing about "the speed of change" and being "on the cutting edge of innovation," could there be a better symbol of the day-to-day reality of Ingentis than this woman?

Delia's replacement was an earnest guy in his early thirties. Jill liked him well enough. He was literate, at least. She didn't think about Delia again until, eight months later, the daily email blast announcing various job changes and promotions within the company was sent around. Jill typically deleted this message without even skimming it; like ninety percent of what arrived in her inbox, it was irrelevant garbage, another distraction. But on that particular Tuesday in November, Delia's name caught her eye. She had been promoted to Associate Director. In addition to what Jill assumed was a rather substantial salary bump, Delia would now have seven people reporting to her.

"God help her underlings," Jill muttered. She deleted the email. That should have been the end of it. Delia was in a different department now. Jill never would have to interact with any of those people. It was their problem and it had nothing to do with her.

But, fuck. Fuck, if it didn't grate at Jill for the rest of the day. It was appalling enough that, despite her unabashed, incontrovertible incompetence, this woman had managed to bounce around the company for almost a quarter century without getting canned. But now she had been promoted? Her inability to formulate a coherent thought in either the written or spoken word, her inability to stay on topic even in personal conversations, her utter lack of any discernable skill set—these were qualities that the organization had deemed worthy of advancement?

Delia was a nice enough older lady. She wasn't a bad person. Jill would never deny that. But what the actual fuck? Jill wasn't jealous. At this point, she had accepted her lot. Her manager's promises about her bright future at the company were empty words, exactly as Lorraine had predicted. Jill would remain exactly where she was, with literally no prospect of change or advancement, unless and until she left the business entirely. And Jill had decided she was okay with that. She had figured out ways to maneuver through the bullshit and finish her responsibilities quickly (but not suspiciously quickly), giving her plenty of free time to work on her various ideas for inventions, computer programs, and apps, and she had committed herself to enjoying Ingentis's job security while she tried to figure out how she could monetize her actual interests and talents as an entrepreneur someday.

At this point, she wouldn't even want a promotion. It would burden her with more pointless responsibilities, without the commensurate increase in income that she would require to pretend like she actually cared about any of it. She had long since ceased dutifully applying for internal job postings that matched her qualifications and would have provided an opportunity to advance or to better utilize her education and skills. When the company stopped bothering to give her courtesy interviews, she took the hint. Instead, she used that time to tinker with her own code, where there was at least some chance of a return on her investment.

And in Jill's mind—at least until she saw the news of Delia's promotion—she and Ingentis had arrived at an unspoken détente. She would continue to competently fulfill her basic job functions and, by staying out of the interpersonal office drama and avoiding or half-assing the litany of time-wasting meetings, email chains, planning sessions, status reports, touch-base calls, strategy huddles, and working lunches that her colleagues used to fill their days in a sorry attempt to convince themselves that they were vital to the organization, she could use the remainder of her working hours to surreptitiously pursue her own projects. Since Jill's substantive work was always completed flawlessly and on time, her boss said nothing. Jill was, to use the consultant-speak that she was quickly mastering in an effort to enhance her ability to bullshit when needed, "actively disengaged" with her job, but the work she did produce was far better than what any of her peers could offer, and she felt more at peace with her current situation than she had during those initial months when she had attempted to care. It seemed like a win-win.

But three weeks later, Delia's promotion was still nagging at her. It would strike her at the oddest times: in the middle of a 10K run before work, while browsing through the precut fruit at Whole Foods, while folding her clothes after laundry day. They promoted her? Delia? Really? REALLY?

Jill told herself that this was the last straw, that Ingentis had gone too far this time. Delia's promotion was a slap in the face, not just to her, but to every intelligent, ambitious person in the company (few though they may have been in that festering cesspool of mediocrity and abandoned dreams). She promised herself she would quit. She reviewed her finances: the $2,000/month deposits from her trust fund that she had received since graduation were contingent on her holding a full-time job, but when combined with her salary and the fact that she had no student loan debt, she had been able to put aside enough in savings to last for at least six months if she lived frugally—and this was assuming she couldn't find another job! Even though the job market was tight, and the prospect of suffering through another series of endless interviews and starting fresh elsewhere was overwhelming, Jill doubted it would take her much longer than a few weeks to find another place that would hire her.

Jill didn't quit.

She was entrenched. Ingentis was the devil she knew, and there was no guarantee that wherever else she might end up would be any less terrible. Maybe a few thousand dollars to break her lease and move to another city wasn't that big of a deal in the grand scheme of things, but it pained her to do it. She had a steady paycheck. Ingentis was a stable job. She had time for her other interests. Jill repeated her justifications to herself again and again, day after day. They remained hollow. The truth was, whether because of cowardice or complacency, the longer she remained at Ingentis, the more difficult it became to leave.

So, Jill stayed. But she remained an outsider, as did most of the other employees who had been forced into Ingentis via various mergers, acquisitions, and insourcings. Her occasional overtures at friendly conversation with colleagues were almost always rebuffed, with varying degrees of decorum. Most of the Corporate Strategy floor either ignored her or treated her with contempt. True, one of the other analysts, Jackson, had a wicked sense of humor and a tendency to direct his scathing commentary at the most flagrant perpetrators of inefficiency and interpersonal shit-stirring—and he was a godsend. Jackson was one of four people who had survived the acquisition of his former employer, a small consulting firm, by Ingentis, and as he told the story, his wife and the mother of his three kids (all under age five) had demanded that he "count his blessings and keep his ass exactly where it is" until their children had made it through elementary school.

Jill also had coffee at least once a week with another guy named Calvin, who had gone to MIT (specifically, Sloan, the business school), who spent his days "making useless pretty little graphs for the idiots in HR," and who seemed to be the only other person who realized that their so-called careers at Ingentis were a crushing failure.

Perhaps a few of the others weren't all bad either. Some of the women occasionally complimented her outfits or her physique when they crossed paths in the women's restroom, although Jill was often dubious about the sincerity of their flattery, particularly when it involved the words "skinny" or "muscle-y." Her boss Donald was okay too. He was a stickler for following company procedure, even at the expense of common sense, but since he treated her with a certain level of kindness (at least compared to most everyone else), she refrained from vocalizing any of her complaints whenever anyone asked what it was like to work for him. She insisted, truthfully, that he was as good of a supervisor as it got at Ingentis.

But none of these people were a replacement for Lorraine. Even Jackson and Calvin probably didn't count as her real friends. It's not like they spent time together socially outside of the office. According to Jackson, some of the younger people on their floor regularly got together for happy hours, attended each other's kids' birthday parties on the weekends, and even went in on season ticket packages to the Patriots games together.

"Not that my wife would let me do any of that stuff," he said bitterly, "but it would be nice to be asked. We're just not in the Cool Kids Club."

"Do you really want to be in their club, though?" Jill had asked. "Do you honestly think that they are 'cool'? Come on, dude. It's the twenty-second floor at an Ingentis Holdings satellite office. Literally no one here is cool. No one. Present company excluded, obviously."

"Obviously."

"Thank God they've never asked me. It spares me the awkwardness of having to think of an excuse to say no."

"I suppose you're right," Jackson sighed.

Jill supposed she was right too. But as much as it made her cringe to admit it, she kind of, sort of, on some level, understood Jackson's point. They were intentionally being excluded. She felt a flicker of irrational anger. She didn't want to be included! But the idea that they were somehow unworthy of being in the presence of the grand Cool Kids Club after normal business hours was absurd, infuriating, and unfair. If nothing else, she was offended on Jackson's behalf. How dare they hurt his feelings! He was the only one of them capable of generating an original thought—or any thought whatsoever, at least without holding six separate hour-long meetings to gather a consensus on what that thought should be. They would be lucky to hang out with him!

And yet, she didn't quit. She found out that the department paid a group of marginally competent outside consultants over $500,000 to spend three weeks performing basic penetration testing on a limited scope of nonconfidential marketing-related data—a task that Jill could have completed by herself, with great enthusiasm and interest, and for free, with two business days of focused work—but she didn't quit. Several of her coworkers began peppering their requests for IT favors with insinuations that she was having an illicit affair with Jackson, but she didn't quit. She was nauseated by the deification of their department head, Ingentis's almighty Senior Vice President of Corporate Strategy, Mr. Samuel Gordon (a name to be spoken by underlings only with hushed reverence), and she could barely restrain herself from rolling her eyes and snickering when supervisors puffed their chests while they boasted to each other about meeting with him, as if his willingness to listen to their pitches for twenty minutes was the ultimate validation of their human worth, but she didn't quit. Then her annual performance review gave her an "acceptable performance" rating, describing her as "unproblematic" and rewarding her with a 0.78 percent raise in salary. She didn't quit. But something in her shifted.

This was the pinnacle of what she could hope to achieve at Ingentis. Blind obedience to cumbersome, outdated systems. Eight dutiful hours a day of busywork. Having a bad case of the Mondays and somnambulating through her life until T.G.I.F. Robotically agreeing with morons like Delia because they were her superiors in the corporate hierarchy and their opinions therefore inherently more valuable. Reorganizing her inbox.

Being unproblematic.

Donald wasn't the worst boss. Much like the way he had lauded Jill for being "unproblematic" (and that remark, Calvin reassured her, was intended as a compliment), Jill considered Donald "harmless." Eleven people, including Jill, reported to him. He was an older white guy—Jill guessed he was in his early sixties, approaching retirement age—with a bit of a stomach paunch that seemed misplaced on his otherwise slim figure. He was married with three grown children. He seemed to adore two of his kids' spouses, but Jill got the feeling he wasn't a fan of his youngest son's wife. Sometimes he shared pictures of his ten-year-old grey cat (which, much to Jill's private amusement, also had slender limbs but an unusually large belly). Sometimes he and Jill talked about racquetball; Donald had an old racquet hanging on the wall of his office, and when Jill was in college, she used to play with her dad when she visited Westport over winter break. It was a small thing, but it was a way to connect.

During her very first midyear performance review, Jill had told Donald that she thought she was being underutilized. She outlined her experience and her skills and offered several suggestions for how she might expand her responsibilities. In polite corporate-speak, honed by years of practice, Donald told Jill to stay in her lane. At the time, Jill was hurt. Two and a half years later, she understood. Donald would never be promoted again. He must have known this and resigned himself to his fate, and he expected Jill to learn to do the same. There wasn't any intentional cruelty in it, only the self-delusion that either of their jobs actually mattered.

Occasionally Donald would reprimand Jill for a minor deviation from the scope of what he referred to as "best practices." Jill would proffer the obligatory words of apology and promises to do better in response, and they would both move on. Donald was harmless and Jill was unproblematic. Donald would never fire her and Jill would never quit.

Until the start of the third and final October Jill would spend as an Ingentis employee.

Donald called Jill's desk phone from his office. It was another one of his innocuous quirks. Jill sat four cubicles away from his office door. She personally would have taken advantage of any opportunity to stretch her legs and walk over to talk in person, but at least he didn't holler her name across the floor to get her attention the way some of the other managers did.

"Hi, Donald. What can I do for you?"

"Please turn your instant messages back on. We've talked about this."

"Okay. I turned them off because I'm trying to focus on finishing cleaning up this spreadsheet by the noon deadline you set." Jill leaned back in her chair and glanced into Donald's office. He looked like someone's sweet old grandpa, and it made Jill feel guilty for being so irritated with him. But the deadline he had set for this particular assignment was both arbitrary and unnecessarily rushed, and she despised the constant pinging of pointless IMs that distracted her from completing the already-asinine task at hand.

"Okay. I see you're back on. I'll message you there." Donald hung up the phone before Jill had a chance to respond. Jill closed her eyes and pressed her right hand into her forehead. Why not just say what he needed to say over the phone? Or, hell, if there was some reason that an electronic paper trail was required, why not send an email? Why, why, why did he insist on these godforsaken IMs?

Almost immediately, an instant message popped up.

RDwyer89w4: is power pt ????

Jill exhaled. Is PowerPoint (presumably)... what? Is it what? She tried to think of why Rachel Dwyer would be messaging her about PowerPoint. Or about literally anything. Jill often volunteered to help others on the floor with their laptop issues when the IT team was backlogged. She didn't have administrative rights to anyone's computer, including her own, so her ability to troubleshoot was limited, but a lot of the problems her coworkers presented to her required only common-sense solutions. As a result, Jill had unintentionally garnered the reputation of being a resource for quick computer fixes without the elevator ride to the third floor of the building, and most likely a week-long wait thereafter, that a visit to the Ingentis IT Help Desk entailed.

So maybe Rachel's PowerPoint program was crashing, or she needed help with one of its functions? Jill scanned through her inbox to double-check whether she had any PowerPoint decks from Rachel that were pending her feedback. As far as she could remember, they weren't supposed to be collaborating on anything.

Jill looked down. Her left hand was clenched so hard that her fingernails had left indentations on her palm. She hated this. She *hated* it. How much time had Rachel saved herself by sending that idiotic riddle of a message, rather than just typing out a full, grammatically correct sentence stating her question or request? Five seconds? Six? And how much time would Jill waste trying to divine what the hell Rachel wanted?

JTorres77r8: ?

Jill muffled a laugh. Two could play this moronic time-wasting game.

RDwyer89w4: ???

JTorres77r8: Rachel, please re-read your message. I don't know what you're asking me. Is there a problem with your PowerPoint or something?

RDwyer89w4: NO

RDwyer89w4: !

RDwyer89w4: will it by fri?

JTorres77r8: Will what by Friday?

JTorres77r8: Look, I'm sorry, I can't chat right now. Donald needs to discuss something with me. I will come by your desk later, or you can send me an email with details of what you need if that's more convenient.

Jill hid her visibility from Rachel before Rachel could send her anything else. Initially, Jill had been worried about offending her coworkers by ignoring their IMs or blocking them from seeing when she was online, but she knew from experience that this useless interaction would carry on for another hour if Jill didn't set certain boundaries.

Jill's IM pinged again before she could get herself any more worked up about Rachel's implicit disregard of the value of her time.

DStrome55j3: You are due for a new laptop Haven't you been getting notifications about this? Now Asset Management is notifying me. You need to return your current laptop to me by the end of this week. You will need to fill out the form to apply for a replacement laptop and have your data transferred over to the new computer between now and then Jill you should of handled this without my reminder

The laptop. The godforsaken laptop. Or, rather, the five godforsaken laptops that Jill had cycled through in the two and a half years since she had started at Ingentis. It took them almost two weeks to get her on the company network with the first one, which was so old and abused that Jill had to duct tape the screen and frame together. It crashed two months later, which led to another two-week wait and another ancient laptop that didn't last six weeks before Jill faced the blue screen of death and a total loss of her data. Her replacement laptop after that debacle was a vast improvement; it was only a year old when Jill inherited it, and it functioned properly without any issues.

Alas, Donald had insisted that Jill return it to Asset Management almost exactly one year ago to the day. Frustrated but, at the time, still a dutiful corporate soldier willing to oblige the company obsession with following procedure at the expense of efficiency and common sense, Jill had reluctantly abided Donald's directions and turned over the laptop. Jill's fourth laptop was the exact same make and model as the one she had just returned, only this one arrived to her without a power cord. Jill swallowed her anger and had a replacement power cord, purchased off Amazon.com for $14.89 and overnighted for an extra $3.99, sent to her home address at her own expense. It wasn't the money that grated at her, it was the principle of it.

By then, Jill had learned to save all her documents and data files to a cloud-based storage space rather than to her desktop, so when she was finally able to power up the new laptop, she was prepared to retrieve her documents and get back to work. Unfortunately, although the hardware was a duplicate of her previous laptop, none of the software she required had been installed. After a week of negotiating with the folks in the IT department either to install at least a few critical programs for her, or to give her administrative rights so that she could install what she needed herself; a week of being told that although they sympathized with her plight, the IT department needed written authorization from her boss's boss to restore her access to the exact same programs that she had used daily on her prior laptop; a week of sitting in her cubicle with virtually nothing she could do other than answer emails, her idleness and boredom punctuated only by the occasional manager scolding her for not turning in her assignments, despite her repeated reminders that she was helpless until her full system and software access was restored; a week of increasing certainty that this must be a sign they wanted her to quit and wishing that they would just give her a severance check and shove her out the door already; at last Jill decided to take matters into her own hands. She bypassed the corporate firewall with disconcerting ease and downloaded Sisense and Yellowfin, which would suffice until IT was able to provide her with full access to all her programs. The network security breach was a fireable offense, but only if she got caught. And even then, it would probably take another month of procedures and protocols and processes for them to actually pull the trigger.

Four months passed. Her boss's boss never did get around to providing the requisite written authorization for the programs. Jill wasn't sure whether she should congratulate herself on her hacking abilities or deride Ingentis's apparent lack of network security and system monitoring, but either way she was relieved that she had taken the initiative to do what was necessary to be able to recommence work.

Then, just as she was starting to feel comfortable, her laptop's CPU was overtaken, in its entirety, by some unseen program that slowed the entire system to a halt. It was possible that someone in IT realized that she had breached their system and, whether as an attempted fix or a form of punishment, had force-installed some sort of patch over the network, which in turn was causing Jill's current issues. Jill debated whether she should resign herself to dealing with an excruciatingly slow laptop that crashed twice a day, or breach the corporate firewall again to try to troubleshoot the problem herself, or risk someone from IT opening an internal investigation if she took the laptop in to be fixed and they inevitably discovered the software she had downloaded without authorization. Before she had a chance to decide, however, she was greeted with another blue screen of death. Total system failure.

And thus, Jill arrived at her current laptop, number five. This one, amazingly, was only six months old, it was delivered with an appropriate power cord, and had all her programs properly installed. And Jill was not giving it up. She was not going to submit herself to another two weeks (or longer!) of begging her superiors to give her the fundamental tools she needed to do her job. Not when this device worked perfectly fine. Not when there was no guarantee that the next laptop she received wouldn't be plagued with a whole new set of problems. All because of some stupid policy that, from what Jill understood, was originally intended to make sure that people with her job title weren't forced to use outmoded technology, but which, thanks to budget cuts and leadership turnover, instead resulted in Jill and her peers unnecessarily cycling computers amongst themselves until the equipment malfunctioned beyond repair. Rather than revising the policy or applying it with a modicum of common sense, everyone suffered.

Jill's eyes were welling up with tears, and she wanted to smack herself. Seriously? After all of the foolishness and disrespect and wasted time that she had suffered stoically for over two years at Ingentis, an IM about trading in her laptop was going to be what finally caused her to melt down at her desk?

JTorres77r8: Hi Donald. I did get a notification or two, but I figured it was an error. I have only had this laptop for a few months and it is still working great!

JTorres77r8: I'm sure you remember how frustrating it has been for everyone including me the last few times I've had laptop issues. Like I said, since this one works perfectly, I think the message was just a mistake.

DStrome55j3: I'm going to need you to follow protocol here. Per the Asset Mgmt notification,

you have until the end of this week to return
it.

    DStrome55j3: Is this something we need to
discuss further?

Jill knew that this was supposed to be a rhetorical question,
but she wasn't ready to concede the fight so easily.

    JTorres77r8: Yes, I guess so. I'll come see
you now.

Jill got up from her desk before Donald had the chance
to protest or make an excuse. He looked more surprised than
annoyed when Jill appeared at his office door moments later.

"Come on in, you can sit," he said.

Jill paused in the doorway for a moment before approaching
the chair. Donald's expression wasn't quite welcoming, but it was
placid. He was wearing a dark green dress shirt, a navy blue and
white plaid tie, and tan trousers. As usual, it was a stylish but not
ostentatious business-casual look; Jill could imagine a man thirty
or forty years his junior wearing the same thing on the pages of
the fall fashion issue of *GQ* magazine. Behind him, an Excel
spreadsheet took up most of his computer monitor screen, but
Jill could see an Internet Explorer window open to his Facebook
homepage peeking out behind it. How naughty of him! Jill wanted
to be angry, to inveigh against Donald's hypocrisy of wasting
company time on social media while insisting on rigid adherence
to corporate policy when it came to Jill's laptop, but she didn't
have the energy anymore. If anything, it was amusing. All this
misdirected attention, all this effort into appearing productive
without actually producing anything, all the posturing and all the
planning to make plans, all of the wasted days collectively running
out the clock while operating under the mass delusion that any of
it mattered? It was, suddenly, just amusing.

"Thanks, Donald." Jill plopped into one of the two chairs
facing his desk. She could feel her lips turning upward into a
smirk and she decided to let him speak first. The rage bubbling
underneath her momentary bemusement wasn't directed toward
him, or at least not exclusively, and regardless of whether a torrent of hysterical laughter or enraged profanity was what would

boil over as a result of today's circus sideshow of imbecility, she wanted to restrain it until she was safely out of earshot.

"There's not much to discuss here, Jill." Donald's tone was matter-of-fact, devoid of any anger but also of any compassion. "We have to follow corporate procedure, even when we don't like it or agree with it."

Jill stared at him in silence.

"I know you've had a few issues with your technology since you started here, but that's exactly what this laptop exchange system was designed to prevent. Most likely, you'll end up with a laptop that's as good or even better than the one you have now."

A hundred different rebuttals to the fallacious logic of the company procedure and Donald's defense thereof blurred together until they formed a soothing, rumbling hum in Jill's mind. She didn't break eye contact and she didn't speak.

"I can see that you're upset and I don't want you to get over-emotional about this. You have two big project deadlines next week, so you're better off making the switch as soon as possible in case there are any hiccups with the new machine. Tech issues won't be an excuse for missing your deadlines."

Jill smiled.

"And we'll keep getting email notifications every fifteen days from Asset Management until you comply," Donald added.

"Okay," Jill said.

"Great, then we're settled here?"

"Okay," Jill said again in a perfectly measured tone. "I will return my machine on Friday. And Friday will be my last day here."

A heavy silence hung over the room as they both processed Jill's words. Jill was as shocked as Donald by her sudden declaration. Sure, she had been toying with the idea of waiting to collect her annual year-end bonus and then immediately tendering her resignation. But she had been toying with that idea since the merger. Why wait that long? It was October and the bonus check wouldn't hit her bank account until February. An extra five or six thousand dollars would be great, but it wasn't worth another four months of misery. Now that she finally had spoken the words aloud, she felt a sense of clarity and resolve that had been conspicuously absent since she first began working at Ingentis. Their measly bonus wasn't enough to entice her to stay for another four days, much less four months.

"I understand you're upset, but let's be rational and not make threats we can't take back. Why don't you close the door all the way?"

Jill stood. She wanted to scream with joy, cartwheel out of Donald's office, kick over a few desk chairs, take a giant celebratory swig out of the bottle of Jack Daniels she kept hidden in the middle drawer of her filing cabinet, and sprint for the exit, hollering "good riddance, motherfucker!" to everyone she passed on the way out of the building for the final, the gloriously final, time. Instead, Jill gently nudged the door shut and sat back down.

"We both know you're not quitting," Donald began.

"I'm afraid that I am," Jill interrupted.

"Do you have another job lined up?" Donald asked.

"Nope." Jill almost felt bad for Donald, he looked so confused and dismayed. "I can give you a full two weeks' notice, if that's helpful to you. I can finish my major projects or set them up in a way that eases the transition for my replacement or whatever."

"Do you have any sort of plan whatsoever?" Donald pressed. "I'm afraid you're letting your emotions get the better of you and you're making a rash decision. Let's take a breath here."

"You've been a good boss, Donald. I don't want to leave you hanging, and like I said, my last day doesn't have to be this coming Friday. It can be the Friday after."

"I don't think you've thought through the consequences of what you're saying right now. Everyone knows you're very book-smart. You have your whole career ahead of you here. Or elsewhere, if that's what you want! But not if you quit on a whim like this."

"It's not really a whim. And it's not just about the laptop." Jill paused. Did she really owe him an explanation? She wasn't capable of shamelessly insulting him or the department or the company to his face, so anything she told him would be a half-truth anyway. She tried to be as diplomatic as possible without

280

outright lying. "I think that I miss the startup environment. It was a better fit for my personality and skill set. But I've really learned a lot about how big corporations work, and I'll take that knowledge with me wherever I go next."

"It'd be a lot easier to search for a new position while you're gainfully employed by one of the most important companies in the nation," Donald said. Jill could sense him trying to suppress his growing agitation. He seemed personally offended that she would want to work anywhere other than Ingentis. "I'm honestly disappointed in you, Jill. This company has given you so much. You have so much potential, and we've been waiting to see it blossom. And now you're just abandoning us? And not even for another opportunity? Just to sit at home and watch TV?"

What, exactly, had this company given her, other than an insecurity complex and the agreed-upon paycheck for services rendered? How could they criticize her for not fulfilling her "potential," when they were the ones who stifled it, stuffed it down, verbally discounted it, ignored it, underutilized it, and undermined it, until she was unsure whether it even existed any-more? Abandoning them? As if they were some kind of family? As if they felt any loyalty to her whatsoever? As if they wouldn't have canned her without a second thought if that's what their balance sheet dictated? And was it truly so inconceivable that she had ambitions, marketable skills, and a diverse set of interests beyond dicking around on her phone while watching reruns of *The Big Bang Theory*, all of which she could finally pursue now that she was escaping this dead-end, demoralizing joke of a job?

Her flash of fury subsided quickly. Lorraine had been right about everything. Jill and Donald and everyone around them had been brainwashed by this place, but Donald was much farther gone than she. Donald would retire here. He was a company man for life. His fate had been sealed decades prior, probably before Jill had been born. Jill couldn't begrudge him defending an insti-tution to which he had dedicated almost forty years of his life. Even though his loyalty was misguided, even though they would probably push him out with a forced early retirement package within the next three years, Jill couldn't resent him for it. She maintained her composure.

"I want to approach this the right way. I will tender a formal letter of resignation to you by the end of today. I can leave now, or on Friday, or the Friday after that. If you want me to prepare a transition package for whoever takes over my responsibilities, I'm more than happy to do so."

"I'll speak with HR," Donald said curtly. "But we won't need you to stay past this coming Friday."

Jill nodded her head. "Okay, that's what I'll plan on, unless you tell me otherwise. I'm going to get a coffee from the Starbucks across the street and have a breath of fresh air, but then I'll be back at my desk. And you can call me on my cell phone if anything urgent comes up in the next fifteen minutes."

"Okay," Donald said between pursed lips. "Please shut the door again on your way out. And please keep this news to yourself until I've had the chance to inform the team on my own terms."

Jill nodded again, closed the door, and walked to her desk. Her head was thumping as the adrenaline she had felt surging through her body started to subside. She could barely remember a single word of what she or Donald had said. Quitting Friday. Starbucks now. That was all that mattered.

Jill grabbed her purse and walked to the elevator before her squeals of joy could escape.

CHAPTER NINETEEN
Jill Torres

Jill hadn't spoken much with either of her parents in the six weeks since she had resigned from Ingentis. Mateo was never one for initiating phone calls, but he always had made it a point to say hello and chat for five or ten minutes when Jill and Jaya were about to say their goodbyes, and Jaya rarely went more than a week without calling her daughter to check in. Now, Jill was lucky to receive a cursory text, amounting to the completion of a family administrative duty, once every week or two:

Mom/M: Your cousin Fatima is engaged!! To that nice boy she met at USC. Everyone is thrilled.

Mom/M: Today is your Grandmother Mnangagwa's birthday. Don't forget to send her a WhatsApp message (in Shona, please).

Mom/M: Your father's boss's son wants to apply to MIT. His name is Derek. We gave him your email address so he can ask questions about the school. Hope that's okay.

They hadn't had a fight or a falling out. Not exactly. But Jaya was less than thrilled with Jill's decision to abruptly quit Ingentis without a new job lined up or a plan to attend graduate school instead, and things had deteriorated from there.

"Over a laptop?" Jaya had pressed after Jill first told her the news. "I don't understand. They wanted to take your work laptop away from you, so you quit? This doesn't make sense."

"Mom!" Jill had responded, exasperated and, truthfully, a bit disappointed that her mom wasn't more excited for her. "I know it sounds like there must be more to the story, but that really is what happened. It's emblematic of the entire corporate culture. They follow policy at the expense of common sense, and in this case their policy was going to dictate that I meet an already unreasonable deadline, while taking away the very tools I needed to complete the project."

"But you gave up? Do you know how many of your high school classmates I see back in Westport, hanging around town and living off their parents' money, unable to find work? They would be thrilled to have a steady job with a good paycheck and health insurance."

"First of all, ninety percent of those kids are spoiled as shit and you know it, Mom."

"Language!"

"Fine. I'm sorry. They're spoiled rotten. But it's true. You know they aren't looking for jobs. The only 'work' they want to do is build their Instagram following. They will live off their parents' teat indefinitely."

"I hope you don't think that's what you're going to do."

"Oh my God, seriously? Of course not. Why does everyone assume that I'm planning to sit around all day, goofing off? There are always startups hiring in Boston, and I just need to find the right one. And I have ideas for my own businesses that I can work on until then. Maybe I will go to grad school, I don't know! You and Dad have all these expectations for my career, and what I'm telling you is that I never would have achieved any of them if I stayed at Ingentis. Never! It was a dead-end job, pleasantly packaged as stability. You think I'm a failure because I quit, but I'm a failure because I didn't do it sooner."

"We don't think you're a failure. I'm just surprised. You've always been so responsible—"

"If quitting a job that literally made me want to kill myself every single fucking day—"

"Young lady, language! You will speak to me with respect and without the cussing or the dramatics. We raised you better than this. I won't warn you again."

"I know, I'm sorry. But it did. You're too far away to understand what working there was doing to me. I was at the point where I woke up every weekday morning wishing I were dead. They were openly disrespectful toward me. All of my assignments were menial tasks and busywork, which they picked apart for arbitrary reasons that had nothing to do with the substance of what I produced. They treated me like trash, and I put up with it for over two years because I didn't want to disappoint you. And because I was scared. And now I'm finally free from it and I just want you to be happy for me for finally having the dignity to get out. Even if you're not proud of me anymore, at least try to understand why I did it."

"Of course we're proud of you." Jaya's tone had softened. "And I'll figure out a way to explain this to your father without upsetting him."

"Okay. Thanks."

"I love you, little one. You are our first and only daughter, nothing changes that. But we will look forward to hearing about your next job, which we expect you to find very soon."

"Okay, Mom. I love you too. Please give Dad an extra hug from me."

When Jill hung up the phone, she resolved not to call her mom again until she was employed. She still wanted to spend the next three or four weeks focusing primarily on exploring her own business ideas, to see if any of them were viable and worthy of pursuit; but after that, she would look for a new job in earnest.

And she would be more careful this time. She had bought into the narrative that TravelBlot was "disrupting" the travel industry, that their applications were "transformative" and "shifting the paradigm" and "industry-leading," and... good God, it was all the same bullshit they said at Ingentis, and yet somehow Jill's tolerance for it while working at TravelBlot had been nearly infinite.

Had she been deluding herself about her entire career? All they were doing at both companies was producing marginally more entertaining or convenient garbage and hastening the already rapid decline of society. Everyone would be slightly dumber, slightly more distracted, and slightly more isolated because of them. Both organizations' business models depended on it.

Sometimes Jill felt ashamed about her role in all this. Other times she thought: good, fucking good, these idiot users make an affirmative (if not entirely informed and conscious) choice to give away their data in exchange for the opportunity to numb their minds for a few hours a day using her former employers' inane but frighteningly addictive products. At least she had made some money off it. Then her conscience would kick in again and she would vow that she'd refrain from accepting any job offer until she was certain that the company wasn't another TravelBlot or Ingentis. Another swindler.

Jill had spent the past three years willfully ignorant, at best, of the moral implications of what she, on behalf of her employers, was creating. She understood this now. She had been too consumed by the false sense of urgency imbued into every decision to reflect on the bigger picture at the time. But she had escaped, and the initial flood of joy and relief in the aftermath of resigning from Ingentis had faded. Her mind finally had quieted enough for her to start to process everything that had unfolded since graduation.

When she had created facial recognition software during her freshman year at MIT, with no motivation other than the self-interested and superficial desire to look more like the beautiful Amanda Wagner, her professor had both praised and cautioned her. Jill's algorithm did a slightly better job than most products commercially available at that time in distinguishing female and minority faces. But, the professor added, almost as an afterthought, had Jill considered how this tech might be used? By the government, military, police forces? Was Jill willing to put these kinds of innovations out into the world, knowing that they might be misused to violate civil liberties or in a discriminatory manner against certain populations? But at the same time, wasn't it better that she be involved in the process, so that she might have some hope of controlling it? Whatever Jill might invent or program, if she didn't do it, sooner or later someone else would, and they might not have the same scruples she did. Wasn't it better that she have some input into how the product functioned and who was granted access?

Jill hadn't thought about that interaction in years. It was a rare conversation about the real-world implications of their work, but from Jill's perspective, it had seemed to the professor like more of a fun thought experiment than a practical problem. But how to approach and resolve those kinds of real-world practical problems was the single most important thing they could have taught her at MIT! What good had being "involved in the process" done for her or for society so far? Was she supposed to play the game for as long as it took her to rise to Donald's level? Or to Senior Vice President Mr. Samuel Gordon's level? Whatever ideals she may have started with would have been stomped out of her by that point. Was it so absurd to think that she could find a decent job, making decent money, that wouldn't putrefy her soul?

Never again. Jill was willing to wait as long as it might take.

Four months after that phone call with her mother, four months after resolving that she wouldn't rejoin the workforce until she had found the right employer and that she would focus on self-improvement in the interim, Jill had nothing to show for her so-called "sabbatical" (a term preferable to "fun-employment," "temporary early retirement," "navigating a career transition," and eventually, just plain "unemployment") other than a half-dozen stagnated or failed projects and a broken lease on a $3,400/month townhouse that she had grown to despise.

The two things were not entirely unrelated. Jill had planned to use one of her rooms as a designated workspace, but that quickly proved untenable. New neighbors had moved into the adjacent townhouse about a month before Jill quit her job at Ingentis. Jill estimated that six to eleven people were living there at any given time, mostly men ranging in age from approximately nineteen to almost sixty, with no apparent familial relation to each other. Two of the younger ones fought incessantly, including rabid brawls that spilled out into the parking lot area in front of the building. The man in his late fifties was a perpetual drunk who tried to break down Jill's front door on four separate occasions, mistaking her townhouse for his own. Based on the number of daily visitors who stopped by for no more than ten minutes, Jill assumed that at least one of them was dealing drugs; and based on the fact that none of them ever wanted to shut up and go to sleep, she further assumed that all of them were sampling the product.

While she had been working full-time, they were a continual annoyance that she did her best to avoid or block out, but as soon as Jill started working from home, their incessant idiocy became inescapable and completely vitiated her ability to form coherent thoughts, much less to complete any sort of productive work.

So, even though she only had another four and a half months left on her lease, Jill decided to pay the $6,500 lump sum early termination fee to break it. She couldn't take it anymore. It would be worth every penny to get away from the stench of weed permeating through their shared walls and clinging to her clothes and her hair; away from the pulsating bass that reverberated through every room of her house and through her skull, overpowering even the best noise canceling headphones and liable to start or stop at any time of the day or night like an auditory version of Chinese water torture; and away from the useless new landlord who ignored not only her petitions that he intervene and put an end to their destructive and sometimes frightening madness, but also her requests that he perform basic maintenance on her faltering heating unit or fix the leaking dishwasher (although he would later refuse to refund the portion of Jill's security deposit that he cited as covering those repairs).

It was, of course, completely illegal and unethical. But Jill no longer had the will to fight it. Maybe someday she'd be in a position to get her revenge on the negligent, thieving landlord and her maniac, methed-out neighbors, but for now—much like when she finally reached her breaking point with Ingentis—she just wanted to be done with it all.

Less than a week after she had decided to abandon her townhouse, she found a single-family home up for rent in the

Bellevue Hill neighborhood. Slightly larger than the townhouse at 1,400 square feet, the home was built in the 1940s and, based on its fixtures and décor, probably hadn't been renovated since the '70s. But it had a cute little yard where she could envision herself doing calisthenics in the sunshine, her neighbors were mostly wholesome young families, and most importantly, she wouldn't have to share a wall with anyone.

She spent another $2,000 in moving expenses, and the home itself cost almost $4,000 per month for a month-to-month lease. Jill didn't tell her parents about any of it. She knew it was border-line sinful to waste that kind of money, but it seemed even worse to try to buy a house when she wasn't sure whether she would still want to live in Boston two months from then. Who knew where her next job might take her? Besides, trying to apply for a home loan while she was unemployed would be futile. As it was, she had to pay the landlord of her new house an extra month's rent up front just to convince her that she wasn't an eviction risk because of her present "self-employed," zero-income status. But it was worth it. She was hemorrhaging money, she could barely bring herself to check her bank account balance, and Jaya and Mateo would never understand or approve, but it was worth it for her sanity.

How different would things have been if Jill had bought a single-family home in Bellevue Hill to begin with? Despite its old age and quirks, she loved her new little house, but she loathed that her money was going into her landlord's coffers rather than toward paying down a mortgage on property she owned. Even within her now blissfully quiet walls, Jill's growing rage remained a distraction from her work—except she couldn't direct her fury at her lunatic neighbors, or really at anyone outside of herself, anymore.

And indeed, Jill did hold herself responsible for all the poor choices she had made that led her to this point. Why had she listened to everyone who insisted that she didn't want what she thought she wanted? When she graduated college, she knew that she wanted a single-family house with a yard, and she knew that she wanted to buy as soon as she could pull together the minimum necessary down payment. Yet, her parents and even the realtor she met with convinced her that she wouldn't want to deal with yard maintenance, that it was unreasonable for a young woman her age to own property, that most people waited to get a sense of the local neighborhoods before permanently committing themselves to home ownership, and that she ought to rent until she met her future husband, otherwise she'd have to deal with the hassle of selling her house once Prince Charming invited her to move into his home. The stupidity and sexism of their reasoning was excruciatingly apparent now, but at the time, Jill had been too overwhelmed to stand up for herself. She capitulated to their arguments, assuming they knew better than she—and long before things at the townhouse had turned so rotten, she had profoundly regretted it.

In the new Bellevue Hills rental, Jill paid a neighborhood kid with a lawnmower fifty bucks a month to mow the grass every other week or so, and that was the end of it. Fifty fucking dollars a month to a teenager had resolved the entire lawn maintenance issue that her father and the realtor kept harping on. Barely one percent of the money she was throwing away on rent every single month, and had been since graduation. That, THAT, was why she allowed herself to be convinced that she didn't want what she knew she wanted. And every single moment she spent at her new single-family home with its cute little yard reminded her how right her instincts had been and how stupid, how fucking stupid, she had been to ignore them.

She had long since forgiven her parents and the realtor for their well-intentioned but misguided advice. But her anger with herself for obediently abiding it, for disregarding her own desires and plans, had been festering for years. Indeed, Jill's longstanding self-directed rage over her submission to their will was one of the first times her conversation with Lorraine had moved from the professional to the personal. It was, in a way, the first step to them becoming actual friends.

"It never changes," Lorraine had said as they hovered by the TravelBlot espresso machine that eventually would become their favorite meeting spot. "I remember one time I was selling my old car to a dealership. To make a long story short, they tried to renege on the contract and I was venting to my mom about the situation. I had it under control, I was just venting. I was frustrated. Her suggestion? That my dad call them on my behalf pretending to be my attorney and fix the situation for me."

"Oh, your dad is a lawyer too?"

"No! Pretending. My father is a corporate accountant. Aside from, like, a high-level awareness of certain SEC and FINRA regs, he has no formal legal knowledge or experience whatsoever. But in my mom's opinion, it would be more effective to have an unqualified man talk shit over the phone, than to have a competent woman who actually is an attorney, who has read the contract and understands the applicable laws, handle the situation. Never mind the fact that impersonating a lawyer constitutes fraud. Never mind the fact that if I were deemed to have encouraged or even allowed it, I would almost certainly be disbarred. Apparently, in her mind, none of that matters because I'm just a dumb girl playing Attorney Barbie dress-up. And that's my own mother. So you can infer how the rest of the world sees us. Nathan and James are far more conscientious than most men in this industry, but we will always be underestimated and second-guessed, and you need to learn to anticipate that and rise above it. Or maneuver around it, as the situation may require."

Lorraine had suggested that, as soon as it was financially feasible, Jill break her townhouse lease and buy the single-family home she truly wanted. Lorraine even had offered to help Jill navigate any contractual legalese she found confusing and to refer her to a good real estate attorney and mortgage broker if she needed it. Jill ruminated on that conversation often in her new rented house. At the time, she had assumed she would take Lorraine up on her offer as soon as her then-current lease expired. But then the acquisition happened, and Lorraine moved away, and she renewed the townhouse lease thinking that she should hold off from any major financial decisions until she was certain she wanted to remain with Ingentis for the long-term, and suddenly two more years had passed and she was stuck exactly where she had been since graduation, with nothing to show for it other than a demoralizing job and a depleted trust fund account. And now, no job and a frozen trust fund, plus rapidly dwindling checking and savings accounts to boot.

Jill alternated between pride that she was betting on herself and her abilities—taking a calculated risk, wagering that with sufficient time and a suitable environment to focus, she would develop a brilliant idea and a multimillion-dollar business plan—and a crippling shame that she was an embarrassment to her parents, that every choice she had made since graduation seemed to sink her deeper into a pit of failure, that she was delusional to think she could achieve anything beyond being a cog in a machine owned and operated by someone else, that she had been propping up her self-esteem on long-past accomplishments that were no longer relevant, that even her birth itself had been a mistake, which Jaya and Mateo had handled with far more grace than they were legally or morally obligated to do, and she couldn't seem to do them the one small courtesy of not being a humiliating waste of space in return.

CHAPTER TWENTY
Jill Torres

The temperature had risen ten degrees overnight, reaching an almost inconceivably warm (for a Boston winter, anyway) fifty-four degrees Fahrenheit, and after a week of gloom, wind gusts, and icy rain, the sun was finally shining. Jill had been distracted all day: her morning run was frustratingly slow despite the ideal weather conditions, she had gotten a math problem wrong on the GRE practice test she took at lunchtime, and she had deleted an entire section of her latest business proposal, deeming it "amateurish, contrived, and just plain stupid," but after two hours of staring blankly at her Word document, she hadn't added anything substantive in its place.

Although she doubted that a change of scenery would have much of an impact on her productivity or her mood, Jill wanted to get out of the house and enjoy what was left of the nicest weather Boston was likely to experience until late spring. She packed up her laptop, applied a hint of mascara to her lashes, and put on a light knee-length jacket over the long-sleeved t-shirt and jeans she was already wearing. She figured she'd stroll through Bellevue Hill Park from the south end to the north, and then try to find a coffee shop or café where she could at least pretend to work.

A mile down Belgrade Avenue, Jill heard vaguely familiar metal music playing on the patio of a restaurant with a sign that read "Confession" out front. She paused and listened until it hit her: Parkway Drive. Jean Paul Woo's favorite band. After their breakup, she had downloaded several of the band's albums and played them on repeat until she had memorized every track. She didn't recognize this particular song, so she figured it was either from a new album or it was the work of a sound-alike band. Either way, Jill decided this would be a good place to stop.

The patio was empty, but with the sun still shining, Jill preferred to work outdoors. She unpacked her laptop and situated herself at an empty table, figuring that if a server hadn't approached her by the time her computer had finished booting up, it would be safe to leave her belongings alone for a few minutes while she went inside to get a drink. Jill didn't mind the solitude; she just hoped the staff wasn't annoyed that she wanted to enjoy the fresh air rather than go inside where, presumably, all of their other customers were.

"Hey there!" The patio door opened and a man who looked to be in his early thirties, with dark, disheveled hair, a tidy beard, and fair skin, wearing a black Whitechapel t-shirt and grey jeans, approached Jill with a slight smile. "Hey," he said again. "Can I help you?"

"Great music!" Jill replied. "This is Parkway Drive, right? It sounds like them, but I can't place the album."

"Huh! Yeah, actually, it is!" The guy's face brightened. "It's off *Reverence*. I got to choose the music today. It's cool you're into it."

"For sure. *Atlas* will always be my favorite, but I'm going to have to download this entire album as soon as I get home."

"I think you'll dig it! Or maybe not," he laughed. "I think it's their best work, but the drummer in my band thinks they went too soft. He didn't like it when I told him he was being a fucking cliché."

"Metal elitism is a real plight. Especially when it keeps you from experiencing legitimately awesome music." Jill grinned and tilted her head toward one of the speakers. "This is badass. It was the whole reason I stopped in. I've never been here before, and I haven't found many places in the neighborhood that play the kind of music I like."

"Right. About that." He quickly glanced back into the restaurant before returning to face Jill. "So, we're not actually open yet. Not until 5:00."

"Oh my goodness, I am so sorry. I thought it was weird I was the only one sitting outside, but I assumed you guys were just slow until the happy hour crowd shows up."

"Don't worry about it! The music is playing, the lights are on, and unless you jumped the fence, I'm guessing the gate was unlocked?"

"It was unlocked and wide open," Jill muttered. "But I'm still so embarrassed. I should've known better."

"No! That was Tara's fault. She was the last one in, and she should have locked us back up until we open. That's on her, not you."

"That's nice of you to say, and I'm really sorry for wasting your time." Jill scrambled to pack up her things.

"Hold on! Now I feel like a dick. You aren't causing any problems out here. You're welcome to stay as long as you'd like. But I'm not sure if it's legal for me to sell you anything with alcohol in it before the bar is officially opened. I know we can't after we're closed, but—"

"I don't want you to get in trouble on my account! God forbid you guys, like, lose your liquor license because I didn't want to wait until 5:00 for a beer. I'm in your way. I can come back some other time."

"No!" His face flushed crimson. "I mean, obviously of course you can get out of here if you want to, but I'm not kicking you out. I don't want you to leave. I mean, it'd be bad to lose a new customer and stuff." He grinned at Jill, who was looking up at him wide-eyed. "You've got your laptop all set up now anyway. I probably shouldn't serve you booze for another hour, but maybe I can bring you a lemonade or a soda? On the house?"

"That's really generous of you. Okay, that'd be awesome. Thank you so much."

"I love that you're a fellow metalhead. I wouldn't have guessed. No offense. Anyway, we have to look out for each other. I'm Alex, by the way. Tara and Glen are the only other people working right now. If either of them hassles you about sitting out here, just tell them I okayed it."

"I don't want to annoy them either! Seriously, I don't mind wandering around or working on a bench in Adams Park or whatever for another hour. I don't want to be a pest."

"Stay, stay!" Alex said, waving his hand. "You're fine. I'll be right back with... a Coke?"

"That's perfect, sure. Thanks again."

Alex returned three minutes later with a soda and a bowl of honey roasted peanuts and pretzel sticks.

"It's the good stuff, for our VIPs," he said as he sat the snacks down in front of her. Jill blushed. "I told Tara and Glen you'd be hanging out here for a while. Tara will be working the patio once we open. She's awesome, aside from occasionally leaving the property totally unsecured so that any stranger off the street can stroll in and make herself at home at our tables." He paused to make sure Jill realized he was being playful. "It's freakishly nice out today, but I'll be behind the bar all night and we'll have the Bruins game on. Once the sun sets and it gets cold, feel free to come hang with me inside. Our patio heater lamps can only do so much when the temperature drops."

"I will!" Jill replied. "And thanks again for all this. You really didn't need to."

"I'd rather chat with a pretty girl than do my sidework or clean. But I guess I ought to get back to it now. I'll see you later?"

"Absolutely," Jill nodded.

Jill turned back to her laptop but found it difficult to concentrate. She wouldn't have thought that Alex was her type, but she wasn't sure she had a type anyway. It had been too long. There had been Jean Paul Woo and Jesse; then a brief period of celibacy followed by a series of flings with random, mostly younger guys; and since then, another long, long period of celibacy. She had been too miserable at Ingentis to think of anyone there in sexual terms, and even when she crossed paths with an attractive stranger at the grocery store or the gym, she had nothing to say. She still didn't have any real friends in Boston that could set her up or introduce her to cool single guys at parties, and seeing how cavalier both TravelBlot and Ingentis were with their clients' personal data made signing up for a dating app a nonstarter. Her parents didn't bother to ask anymore if she was seeing anyone special; they had long since begrudgingly accepted that the answer was always going to be no.

Jill was alone in this life, and she thought she was fine with that. But the fact that she was so charmed by Alex's polite demeanor and mild flirtatiousness—both of which were probably nothing more than learned, habitual behaviors necessary for success at his job—made her wonder if maybe she was not just alone, but lonely too. Did she really have a thing for guys ten years her senior with facial hair and fading arm tattoos, or was she simply grateful for a bit of kind attention? Into what hopelessly pathetic state had her life devolved?

Still, she stayed. She stayed for two mixed drinks on the patio and another three beers inside. She stayed for the entire Bruins game and four rounds of celebratory shots after. She stayed until it dawned on her that the bar had cleared out almost entirely, that the staff was cleaning tables and putting up chairs to vacuum, and that she had almost certainly overstayed her welcome. She abruptly closed out her tab, tipping Alex almost forty percent, and called an Uber. When the 2016 silver Hyundai pulled up to the curb, she sardonically congratulated herself on being sober enough to realize she was far too hammered to try to walk home, and tumbled into the backseat.

The next morning, Jill woke up at 10:30 a.m. to four missed phone calls and a dozen texts from her mom, demanding that Jill call home immediately. Jill felt nauseous. Had something happened to her daddy? The distance and tension between her and her parents over the past few months was, Jill had assumed, a phase that would pass as soon as Jill got her career back on a path her folks could be proud of and all three of them started being a little less stubborn in their expectations of each other.

Jill walked to the kitchen to fetch a Gatorade and an energy drink, both of which were essential to reviving her enough to get through the impending return phone call to her mom. An open bottle of sriracha sauce and a half-eaten microwave meal lay on the counter and a dirty fork was on the floor.

Jill cringed as the end of her evening came back to her in flashes. Midway through her sloppy attempt at eating, Jill had decided that this—2:30 a.m. on a weeknight—was the ideal moment to reinitiate dialogue with her parents. There had been a voicemail message. There had been apologies, accusations, and tears. There had been a level of self-pity and sympathy-baiting that would surely test the outer limits of Jaya's patience, but there also had been slurred but no less sincere words of gratitude and love. Jill could only imagine the scolding she would get from her mother for drinking to the point of inebriation at any time, much less in the middle of the week when she ought to have been sleeping or searching for a job. As if she wasn't already enough of a letdown to them! The thought of hearing the restrained disappointment and anger in her mother's voice was enough for Jill to consider dodging Jaya's calls and ignoring her texts for the indefinite future.

As if on cue, Jaya called again. Jill hesitated, letting the phone ring three times in her hand before deciding to accept the call.

"Hi Mom," Jill said wearily.

"Praise the Lord!" her mother exclaimed. "Mateo! Honey! I've got her. She picked up. I'll put her on speaker."

"Hi Mom," Jill said again. "I'm sorry about that voicemail. I had a rough night and—"

"You're sorry?" Jaya's tone vacillated between relief and fury. "You're sorry? You left us a crazed message at three o'clock in the morning, yelling and crying and apologizing and making no sense at all. We could barely understand you. We thought you might have hurt yourself."

"God forbid it, Jaya." Mateo's voice got louder as he walked closer to Jaya's phone. "Don't speak those words into existence."

"Well, we did! We didn't know what to think after a call like that. And then to go hours without an answer this morning?"

"My ringer was muted, Mom. I woke up not even five minutes ago. I'm literally just now seeing all the missed calls and texts."

"So, we're sleeping until noon on Thursdays now?" Jaya asked.

"I mean, technically it's not even 11:00 yet," Jill muttered.

"What did you just say?"

"You can't do this to your mother," Mateo added. "This behavior is not acceptable."

"Oh my gosh! Dad! I said I was sorry. It was stupid. It's not something I do on a regular basis. I normally don't even go out on the weekends, much less during the week! I was watching a hockey game with some cool people I met at the restaurant where I was working on a business proposal, and we all got carried away."

"And how many of them went home and left their parents terrifying voicemails in the middle of the night?" Jaya asked.

"Most of them were probably doing cocaine or banging their exes around the same time I was trying to leave you a heartfelt message," Jill snapped. She took a breath. "Look, I'm not saying I was right to drunk-dial you guys. Obviously it was a stupid thing to do. But in the scheme of things? Like, that's it? It's really worth getting this mad at me over a dumb but harmless mistake? I didn't even wake you up." Jill could feel her voice cracking, but she tried to press it down. "You've gone weeks without talking to me or doing anything more than sending me some half-hearted texts over the holidays, and now you only bother to call me so you can yell at me? How do you think that makes me feel? I know you never wanted me, I know I was a mistake, and maybe now that I'm grown up, any legal obligation you had to me is over and you just want me to go away. I don't blame you, especially since my whole career and my whole life is a huge failure. But I want you to know that it breaks my heart because I still love you both more than anything. I don't blame you for wanting to be done with me, and I'll leave you alone, I'll delete your numbers if that's what you want, and you can send me all my stuff from my childhood bedroom. This can be the end of it. But I still love you, and I'll miss you, I do miss you, and that's all my stupid message last night was trying to tell you."

Jill paused. The call hadn't been disconnected, so they must have put her on mute while they discussed how, if at all, to respond. Jill could imagine her parents together in their family kitchen, leaned up against the center island's marble countertop, surrounded by white wooden cabinets with silver handles and under ceiling spotlights illuminated by LED bulbs. Unlike the neighboring families, who seemed to undertake new home renovation projects every season, the Torreses' kitchen hadn't been remodeled since Jill was in elementary school. Jaya and Mateo had chosen a timeless style, with a practical layout and durable construction; it was an investment that was meant to last, a perfect symbol for their relationship and the life they were trying to build together.

How small and silly and superficial must life in Westport, Connecticut, have seemed to them all those years? And yet, they had stayed for Jill's sake, so she could enjoy a superior public school that could handle her unique academic gifts. They had stayed so she could play on a well-funded soccer team and run through local parks and neighborhoods alone without having to worry about safety. They had stayed, knowing they'd always be considered outsiders in that town, because they had chosen not to abandon a daughter who by an improbable twist of fate was born looking like an insider, and they wanted her to have the best chance possible to succeed.

No wonder they were so angry with her. Perhaps under other circumstances, a drunken voicemail wouldn't be so bad—Jill could even imagine her dad secretly finding it sort of amusing. But after over four months of unemployment (even though she had been trying to use the time productively), after skipping Thanksgiving and Christmas with them for the first time ever despite living less than three hours away by car (even though she didn't think she would have been welcomed back at the time), after blowing through an unconscionable portion of her savings account and trust fund to pay for a rental house that probably cost more than her parents' monthly mortgage payments (even though they were the ones who convinced her not to buy a home in the first place)? No wonder they weren't bothering to disguise their contempt for her. She was a failure. Jill Torres, after starting with so much promise and potential, was an abject fucking failure. But they weren't going to acquiesce to her self-indulgent self-pity over this fact. If she wanted any chance of salvaging a relationship with them, she needed to convince them that although she may have become a failure, she wasn't an irredeemable one.

"I'm applying to graduate school," Jill mumbled. She could hear her parents breathing and shifting around again, so she knew one of them had clicked the phone off mute. "I spend a couple hours around lunchtime every day studying and taking GRE practice tests. I should be able to get a perfect score on the exam, but I'm holding off until I'm certain I won't mess up anything on the verbal section. I know how disappointed you were when I screwed that up on the SAT."

"Your SAT score was exceptional," Mateo said. "It was almost perfect."

"Right, *almost.* I can do better this time," Jill continued. "And with my undergraduate record, I should be able to get a scholarship. Besides, I swear that what I'm doing now isn't a total waste. Things aren't going as smoothly as I thought they would, but that's partly because I don't have the same resources I did when I was in undergrad. Grad school would change that. I know all you see right now is failure, but these are experiences I can share on my grad school applications. Especially for the West Coast schools. Out there, failure isn't always considered such a bad thing, as long as you're learning from it."

"And are you learning from this?" Jaya asked.

"You're not a failure," Mateo said at the same time. One of them clicked their phone back to mute. Jill's jaw clenched. She was causing her parents to fight.

"I appreciate that, Dad, but you don't need to placate me," Jill said. "There are things that I thought would take me two or three weeks of dedicated work to figure out, and two or three months later I find myself still stuck. So in answer to your question, Mom: yes, I am learning from this, but it's a tougher learning curve than I'd confront compared to if I were at Stanford or Caltech or even back at MIT."

Jill paused. The truth was, she had been studying for the GRE only as a back-up plan. Her hope—maybe it was a childish fantasy—was that she'd be able to launch a startup of her own. But by talking to parents like graduate school was her definitive plan for the future, Jill began to wonder if maybe it ought to be. Why shouldn't it be? Setting aside her fear that her graduate school performance might fail to live up to the standards and expectations she had set with her undergrad success, graduate school was objectively the best option for her. Her abysmal experience at Ingentis was proof positive that she wasn't cut out for the corporate world, and clearly she was still ill-prepared to form and run a business on her own.

"—are glad to hear you talking like you have some direction," her mom was saying. "But why didn't you explain this to us sooner? All you told us was that you spontaneously quit your old job over, what? A fight about the laptop they assigned you? With no new job lined up and no plan whatsoever. And then we barely hear from you for months! For all we know, you've been spending this time flitting around Boston nightclubs like you're Paris Hilton."

Jill wanted to laugh, cry, and scream all at once. "Mom, I really don't want to fight with you. But quitting that job was about so much more than the laptop, and I've already explained that to you several times. And I didn't hear from either of you for months either! Other than, what, a reminder that it was Grandma's birthday and a single text wishing me a 'happy x-mas'? How do you think that made me feel? And to be absolutely fair, to be absolutely one hundred percent fair, so what if I did go to a nightclub? I didn't party in high school, I didn't party in college, and I've barely gone out as an adult. Wasn't the whole point of keeping me in high school instead of sending me to college as a fourteen-year-old so that I could have some semblance of a normal social life? And I still have never had that! I have no friends, no boyfriend, no coworkers I can hang with, no soccer teammates anymore, and the one time I go out and meet some cool people and get a little rowdy watching a hockey game on TV, you decide I'm trying to be a celebutante circa 2005."

"Your graduate school plans sound promising," Mateo interjected. God, Jill adored her dad. Even if, deep down, she knew that everything her mother said and did was out of love, she was forever grateful that, despite the imposing, tough-guy demeanor he portrayed to the rest of the world, her father was a teddy bear who couldn't stand to see his wife and daughter bickering, and this was his way of putting a stop to it. "I think that's a great idea. Have you made a list of potential schools yet? You mentioned Caltech and Stanford, so it sounds like you're interested in California? Obviously we'd love to see you attend our alma mater, but Stanford is a great school too. You know, I think my cousin Beatriz still lives in San Francisco. I'm sure she could show you around and help you adjust. Are you planning on a Ph.D. or a Master's?"

"I'm really not sure yet," Jill admitted. "I don't want to commit myself to something prematurely and then regret it for the next fifty years. I'm looking at programs in math and computer science, obviously, but there's also a lot of interesting work being done in the intersection of neuroscience and AI. Maybe I could do some social good that way. Like, developing a brain-computer interface to create higher-functioning prosthetic limbs for wounded military veterans or something!" Jill paused. She had read an article on the subject in the online edition of the journal *Nature* earlier that week while she was procrastinating from the three hours of debugging code she had scheduled for herself. She found the topic interesting and had clicked two more of the related article links before getting back to the task at hand, but she hadn't considered it a potential new career path until blurting it out on the phone. "I don't know. I haven't ruled out going back to a startup either. I loved working for TravelBlot until we got sold. I just don't want to make the same mistake I did with Ingentis. I wasted over two years of my life there, with nothing to show for it. I know it seems like I'm floundering now, but it would be even worse to let that happen again."

"Mmmmm," Jaya murmured and let out a deep sigh. Jill could imagine her mother standing in the sunlight shining through the kitchen windows, shaking her head. "Well, this is more promising than anything you've said in months. You know we're only concerned because we care? The longer you are without a job and the larger this gap in your résumé becomes, the more difficult it will be for you to explain what happened and find yourself a new position. Any position, much less one worthy of your intelligence and talents. You've had a nice little vacation, but it has lasted long enough. It's time to get back on track."

"You still don't get what I'm trying to achieve right now," Jill snapped. "But okay. Fine. I will submit my résumé to a few startups, okay?"

"It couldn't hurt, right, mija?" Mateo asked. "Wouldn't it be nice to have some extra income until you begin graduate school? Maybe you'll enjoy the work so much that you decide to defer a year!"

"Yeah, maybe," Jill grumbled. "Or maybe I'll hate it as much as I did Ingentis and the entirety of my brainpower will be wasted on counting down the days until I can quit. At least I won't feel guilty about that anymore. I suppose the one thing Ingentis did teach me is that these companies don't give a shit about me, and I'd be crazy to give one about them in return."

"So, see, you did learn something from the experience!" Mateo said with a chuckle. Jill heard her mom give Mateo a light whack on the shoulder, but at least she didn't scold Jill for using a cussword.

"Okay, okay, okay. Point taken." Jill had finished both the Gatorade and the energy drink, but her hangover was starting to hit her in full force and she didn't have the energy to continue this discussion much longer. "So should I, like, not call you until I'm reemployed or have a grad school acceptance letter in hand, or what?"

"Jill!" Jaya exclaimed, exasperated. "You can call us any time, for any reason, and I know you know that. As long as you are not leaving us drunken, disjointed voicemail messages."

"I mean, I don't know that. But thank you for saying it, I guess."

"It's this!" Jaya said with sudden fervor. "More than the lack of a job or direction, more than the drinking, it's this attitude that is worrying us. The helplessness. The self-pity. The lack of confidence. If you can be confident in anything, be confident that your parents love you. But over the past year or two, it's like... like you stopped believing in everything, including yourself."

"Mom! Oh my God." Jill had been so close to getting off the phone, so close to being able to lie in bed half-asleep for the next three hours until the pulsating in her head started to subside, but she couldn't resist. "Are you being serious right now? Tell me, what happened in the past year or two that could have triggered this change? Maybe that I started working that godforsaken job at Ingentis? Where I was treated like I was a moron and I was surrounded by morons, until I was on the brink of becoming a brainwashed moron too? Ingentis was destroying me. And then I quit! I stopped being helpless. I tried to save myself! Whatever flicker of confidence and not-self-loathing that I had left, I clung to it and now I'm trying to rekindle it. I'm trying to believe that I can produce things of value again. I'm trying!"

"Okay," Jaya said.

"Okay?"

"Yes, okay. I don't know if there's much more to be gained by rehashing these same issues again and again. You know how much your father and I love you, right?"

"Yes. I love you guys too. Apparently more than you realize."

"Come back and visit us any time, mija," Mateo said. "Or maybe your mom and I can drive up to Boston to see you for a long weekend?"

God forbid her parents knocked on her old townhouse door, thinking they'd surprise her, only to be greeted by whatever poor soul had taken her place in that increasingly dilapidated dump, with her former neighbors spilling onto the street, fist-fighting and drug-dealing behind them. Maybe then they'd have some sympathy for her. Either way, now was not the time to tell them that she had moved to a more expensive place across town. "I'll come see you soon-ish. I promise. It would be good to get out of the city for a few days."

"Your bedroom is always waiting for you," Jaya said. "We put a few of your things into boxes and we're using your closet for storage now." Mateo cleared his throat. "But overall it's the same. You'll still feel at home."

"You will always have a home here," Mateo added. "We'll put everything back to normal before you come visit, if you want."

"No, Daddy, that's fine. You don't need to do that. It's just—"
Jill's voice cracked. She tried to control herself. "Just, be nice to
me, okay? I hate disappointing you. I'm trying. I really am."

"Okay, little one," Jaya said. "We know. We love you. Go
have some coffee and get to work."

"Okay, Mom," Jill said. "I'm sorry for the voicemail but I'm
glad we talked. I love you guys."

"We love you too," Jaya said.

"I love you, princesa," Mateo added.

"I love you," Jill said again. "Talk soon. Bye."

Jill disconnected and took another Gatorade back to bed with
her. She felt too wretched to think straight, but she was grateful
for the half-reconciliation with her parents. And she was grateful
that they had said 'I love you' back, even if she wasn't entirely
convinced that they meant it.

CHAPTER TWENTY-ONE
Amanda Wagner

Awareness of the Octavia Park controversy had reached a critical mass in Martinsburg and the surrounding townships, and public opinion seemed to be shifting in favor of preservation. Still, Amanda often wondered how much of their supposed progress was simply wishful thinking. Their headway with the local governments was even more opaque: the elected officials who most vociferously asserted their authority (whether in favor of or against conservation) vacillated whenever the opportunity to effect actual policy changes arose, and Amanda and Julie were still struggling to identify and access whoever was wielding the real power behind the scenes. On a day-to-day basis, Amanda sometimes felt like their efforts to preserve Octavia Park were as inconsequential as GRAF's hapless campaigns to lobby Congress for ill-defined environmental reforms.

After spending hours refining her personal profiles, swiping and searching, and exchanging carefully written messages with men who turned out to be catfish, flakes, perverts, spam bots, and shameless "entrepreneurs" trying to market their mix tape, sell their personal training services, or gain Instagram followers, Amanda had given up on dating apps completely. The small potential for reward (everyone had that one friend who had met their soulmate on FarmersOnly.com) couldn't justify the spectacular waste of her time and emotional energy.

But she asked herself: was the Octavia Park project any different? It took her a humiliatingly long time to craft profession-al-sounding emails to potential allies, and half of those messages were completely ignored. The local West Virginia folks were rea-sonably welcoming, particularly when Julie accompanied her or at least set up the introduction, but they clearly preferred to conduct business face-to-face. This, in turn, meant that Amanda needed to make the two-hour trip from Washington, D.C. to Berkeley County, West Virginia, whenever she had a full day off both her jobs. The gas and the mileage on her Versa were adding up, and although Eddie was able to reimburse her fourteen cents per mile for the travel, it didn't cover the full expense of the trip and any money for wear-and-tear repairs would come straight out of her own pocket. Still, every time she pulled out of her building's parking structure, she was once again grateful she had managed to hold on to her faithful old car for all this time. If she had needed to pay for a rental car almost every week, or to try to make her way to Martinsburg and back using public transportation, she probably would've had to step down from her position entirely.

Those solitary car rides to and from West Virginia became sacred, in a way. They were basically the only time she had to pause and reflect. Usually on the way there, she was preoccupied with everything she wanted to accomplish, and the drive gave her an opportunity to clarify her own thoughts and talking points so she could express them more precisely and confidently when she arrived. On the way back, however, her mind naturally drifted. She had started listening to 98.7 WMZQ, the local country music station, which she played softly in the background as a soundtrack to her musings. She had never listened to country music before, but she never thought she'd live in Washington, D.C., or work for a nonprofit or be contentedly (well, more or less contentedly) sin-gle in her mid-twenties either. Country music didn't fit the image she'd had of herself three years—hell, even three months—prior, but she had decided it suited her current mood one evening on the way home, and she quickly grew to like it. Besides, there was no one else in the car whose tastes she needed to accommodate or whom she needed to impress. It was just her and her thoughts.

308

More than once Amanda flashed back to her sophomore year of high school, to her English literature class with... Mr. Erickson? She was pretty sure the teacher's name was Mr. Erickson. His last name didn't actually matter, although it was bizarre that she had forgotten. His class was basically the only academically related component of high school that hadn't long since been discarded from her conscious memory.

Mr. Erickson had assigned them *Invisible Man* by Ralph Ellison, which was one of the only books Amanda had ever bothered to read cover-to-cover, before or since—without skipping pages, without frantically skimming through *CliffNotes* and Wikipedia before each class, without calculating how many gross old dudes she'd have to flirt with at the steakhouse to earn enough in tips to pay for some dork online to write an essay for her on the book's major themes. Unlike many of her other teachers, who would pick on her when she was confused or spacing out during a lecture, Mr. Erickson seemed to know intuitively when Amanda had something valuable to add to the class discussion, and he would call on her then and only then. From kindergarten through college, his was the lone class in which she had received an A+ as her final grade. It was one of a very small handful involving any type of "A," to be honest.

Amanda may have been hazy on her teacher's last name, but she could remember his face as vividly as she could recall the cover of Ellison's book. He was a six foot five lanky white man who was probably in his fifties, although he could have shown his students a driver's license with a birth date indicating he was any- where between ages thirty-eight and sixty-eight, and they would've believed him. He had chipped his top right front tooth years prior while coaching the JV boy's lacrosse team, and his coral-colored khaki shorts were an infamous year-round staple of his wardrobe. His bright red 1989 Jeep broke down in the faculty parking lot at least once a month, and according to school lore, the busted back left window had been covered with duct-taped plastic wrap for over a decade.

Someone said he had inherited several million dollars and promptly gave every cent of it away to the Humane Society,

ASPCA, PETA, and a half dozen other animal rights organizations. Someone else insisted that he used to be a moderately famous TV star in France in the 1980s. Sometimes he would bust out into gangsta rap verses in the middle of a lesson, or play 1940s jazz music on the ukulele he kept in a corner of the classroom while his students were taking their biweekly reading comprehension multiple choice quiz (which was mandated by the school administration, much to his undisguised vexation; he promised his students that their scores would have a negligible impact on their final grade and encouraged them to treat it like the joke that it was).

Amanda had been seated next to Caroline Macafee-Scott in his class. Assigned seating was one of the few faculty conventions that Mr. Erickson did follow, although in retrospect, Amanda realized he had arranged his classroom so that everyone was surrounded by students with whom they were unlikely to have interacted otherwise. Caroline Macafee-Scott, for her part, was well-known as one of the preppiest, wealthiest, most-envied girls in the school. She was the reason that half of the female students in their grade came back from fall break of their freshman year wearing Vineyard Vines polo shirts and pearl (or faux-pearl) necklaces. Her parents bought her a brand new Range Rover for her sixteenth birthday. From a distance, she came across as slightly less snobby than most of her fellow preppy, wealthy, enviable female friends, but Amanda doubted they would have spoken had it not been for Mr. Erickson's class. There, however, they often exchanged glances surreptitiously mocking his antics: who was this nut job and what fresh lunacy was he subjecting them to that day? Indeed, their shared scorn was how they became friendly enough for Amanda to start getting invited to the popular kids' parties.

It was on her fourth or fifth trip back from West Virginia that Amanda realized she had misjudged him. Mr. Erickson was a hero. He was a glorious weirdo. He was bizarre and fun and unconventional. He was brazenly himself. If he was misunderstood, it was either because he preferred it that way or because he was waiting for everyone else to get on his level. And he had appreciated Amanda's essays. He had sensed something in her fermenting under the surface even then, and he had tried to encourage her to cultivate it. To embrace it. He had seen a spark in her—a spark that perhaps couldn't write the first draft of a paper with halfway-decent grammar, and certainly couldn't understand rudimentary algebra or geometry beyond the minimum necessary to get a barely passing C-, but that could instinctively connect with the full range of classic literature, historical autobiographies, avant garde poets, and really anyone with a story to tell, if and when she could force herself to focus on their words long enough for her natural empathy to form a bond to the work's creator.

Had he been hurt when she and Caroline openly snickered at his goofy demeanor, knowing that he was going to hand back her paper with a series of thoughtful, heartfelt comments and encouragement (which did make a profound impression on Amanda, even if she was too "cool" back then to consciously recognize it)? Had he been disappointed in her when she chose the protective bubble of a homogenous small college located in bland, wholesome southern Indiana, instead of doing something more daring after high school graduation? Would he be proud of her now? Why hadn't she thought about him in years? And why was he the first person from Trumbull (other than her parents) that she had thought about in any meaningful way in almost as long? She had long since lost contact with Caroline Macafee-Scott, and all of her high school friends for that matter, outside of social media. And frankly, she barely spoke to her own mom and dad these days.

But Mr. Erickson had given her *Invisible Man*, and *White Teeth* by Zadie Smith, and Alan Turing's biography (which was so, so long, but she managed to finish over half of it without cheating!), and the inkling that perhaps she wasn't as unremarkable as her grades and extracurriculars were leading everyone else to expect. He had seen something in her, almost in the way Eddie seemed to see something in her. Was it antifeminist that she needed to be seen by them—by two men, both of them older than her, white, and in positions of relative authority—to feel like maybe they were right, maybe she mattered?

When she wasn't ruminating on former teachers and faded friendships, Amanda's drive back to D.C. often involved moments of profound discouragement. After the initial excitement of the first few trips to Martinsburg had dwindled, progress often felt excruciating slow. Why was she bothering? After three months of spending nearly every free moment working on the project, she and Julie had achieved a number of small victories, but their ultimate goal—total cessation of any proposed construction at Octavia Park—remained woefully elusive.

In addition to compensating a portion of her travel expenses, Eddie had given Amanda five hundred dollars to pay for "Preserve Octavia Park" shirts and stickers. He had said that there was a line item in Congresswoman Gable's budget allocated for miscellaneous materials and supplies and that it was no big deal, but Amanda privately wondered if he hadn't donated at least a portion of the amount out of his own savings. Regardless of where the money came from, however, the items themselves were a resounding success. Nearly every small business in the Martinsburg area that Amanda and Julie approached agreed to put a sticker or a sign in its storefront window. One café asked for extras; according to the manager-on-duty, a substantial portion of their weekend business was from young people who stopped by for coffee or brunch after a group hike, and he wanted to be able to share the stickers with grassroots supporters.

Most of the local business owners were visibly relieved when Amanda and Julie insisted that they weren't soliciting donations, just public support: signing petitions, writing letters to the editor, showing up for town hall meetings, and pestering their local representatives. Only a small portion of the folks with whom they spoke followed through with any sort of civic action, but it had been enough to bring the growing resistance to the development onto the local politicians' radar.

Other institutional allies soon followed. A church half a mile down the street from the park's main entrance ended up joining the cause when Amanda, Julie, and Julie's friend Cedric, a lieutenant in the Martinsburg fire department and longtime parishioner, met with one of the pastors and explained how the construction and traffic redirection would disrupt weekday and Sunday services, which potentially could lead some parishioners to start attending a different church. Two weeks after that, a mid-sized law firm offered to provide their assistance pro bono if and when legal action became necessary, thanks to a trio of paralegals who met in the park three mornings a week to walk together. And Julie was planning to petition Berkeley Medical Center to lend its support as part of its community outreach for wellness and healthy living. Even if the Center wasn't willing to contribute any funds, Julie and Amanda were cautiously optimistic that the modest involvement of its public relations team would generate additional momentum for the campaign.

And yet, plans for the groundbreaking were not halted. They weren't even officially postponed. Amanda would drive down Route 9, the sun setting in her rearview mirror, and she'd wonder what in the actual fuck she was doing. Why was she meddling in their business? Was she even on the right side of the fight? The more time she spent in West Virginia, the more she came to appreciate the state, but she had no illusions. The residents of Martinsburg and the surrounding area were desperate for jobs. For however misguided the development might be in the long-term, and whatever damage it might do to the viability of nearby local businesses (some of which had been around for generations), the simple fact was, the construction phase of the project would give good people honest work. After construction was completed, Walmart and all of the other stores in the complex would give other good people more honest work. Shouldn't that take precedence?

Still, Amanda pressed on. The members of Ansley Development Corp. were outsiders too. Why should they be allowed to dictate what would happen to the land and people of Berkeley County when they were motivated solely by profit? At least Amanda had been asked by a West Virginia congressional representative and a Martinsburg resident to help organize on behalf of the interests of the Martinsburg community. Julie's and her husband's families both could trace their roots to the region going back nine generations, which, Amanda had learned, meant something in those parts.

Besides, the prior grassroots efforts had failed to gain momentum primarily because they lacked coordination, leadership, and financial resources, and not because, as ADC insinuated, they were part of a bored or destructive or anarchist fringe minority bent on stirring up trouble for its own sake. There had been some "awareness raising" among a foursome of fervid high school students, several rural residents who were enraged that the usage of land and roads so close to their property would be radically changed, and plenty of people who muttered with sincerity "it's such a shame" when the topic came up among friends and colleagues, but none of it had made a substantive difference. All Amanda was doing was helping Julie to organize those various sentiments into action. All she was doing was helping the people whose opinions were being shut out and ignored to be heard and given fair consideration.

Amanda met Congresswoman Gable. Amanda initially thought they would be going out to lunch, but the appointment was pushed back several times until it turned into a twenty-minute meeting in the congresswoman's office. From the beginning, Julie declared that she had neither the time nor the desire nor the disposable income to drive to Washington, D.C., to brownnose some Beltway clown, and she declined the invitation. Amanda had been disappointed initially—she thought the discussion with the congresswoman would be more persuasive if her one of her constituents were present, and Julie was the one who had contacted Representative Gable's office in the first place—but now she was relieved. Julie would have been livid! She would have interpreted the multiple reschedulings and now the congresswoman's extended tardiness as a sign of open disrespect, and probably would have told Congresswoman Gable exactly where she could stick it, using the kind of colorful language that would rival Jasmine and Hugo's back-of-house Spanish cussword training.

Amanda quietly laughed to herself as she sat on a comfortable chair in a dimly lit reception area, where a blond girl with porcelain skin and a satin headband, who Amanda guessed was about nineteen years old, occasionally looked up from her desk to glance at Amanda with disdain and a deep sigh. Eddie had been texting her apologies for the delay and updates about their estimated arrival time. Part of Amanda wanted to snap at the reception room girl and remind her that she had been punctual and she was now the one being inconvenienced. Julie certainly would've done so. But the entire situation was so absurd that any resentment she felt toward the smug, snobby receptionist dissipated almost immediately after it arose. If someone had told Amanda during her senior year at U of Evansville that she would end up here—in Washington, D.C., in a congresswoman's office, with the title of Lead Special Projects Liaison, still waitressing (of course) but also working for a respected environmental nonprofit—she would have said it was impossible. The fact that she had a reason to interact with this girl at all, a reason to sit, expectant and jittery, in a chair that probably cost Congresswoman Gable (or rather, the United States taxpayers) more than the amount of her first two years of GRAF stipends combined, was reason enough to count her blessings.

Congresswoman Gable finally showed up. She didn't apologize or make excuses for the delay. Someone in her position didn't need to. Eddie shook Amanda's hand and gave her a little wink as he made introductions. She thought about it later—was he flirting with her?—but at the time, she was just happy to see a friendly, familiar face. Her nerves temporarily subsided enough for her to blurt out, "Very nice to meet you, Congresswoman Gable," without her voice cracking.

Her anxiety immediately returned as she followed the congresswoman into her private office. She was going to sweat through her blouse. She was going to make an ass of herself and make Eddie look like an idiot for entrusting her with something so important before she was ready. She would never work in this town again, not even as a waitress. She should have begged Eddie and Julie to join her so that she wouldn't have to talk. Nothing in college or at GRAF had prepared her for a meeting like this.

According to Eddie, Congresswoman Gable was impressed. Amanda couldn't fathom why. Literally. She remembered maybe three sentences she had uttered during the duration of their twenty-minute conversation. She did remember Gable indicating that she would "see what she could do to help expedite the process." At the time, Amanda had assumed that this was intentionally noncommittal politician-speak for "I don't care but I want you out of my office so here's a vague promise to conclude this conversation."

Amanda had mentioned an offhand comment that Julie had made at one of their first meetings, that there were several vacant or nearly-vacant lots that had sufficient square footage and some of the preexisting infrastructure necessary to accommodate the Walmart component of the development. According to Julie, some of these abandoned lots were located across the street or conveniently down the road from each other, such that even if Walmart, as the anchor tenant, took up the entirety of one such lot, the structures on a neighboring parcel arguably could be converted into the other retail outlets that Ansley Development Corp. had planned, without a drastic alteration to ADC's original vision. Julie didn't know why these locations already had been dismissed out of hand, but according to her, it was a moot point and they shouldn't bother pursuing it. In recent weeks, Ansley Development Corp. had made it clear that the development at Octavia Park was an all-or-nothing proposition for the region. They had doubled down, insisting that there were no viable alternatives, no plans B or C.

And yet.

It all happened so fast. After so many months of consensus-building, constituent-outreach, town hall appearances, interviews with local bloggers, letters to the editor, social media marketing campaigns, and handing out flyers outside the organic grocery store in forty-degree temperatures with no tangible results, Amanda had what she thought was a disastrous meeting with Congresswoman Gable, and suddenly things changed.

Ansley Development Corp. was reevaluating two plots of land on the southern side of Martinsburg, close to the Eastern West Virginia Regional Airport.

Ansley Development Corp. was in negotiations with the current leaseholders of a twenty-acre lot off Bull Run Road, and with the property owners of the adjacent and unoccupied fifteen-acre tract at the intersection of Bull Run Road and Simmons Drive.

Ansley Development Corp. had purchased all rights to both parcels, as well as an additional eight acres of undeveloped land for spillover parking.

Due to the change in location and strategic approach as mandated by the county government, Ansley Development Corp. was now estimating 220 constructions jobs and 180 retail jobs resulting from the project going forward. (The revised number of construction jobs was, naturally, much closer to what the original estimate ought to have been even prior to the site location change. No explanation was ever given for why the number of retail jobs had shrunk almost in half.)

Ansley Development Corp. was thrilled to announce that on September 6 of that year, the first phase of the revitalization of the ageing and underutilized property along Bull Run Road would begin.

Ansley Development Corp. was a proud defender of this country's natural beauty and public green spaces.

The last one was national news.

Amanda and Julie laughed at the hypocrisy over five rounds of beers at Abolitionist Ale Works. Julie had previously told Amanda that if she ever wanted to spend the night in West Virginia, she could take the master bedroom; Julie's husband could sleep on the couch and Julie would take the floor. (Julie insisted that she had slept in far worse conditions than a carpeted floor in a temperature-controlled room during her twenty years of military service.) Julie had extended the invitation the second time they met, and had twice since mentioned that it was a standing offer, but Amanda had never accepted until that night.

By round six, it was agreed that they needed to leave their cars in the Abolitionist Ale Works parking lot. By round nine, Julie's husband finally arrived to drag their drunk asses home.

"If y'all two can't keep it together, y'all gon be riding home in the bed of this pickup. And if either of y'all puke in here, y'all gon be walking home."

Amanda sat in Julie's lap in the passenger seat, and they both laughed so hard that Amanda was afraid either she would pee on Julie or Julie would pee on her. Frankly, at that point, neither would have known who the culprit was. Amanda almost wished she had held off on that last drink. She was hammered, but she never wanted to forget this night. They had won. The battle was over. It was a reality that they were celebrating, but on some level, they were mourning as well.

In the front seat of that 2010 Toyota Tundra, with Julie's husband in the driver's seat shaking his head in half-serious exasperation, not knowing if the next morning she would remember the swell of love she felt in that moment, Amanda desperately hoped that the end of the Octavia Park project wouldn't mean the end of her friendship with Julie.

CHAPTER TWENTY-TWO
Jill Torres

If this were a movie, maybe Jill would have looked mysterious—lingering at the bar alone in a tight dress, consumed by her own thoughts, awaiting whatever adventure or intrigue the night had in store for her—like a spy or an assassin or a con artist posing as a high-end prostitute sent to steal a billionaire's watch and wallet (along with his heart and maybe his life). In this reality, however, she looked like she had been stood up. She looked pathetic. She looked friendless. She looked like a deranged lunatic, trapped by a festering internal rage that she tried to choke down with another whiskey cola while stuffed into a dark purple bandage dress from French Connection that she should have retired eight pounds ago.

Bring on the singularity, Jill thought. Assuming this shitshow wasn't itself some hapless abortion of a simulation, that is. The world would be better off. Or, at least, it couldn't get any worse than it was right then. No one around her seemed to be living a flesh-and-bones existence anymore anyway. They were all tethered to their phones, most of them probably using and unwittingly sharing their data with some system she had created at TravelBlot, or supported at Ingentis, or independently designed and licensed out in the past. They were more active and invested in their digital lives than their analog ones, and she was one of the architects of the problem.

"Was" being the operative word. Past tense. She was *formerly* one of the architects of the problem. Now, she was nothing. If she had quit because of some crisis of conscience, this might have been a tenable status. But she had been able to ignore the moral ambiguity of TravelBlot's true business objectives, as well as the triviality of her tasks in the lumbering, oafish, unbreakable machine that was Ingentis, because she enjoyed the paycheck. She was an inconsequential casualty when the former company was devoured, and through some sliver of self-preservation she had managed to escape the latter, but she was squandering her newfound freedom. Still. Despite whatever wisdom she smugly thought she held over her former coworkers for figuring out how the machine operated, seeing that its function was to maintain a complacent social order of educated middle and upper-middle class workers as much as it was to accrue unimaginable wealth for a small group of privileged shareholders and C-suite executives, she had done nothing with this knowledge other than angrily ruminate over it while leaning against a barstool at Confession, feigning that she was paying rapt attention to the Bruins game on TV.

Jill glanced around the bar. Alex was off tonight. The dynamic was always different when he was there. He had his bar groupies, a rotating mix of regulars and randoms who were more interested in trying to take him home than they were in having a drink or hanging out with their friends. Jill knew there was plenty of drama among the regulars and some of the staff, although she stayed out of most of it herself and she was reasonably certain that Alex did as well. He did seem to have a particular affinity for her. She was pretty sure she wasn't just imagining it. His special treatment was what induced some of Alex's bar groupies to treat Jill with a sugary sweetness, presumably to demonstrate to him that they weren't like other girls, they would be Chill Girlfriends™, they wouldn't get envious of his friendships with other women.

The proximity of these women (irrespective of their motivations) in turn led to Jill's introduction to several of the straight male patrons: the bar groupies' ex-boyfriends, their current friends with benefits, their "we clearly want each other but you had clumsy sex with Shannon three weeks ago and she's still deluding herself into believing that you might want something serious, so you're off-limits," their "Shannon pissed me off by puking on my jeans and leaving me with the bar tab on Wednesday, so you're fair game now," and countless other relationships that Jill was still uncovering and that seemed to change on a weekly basis.

It was no different than high school, no different than the dorms at MIT, no different than the Cool Kids Club at Ingentis, except, perhaps, for the fact that Jill somehow found herself on the outskirts of the inner circle this time. This had its merits, she supposed, although occasionally she wondered if any of them would still talk to her if she cut back her drinking or stopped buying them rounds. She wondered if they would be quite as nice if she chopped off her long blond hair or stopped applying makeup and changing into a cute outfit before she headed over, or if she gained any more weight (or if she lost the weight she had gained, for that matter). Generally, she tried not to think about it. She knew the answer.

But that night, without Alex behind the bar to snap her out of her reverie, with the other regulars too preoccupied with their own interpersonal nonsense to pay her much attention that evening, Jill fixated on the question. She could formulate it as a mathematical equation (or, at least she could have if her mind wasn't already a convoluted, half-drunken jumble): if X fell below Y—that is, if Jill decided to clean up her act, to start running and lifting every day again, to muster up the ambition to find a job or a project she genuinely cared about, to stop blowing through her entire life savings in a matter of weeks on the assumption that she could always just kill herself once it was gone (and at least then she would go out with a bang)—she would be kicked out of Confession's in-group. They would call her a priss and a snob, possibly to her face and definitely behind her back. They would think that she thought she was better than them. They would resent her for reminding them of how far they too had fallen from their potential, but having resigned themselves to their own fates, they wouldn't stand to see her, through sheer willpower, hard work, and grit, trying to overcome the ruin she had created for herself.

Of course, if X exceeded Y by too great a margin, Jill would become a "trainwreck," a "hot mess," a laughingstock, or someone who was too broke to continue to frequently buy the regular patrons rounds of shots and tip the staff upwards of fifty percent on her nightly tab. Then what purpose would she serve them?

No, in order to maintain the closest thing to a group of friends she'd had since her high school soccer team or her band of fellow programming nerds at TravelBlot (and never minding that this same "group of friends" was currently ignoring her as she sat alone at the bar, thereby allowing her thoughts to meander down this bitter path), the equation must be maintained in perfect equilibrium. It was as exhausting, futile, and self-destructive as trying to devote herself to Ingentis had been.

Had she reached her tipping point at last? How often over the past few months since that horrible, hungover phone call with both her parents had Jill been convinced she was at the threshold of making a real and permanent change, only to end up back at Confession with a triple-digit bar tab that night and a bout of crippling depression the next morning? Three days of running at least a 5K, followed by four days of sloth and overindulgence. Two grad school applications finished in one morning, followed by twelve straight hours of binge-watching reruns of teen dramas on the CW Network. Booze and indecision and untold hours wasting away in this very bar, always justified under the guise of "self-care."

Jill had taken the GRE two weeks earlier and because the test was computerized, she received her results immediately: a perfect 170 on the quantitative reasoning section, a 166 on the verbal reasoning section, and a perfect 6 on the analytical writing section. She felt more relief than excitement about her scores. Nevertheless, it seemed like as good of an excuse as any to reach out to her parents.

Jill had called their landline and Mateo picked up. He said that Jaya was working late that night. Jill could hear a soccer match on TV in the background. Mateo was warm and enthusiastic about the GRE news, and he asked if she had settled on a proposed research agenda yet. Jill had excitedly carried on for several minutes about new developments in the use of machine learning on prosthetic limbs; she could hear it in her own voice, it was the most animated she had been in months. Her dad was, again, loving and supportive, although Jill wondered if he wasn't anxious to get back to his game.

"One more thing," Mateo had asked as they were saying their goodbyes. "Have you changed the oil in your car since the last time we talked, mijita?"

"Yes, Daddy," Jill had replied, forcing back a sudden swell of tears. Her father had been sending her a check for thirty-five dollars every three or four months since she had graduated college, always with a handwritten note that read something along the lines of "For your oil change. Remember: every 3 months or 3,000 miles. Your Dad loves you." Jill realized that at least six months had passed since the last time she had received mail from him. Even if he had sent it to her old address, the post office would have forwarded it to her new home by now. "I mean, I think so," Jill had continued. "I'll double-check my mileage and take the car in this weekend if it's time. Three months or three thousand miles. I haven't forgotten."

Why, now, standing alone in the bar, was this what she dwelled on? Why was this what crushed her heart?

The realization barreled into her so forcefully and so suddenly that she felt lightheaded: she had to get out of Confession. Immediately. Her whole life had been on hiatus since Ingentis. Quitting hadn't resolved her underlying sense of aimlessness and ennui. Things had devolved so far that her own father had to strain to show her the affection and support that had always been a defining characteristic of their relationship. Embracing this surge of motivation to make a change—not "soon," not "when things stabilize" or "when the timing is better," not even "tomorrow morning" when she would have some bullshit "fresh start," but in that moment, before it faded (as it so often did)—would be a small, seemingly insignificant step, but it felt symbolic. This was her tipping point. For real this time.

Jill set down her drink, still half-unfinished, and signaled to the bartender to close out her tab. She left without saying goodbye to anyone, and she wondered if she'd ever return. It didn't matter much either way. She probably wouldn't be missed.

By the time Jill arrived back at her rental house, it was just after 10:00 p.m. She felt more restless than inebriated. She looked inside her refrigerator, then in her pantry, then back to her refrigerator, but nothing seemed appetizing, and she needed to stop drunk-eating anyway. She thought about taking a shower, but she didn't have the energy to get in and she knew she wouldn't have the energy to get out. She checked her email: nothing but mailing list spam. She checked her texts: no new messages, of course. She picked up a book by her bedside, but couldn't focus past the first two sentences. She reloaded her email. She checked the five-day weather forecast. She opened her bank account homepage. This, at least, was interesting enough to maintain her attention, albeit not in a good way.

Jill's trust fund was structured so that she had unlimited access to her money to pay for approved educational expenses. Beyond that, her parents provided that Jill was to receive a monthly allowance of $2,000 starting at age twenty-two, conditioned on Jill holding full-time employment. At age thirty, she would have access to the entire amount without restriction, including the option to withdraw the remainder as a lump sum.

Her parents had carefully and thoughtfully set up the trust this way, as the money was intended to supplement Jill's income, not replace it. They didn't want their daughter to become spoiled or entitled. They couldn't have anticipated that Jill's first job out of undergrad would pay her over $84,000 base salary, plus benefits and bonuses. Jill had been making tens of thousands of dollars more than the average college graduate, even before adding in the trust fund money. With it, she had been able to afford to live without roommates in a nice townhouse in a safe neighborhood (or, at least, it had been nice and safe up until the landlord turnover), despite the high cost of living in Boston. She never had to worry about being able to pay her electric bill on time and in

324

full, even during that one sweltering summer when her energy provider charged her over $400 a month for four months straight. That season, Jill had set the thermostat to seventy-eight degrees, unplugged most of her household appliances, switched to LED bulbs, and wondered how everyone else in the city without her privilege could afford to get by. The trust money didn't let her live extravagantly, but it certainly let her live comfortably. It gave her the freedom and mental energy to think about other things.

At the time, Jill's personal indulgences had seemed like relatively frugal, minor frivolities compared to those of her peers at work or the women she saw walking around the affluent sections of Boston: a hundred dollars for new running shoes every few months instead of thousands of dollars for new designer handbags and heels every season; $250 two or three times a year for tinted SPF 40 sunscreen, retinol cream, and an antioxidant serum from SkinCeuticals, rather than weekly facials, cosmetic dermatologist appointments, and "preventative" Botox; two bookshelves crammed with hardcovers and paperbacks, fiction and nonfiction, purchased from an independent bookstore located down the street from TravelBlot's old workspace, the local public library's annual "yard sale," and late-night Amazon impulse buys, which occupied Jill's nights and weekends in lieu of trendy bars and nightclubs (thereby allowing her to avoid the cover charges, bar tabs, rotating wardrobe, salon-styled hair, professionally applied makeup, and probably a cocaine addiction, which would have been requisite expenditures to assimilate into that scene).

Yes, she probably could have worn down the soles of her running shoes a bit more before replacing them. And she probably could've managed her skincare routine well enough with soap, water, and a decent moisturizer from CVS. She probably could've used her library card instead of her credit card when she wanted something new to read. But why? She knew she wasn't poor, but she didn't feel particularly rich either. She still had access to her fake social media accounts, and many of her former classmates and soccer teammates from Westport had set at least a portion of their pages to public. She could see that their parents had bought them houses in Los Angeles or Dallas or Miami—or, just as often, down the street and still squarely and very much intentionally under their parental authority, in New Canaan or Darien, Connecticut. She could see that they were employed as junior analysts at the same hedge funds where their parents were portfolio managers, despite never having shown a modicum of mathematical aptitude or critical thinking ability in the four years Jill had spent in classes with them. She could see they were set up as art gallery owners or jewelry designers or "content creators" in Williamsburg, Cobble Hill, and the Lower East Side, yet somehow could still afford to jet off to Mykonos or Ibiza or Bali with their latest romantic partner on a whim. Compared to them, Jill's lifestyle was downright modest!

In retrospect, Jill always had known on some level that she was deluding herself with these rationalizations. Since she had graduated from MIT, she had flown to Ecuador three times for family events. Thanks to Ingentis's relatively liberal vacation policies (the corporation's one redeeming factor), she had managed to take week-long solo trips to Ireland, Iceland, Costa Rica, and Morocco. Tens of thousands of dollars in flights and hotel expenses, and she had somehow convinced herself that she was financially responsible because she was spending her money on experiences rather than gadgets and labels and status symbols?

If her parents had given her the trust in a lump sum when she turned twenty-two, maybe she would have spent part of it on a down payment for a house and used the remainder of it to pay for graduate school tuition. Maybe. But maybe she would have blown through it—all of it—even faster. Maybe she would have ended up exactly where she was now—no job, friends who were really nothing more than people she got drunk with, exorbitant rental payments, and parents who might have lost their faith that keeping their blond-haired baby had been the right decision twenty-something years before—but there would have been no money left to pay for Stanford, her first-choice graduate school.

And at this point, the prospect starting over in California was all she had to keep her going. She would live in student housing and work as a TA if she had to. She would even find a roommate if it were necessary. Wouldn't she? Jill thought back to all the petty melodrama in Baker House and even in MacGregor. Yes, she would. She could find another weirdo loner like herself and make it work, because she had no choice anymore but to make it work.

It had felt like her parents cut her off emotionally when they cut her off financially, but Jill knew this was irrational. Technically, they hadn't even been the ones to halt her monthly direct deposits; the executor of the trust had done it, and he was merely following the mandatory terms of the trust document! She wanted to villainize her mom (as she had no doubt that her dad would have readily continued to bankroll her basic living expenses for the indefinite future, notwithstanding her manifest irresponsibility with her trust fund income and her personal savings account), but Jill knew that Jaya had been right. Jill had known that the provisions of the trust dictated that her monthly allowance would cease within thirty days of her termination from Ingentis, and it was probably for the best that her parents couldn't or wouldn't restructure the trust to allow her half-hearted version of "self-employment" to suffice for resuming the bank deposits. Jill stood by her decision to quit Ingentis, but almost every decision she had made in the ensuing months, other than studying for and acing the GRE, was indefensible. More money wouldn't have helped her make better choices. Based on her use of the money she did have, it probably would have made things even worse.

Jill wasn't sure what made her think of Amanda Wagner in that moment, even though Instagram-stalking her high school classmates had turned into a weekly, if not daily, ritual. There had been no way to justify her behavior to herself other than the empty self-reassurances that at least she wasn't as spoiled, sheltered, and completely lacking in self-awareness as they were.

Wasn't she, though? Wasn't that precisely why she had refused to set up a social media profile under her real name for so long? She didn't want anyone to be able to judge her as harshly as she judged her former classmates, or as she judged herself... even though she entirely deserved it.

Why hadn't she checked in on any of Amanda's social media accounts for so long? It wasn't simply because almost everything anyone posted was bullshit (even though it was). It wasn't because she had grown bored with the pictures and posts that Amanda occasionally shared. Jill had prided herself on rooting for her sister, but apparently only when she was confident that she was doing better. When that was no longer clear, and irrespective of what "better" was supposed to mean, Jill had convinced herself that she had lost interest.

The realization that she could be so insecure and petty was less of a shock to her than the fact that she had referred to Amanda, if only in her own head, as her "sister." Why? Why now? Jill had always understood that, from a purely biological standpoint, "sister" was the correct label for their relationship, but she never had allowed herself to think of Amanda that way. Jaya and Mateo were her parents. They were her family. If she were ever to have a sibling, it would be because Jaya got pregnant or because her parents adopted another child.

Was the sudden sense of connection—of joy!—that she felt when thinking of Amanda as her sister disloyal to her mom and dad? For however strained their relationship was at the moment, and probably would be for the foreseeable future, Jill wasn't trying to replace her parents with her sister. Her sister who didn't know she was her sister. Her sister who was barely more than a theoretical construct, an idea of a person formulated out of scattered pictures and captions, of online banality and boasting, which Jill hadn't looked through in almost a year.

So she looked. Jill logged onto her phony Facebook account first. Farhad Razavi was technically still connected to Amanda, but since Jill had last checked, Amanda had readjusted her profile settings so that only a handful of archived posts were viewable anymore. She had better luck with Amanda's Instagram account. There, her profile was still public. Dozens of new photos had appeared. Jill started from the top.

Amanda was still beautiful. Maybe more beautiful than ever. Jill didn't dare check her own appearance in her camera phone to compare. Seeing her own bloated, alcohol-worn face and her chubby-adjacent upper arms would either irreparably break her heart or send her into a blind rage. Either response would inevitably end with her stumbling out of Confession five hours later, one hundred dollars poorer and one thousand whiskey calories fatter, exacerbating the problem in a self-reinforcing cycle that she was only now, finally, seeing a way to escape.

Amanda had, it seemed, found her way. Jill wasn't sure what exactly that phrase was supposed to denote, but as Lorraine would've told her: "it's like pornography, you know it when you see it." And Jill saw it. It wasn't just social media bullshit. The smiles were sincere. The successes were real. Small, maybe, in the scheme of things, but real. Impacting actual people, offline, for the better. And yet Amanda seemed so modest, earnest, hard-working, endearing. And beautiful. Jesus. Jill's bizarre sense of pride outweighed her jealousy. Amanda had become who Jill ought to have been, and Jill was surprised by her (almost entire) lack of bitterness. Complaining that it "wasn't fair" wouldn't change a thing. It was more than fair. Jill had squandered the past three years of her life, and the sooner she acknowledged that fact, the sooner she could rectify it. She was proud of her sister. And, notwithstanding her fury and self-loathing, she was inspired to be more.

If she didn't have the prospect of rebuilding her career, her life, her identity, at Stanford, maybe Jill would have logged off. Maybe she would have refused to allow herself to think about Amanda again for the indefinite future. As it was, Jill was half-convinced that she'd be better off waiting until she was officially enrolled in graduate school and working out regularly again to do anything.

But the simple truth was, she desperately wanted to contact Amanda. She wanted to tell her that she was amazed by what she had accomplished in West Virginia. She wanted to tell her that although she had never visited Washington, D.C., other than a handful of layovers at Dulles, Amanda's pictures provided a better advertisement that the city was a worthwhile place for young professionals to visit than any tourism bureau could have presented. She wanted to tell her that, hey, I think (I know) that we grew up pretty close to each other and people used to get us

329

confused back then, isn't that funny? Isn't it a shame that our paths never randomly crossed? And maybe if we're both back in Connecticut at the same time over Christmas or whatever, perhaps you'd want to grab a coffee or a beer together? Technically, she wouldn't have to admit that they were biologically related to initiate the conversation or extend an invitation to meet, although it probably wouldn't take long for Jill to confess the truth. Amanda was bound to ask if Jill had any theories as to why they looked so much alike, and even if Jill managed to dodge the question in an online exchange, she couldn't imagine lying to Amanda's face about what she knew.

What was stopping her from just leading with the truth? Since Jill had learned the full story over a decade earlier, her parents had reiterated that Jill could never tell anyone what had happened. They had signed legally binding nondisclosure agreements. Jill's trust fund was at stake. The truth would upend two families' lives (and finances) in a way that could never be taken back.

But things had changed since Jill was fifteen. Because her parents had the foresight to have all the settlement money assigned to and deposited in a trust exclusively under Jill's name, Jill was pretty sure that the fertility clinic or the Wagners or whoever couldn't hire lawyers to take back the settlement money out of her mom and dad's life savings. And after Jill paid her tuition and expenses at Stanford? Let them (whoever "they" were) have whatever amounts remained. Jill never deserved any of it to begin with anyway.

Besides, could her parents really have signed an NDA on her behalf? One that would bind her even after she turned eighteen? She should ask Lorraine. It had been months since she and Lorraine had texted, and probably two years since they had last spoken. Assuming that Lorraine wasn't grateful to be in Boise, a couple thousand miles away from Jill's pestering overtures for a continued friendship, this was the perfect excuse to reestablish a connection.

Was it an excuse to call Lorraine, or an excuse to delay writing a message to Amanda? Because, make no mistake, that was Jill's endgame. She had already switched back to Facebook. Trying to connect with Amanda on Instagram—where she probably had strangers' messages delivered directly to her spam folder, lest she be inundated with dozens of messages a day from sketchy guys trying to slip into her DMs with nasty dick pics and shady "business" propositions—would be futile. If Jill were to go through with this, an old-school Facebook private message seemed like the best way, statistically, of getting Amanda to look at her letter and maybe even respond.

Jill paused and stared at her ceiling. Was she really afraid of the potential legal ramifications of contacting Amanda? She was over eighteen, an adult. Indeed, her eighteenth birthday seemed like several lifetimes ago. It's not like Amanda's parents could sue for custody of her. Could they sue Jaya and Mateo for keeping this secret all these years? The last thing Jill needed to do was add another stressor to her already tenuous relationship with her mother and father, and sparking a lawsuit because of her lack of discretion was a strong contender for the most efficient way she could destroy her relationship with her own parents permanently.

Nevertheless, it wasn't clear to Jill how quickly Amanda would tell her folks about Jill, or how they would react when she did. There was a strange dichotomy to Amanda's social media presence: her pages were abundant with pictures of close friends, and she showed a seemingly genuine passion for environmental justice, but photos of her mom, dad, and any siblings, cousins, or other relatives were conspicuously absent. Perhaps Amanda wasn't very close with her extended family. And if that were true, then Jill's existence might be little more than a dinner party anecdote to them. After all, Amanda's mom and dad were Jill's bio parents, but despite the intensity of her desire to get to know Amanda, Jill had, at most, a mild curiosity about the rest of the Wagner family.

Jill scrolled further down Amanda's timeline. Maybe Amanda and her parents had a falling out? In that case, a letter from Jill could be an opportunity for them to reunite, whether in astonishment over their strange situation or banded against Jill and her parents as a common enemy for having withheld the truth from them for so long. Or maybe Jill was reaching. The lack of family photos was possibly nothing more than camera-shyness, or para-noia about their images being posted on the internet, or because they were having such fun and engaging interactions when they were together that they didn't need to pause to post documented proof thereof for the rest of the world to scroll past. Was it worth the risk?

Jill opened a new message but left the subject line blank. She could try to fill it in with something pithy later. Or not. She needed to get the words on the page and hit send before she changed her mind yet again.

"Hi Amanda," Jill began. "We've never met. But my name is Jill, and I am your biological sister."